The Road to Gandolfo

Robert Ludlum

BANTAM BOOKS
NEW YORK · TORONTO · LONDON · SYDNEY · AUCKLAND

This edition contains the complete text
of the original hardcover edition.
NOT ONE WORD HAS BEEN OMITTED.

THE ROAD TO GANDOLFO

A Bantam Book / published by arrangement with
the author

Bantam Export edition / April 1982
Bantam edition / June 1982
Bantam reissue / March 1992

ISBN 0-553-27109-1

Published simultaneously in the United States and Canada

Bantam Books are published by Bantam Books, a division of Bantam Doubleday Dell
Publishing Group, Inc. Its trademark, consisting of the words "Bantam Books" and
the portrayal of a rooster, is Registered in U.S. Patent and Trademark Office and in
other countries. Marca Registrada. Bantam Books, 666 Fifth Avenue, New York, New
York 10103.

PRINTED IN THE UNITED STATES OF AMERICA

RAD   33 32 31 30 29 28 27 26

For John Patrick

A distinguished writer and an honored man whose idea this was.

A WORD FROM THE AUTHOR

The Road to Gandolfo is one of those rare if insane accidents that can happen to a writer perhaps once or twice in his lifetime. Through divine or demonic providence a concept is presented that fuels the fires of his imagination. He is convinced it is truly a *staggering* premise which will serve as the spine of a truly *staggering* tale. Visions of one powerful scene after another parade across his inner screen, each exploding with drama and meaning and . . . well, damn it, they're just plain *staggering!*

Out come reams of paper. The typewriter is dusted and pencils are sharpened; doors are closed and heady music is played to drown out the sounds of man and nature beyond the cell of staggering creation. Fury takes over. The premise which will be the spinal thunderbolt of an incredible tale begins to take on substance as characters emerge with faces and bodies, personalities and conflicts. The plot surges forward, complex gears mesh and strip and make a hell of a lot of noise—drowning out the work of true masters like that Mozart fellow and what's-his-name Handel.

But suddenly something is wrong. I mean *wrong!*

The author is giggling. He can't *stop* giggling.

That's horrible! Staggering premises should be accorded awed respect . . . heaven knows not chuckles!

But try as he may the poor fool telling the tale is trapped, bombarded by a fugue of voices all repeating an old *ars antigua* phrase: *You've-got-to-be-kidding.*

Poor fool looks to his muses. Why are they winking? Is that *The Messiah* he's hearing or is it *Mairzy-Dotes?* What happened to the staggering thunderbolt? Why is it spiraling out of whack in a clear blue sky, hiccuping its way to a diminished . . . *giggle*?

Poor fool is bewildered; he gives up. Or rather, he gives in because by now he's having a lot of fun. After all, it *was* the time of Watergate, and nobody could invent *that* scenario! I mean it simply wouldn't play in Peoria. At that point-in-time, that is.

So poor fool plunges along, enjoying himself immensely, vaguely wondering who will sign the commitment papers, figuring his wife will stop them because the oaf does the dishes now and then and makes a damn good martini.

The *oeuvre* is finally presented and, most gratefully for poor fool, the closeted sound of laughter is heard. Followed by screams of revolt and threats of beyond-salvage termination with extreme-prejudice.

"Not under *your* name!"

Time mandates change, and change is cleansing.

Now it's under my name, and I hope you enjoy. I *did* have a lot of fun.

Robert Ludlum

Connecticut Shore, 1982

A LARGE PART OF THIS STORY TOOK
PLACE A WHILE BACK. AND QUITE A BIT OF IT TOMORROW.
SUCH IS THE POETIC LICENSE OF
LITURGICAL DRAMA.

Part

I

Behind each corporation must be the singular force, or motive, that sets it apart from any other corporate structure and gives it its particular identity.

Shepherd's Laws of Economics:
Book XXXII, Chapter 12

PROLOGUE

The crowds gathered in St. Peter's Square. Thousands upon thousands of the faithful waited in hushed anticipation for the pontiff to emerge on the balcony and raise his hands in benediction. The fasting and the prayers were over; the Feast of San Genarro would be ushered in with the pealing of the twilight Angelus echoing throughout the Vatican. And the bells would be heard throughout all Rome, heralding merriment and good feeling. The blessing of Pope Francesco the First would be the signal to begin.

There would be dancing in the streets, and torches and candlelight and music and wine. In the Piazza Navonna, the Trevi, even sections of the Palatine, long tables were heaped with pasta and fruit and all manner of home-produced pastries. For had not this pontiff, the beloved Francesco, given the lesson? Open your hearts and your cupboards to your neighbor. And his to you. Let all men high and low understand that we are one family. In these times of hardship and chaos and high prices, what better way to overcome but to enter into the spirit of the Lord and truly show love for thy neighbor?

For a few days let rancors subside and divisions be healed. Let the word go forth that all men are brothers, all women sisters; and all together brothers and sisters and very much each others' keepers. For but a few days let charity and grace and concern rule the hearts of everyone, sharing the sweet and the sad, for there is no evil that can withstand the force of good.

Embrace, raise the wine; show laughter and tears and accept one another in expressions of love. Let the world see there is no shame in the exultation of the spirit. And once having touched, having heard the voices of brother and sister, carry forth the sweet memories beyond the Feast of San Genarro, and let life be guided by the principles of Christian benevolence. The earth can be a better place; it is up to the living to make it so. That was the lesson of Francesco I.

A hush fell over the tens of thousands in St. Peter's Square. Any second now the figure of the beloved *Il Papa* would walk with strength and dignity and great love onto the balcony and raise his hands in benediction. And for the Angelus to begin.

Within the high-ceilinged Vatican chambers above the square, cardinals, monsignors, and priests talked among themselves in groups, their eyes continuously straying to the figure of the pontiff seated in the corner. The room was resplendent with vivid colors: scarlets, purples, immaculate whites. Robes and cassocks and head pieces—symbols of the highest offices in the Church—swayed and were turned, giving the illusion of a constantly moving fresco.

And in the corner, seated in a wing chair of ivory and blue velvet, was the Vicar of Christ, Pope Francesco I. He was a plain man of wide girth, and the strong yet gentle features of a *campagnuolo*, a man of the earth. Standing beside him was his personal secretary, a young Black priest from America, from the archdiocese of New York. It was like Francesco to have such a papal aide.

The two were talking quietly, the pontiff turning his enormous head, his huge, soft brown eyes looking up at the young priest in serene composure.

"*Mannaggi'!*" whispered Francesco, his large peasant hand covering his lips. "This is crazy! The entire city will be drunk for a week! Everyone will be making love in the streets. Are you sure we have it right?"

"I double-checked. Do you want to argue with him?" replied the Black, bending down in tranquil solicitousness.

"My God, no! He was always the smartest one in the villages!"

A cardinal approached the pontiff's chair and leaned

4

forward. "Holy Father, it is time. The multitudes await you," he said softly.

"Who—? Yes, of course. In a minute, my good friend."

The cardinal smiled under his enormous hat; his eyes were filled with adoration. Francesco always called him his good friend. "Thank you, Your Holiness." The cardinal backed away.

The Vicar of Christ began humming. Then words emerged. *"Che gelida . . . manina . . . a rigido esanime . . . ah, la, la-laa—tra-la, la, la-laaa. . . ."*

"What are you *doing*?" The young papal aide from the archdiocese of New York, Harlem district, was visibly upset.

"Rodolfo's aria. Ah, that Puccini! It helps me to sing when I am nervous."

"Well, cut it out, man! Or pick a Gregorian chant. At least a litany."

"I don't know any. Your Italian's getting better, but it's still not so good."

"I'm trying, brother. You're not the easiest to learn with. Come on, now. Let's go. Out to the balcony."

"Don't push! I go. Let's see, I raise the hand, then up and down and right to left——"

"*Left to right!*" whispered the priest harshly. "Don't you listen? If we're going on with this honkey charade, for God's sake learn the fundamentals!"

"I thought if I was standing, giving—not taking—I should reverse it."

"Don't mess. Just do what's natural."

"Then I sing."

"Not that natural! Come on."

"All right, all *right*." The pontiff rose from his chair and smiled benignly at all in the room. He turned once again to his aide and spoke softly so that none could hear. "In case anyone should ask, which one is San Genarro?"

"Nobody will ask. If someone does, use your standard reply."

"Ah, yes. 'Study the scriptures, my son.' You know, this is all crazy!"

"Walk slowly and stand up straight. And smile, for God's sake! You're *happy*."

5

"I'm *miserable*, you African!"

Pope Francesco I, Vicar of Christ, walked through the enormous doors out onto the balcony to be greeted by a thunderous roar that shook the very foundations of St. Peter's. Thousands upon thousands of the faithful raised their voices in exultation of the spirit.

"*Il Papa! Il Papa! Il Papa!*"

And as the Holy Father walked out into the myriad reflections of the orange sun setting in the west, there were many in the chambers who heard the muted strains of the chant emerging from the holy lips. Each believed it had to be some obscure early musical work, unknown to all but the most scholarly. For such was the knowledge of the *erudito*, Pope Francesco.

"*Che ... gelida ... manina ... a rigido esanimeee ... ah, la, la-laaa ... tra-la, la, la ... la-la-laaa ...*"

CHAPTER ONE

"That son of a bitch!" Brigadier General Arnold Symington brought the paperweight down on the thick layer of glass on his Pentagon desk. The glass shattered; fragments shot through the air in all directions. *"He couldn't!"*

"He did, sir," replied the frightened lieutenant, shielding his eyes from the office shrapnel. "The Chinese are very upset. The premier himself dictated the complaint to the diplomatic mission. They're running editorials in the *Red Star* and broadcasting them over Radio Peking."

"How the hell *can* they?" Symington removed a piece of glass from his little finger. "What the hell are they saying? 'We interrupt this program to announce that the American military representative, General MacKenzie Hawkins, *shot the balls* off a ten-foot jade statue in Son Tai Square'?— Bullshit! Peking wouldn't allow that; it's too goddamned undignified."

"They're phrasing it a bit differently, sir. They say he destroyed an historic monument of precious stone in the Forbidden City. They say it's as though someone blew up the Lincoln Memorial."

"It's a different kind of statue! Lincoln's got clothes on; his balls don't show! It's not the same!"

"Nevertheless, the White House thinks the parallel is justified, sir. The President wants Hawkins removed. More than removed, actually; he wants him cashiered. Court-martial and all. Publicly."

"Oh, for Christ's sake, that's out of the question." Symington leaned back in his chair and breathed deeply, trying to control himself. He reached out for the report on his desk. "We'll transfer him. With a reprimand. We'll send transcripts of the—censure, we'll call it a censure—to Peking."

"That's not strong enough, sir. The State Department made it clear. The President concurs. We have trade agreements pending——"

"For Christ's sake, Lieutenant!" interrupted the brigadier. "Will someone tell that spinning top in the Oval Office that he can't have it on all points of the compass! Mac Hawkins was *selected*. From twenty-seven candidates. I remember exactly what the President said. Exactly. 'That mother's *perfect*!' That's what he said."

"That's inoperative now, sir. He feels the trade agreements take precedent over prior considerations." The lieutenant was beginning to perspire.

"You bastards kill me," said Symington, lowering his voice ominously. "You really frost my apricots. How do you figure to do that? Make it 'inoperative,' I mean. Hawkins may be a sharp pain in your diplomatic ass right now, but that doesn't wash away what *was operative*. He was a fucking teen-age hero at the Battle of the Bulge *and* West Point football; *and* if they gave medals for what he did in Southeast Asia, even Mac Hawkins isn't strong enough to wear all that hardware! He makes John Wayne look like a pansy! He's *real*; that's why that Oval Yo-yo picked him!"

"I really think the office of the presidency—regardless of what you may think of the man—as commander in chief he——"

"*Horse—shit!*" The brigadier general roared again, separating the words in equal emphasis, giving the crudity of his oath the sound of a military cadence. "I'm simply explaining to you—in the strongest terms I know—that you don't publicly court-martial a MacKenzie Hawkins to satisfy a Peking complaint, no matter how many goddamned trade agreements are floating round. Do you know *why*, Lieutenant?"

The young officer replied softly, sure of his accuracy. "Because he would make an issue of it. Publicly."

"*Bing-go*." Symington's comment sprang out in a high-pitched monotone. "The Hawkinses of this country have a

8

constituency, Lieutenant. That's precisely *why* our commander in chief picked him! He's a political palliative. And if you don't think Mac Hawkins knows it, well—you didn't have to recruit him. I did."

"We are prepared for that reaction, General." The lieutenant's words were barely audible.

The brigadier leaned forward, careful not to put his elbows in the shattered glass. "I didn't get that."

"The State Department anticipated a hard-line counterthrust. Therefore we must institute an aggressive counteraction *to* that thrust. The White House regrets the necessity but at this point in time recognizes the crisis quotient."

"That's what I thought I was going to get." Symington's words were less audible than the lieutenant's. "Spell it out. How are you going to ream him?"

The lieutenant hesitated. "Forgive me, sir, but the object is not to—ream General Hawkins. We are in a provocatively delicate position. The People's Republic demands satisfaction. Rightly so; it was a crude, vulgar act on General Hawkins's part. Yet he refuses to make a public apology."

Symington looked at the report still in his right hand. "Does it say why in here?"

"General Hawkins claims it was a trap. His statement's on page three."

The brigadier flipped to the page and read. The lieutenant drew out a handkerchief and blotted his chin. Symington put down the report carefully on the shattered glass and looked up.

"If what Mac says is true, it *was* a trap. Broadcast *his* side of the story."

"He has no side, General. He was drunk."

"Mac says *drugged*. Not drunk, Lieutenant."

"They were drinking, sir."

"And he was drugged. I'd guess Hawkins would know the difference. I've seen him sweat sour mash."

"He does not deny the charge, however."

"He denies the responsibility of his actions. Hawkins was the finest intelligence strategist in Indochina. He's

9

drugged couriers and pouch men in Cambodia, Laos, both Vietnams, and probably across the Manchurian borders. He knows the goddamned difference."

"I'm afraid his knowing it doesn't *make* any difference, sir. The crisis quotient demands our acceding to Peking's wishes. The trade agreements are paramount. Frankly, sir, we need gas."

"Jesus! I figured that was one thing you *had*."

The lieutenant replaced the handkerchief in his pocket and smiled wanly. "The levity is called for, I realize that. However, we have just ten days to bring everything into focus; to make our inputs and come up with a positive print."

Symington stared at the young officer; his expression that of a grown man about to cry. "What does that mean?"

"It's a harsh thing to say, but General Hawkins has placed his own interests above those of his duty. We'll have to make an example. For everybody's sake."

"An example? For wanting the truth out?"

"There's a higher duty, General."

"I know," said the brigadier wearily. "To the—trade agreements. To the gas."

"Quite frankly, yes. There are times when symbols have to be traded off for pragmatic objectives. Team players understand."

"All right. But Mac won't lie down and play busted symbol for you. So what's the—*input*?"

"The inspector general," said the lieutenant, as an obnoxious student might, holding up a severed tapeworm in Biology I. "We're running an in-depth data trace on him. We know he was involved in questionable activities in Indochina. We have reason to believe he violated international codes of conduct."

"You bet your ass he did! He was one of the best!"

"There's no statute on those codes. The IG specialists have caseloads going back much further than General Hawkins's *ex-officio* activities." The lieutenant smiled. It was a genuine smile; he was a happy person.

"So you're going to hang him with clandestine operations that half the joint chiefs and most of the CIA know would bring him a truckload of citations—if they could talk about them. You bastards kill me." Symington nodded his head, agreeing with himself.

"Perhaps you could save us time, General. Can you provide us with some specifics?"

"Oh, no! You want to crucify the son of a bitch, you build your own cross!"

"You do understand the situation, don't you, sir?"

The brigadier moved his chair back and kicked fragments of glass from under his feet. "I'll tell you something," he said. "I haven't understood anything since nineteen forty-five." He glared at the young officer. "I know you're with Sixteen-hundred, but are you regular army?"

"No, sir. Reserve status, temporary assignment. I'm on a leave of absence from Y, J and B. To put out fires before they burn up the flagpoles, as it were."

"Y, J and B. I don't know that division."

"Not a division, sir. Youngblood, Jakel, and Blowe, in Los Angeles. We're the top ad agency on the Coast."

General Arnold Symington's face slowly took on the expression of a distressed basset hound. "The uniform looks real nice, Lieutenant." The brigadier paused, then shook his head. "Nineteen forty-five," he said.

Major Sam Devereaux, field investigator for the Office of the Inspector General, looked across the room at the calendar on his wall. He got up from the chair behind his desk, walked over to it, and Xed the day's date. One month and three days and he would be a civilian again.

Not that he was ever a soldier. Not really; certainly not spiritually. He was a military accident. A fracture compounded by a huge mistake that resulted in an extension of his tour of service. It had been a simple choice of alternatives: Reenlistment or Leavenworth.

Sam was a lawyer, a damn fine attorney specializing in criminal law. Years ago he had held a series of Selective Service deferments through Harvard College and Harvard Law School; then two years of postgraduate specialization and clerking; finally into the fourteenth month of practice with the prestigious Boston law firm of Aaron Pinkus Associates.

The army had faded into a vaguely disagreeable shadow across his life; he had forgotten about the long series of deferments.

The United States Army, however, did not forget.

During one of those logistic crunches that episodically grip the military, the Pentagon discovered it had a sudden dearth of lawyers. The Department of Military Justice was in a bind—hundreds of courts-martial on bases all over the globe were suspended for lack of judge advocates and defense attorneys. The stockades were crowded. So the Pentagon scoured the long-forgotten series of deferments and scores of young unattached, childless lawyers—obtainable meat—were sent unrefusable invitations in which was explained the meaning of the word "deferment" as opposed to the word "annulment."

That was the accident. Devereaux's mistake came later. Much later. Seven thousand miles away on the converging borders of Laos, Burma, and Thailand.

The Golden Triangle.

Devereaux—for reasons known only to God and military logistics—never saw a court-martial, much less tried one. He was assigned to the Legal Investigations Division of the Office of the Inspector General and sent to Saigon to see what laws were being violated.

There were so many there was no way to count. And since drugs took precedence over the black market—there were simply too many American entrepreneurs in the latter—his inquiries took him to the Golden Triangle where one-fifth of the world's narcotics were being funneled out, courtesy of powerful men in Saigon, Washington, Vientiane, and Hong Kong.

Sam was conscientious. He didn't like drug peddlers and he threw the investigatory books at them, careful to make sure his briefs to Saigon were transmitted operationally within the confused chain of command.

No report signatures. Just names and violations. After all, he could get shot or knifed—at the least, ostracized for such behavior. It was an education in covert activities.

His trophies included seven ARVN generals, thirty-one representatives in Thieu's congress, twelve U.S. Army colonels—light and full—three brigadiers, and fifty-eight assorted majors, captains, lieutenants, and master sergeants. Added to these were five congressmen, four senators, a member of the President's cabinet, eleven corporation executives with American companies overseas—six of which already had enough trouble in the area of campaign contributions—and a square-jawed Baptist minister with a large national following.

To the best of Sam's knowledge, one second lieutenant and two master sergeants were indicted. The rest were— "pending."

So Sam Devereaux committed his mistake. He was so incensed that the wheels of Southeast Asian justice spun off the tracks at the first hint of influence that he decided to trap a very big fish in the corruption net and make an example. He chose a major general in Bangkok. A man named Heseltine Brokemichael. Major General Heseltine Brokemichael, West Point '43.

Sam had the evidence, mounds of it. Through a series of elaborate entrapments in which he himself acted as the "connection," a participant who could swear under oath to the general's malfeasance, he built his case thoroughly. There could not possibly be two General Brokemichaels, and Sam was an avenging angel of a prosecutor, circling in for his kill.

But there were. Two. Two major generals named Brokemichael—one Heseltine, one Ethelred! Apparently cousins. And the one in Bangkok—Heseltine—was not the one in Vientiane—Ethelred. The Vientiane Brokemichael was the felon. Not his cousin. Further, the Brokemichael in Bangkok was more an avenger than Sam. He believed *he* was gathering evidence on a corrupt IG investigator. And he was. Devereaux had violated most of the international contraband laws and *all* of the United States government's.

Sam was arrested by the MPs, thrown into a maximum security cell, and told he could look forward to the better part of his lifetime in Leavenworth.

Fortunately, a superior officer in the inspector general's command, who did not really understand a sense of justice that made Sam commit so many crimes, but did understand Sam's legal and investigatory contributions to the cause of the inspector general, came to Sam's aid. Devereaux had actually filed more evidentiary material than any other legal officer in Southeast Asia; his work in the field made up for a great deal of inactivity in Washington.

So the superior officer allowed a little unofficial plea bargaining in Sam's case. If Sam would accept disciplinary action at the hands of a furious Major General Heseltine Brokemichael in Bangkok, constituting a six-month loss of pay—no criminal charges would be brought. There was just one more condition: to continue his work for the inspector general's office for an additional two years beyond the expiration of his army commitment. By that time, reasoned the superior officer, the mess in Indochina would be turned over to those messing, and the IG caseloads reduced or conveniently buried.

Reenlistment or Leavenworth.

So Major Sam Devereaux, patriotic citizen-soldier, extended his tour of duty. And the mess in Indochina was in no way lessened, but indeed turned over to the participants, and Devereaux was transferred back to Washington, D.C.

One month and three days to go, he mused, as he looked out his office window and watched the MPs at the guardhouse check the automobiles driving out. It was after five; he had to catch a plane at Dulles in two hours. He had packed that morning and brought his suitcase to the office.

The four years were coming to an end. Two plus two. The time spent, he reflected, might be resented, but it had not been wasted. The abyss of corruption that was Southeast Asia reached into the hierarchical corridors of Washington. The inhabitants of these corridors knew who he was; he had more offers from prestigious law firms than he could reply to, much less consider. And he did not want to consider them; he disapproved of them. Just as he disapproved of the current investigation on his desk.

The manipulators were at it again. This time it was the thorough discrediting of a career officer named Hawkins. Lieutenant General MacKenzie Hawkins.

At first Sam had been stunned. MacKenzie Hawkins was an original. A legend. The stuff of which cults were

14

born. Cults slightly to the political right of Attila the Hun.

Hawkins's place in the military firmament was secure. Bantam Books published his biography—serialization and *Reader's Digest* rights had been sold before a word was on paper. Hollywood gave obscene amounts of money to film his life story. And the antimilitarists made him an object of fascist-hatred.

The biography was not overly successful because the subject was not overly cooperative. Apparently there were certain personal idiosyncrasies that did not enhance the image, four wives paramount among them. The motion picture was less than triumphant insofar as it comprised endless battle scenes with little or no hint of the man other than an actor squinting through the battle dust, yelling to his men in a peculiar lisp to "get those Godless . . . [Roar of cannon] . . . who would tear down Old Glory! At 'em, boys!"

Hollywood, too, had discovered the four wives and certain other peculiarities of the studio's on-the-set technical adviser. MacKenzie Hawkins went through starlets three at a time and had intercourse with the producer's wife in the swimming pool while the producer watched in fury from the living room window.

He did not stop the picture, however. For Christ's sake, it was costing damn near *six mill!*

These misfired endeavors might have caused another man to fade, if only from embarrassment, but not so Mac Hawkins. In private, among his peers, he ridiculed those responsible and regaled his associates with stories of Manhattan and Hollywood.

He was sent to the war college with a new specialization: intelligence, clandestine operations. His peers felt a little more secure with the charismatic Hawkins consigned to covert activities. And the colonel became a brigadier and absorbed all there was to learn of his new specialty. He spent two years grinding away, studying every phase of intelligence work until the instructors had no more to instruct him.

So he was sent to Saigon where the escalating hostilities had blossomed into a full-scale war. And in Vietnam—both

Vietnams, and Laos, and Cambodia, and Thailand, and Burma—Hawkins corrupted the corruptors and the ideologues alike. Reports of his behind-the-lines and across-the-neutral-borders activities made "protective reaction" seem like a logical strategy. So unorthodox, so blatantly criminal were his methods of operation that G-2, Saigon, found itself denying his existence. After all, there were limits. Even for clandestine activities.

If *America First* was a maxim—and it was—Hawkins saw no reason why it should not apply to the filthy world of covert operations.

And for Hawkins, America *was* first. Ir-re-fucking-gardless!

So Sam Devereaux thought it was all a little sad that such a man was about to be knocked out of the box by the manipulators who got to where they were by draping the flag so gloriously and generously around themselves. Hawkins was now an offending lion in the diplomatic arena and had to be eliminated in the cause of double-think. The men who should have been upholding the general's point of honor were doing their best to sink him fast—in ten days, to be precise.

Normally Sam would have taken pleasure out of building a case against a messianic ass like Hawkins; and regardless of his feelings to the contrary, he would build a case against him. It was his last file for the inspector general's office, and he was not going to risk another two-year alternative. But he was still sad. The Hawk, as he was known—misguided fanatic as he might be—deserved better than what he was getting.

Perhaps, thought Sam, his depression was brought about by the last "operative" instruction from the White House: find something in the morals area Hawkins can't deny. Check to see if he was ever in the care of a psychiatrist.

A psychiatrist! Jesus! They *never* learned.

In the meantime, Sam had dispatched a team of IG investigators to Saigon to see if they could dig up a few negative specifics. And he was off to Dulles airport to catch a plane to Los Angeles.

All of Hawkins's ex-wives lived within a radius of thirty

16

miles of each other, from Malibu to Beverly Hills. They'd be better than any psychiatrist. Christ! A psychiatrist!

At 1600 Pennsylvania Avenue, Washington, D.C., they were all novocained above the shoulders.

CHAPTER TWO

"My name is Lin Shoo," said the uniformed Communist softly, slant-eyeing the large, disheveled American soldier who sat in a leather chair, holding a glass of whiskey in one hand and a well-chewed cigar in the other. "I am commander of the People's Police, Peking. And you are under house arrest at this moment. There is no point in being abusive, these are merely formalities."

"Formalities for what?" MacKenzie Hawkins shouted from his armchair—the only occidental piece of furniture in the oriental house. He put his heavy boot on a black lacquered table and flung his hand over the leather back, the lighted cigar dangerously close to a silk screen room divider. "There aren't any goddamned formalities except through the diplomatic mission. Go down there and make your complaints. You'll probably have to get in line."

Hawkins chuckled and drank from his glass.

"You have chosen to reside outside the mission," continued the Chinese named Lin Shoo, his eyes darting between the cigar and the screen. "Therefore you are not technically within United States territory. So you are subject to the disciplines of the People's Police. However, we know you will not go anywhere, General. That is why I say it is a formality."

"What have you got out there?" Hawkins waved his cigar toward the thin, rectangular windows.

"There are two patrols on each side of your residence. Eight in all."

"That's a big fucking guard detail for someone who's not going anywhere."

"Small liberties. Photographically, two is more desirable than one and three is menacing."

"You taking liberties?" Hawkins drew on his cigar and again rested his hand over the back of the leather chair. The lighted butt was no more than an inch from the silk.

"The Ministry of Education has done so, yes. You will admit, General, your place of isolation is most pleasant, is it not? This is a lovely house on a lovely hill. So very peaceful, and with a fine view." Lin Shoo walked around the chair and unobtrusively moved the panel of the silk screen away from Hawkins's cigar. It was too late; the heat of the butt had caused a small circular burn in the fabric.

"It's a high-rent district," replied Hawkins. "Somebody in this people's paradise, where nobody owns anything but everyone owns everything, is making a fast buck. Four hundred of 'em every month."

"You were fortunate to find it. Property can be purchased by collectives. A collective is not private ownership." The police officer walked to the narrow opening that led to the single sleeping room of the house. It was dark; where sunlight should have been streaming through the wide window there was a blanket nailed across the frame into the thin surrounding wall. On the floor a number of mats had been piled one on top of another; wrappings from American candy bars were scattered about and there was a distinct odor of whiskey.

"Why the photographs?"

The Chinese turned from the unpleasant sight. "To show the world that we are treating you better than you treated us. This house is not a tiger cage in Saigon, nor is it a dungeon in the shark-infested waters of Holcotaz."

"Alcatraz. The Indians got it."

"I beg your pardon?"

"Nothing. You're making a big splash with this thing, aren't you?"

Lin Shoo was silent for a moment; it was the pause before profundity. "Should someone—who has for years publicly denounced the deeply felt objectives of your beloved motherland—dynamite your Lin-Kolon Memorial inside your Washington Square within your state of Columbia, the robed barbarians on your Court of Supreme Justice would, no doubt, have executed him by now." The Chinese smiled and smoothed the tunic of his Mao uni-

19

form. "We do not behave in such primitive ways. All life is precious. Even a diseased dog, such as you."

"And you gooks never denounced anybody, is that it?"

"Our leaders reveal only truth. That is common knowledge throughout the world; the lessons of the infallible chairman. Truth is not denunciation, General. It is merely truth. All knowing."

"Like my state of Columbia," muttered Hawkins, removing his foot from the lacquered table. "Why the hell did you pick me out? A lot of people have done a lot of goddamned denouncing. Why am I so special?"

"Because they are not so famous. Or infamous, if you will—. Although I did enjoy the film of your life. Very artistic; a poem of violence."

"You saw that, huh?"

"Privately. Certain portions were extracted. Those showing the actor portraying you murdering our heroic youth. Very savage, General." The Communist circled the black lacquered table and smiled again. "Yes, you are an infamous man. And now you have insulted us by destroying a revered monument—"

"Come off it. I don't even know what happened. I was drugged and you goddamned well know it. I was with your General Lu Sin. With *his* broads, in *his* house."

"You must give us our honor back again, General Hawkins. Can't you see that?" Lin Shoo spoke quietly, as though Hawkins had not interrupted. "It would be a simple matter for you to render an apology. A ceremony has been planned. With a small contingent of the press in attendance. We have written out the words for you."

"*Oh, boy!*" Hawkins sprang out of the chair, towering over the policeman. "We're back to that again! How many times do I have to tell you bastards? *Americans don't crawl!* In any goddamned ceremony, with or without the goddamned press! Read that straight, you puke-skinned dwarf!"

"Do not upset yourself. You place far too much emphasis on a mere ceremonial function; you place everyone—*all of us*—in most difficult positions. A small ceremony; so little, so simple——"

"Not to me it isn't! I represent the armed forces of the

United States and nothing's little or simple to us! We don't trip easy, buddy boy; we march straight to the drums!"

"I beg your pardon?"

Hawkins shrugged, a touch bewildered by his own words. "Never mind. The answer's no. You may scare the lace-pants boys down at the mission, but you don't shake me."

"*They* appealed to you because they were instructed to do so. Certainly that must have occurred to you."

"Double bullshit!" Hawkins walked around to the fireplace, drank from his glass and placed it on the mantel next to a brightly colored box. "Those fags were cooking up something with that group of queens at State. Wait'll the White House—wait'll the *Pentagon* reads *my* report. Oh, boy! You bowlegged runts will hightail it to the mountains and then we'll blow *them* up!" Hawkins grinned, his eyes bright.

"You are so abusive," said Lin Shoo quietly, shaking his head sadly. He picked up the brightly colored box next to the general's glass. "Tsing Taow firecrackers. The finest made in the world. So loud, so bright with white light when they go *bang, bang, bang*. Very lovely to watch and to hear."

"Yeah," agreed Hawkins, slightly confused by the change of subject. "Lu Sin gave 'em to me. We shot off a motherload the other night. Before the fucker drugged me."

"Very beautiful, General Hawkins. They are a fine gift."

"Christ knows he owed me *something*."

"But do you not see?" continued the police officer. "They sound like—explosives. Look like—detonating ammunition, but they are neither. They are only show. Semblances of something else. Real in themselves but only an *illusion* of *another* reality. Not dangerous at all."

"So?"

"That is precisely what you are being asked to give. The semblance, not the reality. You have only to *pretend*. In a short, simple ceremony with but a few words that *you* know are only an illusion. Not dangerous at all. And very polite."

"Wrong-o!" roared Hawkins. "Everybody knows what a firecracker is; *nobody'll* know I'm pretending."

"Between the two of us, I must differ. It is nothing more than a diplomatic ritual. Everyone will understand, take my word for it."

"Yeah? How the hell do you know that? You're a Peking cop, not a Kissing-ass."

The Communist fingered the box of firecrackers and sighed audibly. "I apologize for the minor deception, General. I am not with the People's Police. I am second vice-prefect for the Ministry of Education. I am here to make an appeal to you. An appeal to your reason. However, the rest is quite true. You *are* under house arrest, and the patrols outside *are* policemen."

"I'll be goddamned! They sent me a lace-pants." Hawkins grinned again. "You boys are worried, real worried, aren't you?"

The Communist sighed once more. "Yes. The idiots who started this thing have been shipped to mining collectives in Outer Mongolia. It was lunacy; although I'll grant them you were a temptation, General Hawkins. Have you any *idea* the volumes of scurrilous attacks you've made on every Marxist, Socialist, and, forgive me, even vaguely democratically oriented nation on the face of this earth? The worst examples—I should say *best* examples of demagoguery!"

"A lot of that crap was written by the people who paid me to speak," said Hawkins, a bit reflectively. And then he quickly added, "Not that I didn't believe it! Goddamn, I *believe!*"

"You're impossible!" Lin Shoo stamped his foot as a child might. "You're as insane as Lu Sin and his band of growling paper lions! May they all crack many rocks and fornicate with Mongolian sheep! You are simply impossible!"

Hawkins stared at the Communist—both at the furious expression on his face and the brightly colored box of firecrackers in his hand. He had made a decision and both of them knew it.

"I'm also something else, slant eyes," said the lieutenant general, approaching Lin Shoo.

"No! *No!* No *violence,* you idiot——" It was too late for the Communist to scream. Hawkins had grabbed the cloth

22

of his tunic, pulled him swiftly off his feet and chopped Lin Shoo beneath the mandible.

The vice-prefect of the Ministry of Education slumped instantly into unconsciousness.

Hawkins grabbed the box of firecrackers out of Lin Shoo's hand and raced around the lacquered table into the sleeping quarters. He grabbed the blanket nailed across the window, folded back a tiny section on the edge and looked outside at the rear of the house. There were the two policemen chatting calmly, their rifles at their sides. Beyond them was the sloping hill that led down to the village.

Hawkins released the blanket and ran back into the main room, dropping immediately to his hands and knees and scrambling obstacle-style toward the front door. He stood up and silently opened it a crack. The two flanking policemen were about forty feet away and were as relaxed as the troops in the rear. What's more, they were looking down the descending road, their attention *not* on the house.

MacKenzie took the brightly colored box of firecrackers from under his arm, ripped off the lightweight paper and shook out the connecting strings of cylinders. He wound two separate strands together, twisted both fuses into one, and removed his World War II Zippo from his pocket.

He stopped; he sucked his breath, angry with himself. Then, holding the strands of firecrackers at his side, he walked casually past the windows into the bedroom and removed his holster and cartridge belt from another nail in the thin wall. He strapped the apparatus around his waist, removed the Colt .45 and checked the magazine. Satisfied, he shoved the weapon into its leather casing as he walked out of the bedroom. He circled the armchair in front of the Han Shu mantel, stepped over the immobile Lin Shoo, and returned to the front door.

He ignited the Zippo, and held the flame beneath the twisted fuse, then opened the door and threw the entwined strands onto the grass beyond the porch.

Closing and bolting the door softly and swiftly, Hawkins dragged a small red lacquered chest from the foyer and forced it against the thick, carved panel. Then he raced

23

into the sleeping quarters and pulled back a small section of the window blanket and waited.

The explosions were even louder than he remembered; made so, he guessed, from the combined strands bursting against one another.

The guards at the rear of the house were jolted out of their lethargy; their weapons collided in midair as each whipped his off the ground. Rifles in waist-firing position, the two men raced toward the front of the house.

The moment they were out of sight, Hawkins yanked down the blanket, crashed his foot into the thin strips of wood and thinner panes of glass, shattering the entire window. He leaped through onto the grass and started running toward the fields and the sloping hill.

CHAPTER THREE

At the base of the hill was the main dirt road that circled the village. Like spokes from a wheel, numerous offshoots headed directly into the small marketplace, in the center of the town. A semipaved thoroughfare branched outward tangentially from the circling road and connected with a paced highway about four miles to the east. The American diplomatic mission was twelve miles down that highway within Peking proper.

What he needed was a vehicle, preferably an automobile, but automobiles were practically nonexistent outside the highest official circles. The People's Police had automobiles, of course; it had crossed his mind to double back around the hill to find Lin Shoo's, but that was too risky. Even if he found it and stole it, it would be a marked vehicle.

Hawkins circled the village, keeping to the high ground above the road. They would be coming after him. He could stay in the hills indefinitely; that didn't bother him. He had bivouacked underground in the mountains of Cong-Sol and Lai Tai in Cambodia for months at a time; he could live in the forests better than most animals. Goddamn, he was a *pro*!

But it was also pointless. He had to get to the mission and let the Free World know what kind of enemy it was sucking up to. Enough was enough, goddamn it! They could send out radio messages, barricade the whole complex, and fight it out until the offshore carriers sent in air strikes to pinpoint pulverize, even if it meant blowing up half of Peking. Then the copters could come in and get them out.

Of course, the civilians would shit in their pants, but he would control them. Teach the fancy pants how to fight. *Fight! Not talk!*

MacKenzie stopped his fantasizing. Below to the right, coming around the bend in the road about a quarter of a mile away was a lone motorcycle. On it was a *shee-san* police official, a kind of Chinese state trooper. The answer to a prayer!

Hawkins rose from the tall grass and started scrambling down the hill. In less than a minute he was at the edge of the dirt border. The bike was still around the curve out of sight, but he heard it coming closer. He threw himself down on the dirt in the middle of the road, drawing his legs up to appear smaller than he was, and lay perfectly still.

The motorcycle's engine roared as the driver came around the curve, then sputtered as it skidded to a stop. The *shee-san* got off the bike and whipped out the kickstand. Hawkins could hear and feel the quick footsteps as the trooper approached.

The *shee-san* bent over him and touched his shoulder, recoiling at the recognition of the American uniform. Mac moved. The *shee-san* shrieked.

Five minutes later Hawkins had stretched the *shee-san*'s tunic and pants over his rolled-up trousers and shirt. He slipped the trooper's goggles over his eyes and put on the ludicrously tiny visor hat, using the chin strap to hold it in place, a cloth pimple sitting on the crew-cut, grayish black hair. Fortunately for his sense of well-being, he had a cigar. He chewed the end to its desired juiciness and lighted up.

He was ready to ride.

The diplomatic attaché ran into the director's office without saying a word to the secretary or even knocking at the door. The director was threading his teeth with dental floss.

"Excuse me, sir. I've just received the instructions from Washington! I knew you'd have to read them!"

The director of the diplomatic mission, Peking, reached for the cable and read it. His eyes widened and his mouth opened in astonishment. A long strand of dental floss, caught in his teeth, extended down to the desk.

He saw the roadblock cutting off his entry onto the Peking highway. It was about three quarters of a mile down the semipaved thoroughfare; a single *shee-san* patrol car and a line of troopers stretching across the road was all he could distinguish through the fogged-up goggles.

As he drew nearer, he could see that the guards were shouting to each other. One trooper stepped in front of the line and began waving his rifle in the air—hysterically—back and forth, a signal for the approaching rider to stop.

There was only one thing for it, thought Hawkins. If you're going to buy a goddamned grave, buy it *big*! Go out with all weapons on repeat-fire, blazing barrels of thunder and lightning; go out with the screams of the Commie bastards ringing in your ears!

Goddamn! He couldn't see for the fucking dust, and his goddamn *foot* kept slipping off the tiny fucking gas pedal.

He slapped his hand to his holster and pulled out the .45.

He couldn't focus worth shit, but by *Christ*, he could squeeze the trigger! He did so repeatedly.

To his astonishment the *shee-san* did not fire back; instead they dove into the mounds of dirt and sand, screaming like hysterical piglets, scampering into and over the mounds of dirt, burying their asses from the firepower of his single .45 weapon.

Goddamn! *Disgraceful!*

Unless his goggles were playing tricks with the dirt and cigar smoke and the onrushing blurs, even the trooper in front—an officer, by Christ; he had to be—even *he* didn't have the balls to fight back.

An *officer*!

MacKenzie kept the bike at top-throttle and exhausted the clip of the .45. He careened up and over a mound of dirt and sand and cascaded onto a sloping hill of grass. As the bike was in midair he glimpsed the blurs of screaming heads beneath him and wished to hell he had more ammo. He twisted the handlebars violently so he could angle down and zoom diagonally back toward the road.

Goddamn! He hit the surface again! He'd broken through the barricade! He was barrel-assing onto the Peking highway!

The flat concrete was a joy. The spinning wheels of the motorcycle hummed; the wind rushed against his face—clear, intoxicating blasts of clean, dustless air which forced the smoke of his cigar into whirling pockets around his ears. Even the goggles were clear now.

He took the next nine miles like a star-spangled meteor through an unknowing Chincom sky. Another mile and he would turn into the northern side streets of Peking. Goddamn! He was going to make it! And then, by Christ, the Commie bastards would find out what an American counterstrike was!

He raced the bike through the crowded streets and careened off the curb at the entrance to Glorious Flower Square, the final stretch to the mission which stood at the end of the small plaza, fronting the street in alabaster, Oriental splendor. There were, as usual, crowds of Pekingers and out-of-towners milling about, waiting to catch glimpses of the strange, huge pink people that came and went through the white steel doors inside the medium-sized compound.

It wasn't much of a compound at that; there was no brick wall or high metal fence surrounding the mission. Only a thin latticework of decorative wood, lacquered against the elements, enclosing the clipped grass lawn that fronted the steps.

The protection was in the windows and doors: iron grillwork and steel.

MacKenzie revved the bike's engine to maximum, figuring the noise would part the throngs of onlookers.

It did.

The Chinese scattered as he raced down the street.

And Hawkins damn near fell off the bike's saddle at what he saw in front of him; what—in a sense—was rushing toward him at goddamn near fifty miles an hour on that short stretch of pavement in Glorious Flower Square.

There were *three sets of wooden barricades*—elongated horses—in front of the closed latticework gate! Each horizontal plank was a foot or so above the other, forming a receding escalator wall of thick boards backed up by the delicate, filigreed fence.

Standing in a line at port-arms were a dozen or so soldiers, flanked by two officers, all staring straight ahead. At him.

This is it, thought MacKenzie, nothing left but the gesture, the motion—the act itself.

Total defiance!

Goddamn! If he only had some ammo left!

He crouched and headed the bike right into the center of the barricade; he twisted the bar accelerator to the maximum and pressed the foot choke all the way down.

The speedometer's needle wavered in a violence of its own as it quivered and shot up swiftly toward the end of the dial; man and machine burst through the air corridor like a strange, huge bullet of flesh and steel.

Amid the screams of the hysterical crowds and the scattering of the panicked soldiers, Hawkins yanked the handlebars furiously back and slapped the weight of his body against the rear of the saddle. The front wheel rose off the ground like an abstract, spinning phoenix—followed by a mad extension of tail and rider—and crashed into the upper section of the barricade.

There was a thunderous shattering of wood and latticework as MacKenzie Hawkins shot up, into—and through the tiers of obstructions, a maniacally effective human cannonball that dragged the rest of the weapon with him.

The bike plummeted down into the path of washed pebbles that led to the steps of the mission. As it did so, MacKenzie was hurled forward, somersaulting over the bars, rolling on the tiny stones until he thudded into the base of the short flight of steps to the white steel door, the cigar still gripped between his teeth.

Any second now the Chincoms would regroup, the fusillade would begin, and the sharp chops of icelike pain would commence, giving him, perhaps, only seconds before oblivion came.

But the firing did not begin. Only louder and louder screaming from the crowds and the soldiers. Oriental heads peered over the mass of wreckage, above the shattered planks, in front of the smashed latticework. Most of the

29

soldiers who had thrown themselves on the ground were now on their hands and knees.

Yet no one fired a weapon. Then MacKenzie understood: he was, technically, within U.S. territory. If he was shot inside the compound it might be construed as an execution on American soil. It could become an international incident. *Goddamn!* He was protected by lace-pants fol-de-rol! Diplomatic niceties were keeping him alive!

He scrambled to his feet, ran up the steps to the white steel door and began punching the bell and pounding his hand on the metal panel.

There was no response.

He banged louder and kept his free hand on the bell. He yelled to those inside and after what seemed like minutes, the single rectangular slot in the door was opened.

A pair of wide, frightened eyes peered out.

"For Christ's sake, it's *Hawkins!*" roared MacKenzie, putting his screaming mouth inches in front of the panicked set of eyes. "Open the goddamned door, you son of a bitch! What the hell are you doing?"

The eyes blinked, but the door did not open.

Hawkins yelled again, and again the eyes blinked. After several seconds the eyes were replaced by trembling lips.

"No one's home, sir," came the quivering, unbelievable words.

"*What?!*"

"Sorry, General."

The shaking lips were now replaced by the rapid slamming of metal. The slot was closed.

MacKenzie stood there in temporary shock. Then he started pounding once again and yelling again and punching the bell buttons so hard the Bakelite cracked.

Nothing.

He looked back at the crowds and the soldiers, and became aware of the screams and grins and wave after wave of giggles.

Hawkins jumped down the set of steps and began running across the lawn in front of the building. All the windows were not only shut, but the iron inner shutters had been closed behind the grillwork. The whole god-

30

damn mission was sealed tight, an enormous white, rectangular clam.

He raced around the side. It was the same everywhere: closed windows, iron shutters, grillwork.

He rounded the back lawn and ran to the large rear entrance. He began pounding the door and yelling louder than he thought he had ever yelled in his life.

Finally the slot opened and another set of eyes appeared—less frightened than those in front but nevertheless wide and disturbed.

"Open this fucking door, goddamn it!"

Once more lips appeared, and now MacKenzie could see the gray moustache. It was the ambassador.

"Get away from here, Hawkins," said the deep, anglicized voice, cultivated in the Eastern Establishment. "You're just not operative!"

And the slot was closed.

MacKenzie stood there immobilized. Time and space fused into nothingness. He was vaguely aware that the crowds and the soldiers had moved around the latticework fence at the sides and the rear of the mission.

Without really thinking, he backed away from the entrance and looked up at the outside wall of the building and at the roof.

He could do it, using the grillwork of the windows. He jumped to the first window and climbed up the grillwork until he reached the next protrusion of crisscrossing bars.

In several minutes he had scaled the side of the building and pulled himself over the edge of the sloping tiled roof.

He trudged up to the apex and looked around.

The flagpole was centered in the grass on the lawn to the left of the gravel path. The gently waving cloth of Old Glory undulated in the breeze in isolated splendor.

Lieutenant General MacKenzie Hawkins tested the wind and then unzipped his fly.

CHAPTER FOUR

Devereaux smiled at the doorman of the Beverly Hills Hotel, then walked around the huge automobile to the driver's side, tipped the parking attendant, and climbed in behind the wheel, the glare of the sunlight bouncing off the hood. It was all so Southern California: doormen, parking attendants, silent tips, oversized cars and blinding sunlight.

As was the telephone conversation he had held two hours ago with the first Mrs. MacKenzie Hawkins.

He had decided to begin logically, piecing together a progressive disintegration of the man. Surely a pattern would emerge; it would be easier to document this contemporary version of the Rake's Progress if he started with the subject's introduction to the really corrupt world: soft silks and money as opposed to mere killing, torture, and West Point arrogance.

Regina Sommerville Hawkins was that introduction. According to the data banks, Regina was Virginia Hunt Country, spoiled-rich out of Foxcroft and Finch. She had set her cotillion bonnet for the trophy called Hawkins in 1947, when the celebrated youthful warrior of the Bulge had further impressed the nation with dazzling feats on the gridiron. Since Daddy Sommerville owned most of Virginia Beach, and Ginny was an authentic Southern belle—money and magnolia, not just the fragrance—the match was easily arranged. The heroic up-from-the-ranks West Pointer was met, overwhelmed, and temporarily subdued by the lilting drawl, large breasts, and indigenous conveniences of this soft but persistent daughter of the Confederacy.

Daddy knew a lot of people in Washington, so, combined with Hawkins's own talents and track record, Regina expected to be a general's wife within six months. A year at best.

In Washington. Or Newport News. Or New York. Or perhaps lovely Hawaii. With servants and uniforms and dances and more servants and . . .

However, Hawkins was peculiar, and Daddy did not know *that* many people who could curb his odd behavior. The Hawk did not want the la-de-da life of Washington, Newport News, or New York. He wanted to be with his troops. And there was a congressional on his sheet; requests were not denied lightly. Regina found herself in out-of-the-way army camps where her husband furiously trained disinterested draftees for a war that wasn't. So she decided to shed her trophy. Daddy did know enough people to make that easy. Hawkins was transferred to West Germany and Regina's doctors made it clear she could not take the climate. The distance between them just made it feasible to call the whole thing quietly off.

Now, nearly thirty years later, Regina Sommerville Hawkins Clark Madison Greenberg was living in a suburb of Los Angeles called Tarzana with her fourth husband, Emmanuel Greenberg, motion picture producer. On the phone two hours ago she had said to Sam Devereaux:

"Listen, lover, you want to talk about Mac? I'll get the girls together. We usually meet on Thursdays, but what the hell is a day?"

So Sam wrote down the directions to Tarzana and was now on his way in a rented car to Regina's manse. The car radio played *Muddied Waters*, which seemed appropriate.

He found the driveway of the Greenberg residence and entered it, ascending, he was sure, the final crest of the hills. Halfway into the property was an iron gate, operated electrically; it swung open as he approached.

He parked in front of a four-car garage. On the flat asphalt surface there were two Cadillacs, a Silver Cloud Rolls and, in rather obvious counterpoint, a Maserati. Two uniformed chauffeurs were talking idly, leaning against the Rolls. Sam got out of the car with his attaché case and closed the door. "I'm Mrs. Greenberg's broker," he said to the chauffeurs.

33

"This is the *place*, man," laughed the younger chauffeur. "Merrill, Lynch, and The Girls. That's what they ought to call it."

"Maybe they will some day. Is that the path to the door?" Sam gestured toward a flagstone walk that seemed to disappear into a short forest of California fern and miniature orange trees.

"Yes, sir," said the older, dignified chauffeur, as if it were important to cut short the younger man's informality. "To the right. You'll see it."

Sam walked down the path to the front door. He had never seen a pink door before, but if he had to see one, he knew it would be in Southern California. He pushed the doorbell and heard the chimes ring out the opening notes of the *Love Story* theme. He wondered if Regina knew the ending.

The door opened and she stood in the foyer, dressed in tight-fitting shorts and an equally tight, translucent shirt that made her huge breasts burst forward in an absolutely challenging fashion.

Though in her forties, Regina was dark haired, tanned, unlined, and lovely, and she carried her frontage with the assurance of youth.

"You're the m*ay*jor?" she asked, the rank emerging in the low, slow, flat *A* of the Hunt Country.

"Major Sam Devereaux," he confirmed. It was silly to state the name so formally but his attention was on her two titanic challenges.

"Come on in. I reckon you figured we'd all take offense at a uniform."

"Something like that, I guess." Devereaux smiled foolishly, forced his eyes away from the shirt and walked into the foyer.

The foyer was short; the entrance to a huge sunken living room, the far wall of which was nothing but glass. Beyond the glass was a kidney-shaped pool surrounded by a terrace of Italian tile, bordered by an ornate iron fence overlooking the valley.

All this he noticed after, say, fifteen seconds. The first quarter minute was taken up observing three additional pairs of breasts.

34

Each pair was magnificent in its individual style. Full and Round. Narrow and Pointed. Sloping yet Argumentative.

They belonged in turn to Madge, Lillian, and Anne; Regina Greenberg made the introductions swiftly and pleasantly. And Sam automatically related the breasts—the girls to the data in his attaché case.

Lillian was number three. Palo Alto, California.

Madge was number two. Tuckahoe, New York.

Anne was number four. Detroit, Michigan.

A nice cross-section of Americana.

Regina—Ginny—was obviously the oldest, not so much in appearance as in authority. For in truth, all the girls were in that vague age range between middle thirties and the next decade—a span Southern California was expert in obscuring. And each was dressed in sexy Southern California: casual but minutely engineered for that effect.

MacKenzie Hawkins was a man whose tastes and abilities were to be envied.

The courtesies were gotten over with rapidly, courteously. Sam was offered a drink, which he dared not refuse in this company, and seated in a sunken bean bag from which it was impossible to rise. He managed to place the attaché case at his side, but immediately realized that the contortions required to reach over, pick it up, and open it on his lap would tax Plastic Man, so he hoped it would not be necessary.

"Well, here we all are," drawled Regina Greenberg. "Hawkins's Harem, as it were. What does the Pentagon want? Testimonials?"

"There's one we'll all give without reservation," said Lillian brightly.

"Enthusiastically," said Madge.

"*Oooh*," said Anne.

"Yes, well. The general's abilities are enormous," stammered Sam. "I mean—well, I didn't expect to meet you all at once. Together. In a group."

"Oh, we're a real sorority, Major." Madge, Round and Full, sat in a bean bag next to Sam and reached over, touching his arm. "Ginny told you. Hawkins's——"

"Yes, I understood," said Devereaux, swiftly interrupting.

35

"Talk to one of us about Mac, you talk to all of us," added Lillian—Narrow and Pointed—from across the room in a particularly mellifluous voice.

"That's right," cooed Anne—Sloping yet Argumentative—standing outrageously in front of the center pane of glass on the swimming pool wall.

"In the event we don't have a quorum, I act as spokeswoman," drawled Regina Greenberg from a jaguar-skin couch against the right wall. "That's because I was there first and have seniority."

"Not necessarily in years, dear," said Madge. "We won't let you malign yourself."

"It's difficult to know how to begin," said Sam, who, nevertheless, plunged into the difficulty. He touched first, gently, on the abstract hardships of dealing with a highly individualistic personality. He slowly, gently explained that MacKenzie Hawkins had involved his government in a most delicate situation for which a solution had to be found. And although said government was filled with undeniable and undying gratitude for General Hawkins's extraordinary contributions, it was often necessary to study a man's background to help him—and his government—resolve delicate situations. Frequently the partially negative led to the positive, if only to balance and accentuate the affirmative.

"So you want to screw him," recapped Regina Greenberg. "It had to happen, didn't it, girls?"

There was a chorus of yesses and uh-huhs.

Sam knew better than to offer a flat denial; there was more intelligence—or perception—in that room than might have been evident at first. "Why do you say that?" he asked Ginny.

"Gawd Mayjor!" replied Titanic. "Mac's been on a collision course with the high-brass pricky-shits for years! He sees through their manure piles. That's why they like it when those Northern liberals make him out a joke. But Mac's no joke!"

"Nobody thinks he's funny right now, Mrs. Greenberg. Let me assure you."

"What's Mac done?" The question was put defensively by Anne, still silhouetted splendidly at the window.

"He defaced——" Sam stopped; bad choice of word. "He destroyed a national monument belonging to a government we're trying to maintain a détente with. Like our Lincoln Memorial."

"Was he drunk?" asked Lillian, eyes and narrow frontage leveled at Sam; two sets of sharp artillery.

"He says he wasn't."

"Then he wasn't," stated Madge positively from the bean bag beside him.

"Mac can drink a whole battalion under a mess hall slop shoot." Ginny Greenberg's drawl was punctuated by her affirmatively nodding head. "But he never, *never* plays the whiskey game to the disadvantage of that uniform."

"He wouldn't put it into words, Major," said Lillian, "but it was a stronger rule than any oath he ever took."

"For two reasons," added Ginny. "He surely didn't want to disgrace his rank, but just as important, he didn't like for the pricky-shits to laugh at him because of booze."

"So you see," stated Madge in the bean bag, "Mac didn't do what they said he did to the Lincoln Memorial. He just wouldn't."

Sam looked back and forth at the girls. Not one of these ex-Mrs. Hawkinses was going to help him; none would utter a negative word about the man.

Why?

He struggled like hell to get out of the bean bag and tried to assume the stance of a cross-examining attorney. A very soft, gentle attorney. He paced slowly in front of the massive window. Anne went to the bean bag.

"Naturally," he began, smiling, "these circumstances, this group here, evoke several questions. Not that you're under any obligation to answer, but frankly, speaking personally, I don't understand. Let me explain——"

"Let *me* answer," interrupted Regina. "You can't figure out why Hawkins's Harem protects its namesake. Right?"

"Right."

"As spokeswoman," continued Ginny, receiving nods of assent from the others, "I'll be brief and to the point. Mac Hawkins is one great guy—in bed and out, and don't snicker at the bed because most marriages haven't got it.

37

You can't live with the son of a bitch, but that's not his fault.

"Mac gave us something we'll never forget because it's with us every day. He taught us to break our molds. Sounds simple, doesn't it? 'Break your mold.' But, lover, it sets you *free*. 'You're your own goddamned inventory,' he used to say. 'There's nothing you *have* to do and nothing you *can't* do; use your inventory and work like hell.'

"Now, I don't think that all of us believe that's holy writ. But by gawd, he made each one of us try a lot harder. He set us free before it was chic and we haven't done badly. So, you see, there's not one of us—if Mac came knocking at the door—who wouldn't accommodate him. You dig?"

"I dig," replied Sam quietly.

The telephone rang. Regina reached behind the couch to the French phone on the marble table. She turned to Sam. "It's for you."

Sam looked a bit startled. "I left your number with the hotel but I didn't expect..." He walked to the table and took the phone.

"He *what*?!" Blood drained from Sam's face. He listened again. "Jesus! He *didn't*!" And then in the weariness of aftershock: "Yes, sir. I can see he most certainly did.... I'll go back to the hotel and await instructions. Unless you'd rather turn this over to someone else; my tour is up in a month, sir. I see. Five days at the outside, sir."

He hung up and turned to Hawkins's Harem. Those four magnificent pairs of mammaries that both invited and defied description.

"We're not going to need you, ladies. Although Mac Hawkins may."

"I'm your only contact with Sixteen-hundred, Major," said the young lieutenant as he paced—somewhat childishly, thought Sam—the plush Beverly Hills Hotel room. "You can refer to me as Lodestone. No names, please."

"Lieutenant Lodestone, Sixteen-hundred. Has a nice ring to it," said Devereaux, pouring himself another bourbon.

"I'd go easy on the alcohol."

"Why don't you go to China instead? Of *me*, that is."

"You do have a long, long flight."

"Not if *you* make it, I don't."

"In a way, I wish I could. Do you realize there are seven hundred million potential consumers over there? I'd really like to get a see-you shot of that market."

"A who?"

"Close-up look. A real peek-see."

"Ohh. C-U. Not see-you——"

"What an opportunity!" The lieutenant stood by the hotel window, his hands clasped behind his back. *Caveat consumer.*

"Then *go*, for Christ's sake! In thirty-two days I've got a permit to get out of this Disneyland and I don't want to trade my uniform in for a Chinese smock!"

"I'm afraid I can't, sir. Sixteen-hundred needs pro-PR now. All the other slambangs are gone. Some are turning out a crackerjack house organ at Dannemora.... Damn!" The lieutenant turned from the window and walked to the writing desk where there were a half dozen photographs, five by seven. "It's all here, Major. All you need. They're a little hazy, but they show Brand X, all right! He certainly can't deny it now."

Sam looked at the blurred but definable telephotos from Peking. "He almost reached, didn't he?"

"Disgraceful!" The lieutenant winced as he studied the photographs. "There's nothing left to be said."

"Except that he almost made it." Sam crossed to an armchair and sat down with his bourbon. The lieutenant followed him.

"Your head IG investigator in Saigon will fly his reports directly to you in Tokyo. Take them with you to Peking. They've got a lot of real dirt." The young officer smiled his genuine smile. "Just in case you need some final stickum for the coffin."

"Gee, you're a nice kid. Ever meet your father?" Sam drank a great deal of his bourbon.

"You mustn't personalize it, Major. It's an objective operation and we have the input. It's all part of the——"

"Don't say again——"

"... game plan." Lodestone swallowed the words. "Sorry. And anyway, if you do personalize it, what more do you

39

want? The man's a maniac. A dangerous, egotistical madman who's interfering violently with peaceful pursuits."

"I'm a lawyer, Lieutenant, not an avenging angel. Your maniac made several contributions to other—game plans. He's got a lot of people in his corner. I met with eight—*four*—this afternoon." Sam looked at his glass; where did the bourbon go?

"Not any more, he doesn't," said the officer flatly.

"He doesn't what?"

"Whatever constituency he had will disappear."

"Constituency? He's a politician?" Sam decided he needed another drink. He couldn't follow this Buster Brown any longer. So why not get really drunk?

"He *peed* on the Stars and Stripes! That's a Peoria no-no!"

"Did he really reach?"

"We're sending you to China," continued Lodestone, overlooking the question, "in the fastest way possible. Phantom jet aircraft over the northern route, stops in Juneau and the Aleutians, into Tokyo. From there a supply carrier to Peking. I've brought all the papers you need from Washington."

Devereaux mumbled into his bourbon. "I don't like moo goo gai pan and I hate egg rolls. . . ."

"May I suggest you get some rest, sir? It's almost twenty-three hundred and we have to leave for the airbase at oh four hundred. You take off at dawn."

"Wish I'd said that, Lodestone. Nice ring to it. Five hours. And you're down the hall but not *in here.*"

"Sir?" The young man cocked his head.

"I'm going to give you an order. Go away. I don't want to see you until you come to sew in my name tags."

"What?"

"Get the hell out of here." And then Sam remembered and his eyes—though slightly glazed—were laughing. "You know what you are, Lieutenant? You're a pricky-shit. A real, honest-to-God pricky-shit. Now I know what it means!"

Four hours. . . . He wondered.

It was worth a try. But first he needed another drink. He poured it and walked to the writing desk and laughed at the Peking telephotos. The son of a bitch had flair, no question about it. But he was not at the desk to look at the photographs; he opened the drawer and took out his notebook. He turned the pages and did his best to focus on his own handwriting. He walked to the telephone by the bed, dialed nine, and then the number on the page.

"Hello?" The voice was magnolia-soft and Sam could actually smell the oleander blossoms.

"Mrs. Greenberg? This is Sam Devereaux——"

"Well, how're *you*?" Regina's greeting was positively enthusiastic; there was no attempt to conceal her pleasure that the caller was a man. "We were all wondering which one you'd call. I'm really flattered, M*ay*jor! I mean, actually, I'm the elder stateswoman. I'm really touched."

Her husband was probably out, thought Sam through the bourbon, warmed by the memory of her challenging, translucent shirt.

"That's very kind of you. You see, in a little while I'm going to go on a long, long trip. Over oceans and mountains and more oceans and islands and..." *Jesus!* He hadn't figured out how to put it; he hadn't really been sure he could dial her number. Goddamn bourbon fantasies! "Well, it's sheecrit—*secret*. Very covert. But I'm going to talk to your—namesake?"

"Of *cawsse*, lover! And naturally, you didn't get half a ch*ay*nce to ask all those important government questions. I understand, I *really do*."

"Well, several items came up, one in particular——"

"It usually does. I do believe I should do all I can to help the government in its delicate situation. You're at the Beverly Hills?"

"Yes, ma'm. Room eight twenty."

"Wait a sec." She put her hand over the receiver, but Sam could hear her calling out. "*Manny!* There's a national emergency. I have to go to town."

CHAPTER FIVE

"Major! Major Devereaux! Your phone is off the hook. That's a no-no."

An incessant, ridiculously loud knocking accompanied Lodestone's nasal screams.

"What the gawd-almighty hell is *that*?" asked Regina Greenberg, nudging Sam under the covers. "It sounds like an unoiled piston."

Devereaux opened his eyes into the visual abyss of a hangover. "That, dear patron saint of Tarzana, is the voice of the evil people. They surface when the earth churns."

"Do you know what time it is? Call the hotel police, for heaven's sake."

"No," said Sam, reluctantly getting out of bed. "Because if I do, that gentleman will call the joint chiefs of staff. I think they're scared to death of him. They're merely professional killers; he's in advertising."

And before Devereaux could really focus, hands had dressed him, cars had driven him, men had yelled at him, and he was strapped into an Air Force Phantom jet.

They all smiled. Everyone in China smiled. With their lips more than their eyes, thought Sam.

He was met at the Peking airfield by an American diplomatic vehicle, escorted by two flanking Chinese army cars and eight Chinese army officers. All smiling; even the vehicles.

The two nervous Americans that came with the diplomatic car were attachés. They were anxious to get back to the mission; neither was comfortable around the Chinese troops.

Nor did either attaché care to discuss very much of

42

anything except the weather, which was dull and overcast. Whenever Sam brought up the subject of MacKenzie Hawkins—and why not? he had relieved himself on *their* roof—their mouths became taut and they shook their heads in short, lateral jerks and pointed their fingers below the windows at various areas of the automobile. And laughed at nothing.

Finally Devereaux realized they were convinced that the diplomatic car was bugged. So Sam laughed, too. At nothing.

If the automobile *was* fitted with electronic surveillance, and if someone *was* listening, thought Devereaux, that person was probably conjuring up a picture of three adult males passing dirty comics back and forth.

And if the ride from the airfield seemed strange to Sam, his half-hour meeting with the ambassador at the diplomatic mission in Glorious Flower Square was ludicrous.

He was ushered into the building by his cackling escorts, greeted solemnly by a group of serious-faced Americans who had gathered in the hallway like onlookers in a zoological laboratory—unsure of their safety but fascinated by the new animal brought in for observation—and propelled quickly down a corridor to a large door that was obviously the entrance to the ambassador's office. Once inside, the ambassador greeted him with a rapid handshake, simultaneously raising a finger over his slightly quivering moustache. One of the escorts removed a small metal device about the size of a pack of cigarettes and began waving it around the windows as though blessing the panes of glass. The ambassador watched the man.

"I can't be sure," whispered the attaché.

"Why not?" asked the diplomat.

"The needle moved a touch, but it could be the loudspeakers in the square."

"Damn! We have to get more sophisticated scanners. Scramble a memo to Washington." The ambassador took Sam's elbow, leading him back to the door. "Come with me, General."

"I'm a major."

"That's nice."

The ambassador propelled Sam out of the office, across

the corridor to another door, which he opened, and then preceded Devereaux down a steep flight of stone steps into a large basement. There was a single light bulb on the wall; the ambassador snapped it on and led Sam past a number of wooden crates to another door in the barely visible wall. It was heavy and the diplomat had to put his foot against the surrounding cement in order to pull it open.

Inside was a long-out-of-use, walk-in refrigerator, now serving as a wine cellar.

The ambassador entered and struck a match. On one of the racks was a candle, half burned down. The ambassador held the flame to the wick, and the light swelled flickeringly against the walls and the racks. The wine was not the best, observed Devereaux silently.

The ambassador reached out and yanked Sam into the center of the small enclosure and then pulled the heavy door almost shut, but not completely.

His lean, aristocratic features accentuated by the wavering flame of the candle, the ambassador smiled apologetically.

"We may strike you as a touch paranoid, but it's not the case at all, I can assure you."

"Oh, no, sir. This is very cozy. And quiet."

Sam tried to return the ambassador's smile. And for the next thirty minutes he received his last instructions from his government. It was an appropriate place to get them: deep underground, the surrounding earth inhabited by worms that never saw the light of day.

Armed with his briefcase and no courage whatsoever, Devereaux walked out the mission's white steel door, to be greeted by a Chinese officer who waved at him from the foot of the path. Sam saw for the first time the evidence of wreckage—large splinters of wood, several angle irons— lying about on the lawn.

The officer stood outside the border of the property and grinned a flat grin. "My name is Lin Shoo, Major Deveroxx. I will escort you to Lieutenant General Hawkins. My car, should you please."

Sam clinbed into the back seat of the army staff vehicle and settled back, his case on his lap. As opposed to the nervous Americans, Lin Shoo was not at all inhibited about talking. The subject quickly became MacKenzie Hawkins.

"A highly volatile individual, Major Deveroxx," said the Chinese, shaking his head. "He is possessed by dragons."

"Has anyone tried reasoning with him?"

"I, myself. With great and charming persuasion."

"But not with great or charming success, I gather."

"What can I tell you? He assaulted me. It wasn't proper at all."

"And you want a full-scale trail because of *that*? The ambassador said you were adamant. A trial or a lot of hazzerai."

"Hazzerai?"

"It means trouble. It's Jewish."

"You don't look Jewish. . . ."

"What about this trial?" interrupted Sam. "Are the charges centered on assault?"

"Oh, no. That would not be philosophically consistent. We expect to suffer *physically*. Through struggle and suffering there is strength." Lin Shoo smiled; Devereaux didn't know why. "The general will be tried for crimes against the motherland."

"An extension of the original charge," said Sam, making a quiet statement.

"Far more complex, however," replied Lin Shoo, his smile fading into resigned depression. "Willful destruction of national shrines—not unlike your Linkolon Memorials. He escaped once, you know. With a stolen truck he ran into the statuary on Son Tai Square. He is now charged with defacement of venerated artistic craftsmanship—the statuary he ran into was sculptured after the designs of the chairman's wife. And there can be no counterargument concerning drugs for this. He was seen by too many diplomatic people. He made great sums of noise in Son Tai."

"He'll claim extenuating circumstances." No harm in testing, thought Devereaux.

"As with assault, there is no such thing."

"I see." Sam didn't but there was no point pursuing it. "What could he draw?"

"How so? Draw? The sculpture?"

"Prison. What sort of prison sentence? How long?"

"Roughly four thousand, seven hundred and fifty years."

"*What?* You might as well execute him!"

"Life is precious to the sons and daughters of the motherland. Every living thing is capable of contribution. Even a vicious criminal like your maniac imperialist general. He could have many productive years in Mongolia."

"Now just hold on!" Devereaux changed his position abruptly to look Lin Shoo full in the face. He could not be sure, but he thought he heard a metallic click from the front seat. Not unlike the springing of a pistol's safety catch.

He decided not to think about it. It was better that way. He returned his attention to Lin Shoo.

"That's *crazy*! You know that's just plain dumb! What the hell are you talking about? Four thousand—*Mongolia*?" Devereaux's attaché case fell out of his lap; he heard—again—the metallic click. "I mean, let's be reasonable . . ." Devereaux's words drifted off nervously. He picked up the leather case.

"These are the legitimate penalties for the crimes," said Lin Shoo. "No foreign government has the right to interfere with the internal discipline of its host nation. It is inconceivable. However, in this particular case, perhaps, it is not entirely unreasonable."

Sam paused before speaking; he watched the scowl on Lin Shoo's face return slightly, ever so slightly, to its previous polite, unhumorous smile. "Do I detect the beginnings of an out-of-court settlement?"

"How so? Out of court?"

"A compromise. Do we talk about a compromise?"

Lin Shoo now allowed the scowl to float away. His smile came as close to being genial as Devereaux could imagine. "Please, yes. A compromise would be enlightening. There is strength, also, in enlightenment."

"And maybe a little less than four thousand years in Mongolia—in the compromise?"

"Fraught with possibilities. Should you succeed where others have not. After all, it is to our mutual advantage to reach a compromise."

"I hope you know how right you are. Hawkins is a national hero."

"So was your Speeroo Agaroo, Major. Your President said so himself."

"What can you offer? Dispense with the trial?"

Lin Shoo dropped his smile, too suddenly for comfort, thought Sam.

"We cannot do that. The trial has been announced. Too many people in the international community know of it."

"You want to save face, or do you want to sell gas?" Devereaux sat back; the Chinese officer did want a compromise.

"A little of both is a compromise, is it not?"

"What's your little? In the event I can get Hawkins to be reasonable."

"A reduction of the sentence would be one consideration." Lin Shoo's smile returned.

"From four thousand to twenty-five hundred years?" asked Devereaux. "You're all heart. Let's start with probation; I'll concede acquittal."

"How so? Probation?"

"I'll explain later; you'll like it. Give me some real incentive to work on Hawkins." Sam fingered the top of his attaché case, tapping his nails on the leather. It was a silly thing that usually split adversaries' concentration and sometimes produced a hasty concession.

"A Chinese trial takes many forms. Long, ornate, and quite ritualistic. Or very short, swift, and devoid of excess. Three months or three hours. I can, perhaps, bring about the latter——"

"That *and* probation, I'll buy," said Sam quickly. "That's incentive enough to make me want to work real hard. You've got a deal."

"This probation. You will have to define more legalistically."

"Basically, you not only save face and sell gas, but you can show how tough you are and *still* be heroes in the world press. All at the same time. What could be better than that?"

Lin Shoo smiled. Devereaux wondered briefly if there wasn't more understanding beyond that smile than the Chinese cared to show. Then he dismissed the thought;

Lin Shoo distracted him by asking a question and answering it before Sam could speak.

"What could be better than that? Having General Hawkins out of China. Yes, *that* would be better."

"What a coincidence. Because that's one insignificant part of probation."

"Really?" Lin Shoo looked straight ahead.

"You, I can handle," said Sam, almost reflectively. "I've still got to worry about Brand X."

CHAPTER SIX

The cell could be seen clearly through a single pane of unidirectional glass embedded in the heavy steel door. There was a western-style bed, a writing desk, recessed overhead lights, both a desk lamp and bedside light, and a large rug on the floor. There was an open door on the right wall that led to a small bathroom, and a horizontal clothes rack on the left. The room was no more than ten feet by twelve feet, but all things considered, far grander than Sam had visualized.

The only thing missing was MacKenzie Hawkins.

"You see," said Lin Shoo, "how considerate we are; how well appointed are the general's accommodations?"

"I'm impressed," replied Devereaux. "Except I don't see the general."

"Oh, he is there." The Chinese smiled and spoke softly. "He has his little games. He hears the footsteps and conceals himself on either side of the door. Twice the guards were alarmed and made ill-considered entrances. Fortunately, there were several to overcome the general's strength. Now all the shifts are alerted. His meals are delivered through a slot."

"He's still trying. . . ." Sam chuckled. "He's something."

"He is many things," added Lin Shoo enigmatically as he approached a webbed circle beneath the unidirectional glass and pushed a red button. "General Hawkins? Please, General, show yourself. It is your good and gracious friend, Lin Shoo. I know you are beside the door, General."

"Up your ass, slant eyes!"

Lin Shoo released the button momentarily and turned to Devereaux. "He is not always the essence of courtesy."

The Chinese returned to the speaker and pushed the button again. "Please, General, I have a countryman of yours with me. A representative of your government. From the armed forces of your nation——"

"You better check her goddamned purse! Maybe up her skirt! Her lipstick might be a bomb!" came the shout from the unseen general officer.

Lin Shoo turned back to Devereaux in bewilderment. Sam gently moved the Chinese out of the way, pushed the button himself, and yelled into the speaker.

"Get off it, you chickenfucker! Show that hairy ass you call a face or I'll open the slop-shoot and drop in that fucking lipstick! I'll *frag* you, you miserable son of a bitch!—— Incidentally, Regina Greenberg says hello."

The immense head of MacKenzie Hawkins slowly appeared in the pane of unidirectional glass. It merged from the side, huge, crew-cut, leather-lined. Mac's expression was one of utter consternation. A half-chewed cigar was gripped between his teeth, beneath wide, bloodshot eyes that betrayed disbelieving curiosity.

"How so? What do you say?" Lin Shoo's controlled lips were parted in astonishment.

"It's a highly classified military code," said Devereaux. "We only employ it under extreme conditions."

"I will not pursue the matter; it would not be courteous. If you flip the lever on the side of the glass, General Hawkins will see you. When you feel comfortable, I shall admit you. However, I will remain outside, please."

Sam pushed the small handle on the sides of the glass; there was a click. The large, squinting face reacted with instant hostility. Devereaux had the feeling that Hawkins was observing something very obscene but unimportant: Sam, the military accident.

Devereaux nodded to Lin Shoo. The Chinese reached out with both hands, as if to pull with one and push with the other, and unlatched the door. The heavy steel panel opened; Sam walked in.

To an enormous fist that came rushing toward him, on a direct collision course with his left eye. The impact came; the room, the world, the galaxy spun out of orbit into the

50

shimmering of a hundred thousand splotches of white light.

Sam felt the wet cloth over his face before he felt the pain in his head, especially his eye, and he thought that was strange. He reached up, pulled the cloth away and blinked. All he saw at first was a white ceiling. The center light hurt his head, especially his left eye. He realized he was on a bed, so he rolled over and everything came back to him.

Hawkins was at the writing desk, papers and photographs scattered about the top. The general was reading from a sheaf of stapled papers.

Devereaux did not have to move his painful head farther to know that his opened attaché case was somewhere near the general. Nevertheless, he did so and saw it at Hawkins's feet. Open and upside down. Empty. The contents in front of the general.

Sam cleared his throat. He could not think of anything else to do. Hawkins turned; his expression was not pleasant. Somehow absent was that welcoming, manly bond of recognition between comrades–at–arms.

"You little pricky-shits have been busy, haven't you?"

Painfully, Devereaux swung his legs over the side of the bed and touched his left eye. He touched it gently, mainly because he could barely see out of it. "I may be a shit, General, but I'm not so little, as one day I hope to prove to you. Christ, I hurt."

"*You* want to prove something"—Hawkins gestured at the papers and allowed himself the inkling of a cynical grin—" to *me*? With what you *know* about me? You've got moxie, boy. I'll say that for you."

"That phrase is about as antediluvian as you are," muttered Sam as he stood up. Unsteadily. "You enjoying the reading material?"

"It's some goddamned record! They'll probably want to make another movie about me."

"Leavenworth Productions. Film processed in the prison laundry. You *are* a bonafide fruitcake." Devereaux pointed to a blanket draped over the door covering the pane of unidirectional glass. "Is that smart?" He gestured at the blanket.

"It's not dumb. It confuses them. The oriental mind has two very pronounced pressure points: confusion and embarrassment." Hawkins's eyes were level.

The statement startled Sam. Perhaps it was Hawkins's choice of words, or maybe the quiet intelligence behind the voice. Whatever it was, it was unexpected. "I mean it's a little useless; the room is bugged. Bugged, hell! All they have to do is push a red button and they can hear everything we say."

"Wrong, soldier," replied the general as he got out of the chair. "If you *are* a soldier and not a goddamn lace-pants. Come here." Hawkins walked over to the blanket and folded back, first, a corner on the right, then the opposite section of the cloth on the left. In both small areas were barely visible holes in the wall, now very visible with wet toilet paper shoved into the centers. Hawkins dropped the two sections of the blanket and then pointed to six additional plugs of wet toilet tissue—two on each wall, upper and lower—and grinned his leather-lined grin. "I've gone over this fucking cell palm-spread by palm-spread. I've blocked out each mike; there aren't any others. Naturally, I didn't touch 'em before. See how careful the goddamned monkeys were? Even got one right over the pillow in case I talked in my sleep. That was the toughest to spot."

Grudgingly, Sam nodded his approval. And then he thought of the obvious. "If you *have* plugged every one, they'll race in here and move us. You should realize that."

"You should think better. Electronic surveillance in close areas is wired terminally into a single unit. First, they'll figure they've got a short in the unit circuit, which will take 'em an hour to trace—if they don't have to break down the walls and can do it with sensors—and that'll confuse 'em. Then, if they rule out a short, they'll guess *I* plugged 'em and that'll embarrass 'em. Confusion and embarrassment; the pressure points. It'll take 'em another hour to figure how to get us somewhere else without admitting error. We've got at least two hours. So you better do some pretty fine explaining in that time."

Devereaux had the distinct feeling that he had better be capable of some pretty fine explaining. Hawkins was a wily pro and Sam did not relish any confrontation. Certainly not physical or, he was beginning to suspect, mental.

"Don't you want to hear about Regina Greenberg?"

"I've read your notes. You've got lousy handwriting."

"I'm a lawyer; all lawyers have lousy handwriting. It's part of the bar exam. Also I didn't intend to have them typed up."

"I should hope not," said Hawkins. "You've also got a dirty mind."

"You've got terrific taste."

"I don't discuss former wives."

"They've discussed *you*," countered Sam.

"I know the girls. You didn't get anything you could use. Not from the girls, you didn't. Anything else you got is none of my business."

"Do I detect a moral position?"

"In my own crude way. I got a little class, boy." Hawkins pointed to the desk; his arm, hand, and extended finger all were very steady. "Now, start explaining that stuff."

"What's there to explain? You've read it, you say. So do I have to tell you that it represents an airtight case of *persona non grata* on one side, and a large embarrassment for the other? If I do, I just have." Devereaux touched his eye; it hurt like hell, so he sat down again on the bed.

"That stuff in Indochina," growled Hawkins, walking to the desk and picking up the stapled pages, "it's written up like I was working for the fucking gooks!"

"I wouldn't go that far. It raises certain questions as to your methods of operation——"

"That's going *that far*, boy!" interrupted the general. "I was either working for 'em or working with *both* sides, or just pocketing half the pouch money in Southeast Asia! *Or* I was so *dumb* I didn't know what I was doing at all!"

"*Ahh!*" sang Sam in a lilting, false tremolo. "Now we are beginning to understand, said Alice to Cock Robin. A military, really military, man with two Congressional Medals of Honor is a dubious bet for traitor. But all that combat, all those banging noises and that scurrying behind the line and capture and torture and primitive means of brutal survival—the cumulative effect of all *that* would certainly flip out said hero right into laughing land. Very sad, but the human psyche can take only so much."

"Horseshit!" roared Hawkins. "My head's screwed on a hell of a lot tighter than those fuckers who asked for all this crap!"

"Two points for the general," said Devereaux, holding up his fingers in the V sign. "I hereby state for the record that the general's head is screwed better than anyone at Sixteen-hundred. And, I might add, so is the general."

"What does that mean, boy?"

"Oh, come on, Hawkins. You're finished! How and why it happened, I don't know. I just know that you got in the way at a rotten time; you made too much noise and you are *expendable*! Not only expendable, but a goddamned pawn that Sixteen-hundred's giving up loud and clear. You're even an *example*!"

"Horseshit, again! Wait'll the Pentagon gets wind of this!"

"They've—*it's*—already got its nostrils full. The brass noses are colliding with each other, running to the deodorant factories. You don't exist, General! Except maybe as a wayward memory." Sam got up from the bed. The pain in the eye was spreading throughout his head again.

"You can't sell that and I won't buy it," said Hawkins defensively, his voice indicating a slightly diminished confidence. "I've got friends. I've got a career sheet that reads like a recruiting poster. Goddamn it, soldier, I'm a general officer who came up from the ranks—from the fucking mud in Belgium! They won't treat me this way!"

"I'm not a soldier. I'm a lawyer and I'm telling you you've been treated with several layers of forget-me gas. Those telephotos from your buddies in Peking sealed the whole ball of wax. You've bubbled over."

"They've got to prove it!"

"They've got that, too. I was given it in a pitch-black wine cellar about an hour ago. By a psychotic holding a candle. A very solid citizen. They've got you."

Hawkins squinted his eyes and removed the chewed, unlit cigar from his mouth. "How?"

"'Medical records.' That's the hard evidence. Psychiatric and physical. 'Stress collapse' is only the beginning.

54

The Defense Department will issue a statement that says, in essence, you were purposely placed in ambivalent situations so they could ascertain the development. 'Schizoid progression,' I think it's called. Conflicting objectives like the Indochina stuff. Also those pictures of you pissing on the mission's roof have a very complicated psychiatric explanation."

"I've got a *better* one. I was goddamned angry! Wait'll I give my version."

"You won't get a chance to tell it. If the game plan becomes an issue, the President plans to go on the air, praise your past, show your current medical records—with heartbreaking reluctance, of course—and ask the country to pray for you."

"Couldn't happen." The general shook his head confidentially. "*No* one believes a president anymore."

"Maybe not, but he's got the buttons. Not his own, maybe, but enough others. You'll be strapped down in a Nike silo, if he says so." Sam saw that there was a metal mirror in the small cubicle that housed the toilet. He walked toward the door.

"But why should he *do* it? Why would anyone *let* him do it?" Hawkins's cigar was held limply in his hand.

Devereaux looked at the size and hue of the shiner over his left eye. "Because we need gas," he replied.

"Huh?" Hawkins dropped his cigar on the rug. Obviously without thinking, he stepped on it, grinding it into the surface. "Gas?"

"It's too complicated. Never mind." Sam pressed the sensitive flesh around his eye with his fingers. He hadn't had a mouse in over fifteen years; he wondered how long it would take for the swelling to recede. "Just accept the situation for what it is and make the best deal you can. You haven't got much choice."

"You mean I'm supposed to lie down and *take* it?"

Devereaux walked out of the toilet, stopped and sighed. "I'd say the immediate objective was to keep you from lying down in Mongolia. For some four thousand-plus years. If you cooperate, maybe I can pull it off."

"Out of China?"

"Yes."

"How much cooperation? With the gooks *and* Washington?" Hawkins's squint was very pronounced.

"A lot. All the way down the pike."

"Out of the army?"

"No point in staying. Is there, really?"

"Goddamn!"

"I agree. But where does it get you? There's a big world out of that uniform. Enjoy it."

Hawkins crossed back to the desk in angry silence. He picked up one of the photographs, shrugged and dropped it. He reached into his pocket for a fresh cigar. "Goddamn, boy, you're not thinking again. You're a lawyer, maybe, but like you say, you're no soldier. A field commander sucks in a hostile patrol, he doesn't feed it, he cuts it down. Nobody's going to let me enjoy. They'll put me in that Nike silo you mentioned. To keep me from talking."

Devereaux exhaled a long breath through his lips. "It's just possible I can build a shield acceptable to all parties. After you went down the pike over *here*. Full confession, public apology, the works."

"Goddamn!"

"Mongolia, General. . . ."

Hawkins bit into the cigar; the bullet between his teeth, thought Sam.

"What's a 'shield'?"

"Off the top of my head, I figure a letter to the secretary of the army, accompanied by a tape of your reading it—verified by voice print. In the letter, *and* the tape, you state that in moments of complete lucidity you're aware of your illness—et cetera, et cetera."

Hawkins stared at Devereaux. "You're out of your mind!"

"There are a lot of Nike silos in the Dakotas."

"Jesus!"

"It's not as bad as it sounds. The letter and the tape will be buried in the Pentagon. Used only if you publicly make waves. Both to be returned, say, in five years. How about it?"

Hawkins reached into his pocket for a book of matches. He struck one and a cloud of pungent smoke nearly fogged out his face; but his voice was clear behind it. "Down this

Chinese pike of yours, there's no talk about that psychiatric bullshit. No one tries to make me out a nut."

"Hell, no. Nothing like that. Simple fatigue." Devereaux paced back and forth in the small enclosure as he so often did in conference rooms, weaving the fabric of defense. "A little booze, maybe; that's sympathetic, even kind of cute when the client's a ballsy type." Sam stopped, clarifying his thoughts. "The Chinese would prefer an ideological approach; it'd soften them up. You saw the light. They've been generous to you, nice to you. The People's regime is dandy. *And* tolerant. You didn't realize that. You're really sorry for all those nasty things you've said for a quarter of a century."

"Goddamn! You make me *bleed*, boy!" With a technique that escaped Sam, Hawkins actually chewed on his cigar as he roared. And then he removed it and lowered his voice. "I know, I know—. The silos are Mongolia. *Jesus!*"

Devereaux watched the man—painfully. He took several steps toward him and spoke softly. "You've been squeezed, General. By righteous pieces of plastic; nobody knows that better than I do. I've read your file and I agree with maybe one-fiftieth of what you stand for; in many ways I think you're a menace. But one thing you're not is a manipulator. And you're no joke. Remember what you told the girls? You said everyone's his own inventory. That says a lot to me. So let me help you. I'm no soldier, but I'm a damned good lawyer."

Hawkins turned away. In embarrassment, thought Sam. When the words came, there was a defenselessness about them that made him wince.

"Don't know why I'm so concerned about what anybody says—or why I don't settle for a silo *or* Mongolia. Goddamn, boy, I've spent thirty-some years in this man's army. You take off the uniform—no matter what you put me into—I'm as naked as a plucked duck. I only *know* the army; I don't know anything else, not trained for anything when you come right down to it. Never spent any time with the technological—except little stuff in G-two, things like that. Don't know anything about fancy doings like 'negotiations.' All I know how to do is fuck up and trap pouch thieves—those Indochina reports are right about that: I outsmarted the KGB, the CIA, the ARVN, and even the sellouts on the Saigon general staff. But that's different. I can handle personnel, I suppose. But they always gave me the misfits, the stockade products; if they'd been civilians they wouldn't be allowed on the streets. I was always good with them. I could control those devious bastards; I could put myself in their slimy shoes and *use* 'em, *use* their goddamned angling. But there's nothing I can do on the outside."

"That doesn't sound like the man who said everyone's his own inventory. You're better than that."

Hawkins turned and faced Sam. He spoke slowly, reflectively. "Shit, boy. You know what? The only god-damned thing I'm trained for is to be a crook, maybe. And I'd probably fuck that up because I don't give that much of a damn about money."

"You look for challenges. Talented people always do. Money's a by-product; usually the challenge there is in the amounts, what they represent, not what they can purchase."

"I guess so." Hawkins took a deep breath and stretched; his resignation was coming into focus for him, thought Devereaux. He walked past Sam aimlessly, humming the opening notes of *Mairzy-Doats*. Devereaux knew from long experience with clients to let the moment subside, allow the client time to fully accept the decision.

"Wait a minute, boy. *Wait* a minute—." Hawkins took the cigar out of his mouth and leveled his eyes with Sam. "Everybody wants my cooperation. The Chinks, those assholes in Washington—probably a dozen gas conglomerates. I mean they not only *want* it, they *need* it. So much so they'll fake records, build a case—. That ball of wax got out of *control*——"

"Now, hold on. What we're faced with——"

"No, *you* hold on, boy! I'm not going to give you a hard time. I'll make you a better deal than you thought possible." Hawkins shoved the cigar between his teeth, his eyes alive, his voice thoughtful yet intense. "I'll do exactly—*say* exactly, whatever you bastards want me to say and do. Word for word, gesture for gesture. I'll kiss every butt on Son Tai Square, if you want. But *I* want two things. Out of

China *and* the army—they go together. And one thing more: three days in the G-two files back in D.C. Just my *own*, nobody else's. What the hell, I wrote *up* the goddamned things! A last look at my contributions, all the guards you want. I'll be making my final evaluations and additions. Standard procedure for discharging intelligence officers. How about it?"

Sam hesitated. "I don't know. That stuff's classified——"

"Not to the officer who filed it! Clandestine Operations, Regulation Seven Seven Five, Statute of Amendments. Actually, he's *required* to make his final evaluations."

"Are you *sure?*"

"Never more sure of anything in my life, boy."

"Well, if it's standard——"

"I just gave you the regulation! It's military bible, boy!"

"Then I can't see any obstacles——"

"I want it in writing. In exchange for that letter and tape that certifies me so fatigued I eat lizard shit. In fact, *I'll* make the ultimatum: D.C. issues me a written order to comply with CO Reg Seven Seven Five upon my return to the States, or I'll opt for all the silos in Mongolia! I've still got a lot of supporters back home. They may be a little squirrelly, but they're also goddamned noisy."

MacKenzie Hawkins chuckled; his cigar was a mangled pulp of itself. It was Sam's turn to squint.

"What are you thinking of?"

"Not a hell of a lot, boy. You just reminded me of something. Everyone *is* his own inventory. The sum of his parts. There may *be* a big goddamned world out there. And a challenge or two."

Part

II

The closely held corporation—that is, the company whose investors are few, regardless of capitalization— must have at its financial core men of generous heart and stout courage, who will infuse the structure with their dedication and sense of purpose.

Shepherd's Laws of Economics:
Book CVI, Chapter 38

CHAPTER SEVEN

The People's trial went brilliantly for all concerned. MacKenzie Hawkins was the image of converted, reformed hostility; he was a manly pussycat, playing his role to perfection. On his arrival at Travis Air Force Base in California, he emerged from the plane a stoic figure and spoke clearly into the cameras, and at the crowds of press and lunatic fringers; charming the media and defusing the screeching superpatriots.

He stated simply that there came a time when old soldiers—even youngish old soldiers—should step aside gracefully; times changed and values with them. What was perfidy a decade ago was, perhaps, a proper course of action today. The military man, the military *mind* was not equipped—nor should it be trained—for great international issues. It was enough that the military man, a simple warrior in his nation's legions—*sic ... ibid ... in gloria transit* ... MacKenzie Hawkins—adhere to the eternal truths as he saw them.

It was all very refreshing.

It was all very heartfelt.

It was all bullshit.

And Mac Hawkins was superb.

It was remarked that the man in the Oval Office watched from deep down in a sunken armchair with his pet 150-pound dog, Python, protectively on his lap. He laughed and clapped his hands over Python's fur and stamped his feet and giggled and had a wonderful time. His family skipped in and laughed and clapped their hands and giggled and stamped their feet just like daddy. They weren't sure why daddy was so happy, but it was the best fun they'd had since daddy shot that awful little spaniel in the stomach.

Sam Devereaux watched the transformation of MacKenzie Hawkins from roaring bear to passive possum with dubious awe. The Hawk had turned into a soft-bellied mushybeak, and what was basically lacking was the motive. Not that Sam discounted the specter of imprisonment—Mongolia *or* Leavenworth—but once Hawkins had agreed to the plea of guilty, the public apology, the *letter* and gratuitous photographs of his bowed head during the hundred-year sentence of probation, he could have merely resumed his military bearing and let whatever storms rage that might. Instead, he went to extremes to still any controversy. It seemed as though he really wanted to fade away (terrible phrase, thought Devereaux).

Naturally, it crossed Sam's mind that Hawkins's behavior was somehow related to Washington's quid pro quo regarding the G-2 files—the CO Regulation 775, and MacKenzie's access to them. If so, it was an unnecessary effort on the general's part; three intelligence services had looked over the files and found nothing to compromise national security. By and large the entries concerned old-hat Saigon conspiracies, some ancient European network speculations, and a slew of conjectures, rumors, and unsubstantiated allegations—dipsy-doodle nonsense.

If Hawkins honestly believed he could make a compromising dollar—and for what other purpose would he insist on CO 775?—from these out-of-date, unconfirmed recordings, there was no harm in it. What with inflation, the reduced pension he would receive, and the overall untouchability of his status, things were going to be rough enough. So nobody much cared what he did with his old files. Besides, if there was any resulting embarrassment there was also *the letter*.

"Goddamn, it's good to talk to you again, young fella." MacKenzie's voice was loud and enthusiastic over the telephone, causing Sam to jerk the instrument away from his ear. The gesture was part audio-input, part raw fear of association.

Devereaux had left the Hawk over two weeks ago in California, just after the press conference at Travis. Sam

64

had flown back to Washington, his discharge barely three days off, and he had spent the time wrapping up any and all desk matters that might conceivably—even *barely* conceivably—stand in the way of that glorious hour.

Hawkins wasn't a desk matter, but his mere presence was an abstract threat. On general principles.

"Hello, Mac," said Sam cautiously. They had dispensed with the military titles at the beginning of the Peking trial. "You in Washington?"

"Where else, boy? Tomorrow I trek over to G-two for my Seven Seven Five. Didn't you know?"

"I've been pretty busy. There's been a lot to close out here. No reason for anyone to tell me about your Seven Seven Five."

"I think there is," replied the Hawk. "You're escorting me. I thought you knew that."

There was a sudden, huge lump in the middle of Devereaux's stomach. He absently opened his desk drawer and reached for the Maalox as he spoke. "*Escorting* you? Why do you need an escort? Don't you know the address? I'll give you the address, Mac, I've got it right here. Don't go away. *Sergeant!* Get me the address of G-two Archives! Move your *ass*, Sergeant!"

"Hold on, Sam," came the soothing words of MacKenzie Hawkins. "It's just military procedure, that's all. Nothing to get uptight over. Anyway, I *know* the address; you should, too, boy and that's a fact."

"I don't *want* to escort you. I'm a *lousy* escort! I said good-bye to you in California."

"You can say hello again over dinner. How about it?"

Devereaux breathed deeply. He swallowed the Maalox and waved away the WAC who was his sergeant-secretary. "Mac, I'm sorry, but I *do* have a number of things to finish up. Maybe at the end of the week; anytime actually—the day after tomorrow. At sixteen hundred hours to be precise."

"Well, Sam, I thought we ought to go over the G-two routine for tomorrow morning. I mean you *have* to be there, son. It's in the orders. We wouldn't want anything fucked up over there, would we? J*esus*! They wouldn't let either one of us out then."

"Where do you want to have dinner?" asked Devereaux. He grimaced. The Maalox bottle was empty.

You're escorting me. I thought you knew that....It's in the orders. We wouldn't want anything fucked up over there, would we?

No, we certainly would not. Devereaux shook his head. A couple in the next booth were staring at him. He stopped and grinned foolishly; the couple whispered to each other and looked away. Their reaction was clear: You never knew who was being sentenced next.

A tall man came through the curtained arch across the room. It was Sam's turn to stare. In awe.

It was the Hawk. He was sure of it. But the tall man threading his way politely through the crowded room bore little resemblance to the disheveled, cigar-chewing Mac-Kenzie Hawkins who had squinted at him through the glass of a Peking cell. And even less to the close-cropped Hawkins who stood ramrod straight at all times and took each step as though marching to the tune of a thousand pipers—against a strong wind.

To begin with there was the Van Dyke beard. Granted it was new, but the definition was clear and exceedingly well groomed. As was the hair; it was not only growing out, but it had been shaped by tonsorial hands so that the gray swept over the ears in waves. Very, very distinguished. And the eyes—well, one could not really see the eyes because they were covered by tinted, tortoise-shell glasses, a very light tint that was more academic, or diplomatic, than mysterious.

And the man's walk. Good God! Hawkins's ramrod military posture had been replaced by a tasteful, goddamn it, *elegant grace*. There was a softness about the whole bearing, a kind of casual glide that was more Palm Beach than Fort Benning.

"I saw you watching me," said the Hawk as he slid into the booth. "Not bad, eh, boy? Not one of those prickyshits stopped me. How about that?"

"I'm astonished," answered Sam.

"You shouldn't be, son. First thing you learn in infiltration is adaptability. Not just terrain, but a good-sized accent on local customs and behavior. It's a form of psychowar."

"What the hell are you talking about?"

"Behind the lines, Sam. This is enemy territory, don't you know that?"

By the time Mac Hawkins had elegantly spooned his iced vichyssoise he had reached the heart—the core—the bombshell of his reason for dinner with Sam. It was explosively capsuled in a single name.

Heseltine Brokemichael. Late Major General of Command, Bangkok. Currently in limbo, Washington, D.C.

"Yes, Sam, old Brokey was with me in Korea and points east and south. Damn fine officer; a little hot-headed, but then he always had to contend with that stupid bastard cousin of his. What's that idiotic name of his? Ethelred? Can you imagine? *Two* Brokemichaels in the same goddamned army, both with freak names!"

"I'm not hungry any more," said Devereaux quietly. The Hawk continued.

"Yes, sir, you really laid the heavy mortar on Brokey's career. He couldn't get another star on his collar if he bought all the astrologers in the Pentagon. You see, they can never be *sure;* one of the goddamned Brokemichaels is a crook, but, of course, you never proved that, either."

"They wouldn't let me!" Devereaux's whisper carried farther than he cared to think about. The couple in the next booth stared again. Sam grinned again. "I had the evidence; I built the case. They made me drop it!"

"And a good man was cut down just when the joint chiefs were looking kindly on him. I tell you, it's a pity."

"Get off it, Mac. I had that bastard cold——"

"The wrong bastard, boy. And even then you committed serious crimes to get your so-called evidence."

"I took a calculated risk because I was damned angry. I paid for it with two years of my life in that cockadoodle uniform. And that's *it*. I want out."

"That's too bad. I mean, I'm sorry to hear you say that because you may have to spend a little more time over at IG if I——"

"Hold it!" interrupted Devereaux in a whisper that bordered a roar. "I'm out the day after tomorrow! Nothing, *nothing's* going to change that!"

"I certainly hope not. Let me finish. You *may* have to spend time if I can't talk old Brokey out of this crazy idea of his. You see, those charges against you in Bangkok weren't actually dropped; they were sort of suspended because of the complicated circumstances, and what with all those peace freaks screaming against the military. Now, Brokey doesn't hold anything against you, Sam, but he'd really like to clarify his own status, you can understand that. He figures that if he resurrects those charges, you can dig up the files and get the *right* Brokemichael—you'd *have* to or be on a rock pile—and he'd have the JCS smiling nicely on him, just like they used to. Wouldn't take more than, say, six or seven months. A year at the outside—*maybe* eighteen months if the trial was a long one, but you'd both get what you want——"

"I want *out!* That's *all* I want!" Sam wrung his napkin so tightly it squeaked. "I *paid* for my moral indignation. It's past!"

"Past for you, boy. Not old Brokey."

"The facts are *there*. I made a goddamned apology; it's in writing. The day after tomorrow, after sixteen hundred hours, I'll dictate a statement—to a civilian secretary—recapping the whole thing in one-syllable words. I will *not* reopen that case!"

"You will if old Brokey pulls out a certain Bangkok file and issues a directive for your arrest. He *is* a general officer, Sam. Even though he may have pulled duty cleaning out the fucking high-brass latrines, for all I know."

Hawkins had pursed his lips, tsking, and shaking his head slowly; the wide, innocent eyes behind the tinted glasses conveyed anything but innocence.

"All right, Mac. Game time is over. You said, *if* you couldn't talk Brokemichael out of this nonsense. *Can* you talk him out of it?"

"Either talk him out of it, or remove him from the scene for a couple of days. Yes, I can do one or the other. Once you've got that discharge, boy, Brokey'd have a hell of a time convincing anyone to go after you. That paper's sort of a statute of limitations, you know. But I don't have to tell *you* that."

"No, you don't. Just tell me what rotten thing you want from me."

The Hawk removed his tinted glasses and, elegantly, wiped the non-prescription lenses as though he were polishing jade. "Well, as a matter of fact, I've been giving a lot of thought to my immediate future. And I think there's a place for you, but I'm not sure."

"Don't ever be. Next week I'll be back at my desk in Boston with Aaron Pinkus Associates, the best law firm in the Bay State."

"Well, you could take an extra few weeks. Say a month, couldn't you? Je*sus*, boy, it's been four years; what's another month?"

"Aaron Pinkus will one day be on the Supreme Court. Every day with him is an education and I'm not giving up thirty years of paid education. What do you mean, you think there's a place for me? Doing what?"

"I may need an attorney. I think you're the best I ever met."

"I'm probably the only one you've ever met——"

"But you've got a few weak spots, young fella," interrupted Hawkins, replacing his tinted glasses. "I'm sorry to say that, but it's a fact. So I don't know whether to hire you or not. I have to ponder some more about you."

"In the meantime, you'll keep Brokemichael out of the picture?"

"And you'll give some consideraton to acting as my attorney? Just for a couple of weeks? You see, I've got a little money saved up——"

"I know exactly how much money you've got," broke in Devereaux sympathetically. "I *had* to. You want advice for investments?"

"Sort of——"

"Then without qualification I'll help you. I mean that." Sam did. After a lifetime of devotion, risk, and service, Mac had managed to amass the sum total of fifty-odd thousand dollars. No other assets whatsoever. No houses, real estate, stocks. Nothing. That and a reduced pension was all he had for the rest of his life. "And if I can't give you the advice I think you should have, I'll find someone else who can."

"That's mighty touching, son."

Was there a hint of glistening tear in this tough old-line officer's eyes? It was difficult to tell with the tinted glasses.

"It's the least I can do. It may sound corny, but it's the least any taxpayer can do for you. You've given a lot, and you've been shafted by the plastic men. I know that."

"Well, boy," said Hawkins, inhaling deeply, heroically, "everyone does what he has to do in this world. At a given moment of time——*Ouch!* This goddamn faggot suit is tighter than a Memorial Day uniform." The Hawk pulled out a folded, faded magazine from his breast pocket. The pages showing were dog-eared and marked with red pencil.

"What's that?" asked Devereaux.

"Oh, some Chincom propaganda the slants left in my cell. It's the standard Commie crap, misspelled English and all. This is an article that's supposed to show the kind of injustice that's widespread in organized religion. This here Catholic pope has a first cousin—kind of like the Brokemichaels in a way, except they don't have the same names—but they look alike. Actually they're identical, except that this pope's cousin grows a beard to hide the likeness."

"I don't understand. Where's the injustice?"

"This cousin is a small-time singer in a minor opera company and half the time he's out of work. The Chincoms make the obvious comparison. The singer sings his heart out for the people's culture and starves half to death, while his pope cousin eats like a guinea gourmet and steals from the poor."

"It interested you so much you marked it up?"

"Hell, no, boy. I just picked out the inaccuracies to show this priest friend of mine. It may surprise you, but I've been doing a little studying about things I haven't thought much about before. God, and the church, and things like that——. Don't you laugh, now."

Devereaux smiled gently. "I'd never laugh at a thing like that. I don't think it's anything to laugh at. A man's religious thoughts are not only his constitutional right, but often his very real sustenance."

"That's a mighty nice way to phrase it. Real deep, Sam. By the way, just one other thing about this Brokemichael business. Tomorrow morning at G-two. Keep your fucking mouth shut and do as I say."

Hawkins was waiting under the canopy when Sam pulled up to the curb in front of the hotel. He held what looked like a very expensive briefcase in one hand, opened the car door with his other and slid in. There was a broad grin on his face.

"Goddamn! It's a beautiful morning!"

It was not. It was cold and wet and the skies promised a heavy rain.

"Your barometer's a little off."

"Nonsense! The day—like age—depends on how you feel, boy. And I feel just grand!" Hawkins smoothed the lapels of his tweed suit, adjusted the deep red paisley tie over the modish striped shirt, and ran his fingers delicately over the hair above his ears.

"Glad you're in such good spirits," said Sam, starting up the car and entering the flow of traffic. "I don't want to dampen them but you can't take a briefcase with you. You can't remove any papers. Nothing leaves the G-two offices."

Hawkins laughed. He pulled out a cigar from his shirt pocket. "Oh, don't worry your legal head about details," he said, snipping off the end of the cigar with a sterling silver clipper. "I've taken care of all that."

"There's nothing to take care of! I'm responsible for you and I've got twenty-four hours to keep my nose clean." Devereaux took his hostility out on the horn; the sound was returned in good measure by the surrounding vehicles.

"Jesus, you're in a foul temper. You just keep your eyes on the high ground, don't concern yourself with the flanks."

"Goddamn it, doesn't anybody speak English anymore? What goddamned flanks? What does *that* mean?"

"It means what I said last night." MacKenzie spoke as he lighted his cigar. "Do as I say and don't make waves. By the way, would you like to know the name of the fella in

71

charge of the G-two archives? Well, no reason for you to know, but he's a bright son of a bitch, a real genius. Didn't know what I was doing for the service when I got him out of that prison camp west of Hanoi a few years back. He's a Pointer, too. Can you beat that? Class of forty-seven. Same as me. Goddamn! The coincidences in this world——"

"*No!* . . . No, Mac! *No!* No, no, *no!* You can't! I won't let you!" Sam attacked the horn again. Viciously hammering on it. At a crippled old lady who was having a difficult time crossing the intersection. The poor, trembling thing sank her head farther into her quivering shoulders.

"Regulation Seven Seven Five makes it clear that a legal escort is just that. An escort. Not an observer. He takes the clandestine operations officer to and from the place of examination, but he's not permitted inside the room. I guess there're a lot of dishonest lawyers, Sam." MacKenzie took a long, savoring intake of cigar smoke.

"There's *another* thing that's not allowed in that room, you son of a bitch!" Devereaux slammed his hand in fury on the rim of the horn once more. The crippled old lady was now splayed out in the middle of the street. "And that's a *briefcase!*"

"It is, if the officer is making his final contributions. *Nobody* can see those but the ranking archivist of G-two. It's classified material."

"There's nothing *in* there!" yelled Sam, pointing at his briefcase.

"How do you know? It's locked."

Upon entering the offices of army intelligence, Hawkins was escorted quietly, professionally, to the specific room selected for his 775, by two flanking military police. Sam took up the rear. It seemed to Devereaux as formal an exercise as an execution, except that Mac was loose and slightly slouched in his modish tweed suit, not ramrod at all. But once the four of them were inside the room, Hawkins straightened up and replaced his warm civilian tones with the harsh bark of a leather-lined general officer. He ordered the MPs to take Sam into the next room and summon their superior. The MP captains saluted, took Devereaux by the elbows silently into the adjacent room,

72

slammed the door, locked it, checked the corridor, and walked in Wehrmacht unison out into the hallway. They locked that door, too.

He had a vague feeling of *déjà vu*; then he remembered. He'd watched a late night movie on television several weeks ago. *Seven Days in May.* He walked to the single window and looked out. And down. Through the bars. It was four stories to the street. G-2 wasn't taking any chances with legal escorts from the inspector general's office, he thought.

There was the sound of voices from the next room. And then overly masculine laughter accompanied by eruptions of profanity. Old comrades-in-arms recalling the good old days when everyone got his ass shot off, except the generals. Sam sat down in a chair and picked up a dog-eared, worn-out copy of *Let's Stamp Out V.D. in G-2*, and read.

His reading—which was actually rather fascinating—was suddenly interrupted by the steady repetition of another sound from the examination room.

Therump-chump. Therump-chump. Therump-chump.

Devereaux swallowed several times, annoyed with himself for leaving his antacid tablets in the car. The sound he was hearing could not be confused with any other sound in his frame of reference, no matter how hard he tried. It was a Xerox machine.

Why would an examination room for the processing of eyes-only classified files have a Xerox machine?

On the other hand, why wouldn't it?

The first question was infinitely more logical. A Xerox machine was a contradiction—in spirit and in fact—to the purpose of Regulation 775.

Sam went back to his reading, unable to keep his mind even on the pictures.

An hour and twenty minutes later the *therump-chumping* stopped. Several minutes after that a metallic crack of a lock was heard and the door of the examination room was opened. MacKenzie emerged carrying his expensive brief-case, now bulging and strapped together with shining steel G-2 bands, and a foot-long steel chain dangling from the crossbar.

"What the hell is that?" asked Devereaux from the chair, apprehensively and not at all kindly.

"Nothing," replied the Hawk casually. "Just some Fleet-Pac-Com-Sat transfer files."

"And what the hell is that?"

"*Major*," continued MacKenzie, raising his voice, standing suddenly very erect. "I present Brigadier General Beryzfickoosh! *Atten . . . hut!*"

Devereaux shot up from the chair and snapped his hand in salute as a barrel-chested officer with twelve rows of ribbons, an eye patch and, Sam swore, a fright wig on his head, walked swiftly into the room. The salute was returned with a vibrating flourish; the officer then extended a large, muscular hand.

"Hear you're up for discharge, Major," said the general gruffly.

"Yes, sir," answered Devereaux, gripping the outstretched hand.

At which instant Hawkins slapped the briefcase chain over Sam's wrist, securing the triple combination lock between the links, and barked, "First transfer completed, General!"

"*Confirmed*, sir!" shot back the general, still holding Devereaux's hand in an iron grip, his one eye staring at Sam. "Fleet-Pac-Com-Sat is now in your custody, Major! Prepare for second transfer!"

"For what, General?"

"Say!" The general released Sam's hand. "Aren't you the legal prick who shafted old Brokey Brokemichael?"

Devereaux's stomach was suddenly in agony; perspiration formed instantly on his forehead, as the heavy briefcase pulled him halfway to the floor. "There are two sides to that story, sir."

"Goddamned right!" shouted the general. "Brokey's and some shit-ass noncombatant's who *should* be on a stockade rock pile!"

"Now, just a minute, General——"

"*What*, soldier? You being *insubordinate?*"

"No, sir. Not at *all*, sir. I would just like to point out——"

"Point *out*!? You point your ass in the direction of that

74

door an secure the transfer of Fleet-Pac-Com-Sat, or I'll point you right into a court-martial! For insubordination *and* incompetence!"

"Yes, sir! Right away, sir!" Sam tried to salute but the chain and the briefcase were too heavy, so he made a rapid about-face and headed for the door, which was miraculously opened by the two MP captains.

The formalities at the entrance desk were over with quickly. The steel G-2 bands securing the briefcase were some kind of symbol of authority. Devereaux signed the checkout book and the miniature camera silently took his photograph.

Out on the street, Sam turned to the Hawk. "That guy's crazy! Another ten seconds he would have thrown me into solitary! For *what?*"

"Old Brokey's got a lot of friends," said MacKenzie. "Here, I'll drive."

"Thanks." Devereaux reached awkwardly into his pocket and gave Hawkins the keys, his hand still trembling. They walked to the parking lot and got in the car.

Fifteen minutes later, in the middle of a Washington traffic jam, Sam's nerves began to calm down. His panic at being faced with a weird, apoplectic general screwing up his discharge at the last minute was fading. But that concern was being inexorably replaced with another very genuine fear. Brought about partially by the Hawk's silence.

"Mac, now that this pile of fleet-kumquats is in my custody, what the hell am I supposed to do with them? Where's this second transfer taking place?"

"Don't you know?"

"Of course, not."

"The general thinks you do."

"Well, I *don't!*"

"You want to go back and ask him, Sam? Personally, I don't recommend it. Not with the way he feels about you. Jesus! He might dig up all kinds of very serious violations. And you just got your picture taken. One thing always leads to another, you know what I mean? Like the domino theory. Your trial could last for a year or two."

"*What the hell's in here, Hawkins?* Don't bullshit me! What *is it?*"

"Sorry, Sam. I'm afraid I can't discuss it. You understand, boy. It's classified."

Sam sat forward on the couch, his arm stretched out over the coffee table. MacKenzie manipulated the hacksaw back and forth over the chain.

"Once I get this goddamned chain off, we can work on the lock," said Mac comfortingly. "It would be easier with a small blowtorch."

"Not on *my* arteries, you son of a bitch! And thanks for not telling me you didn't have the combination."

"Now, don't worry, I'll have it off in ten or fifteen minutes. The steel's a touch harder than I figured."

An hour and fourteen minutes later the last links were severed, leaving one dangling chain and a triple combination lock around Devereaux's wrist.

"I've got to get in touch with my office," Sam said. "They'll expect me to check in."

"No, they won't. You're with me. Covering my Seven Seven Five. That's what the agreement states. One day minimum, three days maximum."

"But we're not there."

"We went to lunch. . . ." MacKenzie cleared his throat.

"I should still telephone——"

"*Goddamn*, you've no faith in me at *all*! Why the hell do you think I waited until this morning before going to G-two? You've got one day left and *I* account for your time. You can't get in trouble if you're not *there*."

"Of course not. No trouble—just a firing squad."

"Nonsense." Hawkins got up from the floor, carrying the freed briefcase to the hotel writing desk. "You're safer with me. I know those IG close-outs. You think you're winding everything up and some pricky-shit waltzes in and tells you you're not going anywhere until some brief is completed."

Devereaux looked over at the general, now snapping the G-2 bands and opening the expensive briefcase. There was logic in Mac's madness. There *was* sure to be some ball-breaking file or other that a confused superior did not care to have left in his lap. A memorandum could be misplaced—or not read. A confrontation, even a discussion, between legal officers could not be overlooked. Hawkins definitely had a point: Sam was safer away from the office.

MacKenzie removed several hundred Xeroxed pages and put them on the desk beside the briefcase. Devereaux pointed to them and spoke cautiously, "That's all *your* Seven Seven Five?"

"Well, not actually. A lot of it's open stuff that's never been closed out."

Sam was suddenly more uncomfortable than he had been for the past three hours. "Wait a minute. You said back at G-two that it was just raw material on people you'd run across."

"Or people *other* people ran across. I added that, son, I really did. You were just so upset you didn't listen."

"Oh, Christ! You removed raw files on subjects that weren't *yours?*"

"No, Sam," replied the Hawk as he squared off some pages. "*You* did. It says so right at the security desk. Your signature."

Devereaux sank back in the couch. "You devious son of a bitch."

"That kind of says it," agreed Hawkins sadly. "There were times in the field—operating way the hell behind the lines, of course—when I wondered how I could bring myself to do the things I did. But then the answer was always the same. I was trained to survive, boy. And survive I do." The Hawk now had four piles of Xeroxes neatly to the left of the briefcase on the desk. He tapped his fingers over them as if playing a piano and then looked over at Sam pensively. "I think you're going to do real fine. You *will* accept the temporary appointment as my attorney, won't you? Won't be for long."

"And it's a little more complicated than investments, isn't it?" Devereaux remained well back in the couch.

"A mite, I suspect."

"And if I refuse I don't even have to worry about Brokemichael. He's minor. Now there's a small matter of removing classified files from G-two. No statute of limitations on that little caper."

"Don't imagine there is."

"What do you want me to do?"

"Work up some contracts. Pretty simple stuff, I should think. I'm forming a company. A corporation, I guess you'd call it."

Sam inhaled deeply. "That's really kind of amusing, if it weren't so sad. Purpose and intent notwithstanding, there's a not-so-minor item called capitalization required when you form a corporation. I know your finances. I hate to disabuse you but you're not exactly in the corporate assets league."

"No faith, that's your trouble. I expect you'll change."

"And what does that cryptic remark mean?"

"It means I've got the assets figured out to the dollar, that's what it means." Hawkins planted his fingers over the Xeroxes in an elongated press. As if he had found the Lost Chord.

"What assets?"

"Forty million dollars."

"*What!*" In his stunned disbelief, Sam leaped up from the couch. The dangling steel chain followed swiftly and, in a howling instant of pain, the bottom links whipped across his eye.

His left eye.

The room went around and around.

CHAPTER EIGHT

Devereaux ripped open the envelope the instant he closed the hotel door. He pulled out the rectangular slip of heavy paper and stared at it.

It was a cashier's check made out to his name. The amount was for ten thousand dollars.

It was absurd.

Everything was absurd; nothing made any sense at all.

He had been a civilian for exactly one week. There had been no hitches regarding his discharge; no Brokemichael surfaced, and no last-minute problems developed in the office because he had not gone to the office until an hour before his formal separation from the army. And when he arrived he not only had a patch over his left eye, but a thick bandage around his right wrist. From burns.

He had moved out of his apartment, sent his belongings to Boston, but did not follow them because a devious son of a bitch named MacKenzie Hawkins stated that he needed "his attorney" in New York. Therefore Sam had a two-room suite at the Drake Hotel on Park Avenue, reserved and paid for. The suite was leased for a month; Hawkins thought it would be enough time.

For what? MacKenzie was not yet ready to "spell it out." However, Sam was not to worry; everything was "on the expense account."

Whose expense account?

The corporation's.

What corporation?

The one Sam would soon be forming.

Absurd!

Forty million dollars' worth of delusions that screamed for a frontal lobotomy.

And now a cashier's check for ten thousand dollars. Free and clear and no receipt required.

Ridiculous! Hawkins could not afford it. Besides, he had gone too far. People did not send other people (especially lawyers) ten thousand dollars without some kind of explanation. It simply was not healthy.

Sam walked over to the hotel telephone, checked the confusing litany on the pull-out tab beneath the instrument, and placed a call to MacKenzie.

"Goddamn, boy! That's no way to behave! I mean, you might at least say thank you."

"What the hell for? Accessory to theft? Where did you get ten thousand dollars?"

"Right out of the bank."

"Your savings?"

"That's right. Didn't steal from anyone but myself."

"But why?"

There was a slight pause in Washington. "You used the word, son. I believe you called it a retainer."

There was a second pause. In New York. "I think I said I was the only lawyer I knew who had a retainer based in the sort of blackmail that could march me in front of a firing squad."

"That's what you said. And I wanted to correct that impression. I want you to know I value your services. I surely wouldn't want you to think I didn't appreciate you."

"Cut it out! You can't afford it and I haven't done anything."

"Well, boy, I believe I'm in a better position to judge what I can afford. And you *did* do something. You got me out of China some four thousand years before my parole was due."

"That's different. I mean——"

"And tomorrow's going to be your first day of work," interrupted the Hawk. "Not much, but a beginning."

There was now a long pause in New York. "Before you say anything, you should understand that as a member of the bar, I subscribe to a canon of ethics that is very specific. I'll do nothing to jeopardize my standing as an attorney."

Hawkins replied loudly, with no pause whatsoever, "I should hope not! Goddamn, boy, I don't want any slippery shyster in *my* corporation. Wouldn't look good on the stationery——"

"*Mac!*" roared Devereaux in exasperation. "You didn't have stationery printed?"

"No. I just said that. But it's a hell of an idea."

Sam did his best to control himself. "Please. *Please*. There's a law firm in Boston and a very nice man who'll be on the Supreme Court someday who expects me back in a couple of weeks. He wouldn't look kindly on my being employed by—somebody else during my leave. And you said my work for you would be finished in three or four weeks. So no stationery."

"All right," agreed Hawkins sadly.

"Now, what's on for tomorrow? I'll charge you by the day and deduct it from the ten thousand and return the rest at the end of the month. From Boston."

"Oh, don't worry about that."

"I *do* worry. I should also tell you that I'm not licensed to practice in the state of New York. I may have to pay outside attorney's fees; depending upon what you want done. I gather it involves filing for this corporation of yours." Devereaux lit a cigarette. He was happy to see that his hands were not shaking.

"Not yet. We'll get to that in a couple of days. Tomorrow I want you to check out a man named Dellacroce. Angelo Dellacroce. He lives in Scarsdale. He's got several companies in New York."

"What do you mean, 'check out'?"

"Well, I understand he's had business problems. I'd like to know how serious they are. Or were. Sort of find out what his current state of well-being is."

"'Well-being'?"

"Yeah. In the sense of his being around and not in jail, or anything like that."

Devereaux paused, then spoke calmly, as if explaining to a child. "I'm a lawyer, not a private investigator. Lawyers only do what you're talking about on television."

Again MacKenzie Hawkins replied quickly. "I can't believe that. If somebody wants to become part of a corporation, the attorney for the company should find out if the fellow's on the up-and-up, shouldn't he?"

"Well, it would depend on the degree of participation, I suppose."

"It's considerable."

"You mean this Angelo Dellacroce has expressed interest?"

"In a way, yes. But I wouldn't want him to think I was being rude by making inquiries, if you know what I mean."

Devereaux noticed that his hand now trembled slightly. It was a bad sign; better than a pained stomach but still bad. "I've got that strange feeling again. You're not telling me things you should tell me."

"All in good time. Can you do what I ask?"

"Well, there's a firm here in the city that my office uses—used to use, anyway. Probably still does. They might be able to help."

"That's fine. You see them. But don't forget, Sam, we've got a lawyer-client relationship. That's like a doctor or a priest or a good whore; my name doesn't get mentioned."

"I could do without the last reference," said Devereaux.

Damn it. His stomach growled. He hung up.

"Angelo Dellacroce!" Jesse Barton, senior partner, son-of-founder, Barton, Barton and Whistlewhite, laughed. "Sam, you've been away too long!"

"That bad?"

"Let's put it this way. If our mutual Boston friend and your erstwhile employer—I *assume* he's still your employer—Aaron Pinkus, thought you were seriously considering Dellacroce for some kind of money deal, he'd call your mother."

"That bad?"

"I'm not kidding. Aaron would question your sanity and personally remove your name from the office door." Barton leaned forward. "Dellacroce is Cosa Nostra with a capital Mafia. He's so high in the charity rackets the cardinal invites him to the Alfred E. Smith dinner every year. And naturally, he's untouchable. He drives district attorneys and prosecutors right out of their gourds. They can't get him, but not for lack of trying."

"Then Aaron mustn't learn of my very innocent inquiry," replied Sam in confidence.

"Your indiscretion is safe with me. Incidentally, is it an indiscretion? This party of yours, is he really that naïve?"

Sam's stomach began to answer for him. He spoke rapidly to cover the sound. "In my judgment, yes. I'm paying back a debt, Jesse. My client saved my ass in Indochina."

"I see."

"So he's important to me," continued Sam. "And according to you he's naïve. About this Dellacroce."

"Don't take my word for it," said Barton, reaching for his telephone. "Miss Dempsey, get me Phil Jensen downtown, please." Jesse replaced the receiver. "Jensen's second in command at the prosecutor's office. Federal district, not municipal. Dellacroce's been a target over there ever since Phil joined; that was damn near three years ago. Jensen gave up an easy sixty thou' to go after the evil people."

"Commendable."

"Bullshit. He wants to be a senator or better. That's where the real money is——" The telephone rang. Barton picked it up. "Thank you. . . . Hello, Phil? Jesse. Phil, I've got an old friend here; he's been away for a few years. He was asking me about Angelo Dellacroce——"

The explosion on the other end of the line reverberated throughout the office. Jesse winced. "No, for Christ's sake, he's not involved with him. Do you think I'm crazy? . . . I told you he's been away; out of the country, as a matter of fact." Jesse listened for a moment and looked over at Sam "Were you in northern Italy? . . . Where, Phil? . . . Around Milan?"

Devereaux shook his head. Barton continued, one ear at the telephone, his words directed at Sam.

"Or Marseilles? . . . Or Ankara? . . . What about Rashid?"

Devereaux kept shaking his head.

"*Algiers?* . . . Were you in Algiers? . . . No, Phil, you're way off. This is very straight. I wouldn't be calling you if it was anything else, now would I? . . . Simple investment stuff, very legitimate. . . . Yes, I know, Phil. . . . Phil says

83

those bastards will own Disneyland next.... Come on, Phil, that's not kosher; he'll simply walk away from him. I just wanted to confirm Dellacroce's status.... Okay. All right. I've got it. Thanks."

Barton replaced the phone and leaned back. "There you are."

"I touched a raw nerve."

"The rawest. Dellacroce not only skipped free of an airtight indictment last week, but because of a grand jury leak, the prosecutor's office has to issue a public apology. How does that grab you?"

"I'm glad I'm not Jensen."

"Jensen's not. His office will lay off Dellacroce for a couple of months then ring him in again. Won't do them any good; Dellacroce's got his ass in butter. He slides in and out of courtrooms."

"But my client should stay away." Devereaux did not ask a question.

"Several continents," replied Barton. "Clothes don't make the man; his investors do. Ask anyone from Biscayne to San Clemente."

"Well, goddamn, isn't that interesting? You just can't tell anymore, can you?"

"Stay clear of him," said Devereaux, shifting the hotel phone and reaching for the glass of bourbon on the other side of the desk. "He's bad news and you don't want him near you."

"I see what you mean——"

"I'd rather you said 'Yes, Sam, I'll stay away from Angelo Dellacroce.' That's what I'd like to hear you say."

"See what you mean."

"You're not listening. When you pay a lawyer a retainer you listen to him. Now, repeat after me: 'I will not go near——' "

"I know you've had a hard day, but you might put your mind to the next order of business. Just sort of think about it."

"I'm still thinking about Angelo Dellacroce."

"That part's finished with——"

"Glad to hear it."

"——for the time being. Now, I want you to begin roughing

out a kind of standard corporation agreement. A real legal document that has blanks for people putting in money."

"People like Dellacroce?" Devereaux's voice made clear his position.

"*Goddamn*, forget about that guinea bastard!"

"From what I know about him I think you should refer to him as the Roman-blood-royal. But I'd rather you never referred to him again. What kind of corporation? If you want it filed in New York, I'll have to bring in another attorney. I told you that."

"*No, sir, boy!*" Hawkins shouted the words. "I don't want anyone else involved! Just you!"

"I made it very clear: I'm not licensed to practice here. I can't file in the state of New York."

"Who said anything about filing? I just want the papers."

Sam was numb. He was not sure what he was supposed to say; what he could say. "Do you mean to tell me you retained me for ten thousand dollars to prepare legal papers you are not going to execute—strike that—*file?*"

"Didn't say I wouldn't sometime. I'm just not going to worry about it now."

"Then why get a lawyer until you need one? And why the hell am I in New York?"

"Because I don't want you in Washington. For your own good. And when a man raises money for a corporation, he's got to have real legal-looking documents to give for it. I reversed the order of your questions."

"I'm glad you told me. I won't pursue either one. What kind of corporation?"

"A regular one."

"There's no such thing. Every company is different."

"The kind where profits are shared. Among investors."

"In that they're all the same. Or should be."

"That's the kind I want. No monkey business."

"Wait a minute." Devereaux put down the phone and crossed to the chair where he'd left his attaché case. From it he took out a yellow legal pad and two pencils and returned to the desk. "I'll need the specifics. I'm going to ask you some questions so I can rough out this not-to-be-filed, unexecuted legal document."

"Go ahead, boy."

"What's the title? The corporate name."

"I thought about that. What do you think of the Shepherd Company?"

"Not a hell of a lot. I don't know what it means. Not that it makes any difference. Call it anything you like."

"I like the Shepherd Company."

"Fine." Sam wrote out the words. "What's the address?"

"United Nations."

Devereaux looked at the telephone. "What?"

"The address. Whatever the United Nations building is."

"Why?"

"It's . . . symbolic."

"You can't use a symbolic address."

"Why not?"

"I forgot. You're not filing. All right. The depository?"

"Who?"

"The bank. Where the corporate funds will be deposited."

"Leave that blank. A couple of lines. There'll be several banks."

Sam's pencil involuntarily stopped. He forced it onward. "What's the purpose of the company?"

There was a pause in Washington. "Give me some legal-sounding choices."

Now a longer pause in New York. Devereaux's pencil really objected. "Let's start with 'intent.'"

"Obviously, to make money."

"How?"

"By having something people will pay for."

"Manufacturing? Production of merchandise?"

"No, not really."

"Marketing?"

"That's nearer. Keep going."

"Where?"

"Some more words," replied Hawkins.

"I'm not a corporate attorney but if I remember the books, a company's purpose—its motive for profit—is in one form or another of production, manufacturing, marketing, acquisition, services——"

"Hold it! That one."

86

"Services?"

"That's good, but I mean the one before that."

Sam exhaled. "Acquisition?"

"That's it. Acquisition."

"Acquiring at one price, disposing at a second, higher price. You're in brokerage?"

"That's very good, Sam. That's really using the old noodle."

Devereaux pushed the pencil against its inanimate will and wrote on the pad. "If you're a broker, there's got to be a product. Services or real estate or merchandise——"

"Of a deeply religious nature," interrupted MacKenzie, his voice low and solemn.

"What is?"

"The product."

Sam inhaled; it was a long breath. When he exhaled it was with a hum. "Are you saying that you are forming a company to broker the acquisition of religious merchandise?"

"That'll do," answered Hawkins simply.

"Artifacts?"

"That's even better."

"For Christ's sake, *what* is?"

"'Broker the acquisition of religious artifacts.' Goddamn, boy. Perfect!"

Devereaux borrowed the standard New York State forms for a limited partnership agreement from Barton. It was a relatively simple matter to transcribe his notes into the partnership forms and have the hotel stenographer retype the pages as though they had been dictated. Things were looking up, thought Sam as he scrutinized the finished product, replete with its blank lines for investors, depositories, amounts; and the inane description of "brokering the acquisition of religious artifacts."

But it looked as legal as a chapter in Blackstone. Yes, Sam mused as he balanced the envelope containing the gobbledygook he was about to mail to MacKenzie Hawkins. Things *were* looking up. He'd be back in Boston with Aaron Pinkus Associates in a few days; his "legal" work for the Hawk was finished. Altogether it had taken him nine days, some three weeks short of the month Mac had figured.

He had agreed to stay at the Drake a day or two longer, giving Mac sufficient opportunity to approve of his labors. There was no question that approval would come, and it did.

"My word, Sam, that's a mighty impressive looking document," said the Hawk over the telephone from Washington. "I'm downright amazed you were able to write it all up so quickly."

"There are certain guidelines to follow; it wasn't that difficult."

"You're too modest, young fella."

"I'm anxious, that's what I am. Anxious to get back to Boston——"

"I can certainly understand that," broke in Hawkins without the commensurate affirmative that would have curtailed the sudden, growing pain in Devereaux's stomach.

"*Listen*, Mac——"

"I see you made me president of the company. You didn't tell me that."

"There were no other names. I asked you about the corporate officers and you said leave the lines blank."

"What are those titles *secretary* and *treasurer?* Are they important?"

"Not if you're not filing."

"Suppose someday I decided to?"

"The standard procedure is to combine the two. Most states require a minimum of two general partners for a limited partnership agreement."

"But I could have more if I wanted to, couldn't I?"

"Certainly."

"I just wanted to know what's right, Sam. Not important. It's never going to be filed. Just passes the time."

Devereaux thought he detected a note of melancholy in Hawkins's voice. Was Mac beginning to come to grips with his own fantasies? Did he begin to understand that his irrational foray into corporate legalities was simple compensation for the absence of command decision? Sam

88

began to relax. He actually felt sorry for this old war-horse. *Passes the time* was a euphemism for *filling up the days*. "I'm sure it does, General."

"Why, Sam, you haven't called me general in weeks."

"Sorry. A slip."

"I'll be in touch with you tomorrow, boy. You've worked hard. Have a little fun tonight. Remember, it's on the expense account."

"As to that ten thou'. It's very generous of you but I don't want it. I don't need it. I'll deduct whatever legal expenses—stenographer, supplies, that kind of thing—and return the rest. Then there's an investment counselor I know in Washington——"

Devereaux stopped. He realized that the click on the other end of the line had terminated the conversation.

There was no point in not having a good time. He had spent enough weekends in New York to know where the action was: the singles' bars on Third Avenue.

Sam was spectacularly successful. His catch was a nubile young thing who had come out of Omaha, Nebraska—the county seat of Henry Fonda and Marlon Brando—to scale the Broadway heights. She was terribly impressed with a lawyer who did a lot of work for Metro-Goldwyn-Warner-Brothers when he wasn't handling contracts for *Bowling For Dollars* and *Masterpiece Theatre*.

Sam was impressed, too. All during the night, throughout most of the next morning, well into the following afternoon and (with time out for food and limited discussion) into the next evening.

It was 9:27 when the telephone rang; 9:29 when the nubile young thing spoke sleepily. "Sam, the phone's on my side."

"You're very observant."

"Shall I get it?" she asked.

"Since it's on your side, I'd say yes."

"You're sure?"

Sam opened his eyes. The girl had raised herself and was stretching; the sheet had fallen away. "Make it quick," Devereaux said.

"If you're sure."

89

"I have no wife and my mother doesn't know where I am and Aaron Pinkus wouldn't be mad. Get the phone, talk fast, and hang up."

The girl reached for the instrument; Sam reached for the girl.

"There's a man with a raspy voice who wants to talk to you. He says his name is Angelo Dellacroce." She handed Sam the receiver.

"Hey, *you*!" The words spat from the telephone. "You Samuel Deverooze, sec atary-treasurer of this Shepherd Company?"

CHAPTER NINE

Former Lieutenant General MacKenzie Hawkins, twice awarded the nation's highest honor for extraordinary heroism beyond the call of duty in deadly combat against the enemy, cowered like a frightened boy at the sight of former Major Sam Devereaux, military accident.

Hawkins could see Sam getting out of the taxi at the entrance of the North Hampton Golf Club. The brass lamps on top of the stone posts flanking the drive were the only source of light; it was a cold, cloudy night and no moon could be seen. The lamps, however, gave sufficient illumination to reveal the anguished expression on Devereaux's face.

Sam was furious, MacKenzie realized that. But, he thought to himself, he had not actually lied. Not really. He never told Devereaux he *wouldn't* approach Angelo Dellacroce. Only that he had no reason to do so when Sam pressed him on the point. At that moment. Not *later*.

The secretary-treasurer title was something else. It looked terrific on the partnership agreement: *Samuel Devereaux, Esq., Counselor-at-law, Suite 4-F, Drake Hotel, New York*, right above the line reserved for the second most important office in the Shepherd Company. It was for Devereaux's own good; he'd understand that soon enough. But at the moment Samuel Devereaux, Esq., was mad as a caged bull fenced off from heifers in heat.

The Hawk had agreed to Dellacroce's rendezvous because it suited him. The Italian was so concerned about surveillance he had insisted on meeting Mac in the middle of the fairway on hole six at the North Hampton Golf Club between the hours of midnight and one in the morning. But if Hawkins had objected and changed the location to

91

the Bell Telephone Company, Dellacroce would have capitulated.

For Dellacroce had no choice. Mac had a folder on the Mafioso that would have guaranteed a jail sentence worthy of a court in the People's Republic.

Still, a meeting at night in terrain surrounded by thick woods and streams and small lakes appealed to Hawkins. He was at home in such territory. It wasn't Cambodia or Laos, but he could sort of keep his hand in, as it were.

He flew up from Washington in the afternoon and with false identification rented a car and drove out to North Hampton. As soon as it was dark, he circled the golf club and parked at the west perimeter. Dellacroce had told him that the club was closed for the evening and the night watchman would be replaced by one of his men.

Which meant, of course, that Dellacroce would double the patrols everywhere, especially around the area of fairway six.

His pockets stuffed with coils of thin rope and rolls of three-inch adhesive, Hawkins employed an old Ho Chi-minh tactic that had served him well in the past. He began his commando assault at the farthest point inside the hostile area and worked his way toward the front.

At 2300 the enemy patrols started to man their emplacements within the North Hampton Golf Club. There were nine (a few more than Mac had anticipated) spaced out in the rough by the edge of the woods on both sides of fairway six, the line of relay extending back to the clubhouse and the driveway.

One by one, Hawkins immobilized eight patrols; he removed all weapons, bound them, taped their faces—all facial muscles, not just the mouths—and rendered them unconscious with *kai-sai* chops at the base of the skull. Then he worked his way back to the ninth patrol who manned the entrance.

He saved for this man a strategy that was particularly effective against the Pathet Lao. For the guard had to be able to talk.

The man was exceedingly cooperative. Especially after Mac had sliced his trousers from crotch to cuff.

At ten minutes to midnight, Dellacroce's huge black

limousine drove swiftly through the gates and up to the wide, pillared porch. In the darkness the ninth patrol, riveted to a pillar, spoke.

"Everything's fine, Mr. Dellacroce. All the boys are spread good, like you said."

The man's voice was a bit high and a little strained, but Hawkins figured rightly that Dellacroce had other things on his mind.

"Okay. Real good," was the raspy reply as Dellacroce got out of the automobile, flanked by two heavyset body-guards who walked like gorillas with their hands in their fur. "Rocco, you stay here with Augie. You, Fingers, you come with me. And, Meat, you get the fuckin' car back in the lot outta sight."

Before Dellacroce and Fingers had rounded the corner of the building, the ninth patrol was *kai-sai*ed out of commission. By the time Dellacroce and Fingers had disappeared across the lawn, Rocco had joined Augie in peaceful oblivion.

The gentleman named Meat was Hawkins's next dispatchee. It took nearly five minutes, but only because Meat was an experienced combat man. He did not park the limousine at the edge of the lot; instead, he had pulled to a stop in the center. It was good positioning, thought Mac. Meat could observe all his flanks unencumbered by visual shadings or sightline obstructions. Meat was good.

But not good enough.

MacKenzie scrambled diagonally out of the parking area, over the first tee, and left through the rough toward fairway six. Since Dellacroce had made it clear he would be alone, Hawkins knew that Fingers would be hiding in the darkness, no doubt at the edge of the woods, and if he had a brain in his head, across the fairway on the east side for a superior line of fire.

But Fingers did not have such savvy. He remained in the west rough, prone in the underbrush, eliminating any rear flank observation.

Goddamn, thought MacKenzie, it was not much fun taking an asshole like Fingers.

Nevertheless, he took him. Silently. In eleven seconds.

Leaving Angelo Dellacroce alone in the middle of fairway six, the lighted end of a cigar protruding from his fat mouth, his squat body sagging at ease, his plump hands clasped behind his back as though waiting to be served a plate of linguini in a slow trattoria.

Three minutes later Devereaux's taxi was heard on the deserted back road fronting the golf club, and MacKenzie waited behind the pillar.

As Sam walked haltingly up the drive, Hawkins decided not to tell him about the immobilized patrols. It would only worry the ex-major; better to let him think Dellacroce was true to his word: he was alone on fairway six.

"God*damn*! Hello, Sam!"

Devereaux threw himself to the ground, hugging the gravel for dear life. And then he looked up; MacKenzie took out a small but powerful pencil light from his pocket and flicked it on.

The ex-major was certainly angry. His face was kind of pinched and puffed, as if it might explode right out of his skin.

"You unprincipled son of a bitch!" Sam whispered, fury and fear intermeshed. "You lowlife! You're the most devious, despicable form of subhuman that ever lived! What the hell have you done, you *bastard*?"

"Now, now, that's no way to talk. Come on, get up; you look silly down there all splayed out . . ." MacKenzie reached for Devereaux's hand.

"*Don't touch me*, you slug worm! Fucking Mongolian sheep is too *good* for you! I should have let Lin Shoo pry out your fingernails, one by one, for four thousand fucking years!—Don't *touch* me!" Sam staggered to his feet.

"Look, Major——"

"Don't call me that! I don't own a serial number and I don't want to be addressed *ever* by anything *remotely* military! I'm a lawyer, but I'm not *your* goddamned lawyer! Where the hell are we? How many 'torpedoes' have us covered with guns?"

MacKenzie grinned. "There's nobody, boy. Just Dellacroce standing out on the fairway like a nice uncle at a backyard pasta party."

"I don't believe you! Do you know what that gorilla told me on the phone when I said I wouldn't come out here?

That goddamned hood told me my health would take a sudden turn for the worse! That's what he told me!"

"Oh, don't pay any attention to that sort of thing. Those fat slobs always talk tough."

"Horseshit!" Devereaux peered into the darkness. "That maniac said if I was late he'd send a basket of fruit to the hospital—*tomorrow*! And if I tried to leave town, some goon called Meat would find me before the week was up!"

The Hawk shook his head. "Meat's pretty good, but I think you could take him. I'd put my money on you, boy."

"I don't *want* to take him—or *any*body! And don't put any money on *me*! You're never going to see me again! I just wanted to get this over with. I want to meet this Dellacroce; tell him the whole thing's a crazy mistake! I had some typing done for you, and that's all!"

"Now listen to me, son. You're overreacting. There's nothing to worry about at all." Hawkins started walking across the lawn. Devereaux kept pace, his head snapping in the direction of every noise. "Mr. Dellacroce will be exceedingly cooperative. And there'll be no more tough talk, you'll see."

"What was that?" There was a squishing sound.

"Relax, will you? I think you stepped on some dog turd. Do me a favor. Don't start explaining anything until I talk with Dellacroce, okay? It won't take me more than three or four minutes."

"*No!* Absolutely *no*! I don't care to have a promising legal career cut short in the middle of a fairway at some Cosa Nostra golf course! These people don't play games! They use bullets, and chains, and heavy cement! And rivers! What was *that*?" There was a fluttering of wings in the dark trees.

"We alarmed a bird. Let's put it this way. If you just keep your mouth shut until I'm finished, I'll pay you another ten thousand. Free and clear. How about that?"

"You're a lunatic! No, again. Because I can't spend it displacing roots in a Boston cemetery! You could offer ten million; the answer's still no!"

"That's not out of the question——"

"For Christ's sake, have yourself committed before somebody else does!"

"Then I'm afraid I'll have to put it this way. You either shut up until my business with Mr. Dellacroce is finished, or tomorrow morning I call the FBI and tell them there's an ex-major walking around peddling raw-file intelligence documents he illegally removed from the G-two archives."

"Oh, no you don't! Because I'll tell the truth. I'll tell them how you blackmailed me, then conned me, then blackmailed me again. You'd get a lighter prison sentence in Peking!"

"It surely does get complicated, doesn't it? I mean you'd be reopening the Brokemichael business. How would it look? A man violates the espionage laws because he doesn't like spending a little extra time in the service of his country. In a cushy job, not even combat. Pretty weak blackmail, I'd say."

"You *unprincipled*——"

"I know, I know," said the Hawk wearily. "You keep repeating yourself. What you've got to understand is that it doesn't make a whole lot of difference to me. As you said, I've been shafted. How much more shafting can they do?"

Hawkins kept walking. Devereaux followed reluctantly, his eyes darting everywhere, his nerves obviously frayed; a series of whispered squeaks emerged from his throat until he found the words. "Have you no decency, sir? No sense of compassion? No love of your fellow man within your heart?"

"I surely do," said the Hawk. They cut across the third tee onto fairway six. "Now keep that eloquent tongue of yours inactive for a while. If you don't like the way things go, then speak your piece. Can I be fairer than that?"

The overcast sky was thinning out; intermittently the moon shone through. And a hundred yards ahead they could see the squat figure of Angelo Dellacroce, his hands still clasped behind his back, the lighted stub of a cigar still in his mouth.

"He must have ashes all over his front," said Hawkins quietly. Then louder, "Mr. Dellacroce?"

There was a grunt from the obese body in front of them. MacKenzie flicked on his pencil light and held it over his own head, spilling the light on his longish steel-gray hair, throwing shadows down across his precisely barbered Van Dyke.

"You're making us a target!" whispered Sam.

"Who's going to shoot?"

They approached the Italian; Mac extended his hand. Dellacroce made no move to accept it. Hawkins spoke quietly. "Even when I accepted gook surrenders I got a handshake. Sort of separates us from the animals."

Reluctantly Dellacroce pulled his hand from behind his back and the two shook. "I ain't no gook and this ain't no surrender," said the raspy voice.

"Course it isn't," answered MacKenzie brightly. "It's the beginning of a profitable association. By the way, this is my attorney and good friend, Sam Devereaux———"

"Mac!"

"Shut up and shake hands," said Hawkins *sotto voce*. "Goddamn, boys. I said shake *hands!*"

With even greater reluctance, the two hands inched toward each other, touched briefly and separated as though the owners feared infection.

"That's better," said the Hawk enthusiastically. "Now we can talk."

And MacKenzie did. He started by listing the illegal activities—both foreign and domestic—of Angelo Dellacroce. It took him two minutes.

"Now, Mr. Dellacroce, the reason the authorities can't catch up with you is that they don't have access to a single financial clearinghouse that ties in specifically with all these here sundry enterprises. I realize it will sound strange to you, sir, but I believe I have that access. There's a bank in Geneva, Switzerland; the first three numbers on the account happen to be seven, one, five. In this account is something over sixty-two million dollars———"

"Basta! Basta!"

"—and the deposits were made directly from such locales as I've suggested. Now I guess you've studied the new Swiss laws relative to such accounts. They're tricky because fraud in one country may not constitute fraud in Geneva. But goddamn, would you believe there's now a way for Interpol to subpoena the records of those accounts? All the international police have to do is submit a

97

copy of a payment—to a specific account—that's been made by a convicted narcotics dealer. And it surely is wondrous good fortune on my part to have in my possession Xeroxed copies of quite a few such payments——"

"*Basta!* You shut up!" Dellacroce roared. "*Fingers! Manny! Carlo! Dino!* Get out here! *Now!*"

There were only the sounds of the night in reply.

"There's no one there. At least no one that can hear you," said the Hawk softly.

"*What!?——Fingers! Figlio della prostituta!* Get out here!"

Nothing.

"Now, you and I, Mr. Dellacroce, will step away from my friend and attorney, here, so we can talk real private like." MacKenzie touched the Italian's arm, which was instantly yanked away.

"*Meat! Augie! Rocco!* You hear me, boys? Get out here!"

"They're sleeping, too, sir," said Hawkins kindly. "They won't wake up for a couple of hours."

Dellacroce whipped his head toward Mac. "You got cops here? How many cops you got?" The questions overlapped.

"Nobody. Just me and my good friend and attorney——"

"How many? Alone you couldn't!"

"Alone, I did," answered the Hawk.

"My best boys!"

"I'd hate like hell to see your support troops." MacKenzie chuckled. "Now it's time for our private talk."

The Hawk led Dellacroce thirty feet away. He talked quietly for exactly four minutes and thirty seconds.

At which point a rasping, ear-splitting scream shattered the stillness of fairway six.

"*Mannnnaaagggiii!*"

And Angelo Dellacroce fainted right there on the manicured grass.

MacKenzie bent over the man and gently slapped him back into consciousness.

They talked once more with the Hawk holding the obese Italian's neck as though he were a medical corpsman.

The scream came again.

"*Mannnnaaaaggggiii!*"

And Dellacroce fainted again.

So the Hawk revived him again.

And they talked for two minutes more.

"Mannnnaaaaggggiiii'!"

This time MacKenzie lowered the man's head on the grass of fairway six and got up. The moon had broken through the night clouds, revealing a stunned Sam staring at the sight of the fallen Dellacroce. This was it, thought the Hawk, as he walked slowly toward Devereaux. There was no point in procrastinating any longer. Sam would have to be told. There was no other way.

"Well, Sam," began Mac with quiet confidence in the intermittent moonlight on fairway six, "it's a pretty good start. Mr. Dellacroce was eager to subscribe to the full amount reserved for him. The Shepherd Company has its first ten million dollars."

Devereaux's knees buckled. The Hawk rushed forward and caught him before he hit the ground. The ground was not hard but MacKenzie wanted Sam to know he cared; it was always a good idea to let one's superior-adjutant know the commander was concerned for his well-being. "God-damn, son, you've got to stop this kind of thing! You're behaving no better than Mr. Dellacroce! Now that's just not proper; you're cut from a finer tunic!"

Sam's eyes were swimming around and around in the moonlight on fairway six. The words that emerged from his trembling lips were by and large incoherent, but several phrases were repeated often enough to be understood. "Secretary-treasurer!—Oh, my God, I'm a *sec'atary-treasurer*! Ten million dollars' worth of cement! I'm in ten million dollars' worth of shit! I'll be sunk in concrete pajamas! I'm *dead*!"

"Now, now, stop your wailin'. You're a big lawyer, fella; you shouldn't act like this."

"I should never have met you, you squirrelly bastard! That's the only *shouldn't* of my life! Oh, my God! That killer passed out!"

"So did you. Almost. I caught you——"

"*Shhh!* Let's get out of here! I'll send him a letter—I'll get some Bellevue stationery—I'll certify you a lunatic! It was all a lousy joke!"

"Oh, Mr. Dellacroce knows better than that, boy." Hawkins

patted Devereaux's cheek with his right hand while, with his left, he kept an iron grip on the base of Sam's skull, inhibiting any movement above the waist. "Dellacroce's a very religious man, most of these Italian fellas are; doesn't make any difference what they do for a living. That's separate. He knows I told him the truth."

"What the hell are you talking about? What's religion got to do with anything? Get off my neck!"

"Religion helps a man recognize the truth. He may not like it; his *religion* may not like it, or even admit it is the truth, but because he's contemplated, the religious man can separate what's real from what's horseshit. You follow me?"

"Not for a goddamned second! My neck hurts!"

"Sorry. I'll ease up, but it's time we talk." MacKenzie removed his hand. Instantly Devereaux bolted, but the Hawk merely rolled with him, pinning him back to the earth. "I said we've got to *talk*, boy. You're a reasonable person; you can see the logic in that."

"The problem," whispered Sam, straining on the ground, "is that you're *not* reasonable *or* logical! Do you know what you've done? Guys like that—" He gestured with his head; somehow, he could not use his hands. "They freeze people for welching on their bookies! They think nothing about paying for the biggest funeral in town—for a *paisan* who held out on a skim! I *know*. I'm from *Boston*."

"You're overreacting again. Mr. Dellacroce won't do anything like that. He knows where he stands—which is roughly in twenty feet of lye if he doesn't behave. That account in Geneva. He stole from his own people."

Grudgingly, suspiciously, Devereaux stared at Mac in the moonlight. "You're sure of that?"

"It was all in the G-two files. Trouble was nobody put it together. I don't think they wanted to; Dellacroce's crowd are big Pentagon supporters, what with government contracts and union affiliations—. Now, will you listen to me?"

With a reluctance born of fear, but with an assent formed in necessity, Sam nodded. The Hawk helped him up and the two men walked into the rough off fairway six. There was a large oak tree whose leaves filtered the moonlight. Sam sat down against the trunk; Mac fell to one knee in front of him, the line officer clarifying orders at a fire base.

"Remember a couple of weeks ago my telling you how I was looking into things I hadn't thought much about before? God and the church and things like that."

"I remember saying I wouldn't laugh——" Devereaux's reply was flat, wary. A monotone.

"That was very thoughtful, boy. Well, I *was* doing some thinking, but not quite in the way you maybe considered. You and I know that ninety-nine percent of all Commie propaganda is horseshit; everybody knows that. Ours is only—say, fifty to sixty percent, so we're way ahead on that score. But that one percent of the Bolshie feedback got me to wondering. About this Catholic situation. Not what people *believe*, that's their business. But how the organization operates. And it seemed to me that these Vatican fellows got such a good thing going they should spread a little more around. I mean, they got investments, son. When the stock market goes up a couple of points anywhere in the world, they make zillions."

"And if it goes down, they lose zillions."

"Not so! The brokers get 'em out in time or they get canned from the Knights of Malta. It's part of the arrangement. And they can't get their pictures taken with the pope."

"That *is* horseshit."

"If it is, why do all the Catholic brokers on Wall Street have all those initials after their names. You know of any college degrees that start with the letter *K*? Malta, Columbus, Lourdes. And the saints! Je*sus*! Knights of Assisi, Knights of Peter, Matthew—it goes on for pages. It's kind of a social order. The more a fellow on the stock exchange does for the Vatican, the better the *K* after his name. And Wall Street's only one example. It's the same all over the place."

"I think you've been reading some pretty strange books. The *Ku Klux Klanner*, maybe. Nineteen twenty edition."

"Hell, no. I don't cotton to that shit. A man's got a right to believe anything he likes. I'm only talking about the financial part. Then there's real estate. Do you know the sort of real estate the Vatican boys have? I swear they pick up rent from the Ginza to the Gaza strips and most places in between. They own *the* prime properties in New York, Chicago, Hartford, Detroit—'most every place where the micks, the wops, the Polacks and all those kind of people migrated. They always do it the same way. They go in early—before all the ethnics get settled—and buy up land and build a big church. Naturally, all these Ellis Islanders are nervous being in a strange place and all, so *they* build their houses near the church. In a generation or so their kids are lawyers and dentists and own automobile dealerships. So what do they do? They move out to the suburbs and go to work where they once lived, which is now the center of *town*, the *business* district. And the church property skyrockets! It's a regular pattern, boy!"

"I'm trying to find something negative here and I can't," said Sam, staring in the shadows at the excited Hawkins. "What's wrong with the pattern?"

"I didn't say it was wrong. I said it made for one hell of a centralized portfolio."

"'Centralized portfolio'? You've got a new vocabulary."

"Like you said, I've been reading. And not such strange books as you might think. You see, Sam, the product these Vatican boys manufacture—that's not meant disrespectfully, only in a business sense—doesn't change. It may have to adjust a mite now and then, take a tuck here or a nip there, but the basic merchandise stays the same. That reduces a major cost factor and allows for a continuous profit figure with no chance of negative entry——"

"'Negative entry'?"

"That's an accounting term."

"I know it's an accounting term. How do *you* know— don't tell me. Your reading material."

"Maggie's drawers, son."

"What?"

"Never mind. You're on target, that's all. Now, you take an economic situation where the stock exchanges and the real estate markets hold firm, and that means you got the banks, because you control both money *and* land. Prime economic resources. And you add to that a product that requires minimum assembly alterations with maximum purchase growth—hell, boy, it's a worldwide *gold mine*."

"You have been reading. But if you're right, why's there's so much hassle over the parochial schools and *their* costs?"

"That's services, Sam. That's an entirely different entry column. I'm talking about basic portfolios, not annual operating expenditures; they fluctuate with economic conditions. Anyway, it's mostly blackmail."

"That's succinct. They wouldn't like you in Boston."

The Hawk shifted his weight and spoke a little more softly, but with no loss of emphasis. "You mentioned before about something wrong. Well, I don't like to mention it because it only applies to the pricky-shit high brass and not the troops, but there is something that's got a bit of stink to it."

"*You* found a *moral* position?"

"Morality and economics should be more related than they have been; everybody knows that. You take this political thing. Nobody's traded fire power with the Reds any better'n I have. God*damn*, nobody's going to bury me! But it strikes me that these Catholic fellas in the Vatican—and that means all the powerful dioceses—use the Bolshie excuse a mite too freely to oppose a lot of reforms that could make things easier for the peasant slobs scratching a life out of very tough ground."

Devereaux eyed Hawkins skeptically. "That position's a little dated. A great many changes are taking place in the Church. This new pope is opening a lot of windows. Like John the Twenty-third did."

"Not quick enough, Sam. What the Vatican brass needs is a good shake-up in command!"

"You can't change a two-thousand-year pattern overnight——"

"Oh, I understand that," interrupted the Hawk. "And I'm glad you brought up this new pope. This Francesco. Because he's a very popular fellow. Even those who hate his guts—for doing what he's doing—know he's the biggest asset they've got in the whole damn church——that's not meant in a religious sense, of course. I don't take positions that way."

"What positions? What sense?"

"This Francesco," continued Mac, overlooking Devereaux's

103

questions, "is more than just the pope, which is enough to begin with. He's a beloved individual, you know what I'm driving at?"

"I wish you wouldn't say that."

"He's the sort of person every man jack of a Catholic would really sacrifice for, you see what I mean?"

"I don't like that phrase, either."

The Hawk changed knees rapidly; it was good to redistribute weight as often as possible when in an immobile position. "Do you know the estimated total communicant membership of the Catholic Church?"

"The *what?*"

"How many Catholics there are in the world? Never mind, I'll tell you. Four hundred million. Now, taking the median figure of one American dollar—setting a specific date for the rate of exchange; some giving more, most less—that comes to *four hundred million dollars*."

"What does?"

"The projected gross."

"What projected gross?"

"Of the Shepherd Company's business services. This here 'brokering the acquisition of religious artifacts.' It's a clear ratio of ten to one in terms of capitalization, but naturally the profit ratio, as opposed to the gross figure, will be affected by the necessary outlay for equipment and support personnel."

"What the hell are you babbling about?!"

"We're going to kidnap the pope, Sam."

"Whaaat!"

"I've got a trunkful of books, boy. I've really been studying the tactical problems and I think I've got 'em licked. You see, there's this place called Chiesa di San Tommaso di Villanova in Gandolfo—pardon my lousy Italian—and the route from the Vatican is over a kind of country thoroughfare called the Via Appia Antica. It's the road to this here Gandolfo—Castel Gandolfo, they call it. These Italians, they never use one word when they can use two."

"Whaaat?!"

"Now, don't go overreacting. You'll wake up Dellacroce."

"Whaaat?"

"But first we have to corral the remaining capitalization.

104

There's thirty million more coming. I believe I've almost narrowed down the three investors, but I've still got some refining to do." The Hawk clapped his hand over Devereaux's open mouth. "Now, don't start that again. You keep repeating yourself."

Devereaux's eyes bulged above MacKenzie's spread hand, but the rest of his body was frozen. Sort of a form of comatose shock, thought Hawkins. He'd seen a lot of that kind of thing when raw recruits got their first taste of a fire fight. At least Sam wasn't screaming. Or struggling. He was just plain still and kind of cold. The Hawk continued; he had only a few words left to say. The in-depth command analyses would come later. In a way he was glad Devereaux's overreaction was so extreme. In his enthusiasm he had nearly given Sam some tactical information he was not sure he wanted Devereaux to have.

"I didn't choose you lightly. No superior-adjutant is an easy choice for a commander to make, for in many ways the SA is an extension of himself. You got it on *merit*, boy. I don't say you're ideal, you've got deficiencies. I've told you that. But goddamn, your assets outpoint your liabilities. I say that as an honest friend as well as a superior officer.

"Now, there'll be certain executive orders that you'll be asked to carry out, not always knowing precisely why they're vital. You'll just have to accept them. Command is a lonely responsibility; there's not always the time to share the reasons for one's decisions. Ask any frontline officer who sends a battalion into fire. But you'll do splendidly I just know you will. And if by any chance you're tempted to question the orders of your superior officer, or feel that you cannot in conscience implement them, I think you should know that our investor, Angelo Dellacroce, believes that you alone, as the attorney and secretary-treasurer of the Shepherd Company, compiled that list of his illegal activities and furnished me with them. I believe that's why he didn't care to shake hands with you. Coupled with your G-two espionage violations, I'd say your position was somewhat untenable. But if I were you and had my druthers, I'd choose to fight the government treason charges rather than our investor, Mr. Dellacroce. I think that

105

Mafia bastard would cut your balls off, grind 'em up in a blender, and serve 'em as a fancy pâté at your funeral. Like you said earlier, it'd probably be an expensive funeral."

There was no point in the Hawk holding his hand over his superior-adjutant's mouth any longer. Sam had *merfed* and *gleefed* in a spasm of panic and passed out cold.

The moonlight, filtering through the leaves of the large, sturdy oak in the rough off fairway six, cut shafts of yellow and white across Sam's young, peaceful, unmistakably strong features.

Goddamn, thought MacKenzie, the boy's going to be fine! He just needed a little time to absorb the facts. Of course, if a person didn't know any better, he'd think the son of a bitch was dead.

CHAPTER TEN

Sam Devereaux sank despondently into the hotel chair and wished he were dead.

Well, not really, but it certainly would solve a lot of problems. Of course, it was entirely possible that the state of his demise might come about whether he desired it or not. Which brought his eyes back to the insane, unfiled but filled-out limited partnership agreement between the Shepherd Company, MacKenzie Hawkins, President, and the North Hampton Corporation, Mrs. Angelo Dellacroce, President; Depository; the Great Bank of Geneva, Switzerland. He held the legal document in his hand and wondered absently where his fingernails had gone.

Prominently on the first page, directly under the title of president and above the line reserved for the secretary-treasurer, was his name.

Mr. Samuel Devereaux, Counselor-at-law, Suite 4-F, The Drake Hotel, New York City.

He speculated for a moment whether he could alter the Drake's registry and then abandoned the idea. What was the point? On one flank (*flank*?) was the United States government with very specific espionage laws, and on the other was Angelo Dellacroce and his guards-of-honor with their white ties on white shirts and dark glasses and black suits and very *un*specific methods of dealing with the likes of "squeals" such as S. Devereaux, counselor-at-law.

Sam wondered what Aaron Pinkus would do. Then he realized what Aaron would do and abandoned that thought, too.

Pinkus would sit *Shiva* for him.

He got out of the chair and wandered aimlessly through the hotel suite. What the hell *was* he going to do? What in

God's name *could* he do? His gaze fell on the unsigned, typewritten note on the desk.

Copies of this limited partnership agreement have been sent by messenger to MacKenzie Hawkins, Esquire, President, the Shepherd Company, % The Watergate Hotel, Wash. D.C. Instructions cabled: Great Bank of Geneva. Funds transfer awaits presence Sec.-Treas., Shep. Co., Samuel Devereaux in Geneva.

He had been *cabled—internationally.*

In some marble banking hall in Switzerland, a powerful broker of international finance had no doubt already listed him as the bona fide overseer of the transfer of ten million dollars into an account of a nonfiled but very much existing company named Shepherd.

That's what he was going to do whether he liked it or not. It was Geneva, or a lifetime of cracking rocks at Leavenworth, *or* Dellacroce justice—feet-in-cement style.

Kidnap the pope!

My God! That's what the crazy bastard said. He was going to *kidnap the pope!*

All of Mac's other insanities paled by any stretch of comparison! World War Three might be more acceptable! A simple war would be so much—well, simpler. Borders were defined, objectives properly obscured, ideologies flexible. A war was duck soup compared to 400 million hysterical Catholics; and heads of state moaning and groaning their obsequious platitudes, blaming every conceivable inimical faction, extremist or not (secretly glad to be rid of the meddling nuisance in the Vatican) and . . .

My God! World War Three could be a very logical consequence of Hawkins's act!

And with that realization Sam knew what he had to do. He had to stop MacKenzie. But he could not stop him if he were in a maximum security cell in Leavenworth; who would believe him? And he certainly could not stop him if he were at the bottom of one of the deeper sections of the Hudson River, probably upstate, courtesy of Angelo Dellacroce; who would hear him?

No, the only way he could push the Hawk's insanity out of the realm of reality was to find out how the hell MacKenzie intended to pull off his papal score. The most foolish thing here would be to assume he couldn't do it. The Hawk was no joke; anyone who thought he was need only look at a few of Mac's accomplishments—including four extraordinary ex-wives who adored him, and a little matter of an initial capitalization of ten million dollars, to say nothing of military exploits spanning three decades and the same number of wars.

What the Hawk was bringing to the profession of crime were all the strategic resources, the finely honed discipline, and the leadership of an experienced general officer. MacKenzie was starting at the top; no graduate of the lineup he, but instead, a full-fledged criminal commander who had already outsacked a Mafia don in his own backyard.

The son of a bitch had flare. Christ! He had the balls of King Kong smashing the concrete off the Empire State Building as he climbed up the sides.

Kidnap the pope!

Who the hell would believe it?

Samuel Devereaux believed it, that's who believed it. What was left was for S. Devereaux, counselor-at-law, to figure out how to stop it. And stay both alive and outside prison walls so doing. A vague idea was coming into focus, but it was still too blurred to make sense. Yet there was a core of possibility within the outlines.

"Don't be too confident," said Sam out loud. "You're dealing with a living, legal, spinal meningitis!"

But it *was* possible. He could pretend to go along with MacKenzie (always with great reluctance; to act otherwise would be out of character), gather in the diseased money— and, at the last moment, convene the investors and blow the whole operation out of the sky. And to save his hide, there'd be a lot of "in the case of my sudden demise, my own attorneys are instructed to publicly reveal..." any number of things.

Including the translation of the Shepherd Company's "brokering of religious artifacts."

Who would believe it?

"Stop that!" Sam grabbed his wrist, startled by the

109

sound of his own voice. He was further startled by the sound of the telephone. He raced to it like a man facing execution rushing to hear what the governor had to say.

"Goddamn! This must be the attorney *and* secretary *and* treasurer of the Shepherd Company! With assets over ten million dollars! How does that strike you?"

"It's a leading question. I'll not indulge."

"You know something, boy? You must be a pistol of a lawyer!"

"Are you sure you want to talk over the telephone?" asked Devereaux. "It's been given a pretty good FCC rating lately."

"Oh, that's all right. We won't say anything we shouldn't. At least, *I* won't, and I hope to hell you know better. I just wanted to tell you that the additional copies of the partnership agreement are downstairs waiting for you. I sent them up last night with an old master sergeant I used to know——"

"Good *God*, you had *duplicates* made? You damn fool! Those copy places usually keep a set! If they're photostats there'll be negatives!"

"Not where I was. Right down here in the Watergate lobby there's a big machine. You put in a quarter for each page——*Jesus*! You should have seen the crowds gather! They're a little jumpy around here, aren't they? But nobody saw anything. It was kind of weird. Everybody staring; nobody saying anything. Except two guys from the *Washington Post* who came running in from the street——"

"All right!" interrupted Devereaux. "The copies are downstairs. What the hell am I supposed to do with them?"

"Put 'em in your fancy briefcase, the one I gave you. Take 'em to Geneva. You won't need 'em in Switzerland, of course, but there may be one or two other stops on the way back. Namely, London; that's pretty definite. You'll be at the Savoy for a day or two. Airline tickets and everything will be at the hotel in Geneva. When you're in London a gentleman named Danforth will call you. You'll know what to do."

"That's dirty pool. I won't know what to do; I don't know what I'm *doing*! You can't just put me in this crazy

110

situation and not tell me anything. I'm carrying documents! My *name* is on them! I'm involved with the transfer of ten million dollars!"

"Now, calm down," said the Hawk with gentle firmness. "Remember what I told you: There'll be times when, as my adjutant, you'll be asked to carry out orders——"

"*Bullshit!*" roared Sam. "What am I supposed to *say* to people?"

"Well, what's bullshit to one man may be sugar-coated wheat to another. If anyone presses you, you're just helping an old soldier who's quietly raising a few dollars to spread religious brotherhood."

"That's absurd," said Devereaux.

"That's the Shepherd Company," said the Hawk.

MacKenzie lifted up five specific pages from the Xeroxed G-2 files scattered over the hotel bed and took them to the desk across the room. He sat down, picked up a red crayon, and proceeded to mark each copy on the top left border. One through five.

Goddamn! It was the sequence he had been looking for, the pattern he knew was there because a man can't resist going back to his first method of fortune building if the circumstances appear right. And because time minimizes the problems and pressures a person felt decades ago, especially if the profits remain.

The cover intelligence out of Hanoi three years ago had been confusing but authentic. Authentic, that is, on the bottom line; everything else was distorted.

An Englishman was making a killing by brokering hardware and ammunition to North Vietnam.

No big deal; London did not frown on trade to the Commie bloc, although there were specific regulations as to war machinery. But it was a period during that screwed-up, half-assed conflict when the boys in Hanoi *and* Moscow *and* Peking were running slow on the production lines. Money could be made in large bundles by anyone who could divert combat supplies into North Vietnamese ports.

One Lord Sidney Danforth had done just that.

Buying in the United States, West Germany, and France, he sailed under Chilean flag ostensibly for ports in the new African countries. Except the ships did not go anywhere near Africa. They altered their courses in international Pacific waters, sped north, refueled in the Russian out-islands, and headed south to Haiphong as regulation-bound trading vessels.

G-2 could never prove Danforth's involvement because the Communist payments were made directly to the Chilean companies and Danforth stayed well out of sight. And Washington was not about to provoke an incident. Danforth was a powerful Englishman with a lot of clout in the Foreign Office. Nam wasn't worth it.

What had intrigued MacKenzie, however, were the two keys: Chilean flag and African ports. They were covers that had been used before. Thirty years ago. During World War II.

It was common knowledge in intelligence circles that certain South American companies with outside financing had fed war machinery to the Axis at enormous profit during the early forties. In those hectic wartime days the shipping destinations were always Capetown and Port Elizabeth because the manifest records in those harbors were chaotic at best, but usually nonexistent. Scores of ships that were supposed to dock in South Africa altered courses in the southern Atlantic waters and headed into the Mediterranean. To Italy, generally.

Was it possible that one Lord Sidney Danforth had imitated his own operations of three decades past?

It was one thing to chisel a few million out of Southeast Asia in the seventies, something else again to make a fortune out of the holocaust that tested the courage of the British Lion. A man could get his name taken off the Buckingham Palace guest list pretty quickly for something like that.

It was time for the Hawk to have a transatlantic talk with Lord Sidney Danforth, seventy-two-year-old knighted paragon of British industry. And just about the wealthiest man in England.

Goddamn! The Shepherd Company was attracting some of the most interesting investors.

CHAPTER ELEVEN

The Strand was crowded. It was shortly past five o'clock; the legion of office workers were heading home.

Sam had arrived at Heathrow Airport on the 3:40 flight from Geneva and had wasted no time getting to the relaxed comfort of a Savoy suite. He needed it. Geneva had been a nightmare.

He had realized that for any future record, he had to convey a very specific ignorance as to the objectives of the Shepherd Company, cloaking this lack of knowledge in profound respect for the unnamed principals involved; especially the president, who was motivated by deeply–felt religious convictions.

The Geneva bankers were, at first, impressed by his humility. My God, ten million United States dollars and the overseeing lawyer only smiled and spoke convivial banalities, demurring when pressed for identities, nodding soulfully about religious brotherhood when the staggering amount was brought up. So they asked him out to lunch, where there were a lot of winks and drinks and offers of bedroom gymnastics of an incredible variety. This was, after all, Switzerland; a buck was a buck and this hard-nosed approach was not to be confused with yodeling and edelweiss and Heidi in her pinafores. Gradually, thought Devereaux, as the lunches evolved into dinners, the Geneva bankers thought he was either the dumbest attorney ever to practice before the American bar or the most implausibly secretive middleman ever to cross their borders.

He kept up the charade for three days and nights, leaving behind a half-dozen confused Swiss burgomasters, tearfully frustrated over unrequited confidences and terribly sick to their stomachs after too much industrial lubricant. And the strain on Sam was unbearable. He had reached the point where he could not concentrate on anything but his own rigid, blank smile and the necessary quiet control of his fears. He was so preoccupied with himself that when the vice-president of the Great Bank of Geneva saw him off at the airport, Devereaux just smiled and said "Thank you" when the banker threw up over his raincoat.

In his anxiety to get the hell out of Geneva, he had left his shaving kit behind, which explained why he was now on The Strand looking for a drugstore. He walked south for a block and a half, opposite the Hippodrome, and went into the Strand Chemists. His purchases made, he headed back to the hotel, anticipating a long, warm bath, a shave, and a good dinner at the Savoy Grille.

"Major Devereaux!" The voice was enthusiastic, American, and feminine. It came from a taxi which stopped in Savoy Court.

It was Sloping yet Argumentative, the fourth Mrs. MacKenzie Hawkins, the lovely lady named Anne. She hurled herself at Sam, encircling his neck with her arms, pressing her cheek and various other parts against him.

Instantly she withdrew and rather awkwardly composed herself. "I'm awful sorry. Gosh, that was real *forward* of me. Please forgive me. It was just so *terrific* to see a familiar face."

"Nothing to apologize for," said Sam, remembering that Sloping yet Argumentative had appeared to him as the most naïve, as well as the youngest, of the four wives. She had *oohed* a lot, if he recalled correctly. "Are you staying at the Savoy?"

"Yes. I got in last night. I've never been to England before, so I spent the whole day just walking *everywhere*. Gosh, my feet are yelling at me." She parted her very expensive suede coat and frowned at the lovely legs very much in evidence below her short skirt.

"Well, let's get you off them quickly. Into the bar, I mean."

"I can't *tell* you! It's just so *marvy* to see someone you know!"

114

"Are you here by yourself?" asked Devereaux.

"Oh yes. Don, he's my husband—now—is so darned busy with his marinas and restaurants and all those other things that he just said to me last week in LA, he said, 'Annie, honey, why don't you get your pretty little ass out of the way for a while? This is going to be a heavy month.' Well, I thought of Mexico and Palm Springs and all the usual places, and then I figured, damn! Annie, you've never been to London. So off I flew." She nodded brightly to the Savoy doorman and continued as Sam gestured her through the entrance into the lobby. "Don thought I was crazy. I mean, who do I know in England? But I think that was part of it, you know? I wanted to go someplace where there weren't all the usual faces. Somewhere really different."

"I hope I didn't spoil it."

"How?"

"Well, you said I was a familiar face——"

"Oh, my, no! I said familiar, but I didn't mean *familiar*. I mean, one little short afternoon at Ginny's isn't *that* kind of familiar."

"I see what you mean. The lounge is right up those stairs." Sam nodded toward the steps on the left that led to the Savoy's American Bar. But Anne stopped, still holding onto his arm.

"Major," she began haltingly, "my feet are still screaming and my neck is sore from looking up and my shoulder's aching from this darned purse strap. I'd really love to spend a little time straightening myself out."

"Oh, sure," replied Devereaux. "I'm being thoughtless. And stupid. As a matter of fact I was going to do some, er, straightening out myself. I left my shaving gear in Switzerland." He held up the bag from the Strand Chemists.

"Well then, that's *marvy*!"

"I'll call you in about an hour——"

"Why do that? Have you seen the size of those johnnies upstairs? Wow! They're bigger than some of Don's ladies' rooms. In his restaurants, I mean. There's plenty of room. And those big, groovy towels. I swear they're terry cloth sheets!" She squeezed his arm and smiled ingenuously.

"Well, it *is* a solution——"

"The only one. Come on, we'll get some drinks from room service and *really* relax." They started for the elevator.

"It's very kind of you——"

"Kind, hell! Ginny told us you called. She positively *lorded* it over us. Now it's my turn. You were in Geneva?"

Sam stopped. "I said Switzerland——"

"Isn't that Geneva?"

Anne's suite was also on the Thames side, also on the sixth floor, and conveniently no more than fifty feet down the corridor from his.

Switzerland. Isn't that Geneva? Several thoughts crossed Devereaux's mind, but he was entirely too exhausted to dwell on them. And, for the first time in days, entirely too relaxed to let them interfere.

The rooms were very like his own. High ceilings with real moldings; marvelous old furniture—polished, functional—desks and tables and pictures and chairs and a sofa that would do credit to Parke-Bernet; mantel clocks and lamps that were neither nailed down nor with imbedded plastic cards proclaiming ownership; tall casement windows, flanked by regal drapes, that looked out on the river with the lights of small boats, the buildings beyond, and especially Waterloo Bridge.

He was in the sitting room, on the pillowed sofa, with his shoes off and a tall drink in his hand. The London Philharmonic was on BBC1, playing a Vivaldi concerto, and the warmth from a heater filled the room with a splendid comfort. Good things came to the deserving, thought Sam.

Anne came out of the bathroom and stopped in the frame of the doorway. Devereaux's glass was suddenly checked on its way to his lips. She was dressed—if that was the word—in a translucent sheath that at once left little to, yet completely provoked, the imagination. Her Sloping yet Argumentative breasts swelled to blushing points beneath the soft, single layer of fabric; her long, light-brown hair fell casually and sensually over her shoulders, framing her extraordinary endowments. Her tapered legs were outlined under the sheath.

Without saying a word, she raised her hand and beckoned him with her finger. He rose from the sofa and followed.

Inside the huge, tiled bathroom, the enormous Savoy tub was filled with steaming water; several thousand bubbles gave off the scent of roses and wet springtime. Anne reached up and removed his tie, and then his shirt, and then unstrapped his buckle, unzipped his trousers and lowered them to the floor. He kicked them free himself.

She placed her hands on both sides of his waist and pulled down his shorts, kneeling as she did so.

He sat on the edge of the warm tub while she pulled off his socks; and she held his left arm as he slid over the side, his body disappearing under the steaming white bubbles.

She stood up, undid a yellow bow at her neck, and the sheath fell to the floor on top of the thick white rug.

She was utterly magnificent.

And she got into the tub with Sam.

"Do you want to go down to dinner?" asked the girl from beneath the covers.

"Sure," replied Devereaux from under same.

"Do you know we slept for over three hours? It's nearly nine-thirty." She stretched; Sam watched. "After we eat, let's go to one of those pubs."

"If you like," said Devereaux, still watching her, his head on the pillow. She was sitting up now, the sheet had fallen to her waist. Sloping yet Argumentative were challenging all they surveyed.

"Gosh," Anne spoke softly, a touch awkwardly, as she turned and looked down at Sam, who could barely see her face. "I'm being real forward again."

"Friendly's a better word. I'm friendly, too."

"You know what I mean." She bent over him and kissed him on both eyes. "You may have other plans; things you have to do or something."

"Things I want to do," interrupted Devereaux warmly. "All plans are completely flexible, subject only to whim and pleasure."

117

"That sounds sexy as hell."

"I feel sexy as hell."

"Thank you."

"Thank *you*." Sam reached above and beyond her soft, lovely back and pulled the sheet over them.

Ten minutes later (it was either ten minutes or several hours, thought Devereaux) they made the decision: They really did need food, preceded, of course, by short, smoky drams of iced whiskey, which they had in the sitting room, on the pillowed couch, under two soft, enormous bath towels.

"I think the word is 'sybaritic.'" Sam adjusted the terry cloth over his lap. BBC1 was now playing a Noel Coward medley and the smoke from their cigarettes drifted into the sprays of warm orange light from the fireplace. Only two lamps were turned on; the room was dreamed of in a thousand ballads.

"Sybaritic has a selfish meaning," said the girl. "We share; that's not selfish."

Sam looked at her. Hawkins's fourth wife was no idiot. How in hell did he do it? Had he done it? "The way we share, it's sybaritic, believe me."

"If you want me to," she answered, smiling and putting her glass down on the coffee table.

"It's not important. Why don't we dress and go eat?"

"All right. I'll just be a few seconds." She saw his questioning expression. "No, I will. I don't dawdle for hours. Mac once said——" She stopped, embarrassed.

"It's okay," he said gently. "I'd really like to hear."

"Well, he once said that if you try to change the outside too much, you can't help but mix up the inside. And you shouldn't do that unless there's a goddamned good reason. Or if you really don't like yourself." She swung her legs out from under her and rose from the couch, holding the towel around her body. "One, I don't see any reason; and two, I kind of like me. Mac taught me that, too. I like *us*."

"So do I," said Devereaux. "When you're finished, we'll go down to my room and I'll change."

"Good. I'll button your shirt and tie your tie." She grinned and dashed through the foyer door into the bedroom. Devereaux got up naked, throwing the long towel

118

over his shoulder, and went to the side table where the bar was set up in a silver tray. He poured a small quantity of Scotch and thought about Mac Hawkins's barroom philosophy.

Change the outside too much—you mix up the inside.
It wasn't bad, all things considered.

The tiny white light shone between the red and green bulbs on the small panel beside Devereaux's door. Sam and the girl saw it simultaneously as they walked down the corridor and approached his suite. It was the sign that a message was at the front desk for the guest. Devereaux swore under his breath.

Goddamn it! Geneva had not been erased *that* quickly. Or so completely, either. The least Hawkins could do was to let him get a decent night's sleep!

"One of those lights was on for me this afternoon," said Anne. "I came back to change my shoes and found it; it means you have a phone call."

"Or a message."

"Mine was a call. From Don in Santa Monica. I finally got him back; you know, it was only eight o'clock in the morning in California."

"Nice of him to get up and phone."

"Not so. My husband owns two things in Santa Monica: a restaurant and a girl. The restaurant's not open at eight in the morning; forgive my bitchiness. I think Don just wanted to make sure I was really seven thousand miles away." Anne smiled up at him naïvely. He was not sure how to respond, all things considered.

"Seems like a lot of trouble for, well, for checking up." Sam snapped on the light switch in his foyer. Beyond, the sitting room lamps were on, as he had left them five hours ago.

"My husband suffers from a mental illness peculiar to cheap strayers. As a lawyer, I'm sure you're familiar with it. He's paranoid about getting caught. Not morally, you understand; when he's juiced up, he flaunts *that* part. Just financially; he's scared to death some court will make him pay big if I opt for out."

They walked into his sitting room; he wanted to say something but, again, all things considered he was not

119

sure what it should be. He chose the safest. "I think the man's out of his mind."

"You're sweet, but you didn't have to say it. On the other hand, I suppose it's the safest thing you *could* say——"

"Let's find another subject," he interrupted quickly, indicating the couch and the coffee table with the Savoy-supplied newspapers on it. "Sit down and I'll be with you in a minute. I haven't forgotten: You button the shirt and tie the tie." Sam started for the bedroom door.

"Aren't you going to call the desk?"

"It can *wait*," he answered from the bedroom. "I have no intention of letting anything interfere with a quiet dinner. Or for that matter, showing you a pub or two, if they're still open when we're finished."

"You really should find out who's trying to reach you. It could be important."

"*You're* important," shouted Sam, removing a tan double-knit suit from the awkward hanger in his suitcase.

"It could be something vital," said the girl from the sitting room.

"*You're vital*," he replied, selecting a red-striped shirt from the next layer of clothes.

"I can't *ever* not answer a phone, or check for messages, or call back even a name I never heard of; that's being *too* casual."

"You're not a lawyer. Ever tried to get a lawyer the day after you've hired him? His secretary is trained to lie with the conviction of Aimee Semple McPherson."

"Why?" Anne was now standing in the bedroom doorway.

"Well, he's got your money; he's scrounging around for another fee. What the hell, your case probably entails an exchange of letters with the opposing attorney, other explanations notwithstanding. He doesn't want complications."

Anne approached him as he slipped on the red-striped shirt. She nonchalantly began buttoning it. "You're a very cool Clyde. Here you are in strange country——"

"Not so strange," he broke in, smiling. "I've been here before. I'm your tour guide, remember?"

120

"I mean, you've just come from Geneva where you obviously had a bad time——"

"Not so bad. I survived."

"—and now someone is desperately trying to find you——"

"What's desperate? I don't know anybody so desperate."

"For Christ's sake!" The girl yanked his collar as she fastened it. "Things like this make me nervous!"

"Why?"

"I feel responsible!"

"You shouldn't." Devereaux was fascinated. Anne was very serious. He wondered. . . .

And the telephone rang.

"Hello?"

"Mr. Samuel Devereaux?" asked the precise voice of a male Britisher.

"Yes, this is Sam Devereaux."

"I've been waiting for your call——"

"I just got in," interrupted Sam. "I haven't checked my messages yet. Who is this?"

"At the moment, merely a telephone number."

Devereaux paused, annoyed. "Then I should tell you, you would have waited all night. I don't return calls to telephone numbers."

"Come, sir," was the agitated reply. "You're not expecting any other caller of consequence."

"That's a little presumptuous, I think——"

"Think whatever you like, sir! I'm in a great hurry and quite put out with you. Now, where do you wish to meet?"

"I don't know that I want to. Fuck off, Basil, or whatever the hell your name is."

The pause was now on the other end of the line. Sam could hear heavy breathing. In seconds the telephone number spoke. "For God's sake, have pity on an old man. I've done you no harm."

Sam was suddenly touched. The voice had cracked slightly; the man was desperate. He remembered Hawkins's last conversation. "Are you——"

"No *names, please!*"

"All right. No names. Are you recognizable?"

"Extremely. I thought you knew that."

"I didn't. So we meet someplace out of the way."

"Very much so. I thought you knew that, too."

"Stop saying that!" Devereaux was as much annoyed with Hawkins as he was with the Englishman on the telephone. "Then you'd better choose it, unless you want to come to the Savoy."

"Impossible! That's kind of you. I have several apartment buildings in Belgravia. One's the Empire Arms; do you know it?"

"I can find it."

"Good. I'll be there. Flat four seven. It will take me an hour to get into London."

"Don't hurry. I don't want to meet in an hour."

"Oh? At what time then?"

"When do the pubs close these days?"

"Midnight. A little over an hour."

"Shit!"

"I beg your pardon?"

"I'll see you at one o'clock."

"Very well. The Empire security will be alerted. Remember, no names. Just flat four seven."

"Four seven."

"And, Devereaux. Bring the papers."

"What papers?"

The pause was longer now, the English breathing heavier. "That goddamned agreement, you *ass*."

The girl not only accepted the fact that their dinner would be short and that he had to leave the hotel, but she seemed positively elated.

Sam was wondering less and less. The *why* escaped him, but the *what* was becoming clearer. He agreed to have a nightcap with her when he returned. The hour was unimportant, Anne said; she gave him a key.

The taxi stopped at the curb in front of the Empire Arms. At Sam's mention of flat four seven, he was led by a doorman in a series of swift, secretive movements that took him through service doors, a short back staircase, a freight elevator, and the delivery entrance of the flat.

An ominous looking man with a north country accent asked for identification and then led Sam through a pantry, a large living room, a hallway, and finally to a small dimly lit library where a rather ugly little old man sat in shadows by the window. The door closed. Devereaux stood, adjusting his eyes to the light and the unattractive ancient in the armchair.

"Mr. Devereaux—naturally," said the wrinkled old man.

"Yes. You must be the Danforth Hawkins spoke of."

"Lord Sidney Danforth." The ugly little person spat out the ugly words, then suddenly his voice was syrup. "I don't know how your employer pieced together what he did, nor do I for a moment admit *anything;* it's all so preposterous. And so long ago. Nevertheless, I am a good man, a charitable man. Quite a *wonderful* man. Give me the damned papers!"

"What?"

"The agreement, you insufferable bastard!"

Stunned, Sam reached into his breast pocket where he had a folded copy of the Shepherd Company's limited partnership. He crossed to the ugly little person and gave it to him. Danforth swung out a portable desk panel from somewhere at the side of the armchair and snapped on a bright worklight at the top of the board. He grabbed the papers and started scanning them.

"Fine!" said Danforth, wheezing, flipping over the pages. "They say absolutely *nothing!*" The little Britisher reached for a pen and began filling in the blank lines. When he had finished, he refolded the papers and handed them distastefully to Devereaux. "Now, get out! I am a marvelous man, a magnanimous provider; a humble multimillionaire whom everyone adores. I have richly deserved the extraordinary honors heaped upon my person. Everybody knows that. And nobody, I repeat, *nobody* could conceivably associate me with such madness! I am only—spreading brotherhood—do you understand me? *Brotherhood,* I say!"

"I don't understand anything," said Sam.

"Neither do I," replied Danforth. "The transfer will be made in the Cayman Islands. The bank is listed and the ten million will be shifted within forty-eight hours. Then I'm through with you!"

"The Cayman Islands?"

"They're in the Caribbean, you ass."

CHAPTER TWELVE

He could see the tiny white light shining fifty feet down the Savoy corridor. He did not have to get any closer to know it was the door to his rooms; avoiding it was a second, very good reason to let himself into Anne's suite.

"If that's not you, Sam, I've got problems," she called from the bedroom.

"It's me. All your problems are happy ones."

"I like those kind."

Devereaux walked into the large bedroom with the windows overlooking the river. Anne was sitting up, reading a brightly colored paperback by the light of the table lamp. "What's that?" he asked. "It looks impressive."

"A marvelous history of Henry the Eighth's wives. I got it at the Tower this morning. That man was a monster!"

"Not really. A lot of his troubles were geopolitical."

"In his crotch they were!"

"That's more historically sound than you may think. How about a drink?"

"You've got to make a phone call first. I promised; first thing you did when you got back."

The girl turned a page calmly. Sam was not only astonished, he was curious. "What did you say?"

"MacKenzie called. All the way from Washington." She turned another page.

"MacKenzie?" Devereaux could not help himself; he roared. "Just—*MacKenzie called*! You're sitting there like you heard from room service and tell me MacKenzie called. How do *you* know he called? Did he call *you*?"

"Really, Sam, stop being so uptight." Cold as ice, she turned another goddamned page. "It's not as though I didn't know him. I mean, after all——"

"Oh, no! Spare me the odious comparisons! I just want to know about this extraordinary coincidence that has you seven thousand miles from home taking a telephone call from an ex-husband who's calling *me*—three thousand miles from New York."

"If you'll calm down, I'll tell you. If you won't, I'm just going to keep on reading."

Devereaux thought about how much he wanted a drink, but he suppressed his anger and spoke quietly. "I'm calm and I would very much like to have you speak. Please speak."

Anne put the book down on her lap and looked up at him. "To begin with, Mac was every bit as uptight as you are when I got on the line."

"How *did* you get on the line?"

"Because I was worried."

"That's why, not how."

"If you recall, and I think you will if you try real hard, you left me at the table downstairs. You were running late and I insisted. I told you I'd sign the check and go upstairs. Am I right so far?"

"I owe you for dinner. Go on."

"A nice young man in white tie and tails came to the table and said there was an urgent transatlantic call for you. Are they always so dressed up?"

"It's a Savoy custom. What did you say?"

"That you wouldn't be back until very late; I wasn't sure of the time. He seemed upset so I asked him if I could help. He said the caller was a General Hawkins from Washington, and I think the rank and the city made him nervous. Mac always does that; it gets better telephone service. So I told him not to worry about a thing. I'd talk to the old fart. He liked that." Anne returned to her book. "Now, go call him. The number's on the desk in the other room. It's also on the desk in your place and also downstairs. I'm very flattered that you got it here first."

It *was* possible, Sam reflected. Unlikely but within the scope of possibility, as certain radio waves indicated the possibility of additional civilizations in galactic space. "What did Hawkins say? How was he uptight?"

"Oh, just that I was *here*, I suppose," said the girl,

reluctantly taking her eyes off the page. "He started swearing and yelling and giving orders. I said, 'Mac,' I said, 'go wash your mouth out with brown soap!' I always used to tell him that. I mean he uses language we stayed away from in Belle Isle. Anyway, he calmed down and started to laugh." Anne's eyes drifted upward, at nothing. She was remembering, thought Sam, and those memories were not cold ones. "He asked me if I'd gotten rid of the fancy gigolo waiter yet—that's what he calls Don—and if not, *why* not. And how you were such a nice fellow. You know, Mac thinks a great deal of you. Anyhow, it is very important that you call him back. I said it'd be awfully late; maybe not until three in the morning. But he said that was all right; it would only be ten o'clock in Washington."

"Can't it wait until morning?"

"No. Mac was very emphatic. He said if you thought about putting it off I should tell you it had something to do with an Italian gentleman who was asking for you."

"Did he add that he was in the undertaking business?"

"No. But I think you should call him. If you want privacy, you can use the phone in the other room."

"Goddamn, boy! Isn't it a real small world! There you are halfway across the globe and who do you run into but little old Annie. Not that she's old, you understand——"

"I understand," interrupted Sam, "that you've got greetings for me from Dellacroce. What did you tell your deeply religious friend now? That I crucified Jesus?"

"Hell, no. That was just a little psycho-prod, in case you were reluctant to return my call. I haven't even talked to Dellacroce. I don't think he's in favor of any further communications. Does that make you feel better?"

Devereaux lit a cigarette. It helped cover the slight pain that was developing in his stomach. "I'll tell you the truth, Mac. It simply makes me nervous that you called me at all. It makes me feel that you are about to say something that will not bring me any closer to Boston, or my mother, or my real employer, Aaron Pinkus; that's the way your psych-prod makes me feel."

There was a long series of audible tsks from MacKenzie Hawkins in Washington. "You are a very suspicious person. It must be the lawyer in you. How did everything go with Danforth?"

"He's a madman. He blows hot and cold like a psycho. He also signed the papers; he's in for ten million for reasons I can't possibly imagine. The bank's in the Cayman Islands, which is, I assume, the reason for your telephone call."

"You mean you think I'd ask you to go to the Caymans?"

"It crossed my mind."

"I wouldn't do that. The Caymans aren't any fun. Just dinky little hot spots with lots of banks and pricky-shit bankers. They're trying to make the place into another Switzerland. . . . No, I'll fly down there myself and take care of it. And you've got another ten thousand added to your account. Thought you'd like to know that."

"*Mac!*" Devereaux's stomach experienced a sharp, stinging sensation. "You can't *do* that!"

"It's easy, boy. You just make the cashier's check out for deposit only."

"That's not what I mean! You have no *right* putting money into my account!"

"The bank didn't argue——"

"The bank wouldn't argue! *I* argue! I *am* arguing! Christ, don't you understand? It means you're paying me!"

"One-tenth of one percent? Goddamn, boy, I'm cheating you!"

"I don't *want* to be paid! I don't want anything to *do* with any money from you! That makes me an *accessory*!"

"I don't know anything about that, but it's surely not right for one person to call upon the time and the talents of another person and not pay him for it." Hawkins's voice had the ring of a quiet evangelist.

"Oh, shut up, you son of a bitch," said Devereaux, recognizing the inevitability of defeat. "Outside of Danforth, why did you call?"

"Well, now that you mention it, there's a fellow in West Berlin I'd like you to talk with."

"Wait. Don't tell me," interrupted Sam wearily. "The airline tickets and the hotel reservations will be at the Savoy desk before I can say kippered herring."

"By morning, anyway."

127

"Okay, Mac, I know when I'm hung." He was getting in deeper. Somehow, some way, sometime, Sam thought, he would have to climb out.

MacKenzie wrote out the figure numerically.
$20,000,000.00
Then he wrote it in words:
Twenty million dollars.

Strange, but it had no real effect on him. It was merely a means, not an end in itself. Although it had occurred to him that he could easily call it an economic day, wrap it up, and retire to the south of France. Certainly, neither Dellacroce nor Danforth would sue. Not bloody likely. But that wasn't what it was all about; the money was both a conveyance and a by-product. And in its way, a legitimate form of punishment. The two marks deserved their losses.

But time was running short and he could not allow himself to get sidetracked. Summer was only a few months away; there was an enormous amount of work to do. The selection and training of the support personnel would be time-consuming. The leasing and stocking of the maneuver site would be difficult, especially the covert purchasing of equipment. The maneuvers themselves would take a number of weeks. All told, there was a great deal to accomplish in a short time. Because of this it was a natural temptation to veer from the initial strategy and go with less than the full capitalization, but it would be wrong. That's for sure. He had set the figure of forty million not merely for the numerical symmetry to the four hundred million (although it certainly looked proper on the limited partnership agreement, in the blank lines he had filled out), but because forty million took care of *everything*, including last-extremity contingencies.

Otherwise known as quick-witted evacuation of the fire base.

It would have to be forty million. He was just about ready for his third investor.

Heinrich Koenig, Berlin.

Herr Koenig had not been easy. Whereas Sidney Danforth

128

had overworked his modus operandi in Chile, and whereas Angelo Dellacroce had been just plain sloppy with regard to his Mediterranean payments and entirely too ostentatious in his manner of living, Heinrich Koenig had made no obvious errors, and lived the quiet life of a country squire in a peaceful rural town twenty-odd miles from Berlin.

But twenty-two years ago Koenig had played an enormously dangerous game brilliantly. A game that not only netted him a fortune but also insured the capitalization and ultimate success of his various business enterprises.

During the height of the Cold War, Koenig was a double agent-cum-blackmailer. He began by secretly informing on single agents to both sides, then extorting cash—financed through opposing intelligence channels—from those seeking protection from exposure. Soon he was issued exclusive international, nontariff "franchises" for his new companies from scores of countries dependent upon the economic goodwill of both giant factions. Finally, with the grace of Mephistopheles, he forced Washington, London, Berlin, Bonn, and Moscow into declaring his companies *outside* the regulatory legalities that governed other industries. Koenig accomplished this by explaining to each that he would inform the others of its past activities.

And then, to the profound relief of many governments, Koenig retired. He had built his empire on the trampled bodies—deceased and paralyzed—of half the bureaucratic and industrial population of Europe and America. He had remained untouchable because of the very real terror of chain reaction-reprisal. What bureaucrat, what undersecretary, what minister or statesman (indeed, what head of a government) would allow access to the horrors of Pandora's box? So, in retirement, Koenig remained as safe as during his halcyon days of furious activity.

Fear was Koenig's clout. But there was no fear or clout if a man didn't give a good goddamn about reaction or reprisals—governmental, industrial, or international.

And naturally this was Hawkins's weapon.

For there was an international army of victims who would quick-march for the kill if they thought they could do so with impunity, if everyone realized his past sins were known to everybody else. Complete disclosure was Mac's threat.

Koenig would certainly see the logic of this approach; it was the absence of it that had guaranteed his fortunes. He surely could foretell the effects of several hundred lengthy cablegrams sent simultaneously to several hundred inhabitants of the corridors of power throughout the world. Oh, yes! Koenig would be convinced, the instant a barrage of names, dates, and activities was rattled off to him.

MacKenzie picked up the raw-file Xeroxes from the bed, keeping the piles in sequence, and carried them to the coffee table in front of the couch. He sat down and with the red crayon he began circling two or three items on each page.

Things were going beautifully. It was all a question of making a realistic appraisal of one's capabilities and the logistics available to complement those abilities. Simple inventory. He picked up the Xeroxes, moved to the desk, and arranged the papers properly in front of the telephone. He was ready to calmly, dispassionately recite a record of international duplicity that would cause Genghis Khan to blush.

Heinrich Koenig would part with ten million dollars.

His eyes rimmed with black circles of exhaustion, Devereaux went through customs at Berlin's Templehof Airport, fully prepared to have his forehead stamped by the officiously barking neo-Nazi who inspected his papers and luggage. Christ, he thought, give a German a rubber stamp and he went wild.

At one point he stared in amazement at the contents of his own suitcase. Everything was folded neatly and arranged tidily as though packed by Bergdorf Goodman, and he simply did not pack suitcases that way. Then through the fog of dislocation, he remembered that Anne had taken care of everything. She not only had packed for him, she had also accompanied him to the cashier's desk and helped him settle his bill.

She had done all this, reflected Sam, because he was not in condition to do much for himself. The insanity of his predicament had led him into a battle with a bottle of Scotch. He lost. The only thing he did remember to do was to airmail the goddamned limited partnership agreement to Hawkins.

Berlin's Kempinsky Hotel was a Teutonic version of New York's old Sherry-Netherland with a slightly harsher interior; the overstuffed lobby chairs seemed cast more in concrete than leather. Still, it screamed money, polished dark wood, and terribly proper clerks Sam knew hated his weak, democratically oriented, and inferior guts.

The front desk dispensed with him efficiently and swiftly. He was escorted by a disagreeable, aging SS Oberführer who treated his suitcase as though it contained bagels and lox. Once inside the suite (it was enormous; Mac Hawkins did send him first class) the Oberführer snapped up the shades in the various rooms with the authority of a man used to issuing commands to a firing squad. Devereaux, fearing for his life, grossly overtipped him, saw him to the door as if he were a visiting diplomat and bid him a gracious *auf Wiedersehen!*

He opened his suitcase. Anne had possessed the foresight to wrap a full bottle of Scotch in a Savoy towel. If there was ever a time to ingest the indigestible, it was now. Not much; just enough to get the motor running.

There was a knock on the door. Sam was so startled he coughed a mouthful of whiskey over the bed. He corked the bottle and furiously looked for a place to hide it.

Under the pillow! Covered by the bedspread! He stopped. What was he doing? What the hell was the matter with him? What was *happening* to him? *Goddamn you, MacKenzie Hawkins!*

He took a deep breath, and calmly placed the bottle on the dresser top. He took another deep breath, opened the door, and promptly, involuntarily, expelled every bit of air in his lungs.

Standing in the door frame was the blonde Aphrodite from Palo Alto, California, catalogued in his memory as Narrow and Pointed. The third Mrs. MacKenzie Hawkins. Lillian.

"I knew it was you! I said to the man at the desk that it *had* to be you!"

131

Sam was not sure why he had catalogued Lillian as Narrow and Pointed. "Narrow" did the lady an injustice. Perhaps it was a relative adjective, subject to the immediate visual comparison to the other six.

Devereaux was thinking these absurd thoughts and—he was aware—staring like a twelve-year-old at his first *Artists and Models* magazine, while Lillian sat across from him, explaining that she had flown into Berlin three days ago to attend a two-week course in gourmet cooking.

Of course, it was unbelievable. After all, he was a skilled attorney. He had analyzed scores of crime-ridden mentalities, stripping away the layers of fraud from sophisticated deceivers on all levels of the social jungle. In spite of his drained mind and body, he was not a man to be conned easily and he would let the third Mrs. MacKenzie Hawkins know that—in *spades*! He stared at her harder, then mentally shrugged. What the hell!

"So there we are, Sam. I may call you Sam, mayn't I? It's amazing what an interest in really fine cooking can lead to."

"But entirely plausible, Lillian! That's what makes coincidences truly—well, coincidental!" Sam laughed quasi-hysterically, doing his best to control his eyes. He was simply too exhausted to be successful; he just gave up and let his eyes roam freely.

"And I can't think of a better way to see Berlin. If we're lucky, we can find an indoor tennis court! I hear the hotel has a swimming pool; perhaps a gymnasium——" Lillian stopped and Devereaux felt deprived; in his spent condition he was enjoying the soft, breathless, aural massage. "I may be taking far too much for granted. Are you traveling alone?"

He knew he shouldn't. He *shouldn't*.

"More alone than I've ever been in my life."

"Well, we certainly can't have that. If you don't mind my saying so, you look dreadfully tired. I think you've been working half to death. You really need someone to look after you."

"I am only a warm shadow of my substance. . . ."

"You poor lamb. Come over here and let me rub your shoulder blades. It does wonders, it really, really does."

132

"I am a wasted vestige. I am filled with vacuum and molten lead. . . ."

"You're exhausted, my lamb. That's the good boy; stretch out and put your head on Lilly's lap. Oh my, your temples are so warm. And your neck muscles are much too tense. There, that's better; doesn't it feel better?"

It did. He could feel her nimble fingers unbutton his shirt and the gentle hands moving about his chest, caressing his flesh with the touch of angels. What the hell. He opened his eyes, his sight was filled with the unbearable loveliness of two magnificent breasts inches above his face.

"Do you like hot tubs filled with lots of soap bubbles that smell like roses and springtime?" he whispered.

"Not actually," she whispered back. "I'm partial to warm showers. Straight up, as it were."

Sam smiled.

CHAPTER THIRTEEN

The fragrance permeated the air around him; he did not
need to open his eyes to know its source.

If he was able to reconstruct the previous evening with
any accuracy—and the quiescence below his waist convinced him that he could—they had spent most of the
night in the Kempinsky shower.

Sam opened his eyes. Lillian was beside him, sitting up
against the pillows with a pair of horn-rimmed glasses
perched on her lovely upturned nose. She was reading
from an enormous piece of frayed cardboard, the white
sheet covering her chest but not for an instant obscuring
the shafts beneath.

"Hello," he said quietly.

"Good morning!" She looked down at him and positively
beamed. "Do you know what time it is?"

The blonde creature *was* a healthy type, he considered.
It must be all that California surfboarding, or perhaps
MacKenzie Hawkins had taught her to do pushups. "My
watch is under the covers with my wrist. I do not know
what time it is."

"It's twenty after ten. You slept for eleven hours. How
do you feel?"

"Are you telling me we went to bed—I was asleep—by
eleven thirty last night?"

"You could be heard at the Brandenburg Gate. I kept
shoving you to stop your snoring. You were positively
operatic. How's your head?"

"Fairly secure, as a matter of fact. I wonder why?"

"All that steam. And exercise. Actually, you weren't
capable of drinking a great deal. I think your bloodstream

went into revolt." Lillian picked up a pencil from the bedside table and lightly checked the menu.

"You smell terrific," he said after several moments of looking up at her, remembering the sightlines from her lap and the touches of angels over his chest.

"So do you, lamb," she replied, smiling, removing her glasses, and gazing down at Sam. "Do you know, you have a very acceptable body?"

"It has its points."

"I mean you have a fundamentally sound physique, moderately well proportioned and coodinated. It's really a pity you've let it disintegrate." She tapped her glasses against her chin like a doctor studying postoperative conditions.

"Well, I wouldn't go so far as to say disintegrate. I played lacrosse once. I was pretty good."

"I'm sure you were, well over a decade ago. Now look here——" Lilly put down her glasses and peeled the blankets away from Devereaux's chest. "See here. And *here* and here and *here!* Absolutely no tone whatsoever. Muscle pockets that've had no discernible use for years! And *here.*"

"Ouch!"

"Your latissimi dorsi are positively non*existent*. When was the last time you exercised?"

"Last night. In the shower."

"That aspect of your condition cannot be debated. But it's a minor part of the whole being——"

"Not to me it isn't!"

"——relative to the muscular network. Your body is a temple; don't let it crumble and decay with misuse and neglect. Spruce it up! Give it a chance to stretch and breathe and be useful; that's what it's meant for. Look at MacKenzie——"

"I object! I don't want to look at MacKenzie!"

"I'm speaking clinically."

"I knew it," mumbled Devereaux in defeat. "I can't escape him. I'm possessed."

"Do you realize that Mac is well over *fifty*? And take his body. It's taut. It's a coiled spring toned to perfection. . . ."

135

Lilly's eyes drifted up—at nothing. As Anne's had done at the Savoy. She was remembering, as Anne had remembered—and those memories were not cold.

"Well, for God's sake," said Sam. "Hawkins spent his whole life in the army. Running and jumping and killing and torturing. He had to stay in shape so he could stay alive. He had no choice."

"You're wrong. Mac understands the meaning of full capacity, experiencing the total potential. He once said to me—well, never mind, it's unimportant." The girl removed her hand from Devereaux's chest and reached for her glasses.

"No, please." The bedroom in the Kempinsky might have been a bedroom at the Savoy. But the wives were not interchangeable; they were very individual. "I'd like to hear what Mac said."

Lilly held her glasses in both hands, fingering the stems pensively. " 'Your body should be a realistic extension of your mind, pushed to its limit but not abused.' "

"I liked the 'change the outside, mix up the inside' better——"

"What?"

"Something else he said. Maybe I don't understand; the intellectual and the physical are poles apart. I might imagine I could fly off the Eiffel Tower, but I'd better not try it."

"Because that wouldn't be realistic; it would be abusive. But you might train yourself to scale down it in record time. *That* would be the realistic, *physical* extension of your imagination. And it's important to attempt it."

"Scale down the Eiffel Tower?"

"If flying off it is a serious consideration."

"It's not. If I follow this pseudoscholastic doggerel, you're saying that if you think about doing something you should actually translate it as much as possible into physical terms."

"Yes. The main thing is not to remain inert." Lilly waved her arms in emphasis; the sheet plummeted down.

Unbearably lovely, thought Devereaux. But at the moment untouchable; the girl was in debate.

"This is either far more complicated or much simpler than it sounds," he said.

"It's more complicated, believe me," she answered. "The subtlety is in the obviousness."

"You believe in this challenge concept, don't you?" Sam said. "I mean it's fundamentally the necessary satisfaction of meeting the challenge, isn't it?"

"Yes, I suppose it is. For its own sake; to try to reach out for what you can imagine. To test your potential."

"And you believe that." There was no question implied.

"Yes, I do. Why?"

"Because at this moment my imagination is working so hard I can't stand it. I feel the necessity of physical expression; to test my potential. Within reasonable limits, of course." He rose from his base camp until he sat facing her, their eyes level. He reached out and took her glasses, folded them, and dropped them over the side of the bed. He held out his hand and she gave him the menu.

Lillian's eyes were bright, her lips parted in a half smile. "I was wondering when you were going to ask."

And then the Nazi telephone rang.

The voice on the other end of the line belonged to a man brought up in his formative years watching all those war movies from Warner Brothers. Every syllable dripped evil.

"Ve do not—vill not—cannot shpeak on der telephone."

"Go across the street and open a window. We'll shout," replied Devereaux irritably.

"Der time ist der essence! You vill go down to der lobby, to der fart chair in front of der vindow, on der richt of der hentrance! Under der arm carry a folded copy of *Der Spiegel*. Und you vill be crossing der legs every tventy seconds."

"I'm sitting down?"

"You vould look foolish crossing der legs standing up, mein Herr."

"Suppose someone's sitting in the chair?"

The pause conveyed both anger and confusion. There followed a short, strange sound that gave rise to the image

137

of a small pig squealing in frustration. "Remove him!" was the reply that followed the squeal.

"That's silly."

"You vill do as I say! Dere is no time to argue! You vill be contacted. Fifteen minutes."

"Hey, wait a minute! I just got up. I haven't had breakfast; I've got to shave——"

"Fourteen minutes, mein Herr!"

"I'm hungry!"

The connection was broken by a loud click on the line. "To hell with him," said Devereaux, turning back in anticipation to the extraordinary Lillian.

But Lillian was not where she should have been. Instead, she was standing on the other side of the bed in Sam's bathrobe.

"To coin a phrase, my darling, we were saved by the bell. You have things to do, and I really must get ready for class."

"*Class?*"

"*Der erstklassig Strudelschule,*" said Lilly. "Less expert but probably more fun than the Cordon Bleu in Paris. It starts at noon. We're over in the Leipziger Strasse; that's past Unter der Linden. I really should hurry."

"What about——*us?* And breakfast and—don't you shower in the morning?"

Lillian laughed; it was a nice, genuine laugh. "*Der schule* is finished by three-thirty. I'll meet you back here."

"What's your room number?"

"Five eleven."

"I'm five nine."

"I know. Isn't that marvelous."

"Or something. . . ."

The confusion in the Kempinsky lobby was absurd. "Der fart chair in front of der vindow" *was* occupied by an elderly gentleman whose close-cropped, bejowled head kept nodding down into the folds of neck flesh as he dozed. On his lap, unfortunately, was a folded copy of *Der Spiegel*.

The elderly man was, at first, annoyed, then furious at

138

the two men who flanked his chair and told him in no uncertain terms to get up and come with them. Twice Sam tried to intercede, explaining as best he could that he, too, had a folded copy of *Der Spiegel*. It did no good; the troopers were interested only in the gentleman sitting in the huge armchair. Finally, Devereaux stood directly in front of the two contacts and every twenty seconds, crossed and uncrossed his legs.

At which point the bell captain came up to Sam and in perfectly good, loud English gave him the directions to the men's room.

Whereupon a large woman with a striking resemblance to Dick Butkus approached the trio around the armchair and began hitting the two Gestapo men with both a hatbox and an extremely large, black leather handbag.

There was only one thing for it, thought Devereaux. He grabbed one of the contacts around the neck and pulled him away from the fire zone.

"You crazy son of a bitch! *I'm* the one! You're from Koenig, aren't you?"

Thirty seconds later Devereaux was propelled out of the Kempinsky entrance and into a nearby alley.

Halfway down the alley, taking up most of the space between the buildings, was an enormous open truck with a canvas tarpaulin stretched across the rear rigging poles. Under the tarpaulin, from deck to canvas, were hundreds of crates piled on top of one another, filled with thousands (it seemed like thousands) of screeching chickens.

There was a narrow corridor in the center of the van between the crates. It led to the rear window of the cab. In front of the window were two tiny stools.

"Hey, come on! This is ridiculous! It's—goddamn it, it's unsanitary!"

His escorts nodded Germanically and smiled Germanically, and Germanically heaved Sam up into the tiny corridor and shoved him down the eighteen-inch passageway toward the stools.

All around him sharp beaks pecked at his person. The noonday sun was completely blanketed out by the heavy canvas tarpaulin above. The odor of chickenshit was unbearable.

They drove for nearly an hour into the countryside, stopping every now and then to be looked over by cooperative East German soldiers who waved them on, pocketing *deutschmarks* as they did so.

They entered a large farming complex. Cattle were grazing in the fields, silos and barns could be seen, barely, through the opening of the tiny passageway between the crates and the flying feathers at the rear of the truck.

Finally they stopped. Escort number one grinned his Germanic grin and led Sam into the sunlight.

He was marched into a large barn that reeked of cattle urine and fresh manure. He was led—Germanically—down a crisscross series of turns through the stinking building until they came to an empty stall. A row of blue ribbons denoted the residence of a prize steer.

Inside, sitting on a milking stool, surrounded by piles of bullshit, was the heavyset man Sam knew was Heinrich Koenig.

He did not get up; he sat there and stared at Devereaux. In his tiny eyes, surrounded by folds of blemished flesh, were thunderbolts.

"So. . . ." Koenig remained immobile, drawing out the word disdainfully, waving the escorts away.

"So?" replied Sam, his voice cracking slightly, aware of the wet chicken droppings on his back.

"You are the representative from this monster, General Hawkins?" Koenig pronounced the word "general" with a hard Germanic *G*.

"I'd like to clear that up, if I may," said Devereaux with false laughter. "Actually, I'm just a slight acquaintance, barely know the man. I'm a low-profile attorney from Boston; actually not much more than a law clerk. I work for a little Jewish man named Pinkus. You wouldn't like him. My mother lives in Quincy and through the strangest coincidence——"

"Enough!" A very loud fart could be heard in the vicinity of the milking stool. "You are the contact, the intermediary, with this devil from hell!"

"Well, as to that, I would have to debate the legal association; said association subject to the clarification of intent with regard to foreknowledge. I don't believe——"

140

"You are a jackal, a hyena! But such dogs bark loudly if the meat is sufficient. Tell me. This Hawkins. He is a Gehlen operation, *nein?*"

"A who?"

"*Gehlen!*"

Devereaux remembered. Gehlen was the master spy of the Third Reich who bought and sold for all factions after the war. It would not do for Koenig to think there was any connection between Hawkins and Gehlen; for it would mean there was a link to one Sam Devereaux, who was way out of his league.

"Oh, I'm sure not. I don't think General Hawkins ever heard of what's-his-name. I know *I* haven't." The chickenshit was melting under Sam's shirt, all over his fevered back.

Koenig rose slowly from the milking stool, a second flatus loudly proclaiming his ascent. He spoke with quiet, intense hostility.

"The general has my reluctant respect. He has sent me a babbling idiot. Give me the papers, fool."

"The papers—." Sam reached into his jacket pocket for another Xerox copy of the Shepherd Company's limited partnership agreement.

The German fingered the papers silently, squeezing each one as he flipped it. His audible reactions were blunt: a combination of farts and grunts.

"This is outrageous! A great injustice! Political enemies everywhere! All wishing only to destroy me!" Beads of saliva formed at the corners of Koenig's mouth.

"I agree wholeheartedly," said Devereaux, eagerly nodding his head. "I'd throw it away if I were you."

"You would like that? All of you. You are all out to get me! My great contributions that kept peace in the world, enemies in constant touch, that opened hot lines and red lines and blue lines between the great powers—these are forgotten. Now you whisper behind my back. You tell lies about nonexistent bank accounts, even my humble places of residence. You never concede that I earned every *deutschmark* I possess! When I retired, none of you could tolerate it; you did not have me to kick around any longer! And now this! The injustice!"

141

"Oh, I understand."

"You understand nothing! Give me something to write with, you idiot."

He farted and signed.

CHAPTER FOURTEEN

The bells of the Angelus pealed in solemn, vibrant splendor. They echoed throughout St. Peter's Square, floated above Bernini's marble guardians, and were heard in quiet celebration beyond the dome, deep in the Vatican gardens. Seated on a bench of white stone, looking up at the orange rays of the descending sun, was a corpulent man with a face best described as having weathered seven decades good-naturedly, if not always peacefully. The face was full; but the peasant quality of the bone structure under the folds of flesh would tend to deny that the face was pampered. The man's eyes were wide and large and brown and soft; they held nearly equal parts of strength, perception, resignation, and amusement.

He was dressed in the splendid white robes of his office. The highest office of the Holy Apostolic Catholic Church, the descendent of Peter himself, the Bishop of Rome, the spiritual commander of 400 million souls throughout the earth.

Pope Francesco I, the Vicar of Christ.

Born Giovanni Bombalini in a small village north of Padua in the first years of the century. It was a birth that was recorded sketchily, at best, for the Bombalinis were not affluent. Giovanni was delivered by a midwife who, as often as not, forgot to report the fruits of her labors (and her patient's labors) to the village clerk, secure in the knowledge that the church would do *something*; christenings made money. Actually Giovanni Bombalini's emergence into this world might never have been legally recorded at all except that his father had a wager with his cousin Frescobaldi, three villages to the north, that his second child would be a male. Bombalini Senior wanted to

143

take no chances that his cousin Frescobaldi would renege on the bet, so he went to the village hall himself to report the birth of a male child.

As it happened, part of the wager was that Frescobaldi's wife—who was expecting in the same month—would *not* give birth to a boy. But of course she did, and the bet was canceled. This child, Guido Frescobaldi, was born— according to the sketchy records—two days after *his* cousin, Giovanni.

Early in his life Giovanni showed signs of being different from the other children of the village. To begin with he did not care to learn his catechism by verbal repetition; he wanted to *read* it, *then* memorize it. This upset the village priest for it smacked of precociousness and somehow was an affront to authority, but the child would not be denied.

The ways of Giovanni Bombalini were indeed extraordinary. Although he never shirked his labors in the fields, he was rarely too tired to stay up half the night reading whatever he could get his hands on. When he was twelve he discovered the *biblioteca* in Padua, which was hardly the library in Milan, nor Venice, nor certainly Rome, but it was said by those who knew Giovanni that he read every book in Padua, then Milan, then Venice. By which time his priest recommended him to the holy fathers in Rome.

The church was Giovanni's answer to a prayer. And as long as he prayed a great deal—which was easier, though no less time-consuming than laboring in the fields—he was allowed to read more than he ever thought would be allowed him.

By the age of twenty-two, Giovanni Bombalini was an ordained priest. Some said the best-read priest in Rome, an *erudito fantastico*. But Giovanni did not possess the properly stern visage of a proper Vatican *erudito*; nor did he assume the proper attitudes of certainty with regard to everyday truths. He was forever finding exceptions and flexibilities in liturgical history, pointing out (some said mischievously) that the writings of the church found their strength in honest contradictions.

At twenty-six Giovanni Bombalini was a sharp pain in the large Vatican ass. Aggravated further by his matured appearance, which was the antithesis of the gaunt, academic image so desired by Rome's *eruditi*. He was, if anything, the caricature of a field peasant from the northern districts. Short of stature, stocky, and wide of girth, he looked like a farmhand more at home in the goat stables than in the marble halls of the various Vatican *collegia*. No amount of theological erudition, or good nature, or, indeed, deep belief in his church could counteract the combined aggravation of his mind and appearance. So posts were found for him in such unlikely locations as the Gold Coast, Sierra Leone, Malta, and, through an error, Monte Carlo. An exhausted Vatican dispatcher misread the name Montes Claros and inserted Monte Carlo—no doubt because he had never *heard* of Brazil's Montes Claros—and the fortunes of Giovanni Bombalini turned.

For into the cauldron of high stakes and high emotions wandered the simple looking priest with the bemused eyes, gentle humor, and a head packed with more knowledge than any twelve international financiers put together. He'd had little to do in the Gold Coast, Sierra Leone, and Malta, so he had occupied his time, when not praying or teaching the natives, by subscribing to scores of reading services and adding to his already extraordinary memory bank.

It is common knowledge that people who live with constant motion, and high risk, and a great deal of alcohol, occasionally need spiritual consolation. So Father Bombalini began to comfort a few stray lambs. And to the amazement of these first few strays, they found not so much a simple priest who outlined penance, but a most amusing fellow who could discourse at length on almost any subject: economic conditions of world markets, historical precedents for anticipated geopolitical events, and, particularly, food. (Here he favored the more basic sauces, eschewing the artifices of the often inappropriate *haute cuisine*.)

Before too many months had passed, Father Bombalini was a regular guest at many of the larger hotel suites and great houses of the Côte d'Azur. This rather odd-looking, rotund prelate was a marvelous raconteur, and it always made everyone feel better to have him around before going out to covet—successfully—his neighbor's wife.

And a number of excessively large contributions to the

145

church were made in Father Giovanni's name. With increasing frequency.

Rome could no longer overlook Bombalini. The exchequers of the Vatican treasury said so.

The war found Monsignor Bombalini in various Allied capitals and occasionally attached to various Allied armies. This was brought about for two reasons. The first was his adamant deposition to his superiors that he could not remain neutral in light of the known Hitlerian objectives. He catalogued his thesis with sixteen pages of historical, theological, and liturgical precendents; none but the Jesuits could understand it, and they were on his side. So Rome shut its eyes and hoped for the best. The second reason for his wartime travels was that the international rich of Monte Carlo in the thirties were now colonels and generals and diplomats and ambassadorial liaisons. They *all* wanted him. There were so many intra-Allied requests for his services that in Washington, J. Edgar Hoover marked Bombalini's file: *Highly Suspect. May be a fairy.*

The postwar years were a time of rapid acceleration up the Vatican ladder for Cardinal Bombalini. Much of his success was due to his close friendship with Angelo Roncalli, with whom he shared a number of unorthodox views, as well as a penchant for decent, but not necessarily exclusive, wine and a good game of cards after the evening prayers.

As he sat on the white stone bench in the Vatican gardens Giovanni Bombalini—Pope Francesco—reflected that he missed Roncalli. They had accomplished much together; it had been good. And the similarities of their respective ascendencies to the chair of St. Peter never ceased to amuse him. Roncalli, John, would have been amused, too; no doubt, was, of course.

They were both compromises offered by the stern, orthodox constituencies of the Curia to quiet the fires of discontent within the global flock. Neither compromise expected to reign very long. But Roncalli had it easy; he had only theological arguments and undeveloped social reformers to contend with. He didn't have damn fool young priests who wanted to marry and have children and, when of other persuasions, run homosexual parishes! Not

146

that any of these personally bothered Giovanni; there was absolutely *nothing* in theological law or dogma that actually prohibited marriage and offspring; and, as far as the other, if love of fellow man did not surmount biblical ambiguities, what had they learned? But, Mother of God, the fuss that was made!

There was so much to do—and the doctors had made it clear that his time was limited. It was the only thing they *were* clear about; they could isolate no specific illness, no particular malady. They just conferred and confirmed that his "vital signs" were slowing down at an alarming rate. He had demanded openness from them; Mother of God, he had no fear of death! He welcomed the rest. He and Roncalli could plow the heavenly vineyards together and take up their baccarat again. At last count Roncalli owed him something over six hundred million lire.

He had told the doctors that they looked too long in their microscopes and too little at the obvious. The machine was wearing out; it was as simple as that. Whereupon they nodded pontifically and uttered somberly: "Three months, four at the most, Holy Father."

Doctors. *Basta!* Veterinarians with *cugini* in the Curia! Their bills were outrageous! The goatherders of Padua knew more about medicine; they had to.

Francesco heard the footsteps behind him and turned. Walking up the garden path was a young papal aide whose name escaped him. The youthful priest carried a clipboard in his hand. There was a painted crucifix on the underside; it looked silly.

"Your Holiness asked that we resolve some minor matters before the vesper hour."

"By all means, Father. What are they?"

The aide rattled off a series of inconsequential functions, ceremonial in nature, and Giovanni flattered the young prelate by requesting his opinion on most of them.

"Then there is a request from an American periodical, *Viva Gourmet*. I would not mention it to the Holy Father except that the inquiry was accompanied by a strong recommendation from the United States Armed Forces Information Service."

"That is a most unusual combination, is it not, Father?"

147

"Yes, Your Holiness. Quite incomprehensible."

"What was the request?"

"They had the effrontery to ask the Holy Father to submit to an interview with a lady journalist regarding the pontiff's favorite dishes."

"Why is that an effrontery?"

The young prelate paused; he seemed momentarily perplexed. Then he continued with confidence. "Because Cardinal Quartze said it was, Holy Father."

"Did the learned cardinal give his reasons? Or, as usual, did he commune with God all by himself and simply deliver the divine edict?" Francesco tried not to overdo his perfectly natural reaction to Ignatio Quartze. The cardinal was a loathsome fellow in just about every department. He was an *erudito aristocratico* from a powerful Italian-Swiss family, who had the compassion of a disturbed cobra. Looked like one, too, thought Giovanni.

"He did, Holy Father," replied the priest. And the instant he spoke, the aide was struck by a sudden embarrassment. "He—he——."

"May I suggest, Father," said the pontiff with graceful understanding, "that our splendidly berobed cardinal offered the opinion that the pope's favorite dishes were less than impressive?"

"I—I——"

"I see he did. Well, Father, it is true that I subscribe to simpler cooking than does our cardinal with the unfortunate nasal drip, but it is not due to lack of knowledge. Merely lack of, perhaps, ostentation; not that our cardinal, who is afflicted with that unfortunate eye that strays to the right as he talks, is ostentatious. I don't believe it ever crossed his mind."

"No, of course not, Holy Father."

"But I think that during these days of high prices and widespread unemployment, it might be a fine idea for your pontiff to outline a number of inexpensive, though I assure you, quite excellent dishes. Who is this journalist? A lady, you say? Don't ever tell anyone I said it, Father, but they are not the best cooks."

"No, surely not, Your Holiness. The nuns of Rome are strenuous——"

148

"Galvanizing, Father. Positively galvanizing! Who is the journalist from this gourmet periodical?"

"Her name is Lillian von Schnabe. She is American, from the state of California, married to an older man, a German immigrant who fled Hitler. As coincidence would have it, she is currently in Berlin."

"I merely asked who she was, Father. Not her biography. How do you know all this?"

"It was in the recommendation from the United States Army Information Service. The military think highly of her, apparently."

"More than apparently. So, her husband fled Hitler? One does not turn away from such compassionate women. Coupled with the state of food prices—a number of inexpensive papal dishes is called for. Set up an appointment, Father. You may tell our resplendent cardinal, who suffers from the unfortunate affliction of a high-decibeled wheeze, that we truly hope our decision is not an affront to him. *Viva Gourmet*. The Lord God has been good to me; it is a mark of recognition. I wonder why its correspondent is in Berlin? There's a monsignor in Bonn who makes an excellent *Sauerbraten*."

"I swear, you've got feathers in your teeth!" said Lillian as Sam walked into the room.

"It's better than chickenshit."

"What?"

"My business contact had a strange method of transportation."

"What are you talking about?"

"I want to take a shower."

"Not with *me*, honey!"

"I've never been so hungry in my life. They wouldn't even stop for a—what the hell is it? A strudel. Everything was *ein, zwei, drei*! *Mach schnell*! Christ, I'm starved! They really think they won the war!"

Lillian backed away from him. "You are the filthiest, most foul-smelling man I've ever seen. I'm surprised they let you in the lobby."

"I think we goose-stepped." Sam noticed a large white business envelope on the bureau. "What's that?"

149

"The front desk sent it up. They said it was urgent and they weren't sure you'd stop for messages."

"I can only conclude your ex, the fruitcake, has been busy." Devereaux picked up the envelope. Inside were airline tickets and a note. He didn't really have to read the note; the airline tickets said it all.

Algiers.

Then he read the note.

"*No!* Goddamn it, *no!* That's less than an hour from now!"

"What is?" asked Lillian. "The plane?"

"What plane? How the hell do *you* know there's a plane?"

"Because MacKenzie called. From Washington. You can imagine his shock when I answered——"

"Spare me your inventive details!" roared Devereaux as he raced to the telephone. "I've got several things to say to that devious son of a bitch! Even convicts get a day off! At least time for a meal and a shower!"

"You can't reach him now," said Lillian quickly. "That was one of the reasons he called. He'll be out for the rest of the day."

Sam turned menacingly. Then he stopped. This girl could probably cut him in two. "And I suppose he offered a suggestion as to why I should be on that plane. Once he got over the shock of hearing your lovely voice, of course."

Lillian looked puzzled. It crossed Devereaux's mind that the puzzlement was not entirely genuine. "Mac mentioned something about a German named Koenig. How anxious this Koenig was for you to leave Berlin—one way or the other."

"The less controversial method being Air France to Paris and from Paris to Algiers?"

"Yes, he did say that. Although not in those exact words. He's terribly fond of you, Sam. He speaks of you as a son. The son he never had."

"If there's a Jacob, I'm Esau. Otherwise, I'm fucked as Absolom."

"Vulgarity isn't called for——"

"It's the only thing that *is* called for! What the hell is in Algiers?"

150

"A sheik named Azaz-Varak," answered Lillian Hawkins von Schnabe.

Hawkins left the Watergate in a hurry. He had no desire to talk to Sam; he had absolute faith in Lillian, in all the girls, actually. They were doing their jobs splendidly! Besides, he was to meet with an Israeli major who, with any luck, could put the final pieces of the puzzle together for him. The puzzle being Sheik Azaz-Varak. By the time Devereaux reached Algiers a telephone call would have to be made. The Hawk could not make it without that final item which would insure the last of the Shepherd Company's capitalization.

That Azaz-Varak was a thief on a global scale was nothing new. During the Second World War he sold oil at outrageous prices to the Allies and the Axis simultaneously, favoring only those who paid instantly in cash. This did not make him enemies, however; instead, his policies engendered respect, from Detroit to Essen.

But the war was ancient history. That war. It was Azaz-Varak's behavior in a far more recent conflagration that interested Hawkins: the Mideast crisis.

Azaz-Varak was nowhere to be found.

While oaths were hurled across the lands of the Middle East, and the world watched armies clash against armies, and crisis-laden conferences took place, and outrageous profits were made, the greediest sheik of them all claimed to have a case of shingles and went to the Virgin Islands.

Goddamn! It didn't make sense! So MacKenzie went back into Azaz-Varak's raw files and studied them with the eye of a professional. He began to find the pattern in the years between 1946 and 1948. Sheik Azaz-Varak had apparently spent a considerable amount of time in Tel Aviv!

According to the reports, his first few trips were made quite openly. It was supposed that Azaz-Varak sought Israeli women for his harem. Thereafter, however, Azaz-Varak continued to fly into Tel Aviv, but not openly; landing at night in outlying private airfields that could accommodate his most modern and expensive private planes.

More women? Hawkins had researched exhaustively and was unable to unearth the name of a single Israeli female

151

who ever went back to the sheikdom of Azaz-Kuwait.

Then, what had Azaz-Varak been doing in the state of Israel? And why had he traveled there so frequently?

MacKenzie's breakthrough came, strangely enough, from information supplied by naval intelligence on the island of St. Thomas, where Azaz-Varak had fled during the Mideast war. There, he tried to buy up more property than anyone wished to sell. Rebuffed, he became furious.

The islanders had enough trouble. They did not need Arabs with harems and slaves. Jesus! *Slaves!* The very idea sent the bureau of tourism into apoplexy; visions of all that kitchen help in revolt were positively nauseating. Azaz-Varak was systematically prevented from buying two buckets of sand. When it was suspected he was trying to negotiate through second and third parties, covenants were included that would have made Palm Beach green with envy and the ACLU purple with rage. Simply put: no fucking Arabs could own, lease, sublease, visit, or trespass.

So in his frustration, the acquisitive sheik angrily, and hastily, brought in an American holding company called the Buffalo Corporation and tried to negotiate through it. There *were* laws and St. Thomas was a United States possession. And it did not take much research on Hawkins's part to uncover the fact that the Buffalo Corporation— address: Albany Street, Buffalo, New York; telephone: unlisted—was a subsidiary of an unknown company called Pan-Friendship, main office: Beirut; telephone: also unlisted.

Subsequent overseas calls to several Israeli clearinghouses made stunningly clear what Azaz-Varak had been doing during all those visits to the Jewish homeland. He owned half the real estate in Tel Aviv, much of it in the poorer sections of town. The sheik was a Tel Aviv slumlord.

The Buffalo Corporation collected rents from all over the city. *And* if the Israeli major—who was in ordnance and supply—confirmed a report the Hawk had received from some old Cambodian buddies in the CIA, the Buffalo Corporation was also in another business. One that held most unfortunate implications for the owner of said Buffalo

Corporation, insofar as he was the very Arab who scared hell out of the realtors in St. Thomas.

The report was simple; all MacKenzie needed was one military official to corroborate it. For the CIA boys learned that a major expeditor of petrochemicals and fuel for the army of Israel during the Mideast war was a little-known American company called the Buffalo Corporation.

Sheik Azaz-Varak not only owned half the real estate in Tel Aviv, but at the height of the conflict, he fed the Israeli war machine so the maniacs in Cairo wouldn't damage his investments.

It was the sort of information that simply demanded a long-distance call, thought MacKenzie Hawkins. To the sheikdom of Azaz-Kuwait.

Devereaux appreciated the sympathy from the Air France stewardess, but he would have appreciated food more. There were no supplies in the galley of the 727, a conditiion that would be corrected in Paris. Apparently—and there was no way to be sure he understood correctly—the Boche catering trucks that serviced Air France had been tied up in a Russian-induced traffic jam on the autobahn, and what had been left in the galley had been stolen by the Czechoslovakian ground crew in Prague. And besides, the food was better in Paris.

So Sam smoked cigarettes, caught himself chewing bits of tobacco, and tried to concentrate on the doings of MacKenzie Hawkins. His seatmate was some kind of Eastern religious, perhaps a Sikh, with brown skin tinged with gray, a very small black beard, a purple turban, and darting eyes that were as close as a human's could be to those of a rat. It made thinking about MacKenzie easier; there would be little conversation on the trip to Paris.

Hawkins had raised his third ten million. And now there was an Arabian sheik who was the fourth and final mark. Whatever it was that MacKenzie had culled from the raw files had the effect of thermonuclear blackmail. Christ! *Forty million!*

What was he going to *do* with it? What kind of "equip-

153

ment and support personnel" (whatever the hell *they* were) could possibly cost so much?

Granted one did not kidnap a pope with a dollar and a quarter in his pocket, but was it necessary to cover the Italian national debt to do it?

One thing was certain. The Hawk's plan for the kidnapping included the exchange of extraordinary sums of money. And whoever accepted such sums were *ipso facto* accessories to the most outrageous abduction in history! It was another avenue he, Sam, could explore. And a pretty good one at that. If he could obtain the names of even a few of Mac's suppliers, he could scare them right out of the picture. Certainly the Hawk was not going to say to someone: *Yes, I'll buy that railroad train because I'm going to kidnap this pope fellow and it'll be a big help*. No, that was hardly the way of an experienced general officer who had drugged half the pouch couriers in Southeast Asia. But if he, Sam, reached that same someone and said: *You know that train you're selling to that bearded idiot? It's going to be used to kidnap the pope. Have a good night's sleep*—well, that was something else again. The train would not be sold. And if he could prevent a train from being sold, perhaps he could prevent other supplies from reaching the Hawk. MacKenzie was army; lines of supply were paramount to any operation. Without them whole strategies were altered, even abandoned. It was military holy writ.

Yes, reflected Devereaux, gazing out into the German twilight from the foodless Air France plane, it was a very decent avenue to explore. Coupled with his first consideration—finding out how the Hawk intended to pull off the kidnapping, and the second consideration—finding out what specific blackmailing material MacKenzie held over his investors, the suppliers were a third, powerful ingredient. In preventive medicine.

Sam closed his eyes, conjuring up visions of long ago. He was in the basement of his home in Quincy, Massachusetts. On the huge table in the center of his room was his set of Lionel trains, going around and around, weaving in and out of the miniature shrubbery and over the tiny bridges and through the toy tunnels. But there was something strange about the sight. Except for the engine and the caboose, all the other vehicles were marked identically: "Refrigerator Car. Food."

At Orly Airport, the passengers to Algiers were told to remain on the plane. For Devereaux nothing mattered once he saw the white truck pull up alongside the aircraft and men in white coats transferring immaculate steel containers into the galley. He even smiled at Rat Eyes beside him, noticing as he did so that his seatmate's purple turban had slipped somewhat over his brown forehead. Sam might have said something—he'd learned long ago that even strangers appreciated it when you told them their zippers were open—but since several other turbaned acquaintances who'd boarded at Orly had come up to pay their respects and had said nothing, Devereaux felt it wasn't his place. Besides most of the other purple turbans seemed a touch lopsided. Perhaps it was a custom indigenous to the particular religious sect.

Regardless, all Sam could think about were the immaculate steel trays, now securely in the Air France galley broilers, sending out deliriously inviting wafts of *escalope de veau, tournedos, sauce Béarnaise*, and, if he was not mistaken, steak *au poivre*. God was in his heaven and on Air France as well. Good Lord! Devereaux vaguely calculated the hours since he'd eaten: It was nearing thirty-six.

Unintelligible words droned over the cabin loudspeakers; the 727 taxied out onto the field. Two minutes later they were airborne and the stewardesses went about the business of distributing the most meaningful literature Sam could think of: menus.

His order took up more time than anyone else in the cabin. This was partially due to the fact that he salivated and had to swallow as he spoke. There followed an agonizing hour. Normally it was not agonizing to Sam, for it was taken up with cocktails. But today he could not drink. His stomach was too empty.

At length, dinner approached. The stewardess went down the aisle spreading the miniature tablecloths, placing the napkin-enclosed silverware, and reconfirming the choice of dinner wines. Sam could not help himself; he kept craning his neck over the edge of the seat. The scents from the galley were driving him crazy. Every odor was a banquet to his nostrils; the juices ran down his throat at each recognizable smell.

And naturally it had to happen.

The weird looking Sikh beside him lunged from his seat and unraveled his purple turban. Out of the cloth fell a large, lethal revolver. It crashed to the deck of the aircraft; Rat Eyes lunged down, retrieved it, and screamed.

"Aiyee! Aiyee! Aiyee! Al Fatah! Al Fatah! Aiyee!"

It was the signal; a screeching symphony of "Aiyees" and "Fatahs" could be heard behind first class, throughout the tube of the long fuselage. From somewhere in his trousers, Rat Eyes pulled out an extremely long, murderous looking scimitar.

Sam stared numbly. In complete defeat.

So the man wasn't a Sikh. He was an Arab. A goddamn fucking Palestinian Arab.

What else?

The stewardess now faced the murderous blade; the barrel of the huge pistol was jammed between her breasts. She did her best, but the terror could not be concealed.

"On the wires! On the wires to your captain!" screeched the Palestinian. "This aircraft will proceed to Algeria. This is the wishes of Al Fatah! To Algiers! Only Algiers! Or you will all die. *Die! Die!"*

"Mais, oui, monsieur," screamed the stewardess. "The aircraft *is* proceeding to Algiers! *That* is our destination, monsieur!"

The Arab was crestfallen. His wild, piercing eyes became temporary pools of dull mud, the frustration conveyed by the tiny dots of questioning chaos in the center of the mud.

Then the eyes sprang back once more to the vivid, cruel, violent exuberance.

He slashed the air with the huge scimitar and waved the pistol maniacally.

His demonic, defiant screams were worthy of shattering the high-altitude glass, but fortunately did not.

"Aiyee! Aiyee! Arafat! Hear the word of *Arafat!* Jewish

156

dogs and Christian pigs! There will be no food or water until we *land! That is the word of Arafat!"*

Deep within the recesses of Sam's subconscious a small voice whispered: *You're fucked, babe.*

CHAPTER FIFTEEN

The stage manager winced; two violins and three horns went sour during the crescendo of "Musetta's Waltz." The act's finale was ruined. Again.

He made a note for the conductor who he could see was smiling blissfully, unaware of the grating dissonance. It was understandable: the man's hearing wasn't so good anymore.

As the stage manager looked out, he saw that the spotlight operator had dozed off again; or had gone to the toilet. Again. The shaft of light was angled down, immobile, into the pit—on a confused flautist—instead of on Mimi.

He made a note.

On the stage itself was another problem. Two problems. The swinging gates into the cafe had been hung upside down, the pointed tops inverted so that they vee'd up from the floor, providing the audience a clear view behind the scenery where numerous bare feet were being rubbed and not a few extras scratched themselves in boredom. The second problem was the step unit on stage left; it had become unhinged so that Rodolfo's leg plummeted down into the open space causing his tights to rip up to his crotch.

The stage manager sighed and made two more notes.

Puccini's *La Boheme* was being given its usual performance by the company. *Mannaggia!*

As he finished putting three exclamation points after his twenty-sixth note of the evening, the assistant box-office manager approached his lectern and handed him a message.

It was for Guido Frescobaldi, and because any distraction was preferable to watching the remainder of the act, the stage manager unfolded the paper and read it.

Instantly, involuntarily, he caught his breath. Old Frescobaldi would have a fit—if it was possible for Guido to *have* a fit. There was a newspaper reporter in the audience who wanted to meet with Frescobaldi after the performance.

The stage manager shook his head sadly, recalling vividly Guido's tears and protestations when the last (and only) newspaper reporter interviewed him. There were two reporters actually: a man from Rome and a silent Chinese colleague. Both Communists.

It was not the interview that had upset Frescobaldi, it was the article that came out of it.

Impoverished Opera Artist Struggles for Peoples' Culture as Cousin, the Pope, Lives in Indolent Luxury off the Honest Sweat of Oppressed Workers!

That had been for openers. The front page headlined the story in the Communist newspaper, *Lo Popolo*. The article had gone on to say that diligent investigative reporting on the part of *Lo Popolo*'s journalists—ever alert to the inequities of capitalism's unholy alliance with savage organized religion—had uncovered the crass injustice done to this look-alike relative of the world's most powerful and despotic religious leader. How one Guido Frescobaldi sacrificed for his art while his cousin, Pope Francesco, stole everyone blind. How Guido contributed his great talent for the good of the masses, never seeking material rewards, satisfied only that his contributions uplifted the spirit of the people. So different from his cousin, the pontiff, who contributed nothing but new methods to extract money from the frightened poor. Guido Frescobaldi was the earthly saint; his cousin the subterranean villain, no doubt with orgies in the catacombs, surrounded by treasures.

The stage manager did not know a great deal about Guido's cousin, or what he did in the catacombs, but he did know Frescobaldi. And *Lo Popolo*'s reporter had etched a portrait that was somewhat at variance to the Guido they all knew. But it was *this* Guido the world outside of Milan read about. *Lo Popolo* stated in an editorial that the

159

shocking story was to be reprinted in all the Socialist countries, including China.

Oh, how Frescobaldi had screamed! His roars had been the protestations of a thoroughly embarrassed man. The stage manager hoped that he could catch Guido during the act change and give him the message, but it was not always easy to find Guido during an act change. And it was useless to put the note in his dressing room for he would never see it.

For the role of Alcindoro was Guido Frescobaldi's moment in the operatic sun. It was his single triumph in a lifetime devoted to his beloved *musica*. It was proof that tenacity really did overshadow talent.

Guido was usually so moved by the events on stage—as well as his own performance—that he waddled in a trance behind the scenery until the confusion of an act change was over, his eyes invariably moist, his head held high in the knowledge that he had given his all for the audience of La Scala Minuscolo, the fifth-string company of the world-renowned opera house. It was both a training ground and a musical cemetery, allowing the inexperienced to flutter their vocal wings and the over-the-hill to stay occupied until the Great Conductor summoned them to that glorious festival in the sky.

The stage manager reread the note to Guido. In the audience that night was a lady journalist named Signora Greenberg who wished to chat with Frescobaldi. He had been recommended to her by no less a distinguished source than the United States Army *Information Servizio*. And the stage manager knew why this Signora Greenberg included the recommendation in her note. Ever since the Communists wrote that terrible article, Guido refused to talk to anyone from the newspapers. He had even grown a huge walrus moustache and beard to lessen the likeness between himself and the pontiff.

The Communists were stupid. *Lo Popolo*, through habit, was always picking a fight with the Vatican, but they soon learned what everyone else knew: Pope Francesco was not a man to vilify. He was simply too nice a fellow.

Guido Frescobaldi was a nice fellow, too, thought the

stage manager. Many a late night they had divided bottles of wine together; a middle-aged signaler of cues and the elder character actor who had given his life for music.

What a drama was in the *real* story of Guido Frescobaldi! It was worthy of Puccini, himself!

To begin with, he lived only for his beloved opera; all else was inconsequential, necessary solely to keep body and musical soul together. He had been married years ago. And six years later his wife had left him, taking their six children with her back to her native village near Padua and the security of her father's not immodest farm. Though Frescobaldi's circumstances, which by tradition meant the circumstances of his family, had not been destitute. And if his own income was currently less than adequate for *him*, it was by choice, not necessity. The Frescobaldis were actually quite well off; their cousins, the Bombalinis, had been sufficiently wealthy to allow their third son, Giovanni, to enter the church, and God knew that took a little money.

But Guido turned his back on all things clerical, mercantile, and agricultural. He wanted only his music, his opera. He badgered his father and mother to send him to the academy in Rome, where it was soon discovered that Guido's passion far outdistanced his talents.

Frescobaldi had the Latin fire and the soul, perhaps, but he also possessed a rotten musical ear. And Papa Frescobaldi was getting nervous; so many Guido associated with were *non sono stabile*—they wore funny clothes.

So at the age of twenty-two, Papa told Guido to come home to the village north of Padua. He had been studying in Rome for eight years; no noticeable progress had been made. No jobs—at least in music—had been offered, no musical future seemed to hold promise.

Guido did not care, however. It was the total immersion in things musical that counted. Papa could not understand. But Papa would no longer pay, so Guido came home.

The elder Frescobaldi told his son to marry his nice village cousin, Rosa Bombalini, who was having a little trouble finding a husband, and Papa would give Guido a

161

fonografo for a wedding present. Then he could listen to all the music he wished. Also, if he did not marry Cousin Rosa, Papa would break his ass.

So for six years, while his cousin and brother-in-law, Father Giovanni Bombalini, studied in the Vatican and was sent to strange places, Guido Frescobaldi endured a forced marriage to the three-hundred-pound bundle of self-indulgent hysteria named Rosa.

On the morning of his seventh anniversary, he gave up. He awoke screaming; he smashed windows, broke furniture, threw pots of linguini against the walls, and told Rosa that she and her six children were the most repulsive human beings he had ever met.

Basta!

Enough was enough!

Rosa gathered the children together and fled to the village farm; and Guido walked downtown to his father's pasta shop, picked up a bowl of tomato sauce, heaved it in Papa's face and left Padua forever. For Milan.

If the world would not let him be a great operatic tenor, he at least would be near great singers, great music.

He would clean toilets, sweep stages, sew costumes, carry spears. Anything.

He would make his life at La Scala!

And so it had been for over forty years with Frescobaldi. He had risen slowly but happily from toilets to brooms, from stitching to spears. Finally he was awarded those first few words on stage—*Not so much to sing, Guido! More like talk, you see?*—and the sheer openness of his emotion made him an instant favorite of less discriminating operagoers. Of La Scala Minuscolo. Where the ticket scale was lower.

In his way Frescobaldi became a beloved fixture as well as a devoted participant. He was always available to help in rehearsals, to cue, to stand in, to recite, and his knowledge was formidable.

Only once in all the years did Guido cause any trouble for anyone, and it wasn't really his fault. That, of course, was the *Lo Popolo* attempt to embarrass his cousin, the pope. Luckily, the Communist writer had not discovered Frescobaldi's early marriage to the pontiff's sister. It would have been difficult for him, however, because Rosa Bombalini had died of overeating three decades ago.

Hurriedly, the stage manager made his way to Frescobaldi's dressing room. He was too late. The lady speaking to Guido surely was the Signora Greenberg. She was very American and, indeed, very well endowed. Her Italian was a little strange, however. Her words were drawn out like yawns, but the lady did not appear sleepy.

"You see, Signore Frescobaldi, the purpose will be to counteract those nasty things the Communists wrote."

"Oh, yes, *please*!" cried Guido imploringly. "They were infamous! There is no finer man in the world than my dear cousin, *Il Papa*. I weep for the embarrassment I caused!"

"I'm sure he doesn't feel that way. He speaks so well of you."

"Yes—yes, he would," replied Frescobaldi, the moisture clouding his blinking eyes. "As children we would play in the fields together, when our families visited. Giovanni—excuse me, Pope Francesco—was the best of all the brothers and cousins. He was a good *man* even as a *boy*. Does that make sense? And brains!"

"He'll be happy to see you again," said the Signora. "We haven't scheduled the exact time yet, but he hopes you'll meet with him for the photographs."

Guido Frescobaldi could not help himself. Although he lost not a dram of dignity, he wept—quietly, without a sound or a gesture. "He is such a kind man. Did you know that when that terrible magazine came out he sent me a note, in his own hand. He wrote to me: 'Guido, my cousin and dear friend: Why have you hidden yourself all these years? When you come to Rome, please call on me. We will play some bocce. I put a course in the garden. Always, my blessing, *Giovanni*.'" Frescobaldi dabbed his eyes with the edge of the makeup towel. "Not a hint of anger or even displeasure. But of course I would never disturb so great a personage. Who am I?"

"He knew it wasn't your fault. You understand that your cousin would rather not have it known that we're planning this anti-Communist story. With politics the way they are——"

"Not a *word*!" interrupted Guido. "I say *nothing*. I wait

163

only to hear from you and I shall come to Rome. If need be—and I am scheduled to perform—I shall allow my understudy to take my place. The audiences may throw vegetables, but for Francesco, *anything!*"

"He'll be touched."

"Did you know," said Frescobaldi, leaning forward in the chair, lowering his voice, "that under this moustache of mine, the face is very like my exalted cousin's?"

"You mean you *really look alike*?"

"It was ever so since we were children."

"It never would have crossed my mind. But now that you mention it, I do see a resemblance."

The stage manager closed the door silently. It had been partially open; they had not seen him and there was no point in interrupting. Guido might be embarrassed; the dressing room was small. So Frescobaldi was going to see his cousin, the pope. *Buonissimo!* Perhaps he might beseech the pontiff to allocate some funds to La Scala Minuscolo. They could use the money.

The singing was really terrible.

"Aiyee! Al Fatah! Arafat!"

The screaming Palestinian revolutionaries dashed through the exit doors and down the steps to the concrete of Dar el Beida airport. They hugged and kissed each other and slashed at the night air with their blades. One unfortunate had his finger sliced off in the rejoicing, but it did not cause much conern. Under the leadership of Rat Eyes the group made a dash for the fence that surrounded the field.

No one tried to stop them. Indeed, the searchlights were swung in their direction to help them see their way over the fence. The authorities understood that it was desirable for the idiots to leave the field this way. If they walked into the terminal and out through the doors, a large degree of face would be lost. Besides, the quicker they left the better. They were doing nothing for the tourist trade.

The instant the final Palestinian raced out of the aircraft, Sam had lurched into the Air France galley. To no avail. In the midst of crisis, Air France had kept its head—and its financial acumen. The gleaming mental trays were in place for the next contingent of passengers.

"I paid for some goddamned food!" yelled Sam.

"I'm sorry," said the stewardess, smiling blankly. "Regulations prohibit the serving of food after landing."

"For God's sake, we were hijacked!"

"Your ticket reads Algiers. We are in Algiers. On the ground. After landing. There can be no food."

"That's inhuman!"

"That is Air Frawnce, monsieur."

Devereaux staggered through the Algerian customs. He held four American five-dollar bills in his hand, separated as though they were playing cards. Each of the four Algerian inspectors down the line took one, smiled, and passed him on to the next man. No luggage was opened; Sam grabbed his suitcase off the conveyor and looked frantically for the airport restaurant.

It was closed. For a religious holiday.

The taxi ride from the airport to the Aletti Hotel on Rue de l'Enur El Khettabi did nothing to calm his nerves or soothe his agonizingly empty stomach. The vehicle was ancient, the driver more so, and the road down into the city steep and filled with winding curves and hairpin turns.

"We're terribly sorry, Monsieur Devereaux," said the dark-skinned desk clerk in overly precise English. "All of Algiers is in a state of fasting until the sun rises in the morning. It is the will of Mohammed."

Sam leaned over the marble counter and lowered his voice to a whisper. "Look, I respect everyone's right to worship in his own way, but I haven't eaten and I've got a little money——"

"Monsieur!" The clerk's eyes widened in Algerian shock as he interrupted and drew himself up to his full height of roughly five feet. "The will of Mohammed! The way of Allah!"

"Good Lord! I don't believe my *eyes*!" The shout came from across the Aletti lobby. The light was dim, the ceiling high. The figure was obscured in shadows. The only thing Sam knew was that the voice was deep and feminine. And

165

deeply feminine. Perhaps he had heard it before, he could not be sure. How could he be sure of anything—at that moment—in such an unlikely spot as an Algerian hotel lobby—during an Algerian religious holiday—in the last stages of starvation. All was beyond sureness.

And then the figure walked through the hazy pools of light, led by two enormous breasts that cleaved the air in majestic splendor.

Full and Round. Naturally; why did he even bother to act surprised? Ten million—thirty million, forty million dollars no longer shocked him. Why should the sight of Mrs. MacKenzie Hawkins, number two?

She pressed the cool, wet towel on his forehead; he lay back on the bed. Six hours ago she had taken off his shoes and socks and shirt and told him to lie back and stop shaking. In truth, she'd *ordered* him to stop shaking. And while he was at it, to stop babbling incoherently about crazy things like Nazis and chicken droppings and wild-eyed Arabs who wanted to blow up airplanes because they flew where they were supposed to fly. Such talk!

But that had been six hours ago. And during the interim she had taken his mind off food, and MacKenzie Hawkins, and some sheik named Azaz-Varak, and—oh my God!—the *kidnapping of the pope*!

She had reduced the dimensions of the whole insanity to the simpler proportions of a terrifying nightmare.

Her name was Madge; he had remembered that. And she had sat next to him on the bean bag in Regina Greenberg's living room; and she had reached over to touch him every time she emphasized a point. He remembered that distinctly because each time she had leaned toward him, Full and Round seemed to burst out of her peasant blouse, as they seemed now about to burst out of the silk shirt she wore.

"Just a bit longer," she said in her deep, somewhat breathless voice. "The desk clerk promised you'd be the first tray out of the kitchen. Now just relax."

"Tell me again."

"About the food?"

"No. About how come you're here in Algiers. It'll take my mind off the food."

"Then you'll just start babbling again. You simply won't believe me."

"Maybe I missed something——"

"You're teasing me," said Madge, leaning over dangerously, adjusting the towel. "All right. Short and to the point. My late husband was the leading West Coast importer of African art. His gallery was the largest in California. When he died he had over $100,000 tied up in seventeenth-century Musso-Grossai statuary. What the hell am I going to do with five hundred statues of naked pigmies? I mean *really!* You'd do just what I'm doing. Try to stop the shipment and get your money back! Algiers is the clearing house for Musso-Grossai——Now, damn it! There you *go* again!"

Devereaux could not help himself. Tears of laughter rolled down his cheeks. "I'm sorry. It's just that it's so much more *inventive* than a sudden London vacation from a philandering husband. Or a gourmet school in Berlin. My God, it's beautiful! Five hundred naked pigmies! Did you think it up, or did Mac?"

"You're too suspicious." Madge smiled gently, knowingly, and lifted the towel from his forehead. "That's no way to live. Here, I'll soak this with some cool water. Breakfast should be here in fifteen or twenty minutes." She rose from the bed and looked over at the window in silent thought. The orange rays of the new day were streaming through the window. "The sun's up."

Devereaux watched her; the dawn's light washed over her striking features, heightening the sheen of her auburn hair and adding a soft, deep glow to her face. It was not a young face but it had something better than youth. An openness that accepted the years and could laugh gracefully at them. There was a directness that touched Sam.

"You're a terrific looking person," he said.

"So are you," she replied quietly. "You've got what an old friend of mine used to call a face you'd like to know. Your eyes level. My friend used to say 'watch the eyes, especially in a crowd; see if they listen.' Actually, Mac said

167

it. A long time ago. I suppose that sounds silly, eyes listening."

"It doesn't sound silly at all. Eyes do listen. I had a friend who used to go to Washington cocktail parties, and he'd repeat the word 'hamburger' over and over again— just 'hamburger,' nothing else. He swore that ninety percent of the time the people around him would say things like, 'Very interesting. I'll check the statistics on that'; or 'Have you mentioned it to the undersecretary?' He always knew who'd say those things because their eyes were moving so fast; you see, he wasn't very important."

Madge laughed softly; their eyes locked and she smiled. "He sounds very important to me."

"You're a *nice* person, too."

"Yes, I try to be." She looked over at the window again. "MacKenzie also said that too many people run from their perfectly natural inclination to be concerned human beings. As if concern was a sign of weakness. He said: 'Goddamn, Midgey, *I'm* concerned and no son of a bitch better call *me* weak!' And no one ever did."

"I suppose being concerned is another way of being nice," added Devereaux, mulling over the latest homily.

"There's no better way," said Madge, carrying the towel into the bathroom. "I'll be out in a minute."

She closed the door. Sam repeated the words to himself: *Too many people run from their perfectly natural inclination to be concerned human beings*. MacKenzie was a man of more complications than Devereaux cared to think about. At least, until breakfast arrived.

The bathroom door opened. Madge stood in the door frame and smiled deliberately, a sense of marvelous fun in her eyes, very much aware of the picture she presented. She no longer wore her skirt. Instead her breasts were now lovingly encased in an ivory-colored brassiere made of webbed lace. Below, her short slip accentuated the curve of her hips and bore witness to the soft white flesh that touched—and wanted to be touched—between her upper thighs.

She walked around to the side of the bed and took his immobile hand. She sat down gracefully and leaned over, her incredible spheres touching him, sending electricity through him causing him to suddenly inhale very short breaths. She kissed him on the lips. She pulled back and undid his belt and with the swift, graceful movements of a dancer, pulled down his trousers.

"Why Major, you have been thinking nice thoughts——"

And the Algerian terrorist telephone rang.

The galaxy went out of whack again. Sanity vanished in a sudden rush of hysteria. Sweet reason and laced brassieres and soft flesh were no more. Instead, screams in Arabic, commands that threatened unbelievable violence should they be disobeyed.

"If you'll stop yelling about pigs and dogs and vultures for a second, maybe I can figure out what you're trying to say," said Sam, holding the phone away from his ear. "All *I* said was that I couldn't come down right now."

"I am the emissary from Sheik Azaz-Varak!"

"What the hell is that?"

"Dog!"

"It's a dog? You mean a puppy dog?"

"Silence! Azaz-Varak is the god of all khans! The possessor of the desert winds, the eyes of the falcon, the courage of all the lions of Judea, the prince of thunder!"

"Then what does he need me for?" ventured Sam hesitantly, reluctantly recognizing the name of the Hawk's fourth mark. The final ten million. Jesus! He thought about it now with no more emphasis than ten boxes of Pop Tarts!

"Silence, dog! Or both your ears will be cut from your head and placed with hot irons up your unspeakable."

"Now, goddamn it, that's not friendly! You talk nicer or I'm going to hang up; there's a lady here."

"Please, Mr. Deveroo," said the Arabic voice, suddenly quite gentle with a trace of a whine. "In the name of Allah, for the *love* of Allah, do not be difficult. It will be *my* ears in unspeakable places if you are difficult. We must leave for Tizi Ouzou immediately."

"Tizi—who?"

"Ouzou, Mr. Deveroo."

"Ouzoo? Did you say Ouzoo?"

Suddenly, without any warning whatsoever, the most unexpected thing Sam could imagine happened. Madge grabbed the telephone from him.

"Give me that!" she ordered. "I know Tizi Ouzou; my husband and I stayed there once. It's a dreadful place!— Listen here, whoever you are, you'd better have a damn good reason to ask my friend to go to Tizi Ouzou. It's the godforsaken end of nowhere! Without a decent hotel *or* restaurant, to say nothing about toilet facilities!"

The girl held the phone to her ear, nodding briefly every three or four seconds. The whine on the line became very audible.

"Really, Madge, I can handle——"

"Be quiet. This son of a bitch isn't even Algerian . . . Yes. Yes. . . . All right. Then we'll *both* be down! . . . Take it or leave it, you desert gnat, that's the only way it's going to be. . . . They're *your ears*, sweetie. . . . And one other thing. The minute we get there, I want a huge meal waiting for my friend here, do you understand? . . . And no biscuits of camel dung, either! All right. Five minutes."

She hung up and smiled at Devereaux, who was mostly naked and completely pale.

"That was very generous of you, but it's not necessary——"

"Don't be silly. You don't know these people; I do. You have to be firm; they're quite harmless, despite those goddamned knives. Besides, do you think I'd let you out of my sight for a minute? After I've seen what nice thoughts you've been thinking? And in your condition." She leaned over and kissed him again. "It's really very touching."

Devereaux realized that in his weakened condition he might be subject to hallucinations; but he was not prepared for the two robed Arabs that met them in the Aletti lobby.

Peter Lorre and Boris Karloff. Quite a bit younger than the more recent photographs Sam remembered, but otherwise unmistakable.

The next twenty minutes were a blur. Yet he *had* to be able to think clearly. Azaz-Varak (*who*ever and *wher*ever he was) signified the last of the investors. He had to begin putting together the pieces of his counterstrategy.

Peter Lorre sat in the front seat next to Boris, who drove. The car sped through the streets and careened dangerously around the corners of early morning Algiers. They were halfway up a winding, steep hill when Devereaux realized they were heading for Dar el Beida airport.

"We going on a plane?" asked Sam apprehensively.

Madge answered beside him. "Oh sure, sweetie. Tizi Ouzou's like two hundred miles east. You wouldn't want to drive. Remember, I've *been* there."

Devereaux looked at her. He wondered, and whispered, "I remember. What I can't understand is why you're here. Do you know what you're involved with? Do you know what you're *doing*?"

"I'm trying to be helpful."

"So was Rose Mary Woods."

The interior of the helicopter was only slightly smaller than the main level of Pennsylvania Station. Pillows were everywhere and beside each seat was an elaborate water pipe attached to the wall with a kind of Bunsen burner underneath it. An open galley was at the rear.

And after three minutes in the air, Sam was given the first sustenance he could recall. A small cup of acrid, black liquid that vaguely smelled of coffee, but more of bitter licorice mixed with stale sardines.

He drank it in one swallow, grimaced, and looked at the tiny person wrapped in sheets who had poured it for him. The tiny person manipulated several wheels around the water pipe in the wall and held a match to the burner beneath. A long rubber tube with a mouthpiece was reeled from somewhere and held out for Sam.

He took it and wondered. It probably would not do him any good, but on the other hand it was something to put in his mouth, and nothing of that nature at this point could be any worse than the numbed agony he was experiencing. He inserted the mouthpiece between his teeth and drew on it.

It wasn't smoke exactly; it was more a vapor. Sweet and pungent at the same time. Really very pleasant. Actually quite delightful. Rather diverting in its way.

He drew more heavily; and then more rapidly; he looked across at Madge, sitting opposite him in a bank of

171

pillows. "Would you mind, my dear?" he heard himself saying calmly. "Please remove all your clothes."

"I'd go easy on that," replied the girl in her most provocative, breathless whisper.

Was she whispering? Her voice seemed to arrive at his ears on different levels of sound.

"Your blouse first, if you please." Again he was not quite positive he had said what he heard himself saying. "Then perhaps if you would remove your shirt while performing a small, undulating dance. That would be very accommodating."

"Put that damn thing down."

"It's up?" He could actually smell her perfume. And the pains were gone from his stomach. Instead he could feel a surging force of great strength pulsating throughout his body. He was capable of giant deeds; he was—what was it?—the possessor of the desert winds. A prince of thunder, a hurler of lightning. With the courage of all the lions of Judea.

"That's not a Lucky Strike you're pulling on. It's pure hashish."

"Who . . . ?" The information reached that small section of his brain that was functioning. *What the hell was he doing?* He spat out the mouthpiece and tried to stabilize the aircraft; it had to be the helicopter because *something* was suddenly going around and around. The lion of Judea was shrinking. A mangy pussycat was taking its place.

And then he heard the whining words of Peter Lorre, who had walked back from the pilot's area. "We are on a heading south-southeast of Tizi Ouzou."

"How come?" Madge was upset and did not bother to conceal it. "You said Tizi, not someplace else. I've got friends on Rue Joucif, you fly! My late husband did a lot of favors for the Algerian government!"

"A thousand nights of blissful pardons, lady of Deveroo, but my government is Azaz-Kuwait. My sheik is the sheik of all sheiks, the god of all khans, the eyes of the falcon, the courage——"

"*When you're calling mee, calling meee, calling meeee!*" Sam suddenly found himself bursting forth in song; at least, it sounded like him. It *was* a song.

172

"Shut up, Major!" shouted Madge.

"Alone—alonnnnne on this night that was meant for——"

"Will you be quiet!" yelled the girl.

"It seemed appropriate," mumbled Sam.

"Where are we going?" asked Madge of the whining Arab, who was looking at Devereaux as though the American should be watched closely.

"Seventy miles southeast of Tizi Ouzou is a stretch of desert that is traversed only by Bedouin tribes. It is very remote and lends itself to confidential rendezvous. An eagle's tent has been spread for the sheik of all sheiks, the god of all knans. Azaz-Varak, the magnificent, is flying in from his holiest of kingdoms to meet with the unspeakable dog named Deveroo."

"When I'm calling yoooo—Deveroo—only yooooo——"

"Will you shut up!"

CHAPTER SIXTEEN

There were maps everywhere, covering the Watergate bed, spilling over the coffee table, scattered about the floor, propped up against the bureau mirror, and draped over the hotel sofa. There were gasoline road maps, railroad maps, elevation charts, geological and vegetation carto-analyses; even aerial photographs from sequential altitudes of 500, 1,500, 5,000 and finally 20,000 feet.

These plus 363 ground-level photographs of every inch of the terrain under study.

Nothing could be left to chance.

Five minutes ago he had made his final decision. The real estate broker from the highly confidential, international firm of Les Châteaux Suisse des Grands Siècles would be arriving imminently. Naturally, secretly; the first law of Les Châteaux Suisse was absolute secrecy.

Mac had selected a remote château in the canton of Valais, south of Zermatt, in the countryside near Champoluc. The surrounding lands—two hundred acres—were in the cartographical shadow of the Matterhorn and were virtually inaccessible.

What was uppermost in his mind were two factors. The first was terrain. It would have to come as close as possible to duplicating Ground Zero, as Hawkins had decided to name it. Every turn and curve and rise of the road; each slope and hill that might play a part in the approach to or the escape from Ground Zero would have to be simulated as precisely as possible. Maneuvers were useless if the training grounds did not reflect the combat zone.

The second factor was the inaccessibility. His base of operations, as Mac had come to think of the leased property, had to be completely concealed from the outlying country

174

roads as well as from the air. The area had to be one where huge pieces of equipment could be hidden in seconds; where a complement of at least a dozen men could live and train for a minimum of eight weeks.

The château in question possessed these specifics. And it was not that far from Zurich. The Shepherd Company's capital would be transferred to Zurich. Devereaux would have to see to this centralization of finances. As well as the vetting of the château's lease.

There was a discreet knock at the hotel door. MacKenzie stepped carefully over the maps and photographs on the floor and went to it. He stood close to the panel and spoke.

"Monsieur D'Artagnan?" Les Châteaux Suisse used pseudonyms all the time.

"Oui, mon général," was the quiet reply from the corridor.

Hawkins opened the door and a middle-aged, nondescript, portly man entered. Even his slightly waxed moustache was nondescript, thought MacKenzie. He'd be a tough fellow to spot in a crowd; there was absolutely nothing outstanding about him.

"I see you have perused the information we sent you," said Monsieur D'Artagnan in an accent formed west of Alsace-Lorraine. He was obviously a man who wasted no time on the amenities, and the Hawk was grateful for that.

"Yes, I have. I've made my decision."

"Which property?"

"Château Machenfeld."

"Ahh, *Le Machenfeld! Magnifique—extraordinaire!* What history has been played on its rolling fields; what battles won and lost in front of its towering parapets of granite! And the indoor plumbing has been kept most functioningly modern. An exquisite choice. I congratulate you. You and your coterie of religious brothers will be very happy." D'Artagnan removed the fattest envelope Hawkins had ever seen from his inner jacket pocket. The highly secretive firm did not carry briefcases, Mac remembered; so much confidential information crammed into one repository was too dangerous. The brokers carried only those papers of immediate concern.

175

"Are those the leasing arrangements?"

"*Oui, mon général.* All completed and ready for your chosen and agreed-upon mark. And the six months' deposit, of course."

"Well, before we get to that, let me go over the conditions——"

"There are *new* ones, monsieur?"

"No. I just want to make sure you understand the old ones."

"But, my *général*, everything *was* understood," said D'Artagnan, smiling. "You dictated the specifications; I transcribed them myself, as is our policy, and you approved the transcript. Here. See for yourself." He handed Hawkins the papers. "I think you know we would never alter our clients' demands. We have only to fill in the specific château and cross-check to make sure the demands are not in conflict with the owner's conditions of lease. I have done so with all potential locations; there are no conflicts."

MacKenzie took the papers and picked his way between the maps and photographs to the sofa. With one hand he removed two huge elevation charts and sat down.

"I want to be positive that what I'm reading is what I heard."

"Ask any questions you wish. As is the policy of Les Château Suisse des Grands Siècles, each broker is completely familiar with all conditions. And when our business is concluded, the papers are microfilmed and placed in the company vaults in Geneva. We suggest you make similar arrangements with your copies. Untraceable."

Hawkins read aloud. "Whereas the party of the first part, hereafter known as the lessee, takes possession *in-nomen-incognitum.* . . ." Mac's eyes skimmed downward. "In the absence of . . . *communicatum-directorum* between the party of . . . and the party of . . . Goddamn! You boys got your training in clandestine operations."

D'Artagnan smiled; the waxed moustache stretched a little. "Ask your questions, monsieur."

And so it began.

Les Châteaux Suisse des Grands Siècles was nothing if not thorough and specific—in the language of a lease that would never from that moment on see the light of day.

To begin with all identities were held sacrosanct, never to be divulged to any individual, organization, court, or government. No law, national or international, superseded the agreement; *it* was the only law. Payments were made to the firm either in cash or treasurer's checks; in the case of the Shepherd Company, from a Cayman Island depository.

Whenever explanations of "source" were desirable, they would be expedited where necessary and in the interests of controlling outside curiosity. In the case of the Shepherd Company, the sole explanation of "source" was a loose federation of international philanthropists interested in the study and promulgation of an historic religiosity.

All supplies, equipment, transportation, and services would be expedited in complete confidentiality by Les Châteaux Suisse des Grands Siècles and consigned to branch offices in Zermatt, Interlaken, Chamonix, or Grenoble. Any and all deliveries of consequence to Le Château Machenfeld would be made between the hours of midnight and 4 A.M. Drivers, technicians, and laborers, where possible, would be from the ranks of the Shepherd Company's brotherhood, who would be sent down from Le Machenfeld to the branch offices. In the absence thereof, only employees of Les Châteaux Suisse who had no less than ten years acceptable service with the firm would be assigned the deliveries.

All payments were to be made in advance, based on book retail value, with a surcharge of 40 percent for the confidential services of Les Châteaux Suisse.

"That's a lot of percent," said MacKenzie.

"It's a very wide boulevard," replied D'Artagnan. "We don't avail ourselves to those who drive in narrow streets. We think our consultation fee is ample proof of this."

It was, thought the Hawk. The "consultation fee"— applied against whatever lease was arrived at, *if* a lease *was* signed—was $500,000.

"You do mighty fine work, Mr. D'Artagnan," said Hawkins, taking up a fountain pen.

"You're in good hands. In a few days you will, as it were, vanish from the face of the earth."

177

"Don't worry. Everybody I know—that's *everybody*—will be extremely grateful never to hear from me again. Seems I generate complications." The Hawk laughed quietly to himself. He signed his name: *George Washington Rappaport*.

D'Artagnan left with MacKenzie's treasurer's check drawn on the Cayman Islands' Admiralty Bank. The amount was for $1,495,000.

The Hawk picked up a handful of photographs and walked back to the hotel sofa. As he sat down, however, he knew he could not dwell on the majesty of Machenfeld. There were other immediate considerations. Machenfeld would be worthless without the personnel to train within its borders. But former Lieutenant General MacKenzie Hawkins, twice winner of the Congressional Medal of Honor, knew where he was going and how to get there. Ground Zero was several months away. But the journey had begun.

He wondered how Sam and Midgey were doing. Goddamn, that boy was getting around!

The helicopter descended, dropping straight down and causing torrential clouds of sand to blast up in increasingly furious layers from the desert floor. So thick was the enveloping storm that the only way Sam knew they had landed was the jarring thud of the undercarriage as it met and was swallowed by the dunes.

They had been in the air somewhat longer than had been anticipated. There had been a minor navigational problem: The pilot was lost. It had to be the pilot since it was unthinkable to admit the possibility that the eagle's tent of Azaz-Varak was in the wrong place. But at last, they saw the complex of canvas below.

The sand settled and Peter Lorre opened the hatch. The desert sun was blinding. Sam held Madge's arm as they stepped out of the aircraft; if the sun was blinding, the sand was boiling. "Where the hell are we?"

"Aiyee!" "Aiyee!" "Aiyee!" "Aiyee!"

The screams were everywhere, and *from* everywhere there was rushing movement. Turbaned Arabs, their sheets flying in the wind like a hundred white sails, raced out of

178

the various tents toward them. Peter Lorre and Boris Karloff flanked Sam, gripping his arms as if displaying an animal carcass. Madge stood in front, somewhat protectively, thought Devereaux uncomfortably, as though she were about to give instructions to a slaughterhouse butcher. The racing battalion of sheets and turbans formed two single lines that created a corridor leading slightly uphill in the sand to the largest of the tents, about fifty yards away.

Peter Lorre's nasal shriek filled the air. *"Aiyee!* The eye the falcon! The hurler of lightning! The god of all khans and the sheik of all sheiks!" He turned to Sam and screamed even louder. *"Kneel! Unworthy white hyena!"*

"What?" Devereaux wasn't arguing; he just thought the sand would melt his trousers.

"It is better to kneel," said the deep-throated Boris Karloff, "than to find yourself standing on stumps."

The sand was, indeed, uncomfortable. And Sam, in an instant of real human concern, wondered what Madge was going to do; she wore a very short skirt above her desert boots. He squinted and looked at her.

He need not have indulged in human concern, he thought. Madge was not kneeling at all. Instead she had moved slightly to the side and was standing erect. She was spectacular.

"Bitch," he whispered.

"Keep your head," she answered quietly. "That's meant figuratively—I think."

"Aiyee! Behold the prince of thunder and lightning!" shrieked Peter Lorre.

There was movement at the tent at the end of the corridor of abus and turbans. Two minions swept back the front flap and prostrated themselves on the ground, their faces in the sand. From the shadowed recesses emerged a man who was a major disappointment, a walking anticlimax, to the dramatic preparations for his entrance.

The prince of thunder and lightning was a spindly little Arab. Peering out from the shrouds was about the ugliest face Devereaux had ever seen. Below the outsized, narrow, hooked nose, Azaz-Varak's lips were curled—actually *curled*—so that his thick black moustache seemed fused to his nostrils. The pallor of his skin (what could be seen) was

179

a sickly beige, which served to emphasize the dark, deep circles under his heavy-lidded eyes.

Azaz-Varak approached, lips pressing, nostrils sniffing, head bobbing. He looked only at Madge. When he spoke there was a certain authority in his whine.

"The wives of the lion's lair, the royal harem—none understand the awesome responsibilities that befall my generous person. Would you like a camel, lady?"

Madge shook her head with a certain authority of her own. Azaz-Varak continued to stare.

"Two camels? The airplane?"

"I'm in mourning," said Madge respectfully but firmly. "My wealthy sheik passed away just after the last crescent moon. You know the rules."

The heavy-lidded eyes of Azaz-Varak were filled with disappointment; his curled-up lips smacked twice as he replied. "Ahh, it is the awesome burdens of our faith. You have two crescents of the calendar to survive. May your sheik rest with Allah. Perhaps you will visit my palaces when your time has passed."

"We'll see. Right now, my escort is hungry. Allah wants him to protect me; he can't do that if he faints."

Azaz-Varak looked at Sam as though studying the preslaughtered carcass. "He has two functions, then. One worthy, one despicable. Come, dog. To the eagle's tent."

"That's where the food is, isn't it?" Devereaux smiled his best, most ingratiating smile as he scrambled to his feet.

"You will partake of my table when our business is concluded. Pray to Allah that it is finished before the northern snows come to the desert. Did you bring the unmentionable agreement?"

Devereaux nodded. "Did you bring any hot corned beef?"

"*Silence!*" shrieked Peter Lorre.

"Lady," said Azaz-Varak, addressing Madge, "my servants will see to your every wish. My palaces are lovely; you would like them."

"It's tempting. We'll see where I am in a month or so." She winked at Azaz-Varak. His lips went through a series of wet pressings before he snapped his fingers and proceeded toward the eagle's tent.

The minutes stretched into quarter hours, those to the inevitable hour, and then two more of them. Devereaux honestly believed he had reached the end. A promising legal career was being snuffed out, starved out, in the middle of some godforsaken stretch of desert, seventy miles south of a ridiculously named place called Tizi Ouzou in North Africa.

What made the ending so ludicrous was the sight of Azaz-Varak poring over each sentence of the Shepherd Company's limited partnership papers, with eight to ten screeching Arabs looking over his shoulder, arguing vehemently among themselves. Every page was treated as though it were the only page; every convoluted—and unnecessary—legalism torn apart for a meaning that was not there. Sam saw clearly the terrible irony: the esoteric, legalistic nonsense that was the essence of every lawyer's livelihood was keeping him from his own survival.

An insane thought went through his pained brain: if all legal documents were written to be understood between meals—all meals postponed until said understanding was clear—the state of justice would be on a much higher plane. And most lawyers of his acquaintance out of work.

Every now and then one of Azaz-Varak's ministers would carry over a page and point to a particular paragraph, asking him in excellent English what it meant. Invariably Devereaux would explain that it was a standard clause— which invariably it was—and not important.

If it was not important, why was the language so confusing? Only significant items were in confusing words; otherwise there was no need for the confusion.

And, too, good things were stated clearly; unworthy things were often obscured. Did standard mean unworthy?

And so it went. Until at one point Sam screamed.

Nothing else; he simply screamed.

Azaz-Varak and his gaggle of ministers looked over at him. They nodded as if to say, "Your point is well taken." And then went back to screaming at each other.

At the instant the darkness started to cloud his vision, his last look at living things, thought Sam, he heard the words, whined by the sheif of sheiks.

"The northern snows have reached the desert, unspeakable one. These foul papers are like camels' prints in storms of sand: They are without meaning. Not any meaning that would bring the wrath of Allah, or certain international authorities. My generous, all-knowing person has signed them. Not that I subscribe to the despicable suggestions made to my ear, but only to help unite the world in love, you hated dog."

Azaz-Varak rose from the mountain of pillows beneath him. He was escorted to a screened-off section of the enormous tent by several hunched-over ministers and disappeared beyond the silks.

Peter Lorre came up to Sam, the limited partnership agreement in his hands. He gave it to Devereaux and whispered, "Put this in your pocket. It is better that the eye of the falcon not fall on it again."

"Is falcon edible?"

Perplexed, the tiny Arab looked at Sam. "Your eyeballs are swimming in their sockets, Abdul Deveroo. Have the faith of the Koran, first paragraph, book four."

"What the hell is that?" Sam could hardly speak.

"'The feasts were brought among the unbelieving infidels and no longer were they unbelieving.'"

"Does that mean we eat?"

"It does. The god of all khans has ordered his favorite: boiled testicle of camel braised with the stomach of desert rat."

"*Aiyeeeeee!*" Devereaux blanched and leaped up from the floor of the eagle's tent. The spring had been sprung; there was nothing left but self-annihilation. The end was at hand; the forces of destruction called for his finish in an explosion of violence.

So be it. He would meet it swiftly. Surely. Without thought, only blinding fury. He ran around the pillows and over the rugs and out onto the sand. It was sundown; his end would come with the orange sun descending over the desert horizon.

Boiled testicles! Stomach of rat!

"Madge! *Madge!*"

If he could only reach her! She could bring back news of his demise to his mother and Aaron Pinkus. Let them know he died bravely.

"*Madge!* Where are you?!"

When the words came he felt stirrings of bewilderment that were contradictory to the last thoughts of those who were about to perish.

"Hi, sweetie! Come on over. Look what I've got *here*. It's a *gas!*"

Sam turned, his ankles deep in sand, his caked lips trembling. Fifty yards away a group of Arabs were gathered around the front of the helicopter, all peering into the pilot's cabin.

In a trance of confusion, Devereaux staggered toward the bewildering sight. The Arabs squealed and grumbled but let him through. He gripped the ledge of the window and peered inside. It was easy; the aircraft had sunk into the dune upon landing.

It was not his eyes, however, that were assaulted. It was his ears.

There was a continuous, deafening crackle of static from the helicopter's panel that filled the small enclosure like jack hammers in a wind tunnel. Madge was in the co-pilot's seat, her blouse neckline lowered another several buttons.

Then he heard the words riding through the static and Sam froze, his hunger and exhaustion replaced momentarily by a kind of hypnotic terror.

"Midgey! Midgey, girl! You still there?"

"Yes, Mac, still here. It's just Sam. He's finished with what's-his-name."

"*Goddamn!* How is he?"

"Hungry. He's a very hungry boy," said Madge, expertly manipulating switches and dials on the radio panel.

"There'll be plenty of time for rations later. An army travels on its stomach, but first it's got to evacuate the fire zone! Before it gets its ass shot off! Does he have the papers?"

"They're sticking out of his pocket——"

"He's a fine young attorney, that boy! He'll go far! Now,

get out of there, Midgey. Get him to Dar el Beida and on that plane for Zermatt. Confirm, and over and out!"

"Roger—confirm, Mac. Out." Madge whipped through several dozen switches as though she were a computer programmer. She turned her face to Devereaux and beamed. "You're going to have a nice rest, Sam. Mac says you really deserve a vacation."

"Who? Where . . . ?"

"Zermatt, sweetie. It's in Switzerland."

PART

III

The smooth-running corporation is largely dependent on its executive personnel, whose backgrounds and allegiances are compatible with the overall objectives of the structure and whose identities can be submerged to the corporate image.

Shepherd's Laws of Economics:
Book CXIV, Chapter 92

CHAPTER SEVENTEEN

Cardinal Ignatio Quartze,. his thin, aristocratic features bespeaking generations of *noblesse oblige,* stormed across the rugs of his Vatican office to the large balconied window overlooking St. Peter's Square. He spoke in fury, his lips compressed in anger, his nasal voice searing like the screech of a bullet.

"The Bombalini peasant goes too far! I tell you he is a disgrace to the college which—God help us all—elevated him!"

The cardinal's audience was a plump, boyish-looking priest who sat, as languorously as his habit allowed, in a purple velvet chair in the center of the room. His pink cheeks and pursed, thick lips bespoke, perhaps, a less aristocratic background than his superior but not less a love of luxury. His speech was more a purr than a voice.

"He was and remains only a compromise, Cardinal. You were assured his health would not permit an extended reign."

"Every *day* is an extension beyond endurance!"

"He has certain... humilities that serve us. He has quieted much hostile press. The people look upon him warmly; our worldwide contributions are nearly as high as they were with Roncalli."

"Please! Not that name! What good is a treasury that expands and contracts like a thousand concertinas because the Holy See subsidizes everything he can put his fat peasant hands on! And we don't need a friendly press. Division is far better to solidify our own! Nobody understands."

"Oh, but I do, Cardinal. I really do——"

"Did you see him today?" continued Quartze as if the

priest had not spoken. "He openly humiliated me! In audience! He questioned my African allocations."

"A patently obvious ploy to appease that terrible black man. He's forever complaining."

"And afterward he tells jokes—*jokes*, mind you—to the Vatican guard! And waddles into the museum crowds and eats an ice—*eats* an *ice*, mind you—offered by some Sicilian brood mare! Next he'll drop lira in the men's room and all the toilet seats will be stolen! Such indignities! What he does to the bones of St. Peter! They will turn to dust!"

"It cannot be very long, my dear Cardinal."

"Long enough! He'll deplete the treasury and fill the Curia with wild-eyed radicals!"

"You are the next pontiff. The negative reactions of the broad middle hierarchy support you. They are silent, but resentments run deep."

The cardinal paused; his mouth curved slightly downward as he stared out into the square, his jaw jutted forward below the dark hollows of his deep-set eyes. "I do believe we have the delegates. Ronaldo, get me the plans for my villa at San Vincente. It calms my nerves to study them."

"Of course," said the priest, rising from the purple chair. "You must remain calm. And when summer comes you will be rid of the Bombalini peasant. He will stay at Castel Gandolfo for at least six weeks."

"The *plans*, Ronaldo! I'm very upset. Yet in the midst of chaos, I remain the most controlled man in the Vatican—— The plans, you transvestite!" screamed the cardinal.

The moment the papal aide with the ever present clipboard left the room, Pope Francesco I got out of the elevated, high-backed, white velvet chair (a repository that would have frightened Saint Sebastian) and sat next to the lady from *Viva Gourmet* on the couch. He was struck immediately by the beauty of her voice; it was warm and lilting. Very lovely. It befitted such a healthy looking woman.

The aide had suggested that the interview be limited to twenty minutes. The pontiff had suggested that it should end when concluded. The lady journalist had reddened slightly with embarrassment, so Giovanni put her at ease by switching to English and asking her if she thought there was a market for clipboards with crucifixes painted on the undersides. She had laughed while the aide, who did not understand English, stood by the door, the clipboard clutched to his breast like a plastic stigmata.

The aide would have to be replaced, thought the pope. He was another young prelate seduced by the pretensions of Ignatio Quartze. The cardinal was too obvious; he was moving his charges into the papal apartments before the papal funeral was arranged. But Francesco had made up his mind. The Church was not going to be left in the pontifical hands of Ignatio Quartze. To begin with, they held the chalice at Mass as though wringing the neck of a chicken.

The interview with *Viva Gourmet*'s Lillian von Schnabe was productive and pleasant. Giovanni expounded on two of his favorite subjects: that good, substantial meals could be created from inexpensive stock and flavored with simple, spiced sauces; and that in these difficult days of high prices it was a mark of distinction—to say nothing of Christian brotherhood—to share one's table with one's neighbor.

Mrs. von Schnabe saw immediately what he was trying to communicate. "Is this a form of 'the loaves and the fishes,' Your Holiness?"

"Let us say He was not preaching to the wealthier sections of Nazareth. A number of His miracles were based in sound psychological principles, my dear. I open my basket of fruit, you open your basket of pasta; we have fruit *and* pasta. The simple addition alone gives variety. Variety we rightfully equate with more rather than less."

"And the diet's improved," agreed Lillian, nodding.

"*Perfetto.* You see? Two *principios:* reduce the cost and share the supply."

"That sounds almost socialistic, though, doesn't it?"

"When stomachs are empty and prices are high, labels are foolish. In the *Borsa Valori*—the stock exchange, you call it—they are not prone to open baskets; they sell them. It is fitting that they do so, considering the nature of their labors. But I do not address such people. They eat at the Grand Hotel, on each other's expense accounts. I believe that, too, is a derivative of the 'loaves and fishes' principle."

They discussed numerous recipes based on the village dishes from the pope's past. Giovanni could see that the nice lady with the lovely voice was impressed. He had done his nutritional homework; carbohydrates, proteins, starch, calories, iron, and all kinds of vitamins were to be found in his recipes.

Lillian filled half a notebook, writing as rapidly as the pope spoke, stopping him occasionally to clarify a word or a phrase. After nearly an hour had passed, she paused and asked a question Giovanni did not understand.

"What about your own *personal* requirements, Your Holiness? Are there any restrictions or specific necessities called for in the meals brought to you?"

"*Che cosa?* What do you mean?"

"We are what we eat, you know."

"I sincerely hope not. I am in my seventh decade, my dear. An excess of onion or olive or pimento. . . . But such information is not needed for your article. People my age quite naturally gravitate to and regulate their personal needs in this area."

Lillian put her pencil down. "I didn't mean to pry, but you're so fascinating a man—and I *am* considered one of the best nutritional experts in America. I suppose I just wanted to approve of the way your kitchen treats you."

Ahh, thought Giovanni Bombalini, *how many years it has been since a lovely person of the opposite gender has been concerned about him! He could not remember, it was so long ago! Pinched-faced nuns and officious nurses, yes. But so attractive a lady, with such a lovely voice. . . .*

"Well, my dear, these outrageous doctors *do* insist on certain foods. . . ."

Lillian picked up her pencil.

And they talked for another fifteen minutes.

At the end of which time there was a knock on the door of the papal apartment. Francesco rose from the couch and returned to the elevated, high-backed, white velvet chair that belonged in one of those Cinecitta biblical spectaculars.

An agitated Cardinal Ignatio Quartze stood in the doorway, a handkerchief dabbing his aquiline nose, noises emerging from his throat. "I am sorry to interrupt, Holy Father," he said in both Italian and high dudgeon, giving the word "holy" a rather profane but eminently courteous connotation, "but I've just been informed that Your Holiness has seen fit to disagree with my instructions regarding the convocation of the Bankers for Christ."

"'Disagree' is too strong a term. I merely suggested that the convocation committee reconsider. To occupy the Sistine Chapel for two days at the height of the spring tourist season seems unwarranted."

"If you will forgive my contrary observation, the Sistine is the most favored *and* frequented site we possess. All convocations of merit convene there."

"Thus denying thousands every year of its beauty. I'm not sure there's merit in that."

"We are *not* an amusement park, Pope Francesco." Strange noises continued to come from the area of the cardinal's throat; he blew his nose with aristocratic vigor.

"I sometimes wonder," replied Giovanni. "We sell such a diversity of baubles everywhere. Did you know there's a stand featuring rhinestone rosary beads?"

"*Please*, Your Holiness. The Bankers for Christ. They *expect* the Sistine. We are finalizing extremely important matters."

"Yes, my dear Cardinal, I received the memorandum. 'Accruals for Jesus' is somewhat labored, I think, but I suppose these are certain tax advantages." Giovanni's attention was suddenly drawn to Lillian. She had closed her notebook politely but firmly; she was anxious to leave. *Ahh*, it had been such a pleasant interlude! And Quartze was not going to spoil it; he could wait. He addressed the attractive lady with the lovely voice. In English, of course; a language only barely understood by Quartze. "How rude we are. Do forgive us. The agitated cardinal with the propellers in his nasal passages has once again found my judgments lacking."

191

"Then I would have to say *his* judgment left much to be desired," said Lillian, rising from the couch and placing her notebook in her purse. She looked into Giovanni's eyes and spoke softly with feeling. "I suppose this isn't a proper thing to say but since I'm not Catholic, I'll say it anyway. You're one of the most attractive men I've ever met. I hope you're not offended."

Giovanni Bombalini, Pope Francesco, Vicar of Christ felt the stirrings of memories of fifty years ago. And they were good. In a profoundly sacred sense—for which he was grateful. "And you, my dear, possess an honesty—however erroneous your present opinion—that walks in the warm light of God."

"If I do, it's because I was taught by someone quite like you, I think. Although few would recognize the similarity."

"I am flattered. This—someone, give him the blessings of a farmhand-priest."

Lillian smiled. She started for the door, where Quartze's handkerchief fluttered a tattoo in front of his agitated face and the sounds of mucus still could be heard beyond his aquiline nose and very thin lips. The prelate sidestepped to let her pass, doing his best to ignore her. So Lillian paused briefly, forcing him to look at her. When he did so, she winked.

As she closed the door the words from Pope Francesco were clear and firm. For in his anger, the pontiff raised his voice, in English.

"Talk to me not of the Sistine, Ignatio! Instead, discuss these plans I requested for your waterfront home at Sam Vincente! What are 'security arrangements'? They include a *steam bath*?"

Hawkins had reserved both seats in the first-class section of the Lufthansa 747. Since he needed elbow room, there was no point in inconveniencing a fellow passenger. This way, he was able to place file folders beside him for quick referrals.

He had specifically chosen the night flight to Zurich. The travelers, by and large, would be diplomats, bankers, or corporate executives used to transatlantic flights; they would use the night for sleep, not socializing. He would have a minimum of interruptions.

For selections would have to be made, offers of recruitment dispatched immediately from Zurich.

MacKenzie's briefcase contained assorted personnel profiles from which he would choose his troops. They were the last of the files he had Xeroxed at the G-2 archives. Those fortunate enough to be chosen would be his brigade; his personal army that would be privileged to engage in the most unusual maneuver in modern military history.

And each soldier would return from the engagement one of the richest men in his part of the world.

For, where possible, they would *be* from separate parts of the world. For the inviolate condition of recruitment was that none would ever acknowledge the existence of the others once the engagement was completed. It would be better if they came from different places.

The dossiers in the Hawk's briefcase were those of the most accomplished double and triple agents in the U.S. Army data banks. And there was a common denominator running through each file: All were in forced retirement.

The state of double and triple agenting was at a low ebb. The experts described in the dossiers had not had really gainful employment for some time, and for such men inactivity was anathema. It meant not only a loss of prestige within the community of international criminals, but also a reduced scale of living.

The prospects of $500,000 per man would not be lightly dismissed. And each potential recruit was worth it. Each was the best at his specialty.

It was all a question of logistics. Think—then *out*think. Every function handled by an expert, every move timed to the split second.

And that required a commander who demanded flawless precision from his troops. Who trained them to perform at peak efficiency levels. Who did not stint when it came to equipment and simulation; who would duplicate as far as technically possible the *exact conditions* projected for the assault. In essence, a general officer of the first rank. Himself. *Goddamn!*

Once the brigade was selected and assembled, Mac would outline the basic strategy. Then he would allow his officers to offer suggestions and refinements. A good commander always listened to his subordinate officers but, of course, reserved final judgment for himself.

The weeks of training would show where the strengths and weaknesses lay; the objective was merely to eliminate all weakness.

The fewer troops the better, but not so few as to impair the efficiency of the mission. Which was why there was only one payment for each soldier: $500,000. There would be no rewards if they were caught. At least, not the kind they were after. There *would* be certain family allotments in the case of capture. It was the sort of thing all armies had learned to take for granted. Men performed better under combat conditions if their minds were free of concern about their families. It was a good thing, too. It was another proof of separation between the species.

The Shepherd Company would bank funds for dependents in advance of Ground Zero; to be deducted, of course, from all final payments upon the successful completion of the operation.

Goddamn! He was not only pro, he was a very thorough pro at that! If those idiots in the Pentagon had turned over the whole U.S. Army to him, they would not be having all that trouble with volunteer enlistments. The Pentagon pricky-shits did not really understand "the book." If a soldier took the book for what it was and didn't try to bend it politically, or find ambiguities to hide behind—well, it was a goddamned good book. Flawed but workable.

He had no time to think about pricky-shits. He had about refined his brigade. The required areas of expertise were seven: camouflage, demolition, sedative medicines, native orientation, aircraft technology, escape cartography, and electronics.

Seven experts. He had narrowed the dossiers down to twelve. Before he reached Zurich he knew he would have the seven. It was just a question of reading and rereading. He would send out his offers from Zurich, not from the

Château Machenfeld; nothing could be traced to Machenfeld.

He even had to be careful in Zurich. Not with regard to traces, however; he could handle that problem. But he had to make damn sure he didn't run into Sam Devereaux. Sam was due within hours of his own arrival; he wasn't ready for Sam's kind of panic. He could handle *that* problem better within the confines of Machenfeld.

But then, thought the Hawk, he didn't really have anything to worry about. Devereaux was the girl's problem and they had—each and every one—carried out their assignments with real know-how.

Goddamn! They were splendid! A man had to count himself fortunate, indeed, to have such a quartet of fine women behind him. "Behind every great man ..." they said. Behind *him* there wasn't *one* fine lass, there were *four*.

And a grander, more upstanding group of girls there never were! Sam was a lucky fellow and he didn't know it. Hawkins made a mental note to tell him when he saw Sam at Machenfeld.

Tomorrow, if the schedule held.

Devereaux walked down the station platform looking for the correctly numbered railway car. The task was made difficult because he could not stop belching. He had eaten his way from Tizi-whatever-the-hell-it-was, through Algiers, past Rome, into Zurich. Madge had seen him off at Dar el Beida airport admitting no more during their good-byes than she had saying hello in the Aletti Hotel room.

But Sam had made up his mind not to speculate any further about the girls. Whatever propelled them to do what they did for the Hawk could be left to Krafft-Ebing; he had other things to concentrate on.

The capitalization of forty million dollars was committed. Hawkins now had his marbles (no, he did not have his marbles, but that was another question), and he would start playing the game. The Hawk would begin his final arrangements, make his purchases, recruit his—what was it?—"support personnel."

Jesus! Support personnel!

So he could kidnap the pope!

Oh, my God! The whole world was an enormous fruit-cake!

There was only one thing to bear in mind, one objective to keep in focus: How to stop MacKenzie Hawkins.

Two objectives: Stay out of jail himself. And out of the homicidal clutches of the Mafia, the Peerage, the Nazis, and particularly those Arabs who wanted to stuff his unmentionables into unspeakables.

He found his compartment, the sort made famous by Rex Harrison and Margaret Lockwood. Shadows and black velvet collars and the incessant *therumping* of the metal wheels against the metal tracks below signifying the inevitable approach of terror. And large windows on the sliding doors, with curtains suddenly drawn back revealing the faces of evil.

Night Train, Orient Express—with slow dissolves to hands inching into folds of dark overcoats, ever so slowly withdrawing the black steel of murderous pistols. The train started.

"Well, Ah declare! Ah said to myself, Ah simply *don't beleeve it*! It's the *mayjor*! Right here in *li'l ole Zurich*!"

There was no reason to be the least astonished. After all, *Titanics* was on schedule.

Regina Sommerville Hawkins Clark Madison Greenberg stood in the corridor outside the railroad compartment and spoke through the wood-framed window. She slid the door open and filled the small enclosure with remembrances of magnolia blossoms. Sam sat down calmly by the window, amazed at his own casualness. "Your timing's nothing short of brilliant. The train rolls and so do you. If I tried to get off at Lucerne I have an idea you'd start screaming 'rape!'"

"Why, what a peculiar thing to say. I hope you haven't forgotten the Beverly Hills Hotel; I never will."

"My memories have no beginnings, no middles, no ends. The world fornicates in a thousand broken mirrors; we abuse ourselves in the reflections of Sodom and Gomorrah. . . .

"Now, tell me why you just *happen* to be in Zurich. At

196

the Hauptbahnhof, on this particular train, in this particular car."

"Oh, that's easy. Manny's shooting a picture in Geneva. For UA. I think it's so porn they had to make it outside the States."

"That's Geneva; this is Zurich. You can do better than that. Let's have it for Hawkins's Harem. A little imagination, please."

"Honestly! Now you're downright offensive!" Regina swept her vicuña back and placed her hands defiantly on her hips. Two cannons had Devereaux in their sights. "I don't think you've got a damn thing to complain about. We root outselves up out of *very* comfortable circumstances, traipse *all* over the world, subject ourselves to every kind of inconvenience—*rush, rush, rush*—check on everything— look after you, body *and* soul—make sure no one hurts you—see to your every comfort—. Oh, Lawdy, what more could we do?! And for what? *Abuse!* Just plain, big ole abuse!"

Regina dropped her defiant pose and began to cry. She opened her purse, withdrew a Kleenex, and sat down opposite Sam, dabbing her eyes.

A lost, hurt little girl.

"Hey, come on. That's not fair."

As are most men, Sam was helpless before a tearful woman.

Regina sobbed; her chest throbbed. Devereaux got out of his seat and knelt in front of her. "It's okay. It's all right. Don't cry, please."

Between subsiding gasps, the girl looked at him gratefully. "Then you don't hate me? Say you don't hate me."

"How could I hate you? You're lovely—and sweet—and for Christ's sake, please stop crying."

She put her face next to his and her lips against his ear. "I'm sorry. It's just that I'm exhausted. The pressure's been simply God-awful. I've stayed by the telephone night and day, always worryin'—and, of course, wonderin'. I really missed you."

Ginny's coat was like a warm, comforting blanket between them. The huge, soft lapels came close to enveloping

Devereaux's arms. She took both his hands and guided them between the folds of thick fabric and placed them on the softer, warmer, more comforting swells of loveliness that were beneath the silk of her blouse.

"That's better. Stop crying now." It was all he could think to say, so he said it softly.

She whispered into his ear, causing all kinds of things to happen to his metabolism. "Do you remember those marvelous old English movies that took place on trains like this?"

"Sure. Rex Harrison saving Margaret Lockwood from the evil Conrad Veidt——"

"I think you can slide the door closed and lock it. And there are curtains. . . ."

Devereaux rose from the floor. He locked the door, closed the curtains, then turned back to Regina. She had removed her vicuña coat and spread it invitingly over the soft seat of the railroad compartment.

Beneath them the *therumping* sounds of the metal against metal signified the inexorable journey, the beat somehow sensual. Outside, the lovely countryside of Switzerland whipped by, bathed in a Swiss twilight.

"How much time do we have before we reach Zermatt?" he asked.

"Enough," she replied, smiling. She began unbuttoning her silk blouse. "And we'll know. It's the last stop."

CHAPTER EIGHTEEN

Hawkins registered at Zurich's Hotel D'Accord with a counterfeit passport. He'd purchased it in Washington from a CIA agent who realized the courts would not let him write a book when he retired; the man also offered a selection of wigs and hidden cameras but MacKenzie demurred. On settling into the room, his first act was to go right down to the lobby again and negotiate with the head switchboard operator: cash for cooperation. Since the cash was one hundred dollars, it was agreed that all his calls and cablegrams would be routed through her board.

He returned to the room and spread the seven dossiers (his final selections) over the coffee table. He was immensely pleased. These men were the most devious, experienced *provocateurs* in their fields. It was now merely a question of enlisting them. And MacKenzie knew he was an exceptionally qualified recruiter.

Four he knew he could reach by phone. Three by cable. Admittedly, the telephone contacts would be difficult, for in no case would one call find the expert in. But he would reach them by using various codes from the past. One call would be made to a Basque fishing village on the Bay of Biscay; another to a similar coastal town in Crete. A third would be placed to Stockholm, to the sister of the espionage expert who was currently living as a minister of the Scandinavian Baptist Church. The fourth call would be to Marseilles where the man sought was employed as a tugboat pilot.

And the geographical diversity! In addition to those he could reach by telephone (Biscay, Crete, Stockholm and Marseilles), there were the cablegrams: to Athens, Rome, and Beirut What a spread! It was an intelligence director's dream!

MacKenzie took off his jacket, threw it on the bed, and withdrew a fresh cigar from his shirt pocket. He chewed the end to its proper consistency and lighted up. It was just nine-fifteen; the afternoon train to Zermatt was at four-fifteen.

Seven hours. Now that was a good omen if ever one existed! Seven hours and seven subordinate officers to recruit.

He carried the three dossiers to the desk and arranged the files in front of the telephone. The cablegrams would be sent first.

At precisely twenty-two minutes to four the Hawk replaced the telephone and made a red check mark on the dossier titled *Marseilles*. It was the last of the phone contacts; he needed only two replies—to the cables to Athens and Beirut. Rome had responded two hours ago. Rome had been out of work longer than the others.

The calls had gone smoothly. In each case the initial conversations with the middlemen—and women—had been reserved, polite, general, almost abstract. And with each MacKenzie employed just the right words, quietly, confidentially. Each expert he had wanted to reach called him back.

There had been no hitches with anyone. His proposals were couched in the same universally understood language; the term *yellow mountain* the springboard. It was the highest score an agent could make for himself. The *yellow mountain* figure was a "five hundred key" with advance funds banked against contingencies. The *security controls* included "inaccessible clearinghouses" that maintained no connections with international regulatory agencies. The *time factor* was between six and eight weeks, depending on the "technological refinements called for in the sophisticated engineering process." And finally, as leader, his own background encompassed wholesale service to entire governments in most Southeast Asia, proof of which could be confirmed by several accounts in Geneva.

He had done his research well. To a man, they all needed to mine the *yellow mountain*.

Hawkins got up from the desk and stretched. It had been a long day and it wasn't over yet. In twenty minutes he would have to leave for the railroad station. Between now and then he would speak with the switchboard operator and give her instructions for those callers who might try to reach him. The instructions would be simple: he had reserved the room for a week; he would return to Zurich in three days. The callers could contact him there, or leave numbers where they could be reached. MacKenzie did not want to return to Zurich, but Athens and Beirut were exceptional recruits.

The telephone rang. It was Athens.

Six minutes later Athens was in.

One more to go.

The Hawk moved his untouched luggage to the door and repacked his briefcase, leaving Beirut's dossier in a separate, easily accessible spot. He looked at his watch: three minutes to four. There was no point in procrastinating any longer. He had to leave for the station. Returning to the desk he dialed the switchboard operator and told her he wanted to leave a few simple instructions——

The operator interrupted politely.

"Yes, of course, mein Herr. But may I take them later? I was about to ring your room. An overseas call has just come in for you. From Beirut."

Goddamn!

Sam opened his eyes. The sun was streaming through the huge French doors; the breeze billowed the drapes of blue silk. He looked around the room. The ceiling was at least twelve feet high, the fluted columns in the corners and the intricately carved moldings of dark wood everywhere bespoke the word "château." It all came into focus. He was in a place called Château Machenfeld, somewhere south of Zermatt. Outside the thick, sculptured door of his room was a wide hallway with Persian prayer rugs scattered over a glistening dark floor, and muted candelabra on the walls. The hallway led to an enormous winding staircase and a proliferation of crystal chandeliers above a great hall the size of a respectable ballroom. There, among priceless antiques and Renaissance portraits, was the entrance—

gigantic double doors of oak opening on a set of marble steps that led to a circular drive large enough to handle a funeral for the chairman of General Motors.

What had Hawkins *done*? How did he do it? My God. *Why*? What was he going to use such a place for?

Devereaux looked at the sleeping Regina, her dark brown hair lying in waves over the pillow, her California-tanned face half buried under the eiderdown quilt. If she had any answers, she wouldn't tell him. Of all the girls, Ginny was the most outrageously manipulative; she had orchestrated him right down to the moment of sleep. Partially, granted only partially, because he was fascinated by her. There was a will of steel beneath the soft magnolia exterior; she was a natural leader who, as all natural leaders, took delight in her leadership. She used her gifts, mental and physical, with imagination and boldness, and a considerable dash of humor. She could be the strong moral proselytizer one moment, and the lost little girl in the middle of burning Atlanta the next. She was the laughing, provocative siren in the plantation moonlight, and with the flick of a switch, a conspiratorial, whispering Mata Hari giving orders to a suspicious looking chauffeur in the shadows of the Zermatt railroad station.

"Mack Feldman's ass is in the bitter seltzer!"

To the best of Sam's recollection those had been the words Ginny had whispered to the strange man in the black beret, with the gold front tooth, whose catlike eyes riveted themselves to the front of her blouse.

"Mac's in felt!" had been the whispered reply. *"His sight's in an auto bomb's flower pot!"*

With that less-than-articulate rejoinder, Ginny had nodded, grabbed Devereaux's arm, and propelled him into the Zermatt street.

"Carry your suitcase in your left hand and whistle something. He'll turn into an alley and we'll wait at the corner for him to bring out the car."

"Why all the nonsense? The left hand. The whistling ——"

"Others are checking. To make sure we're not being followed."

The *Orient Express* syndrome was being somewhat

overdone, Sam had thought at the time, but nonetheless he'd switched the suitcase to his left hand and started whistling.

"Not *that*, you ninny!"

"What's the matter? It's some kind of hymn——"

"Over here it's called 'Deutschland Uber Alles'!"

He'd switched to "Rock of Ages" as another man, this one in a real Conrad Veidt overcoat complete with velvet lapels, came up to Regina and spoke softly.

"Your warts are in the wagon."

"Mack Feldman's ass surely has sweet sheckles," she had answered quietly, rapidly. And within seconds a long black automobile raced out of the dark alley and they had climbed in.

That was how the tortuous, two-hour drive had begun. Miles of winding, uphill roads cut out of the Swiss mountains and forests, intermittently illuminated by the eerie wash of moonlight. Until they reached some kind of massive gate that wasn't a gate; it was an honest-to-god *portcullis*. In front of a *moat*.

A real moat! With heavy planks and the sounds of water below. Then another winding, uphill road that ended in the enormous circular drive in front of the largest country house Sam had seen since he toured Fontainebleau with the Quincy Boy Scouts. And even Fontainebleau didn't have parapets. This place did, certainly high and definitely stone, with the sort of cutout patterns one associated with *Ivanhoe*.

Quite a place, Château Machenfeld. And he had only seen it at night. He wasn't sure he wanted to see it in daylight. There was something frightening about the mere thought of such a massive edifice when related to one MacKenzie Hawkins.

But where did the château fit in? What was it for? If it was going to be the son of a bitch's command post, why didn't he just rent Fenway Park and be done with it? It had to take an army of minions to keep the place running; minions talked. Ask anyone at Nuremberg or in Sirica's courtroom.

But Regina wouldn't talk. (Of course, she wasn't a minion; in no way did the word fit.) Yet he had tried. All the way down from Zurich—well, perhaps not every moment—and half the night in Machenfeld—perhaps less than half—he had done his best to get her to tell him what she knew.

They had sparred verbally, each talking obliquely, neither coming to grips with any positive statements that could lead to any real conclusions. She admitted—she had no choice—that all the girls had agreed to turn up in the right places at the right times so that he, Sam, would have company and not be led into temptations that could be debilitating on such a long business trip. And have someone trustworthy to take messages for him. And watch out for him. And where the goddamned cotton-pickin' hell was the harm in *that*? Where was he going to find such a concerned group of ladies who had his best interests at heart? And kept him on schedule?

Did she know what the *business trip* was about?

Lawdy, no! She never asked. None of the girls asked.

Why not?

Landsakes, honey! The Hawk told them not to.

Couldn't any of them draw . . . certain inferences? I mean, my God, his itinerary wasn't exactly that of a New England shoe salesman.

Honeychile! When they were married to the Hawk—individually, of course—he was always involved with top-secret army things they all knew they shouldn't ask questions about.

He wasn't *in* the army now!

Well-live-and-die-in-Dixie! That's the *army's* fault!

And so it went.

And then he began to understand. Regina was no patsy. None of the girls was. *Fall guy* was not in their collective vocabulary. If Ginny, or Lillian, or Madge, or Anne knew anything concrete they weren't about to say so. If they perceived a lack of complete integrity, each put on blinders, and her own particular activity remained unrelated to any larger action. None certainly would discuss anything with *him*.

There was another problem in the midst of the Hawk's insanity: Sam genuinely liked the girls. Whatever the whack-a-doo furies were that drove them to do MacKenzie's bidding, each was her own person, each an individual, each—God help him—had an honesty he found refreshing. So, if he did spell out what he knew, the instant he did so they were accessories. To a *conspiracy*. It didn't take a lawyer to know that. What was he thinking about; he *was* a lawyer.

As of this . . . point in time . . . each girl was clean. Maybe not like a hound's tooth; maybe not even like a wino's bridgework, but legally it could be argued that each had operated in a vacuum. There was no conspiracy under the circumstances.

Thank you, Mr. Defense Attorney. The bench suggests that you reclaim your tuition from law school.

Sam got out of the ridiculously oversized, canopied bed as quietly as possible. He saw his shorts halfway across the room toward the French doors, which was where he was heading, anyway, and briefly wondered why they were so far from the bed. Then he remembered, and he smiled.

But this was morning, a new day, and things were going to be different. Ginny had given him one specific to hang onto: Hawkins would arrive by late afternoon or early evening. He would use the time until then to learn whatever he could about Château Machenfeld. Or more precisely, what the Hawk was planning for Château Machenfeld as it related to one Pope Francesco, Vicar of Christ.

It was time for him to mount his own counterstrategy. Hawkins was good, no question about it. But he, Sam Devereaux from the Eastern Establishment's Quincy-Boston axis, wasn't so bad, either. Confidence! Mac had it; so did he.

As he put on his shorts, the obvious first move in his counterstrategy came into focus. It wasn't just obvious, it was blatant; bells rang! Such an extraordinary place (mansion, estate, compound, small country) as Machenfeld would demand an unending series of supplies to keep it functioning. And suppliers were like minions, they could see, and hear, and bear witness. The Hawk's proclivity for massiveness could be the most vulnerable aspect of his plans. Sam had considered disrupting Mac's supply lines as *one* of his options, from a military point of view, but he had no idea how positively logical it was. It might be all he needed.

He'd circulate rumors as massively dangerous, as gigantically outrageous, as the sight of Machenfeld itself. He'd start with the servants, then the suppliers, then everyone else who came near the château, until a state of isolation was brought about and he could come to grips with a deserted Hawkins and—*what the hell was that noise*?

He walked rapidly to the French doors and through them to the small balcony beyond. It overlooked the rear of Château Machenfeld. He assumed it was the rear; there was no circular drive below. Instead, there were gardens in spring bloom, with graveled paths and latticed arbors and scores of small fishponds carved out of rock. Beyond the gardens were green fields that merged into greener, darker forests, and in the distance were the majestic Alps.

The noise continued, spoiling the view. He could not, at first, determine where it came from, and so he squinted in the sunlight. And instantly wished to hell he hadn't. Because he could now see what was making the noise.

One, two, three . . . five, six . . . eight, nine! Nine assorted—*insanely* assorted—vehicles were slowly going down a dirt road that bordered the fields, progressing south toward the surrounding forests.

There were two long black limousines, a huge earthmoving bulldozer, an outsized tractor with pronged forks in front, and five—goddamn it, yes, five motorcycles!

It didn't take a lot of imagination to get the picture. The Hawk was about to enter maneuvers! He had bought himself his own personal *papal motorcade*! Plus equipment that could shove the ground around into any design he liked: The route of said papal motorcade!

But he hadn't even arrived at Machenfeld! How the hell was he able to—and what the hell was *that*?

In his anger and confusion, Devereaux gripped the balcony, shaking his head in frustrated bewilderment. His eyes were arrested by an extraordinary sight fifty yards away.

Within a kind of patio, outside a pair of open doors that looked like the entrance to some sort of enormous kitchen, stood a large man wearing a chef's hat, who was in the process of checking off items from a thick sheaf of papers in his hands. In front of the man was a mountain of crates and cartons and boxes that must have reached the height of fifteen feet!

Lines of supply, *shit*!

There wasn't anything left in Europe for Hawkins to buy. There was enough food down there to eliminate half the famine on the Ganges! The son of a bitch had requisitioned enough rations for an army, goddamn it, an army setting out on a two-year bivouac!

Limousines, motorcycles, bulldozers, tractors, food for the entire Lost Battalion! Sam's counterstrategy move number one was shot to hell by a parade of nine idiotically assorted vehicles and some gasping eccentric in a chef's hat.

The only state of isolation in the foreseeable future was from any and all lines of supply. They were totally unnecessary.

That left the minions. The dozen or so servants that had to be around to keep Machenfeld afloat. Kitchens, gardens, fields (that probably meant barns, maybe livestock), and at least thirty to forty rooms with cleaning and waxing and polishing and dusting. Christ! There *had* to be a staff of twenty!

He'd begin right away. Perhaps with the drivers of the nine vehicles; convince them to get the damn things off the château's grounds before it was too late. Then he'd rapidly go from one group of servants to another. Let them know in ominous terms, which meant legal terms, that if they knew what was good for them they'd get the hell out of Machenfeld before all the agents of Interpol descended.

All the food in Switzerland wouldn't do the Hawk any good if there was no one on the premises. To *run* the premises. And a few well-chosen words to those manning the vehicles, words like "international violations," "personal accountability," and "life imprisonment," would surely cause that stream of motorcycles and limousines and trucks to barrel-ass back over the moat into safer territory.

Sam was so preoccupied with his new strategy that he wasn't really aware that his undershorts kept sagging, causing him to hold them up with a free hand. He was forced to be aware of it now because as he gripped the railing his shorts had plummeted down to his ankles. Swiftly, he retrieved his modesty, noting with a degree of self-satisfaction that the games with Ginny Greenberg must have been pretty damned exciting indeed. But it was no time for pleasant reminiscence; there was work to do. His watch read nearly eleven; he hadn't realized he'd slept so long—the games were not only exciting, but exhausting. He had barely five or six hours to get everybody out. Such a large staff of servants probably had lots of personal belongings. That would mean transportation, perhaps more complicated than he had considered. But one thing had to be clear: when the minions left the grounds of Machenfeld, they were *not to return*. For *any* reason. Anything less would weaken his basic premise: Machenfeld was a threat to everyone who remained, therefore no one was to do so.

Evacuation!

The château was to be deserted!

Then what the hell was MacKenzie going to do?

Stew in his cigar juice, *that's* what he was going to do!

It was merely a question of logistics and execution.

Goddamn! Logistics and execution! He was beginning to *think* like the Hawk! And have the confidence of the Hawk! Be bold! Be outrageous! Take fate by the balls and . . .

Shit! Before anything could happen, he had to get dressed. He raced through the French doors into the room. Ginny stirred and moaned a little and then buried her head farther into the eiderdown quilt. He stepped out of the torn underwear, and crossed quietly to his suitcase which was on an overstuffed armchair against the velour-covered wall.

It was empty.

There wasn't a goddamn thing in his suitcase.

He looked around for the closet.

Closets. There were four.

Empty. Except for Ginny's dresses.

Shit!

He ran as quietly as possible to the sculptured door and opened it.

Sitting across the wide hallway was the black beret with

the gold front tooth and catlike eyes which were now focused on Sam's lower extremities. In the confusion that, perhaps, was understandable. The sneer was not.

"Where are my clothes!?" whispered Devereaux, partially closing the door, leaning against it.

"In the *launtree*, mein Herr," replied the black beret in an accent formed in some Swiss canton run by Hermann Göring.

"Everything?"

"Courtesy of Château Machenfeld. All was dirty."

"That's ridiculous!" Sam tried to keep his voice low. He did not want to wake Ginny. "Nobody asked me——"

"You were asleep, mein Herr," interrupted the black beret, grinning suggestively, his gold tooth gleaming. "You were very tired."

"Well, now I'm very angry! I want my clothes back. Right away!"

"I cannot do that."

"Why not?"

"It is the *launtree's* day off."

"What? Then why did you take them?"

"I told you, mein Herr. They were dirty."

Sam stared at the catlike eyes across the hallway. They had narrowed ominously; and the gold tooth was no longer seen because the grin had disappeared, replaced by an adamant mouth. Sam closed the door. He had to think. Quickly. As Mac would say, he had to weigh his options. And he had to get out.

He did not consider himself a brawler, yet he was not a physical coward. He was a pretty big fellow, and regardless of what Lillian said in Berlin, he was in fair shape. Still, all things considered it was a good guess that the black-bereted maniac across the hall could beat the shit out of him. Even naked, he could not leave by the stairs.

Option One considered and rejected.

That left the windows, more specifically the small balcony beyond the French doors. He grabbed his shorts off the floor, put them on, held them up, and walked silently outside. The room was three stories off the ground, but directly below was another balcony. With sheets, or drapes, tied together he could make it with reasonable safety.

Option Two was feasible.

He went back inside and studied the drapes. As his mother in Quincy would say, they were spring drapes. Silk, billowy, not strong. Option Two was fading. Then he looked at the bed sheets, ignoring the inviting sight of Regina who was now more outside the eiderdown quilt than under. If the sheets were combined *with* the drapes, this would probably hold him. Option Two was reemerging.

Battle dress.

That was a problem. There was nothing *but* dresses.

So, assuming Option Two succeeded and he reached the ground, he had Options Three and Four to consider. And as he considered them there was a sinking feeling in his stomach. He could race around Machenfeld in underwear that kept falling down to his ankles or he could put on one of Ginny's Balenciaga prints and hope the zipper held.

A man running around spreading alarms in disheveled underwear, *or* a Paris original, was not likely to be taken too seriously. There might even be Options Five and Six to contend with: be locked up, or be raped.

Shit!

He had to keep his head; he had to get hold of himself and think things out. Slowly. He could not allow a minor item like clothing to stand in the way of evacuation. What could the Hawk do? What was that goddamned term he used so frequently?

Support personnel! That was it!

Sam raced back out on the balcony. The man in the chef's hat was still checking off items on his list. It'd probably take him a week.

"Psssst! Psssst!" Devereaux leaned over the railing, remembering at the last instant not to let go of the underwear. "Hey *you!*" he whispered loudly.

The man looked up, startled at first, then smiled broadly. "Ahh! Bonjour, monsieur! Ça va?" he shouted.

Sam held his finger to his lips. "Shhh!" He gestured for the chef to come closer.

He did so, carrying his papers, making a last notation as he walked. "Oui, monsieur?"

"I'm being held prisoner!" whispered Devereaux with solemn urgency and much authority. "They've taken my

210

clothes. I need *clothes*. And when I get down I want you to get everyone who works here into the kitchen. I've got some very important things to say. I'm a lawyer. *Avocat*."

The man in the chef's hat cocked his head. "*Je ne comprends pas, monsieur. Desirez-vous le petit déjeuner?*"

"Who?—No. I want *clothes*. See? All I've got is this, *these*." Sam stretched his torn undershorts so they could be seen between the rails; then he pointed to his legs. "I need pants, *trousers*! Right away. *Please!*"

The expression on the man's face changed from bewilderment to suspicion. Perhaps even distaste mingled with hostility. "*Vos sous-vêtements sont très jolis,*" he said, shaking his head, turning back toward the patio and the crates of food.

"Wait! Wait a minute!"

"The chef is French, mein Herr, but not *that* French." The voice came from below, from the balcony directly underneath. The speaker was an immense, bald man with shoulders nearly as wide as the depth of the railing. "He thinks you are making a most peculiar offer. I can assure you he's not interested."

"Who the hell are *you*?"

"My name is unimportant. I leave the château when the new master of Machenfeld arrives. Until then his every instruction is my command. His instructions do not include your clothing."

Devereaux had an overpowering urge to let his shorts fall and copy Hawkins's action on the roof of the diplomatic mission in Peking, but he controlled himself. The man on the balcony below was huge. And obviously couldn't take a joke. So instead he leaned over and whispered the words conspiratorially.

"Heil Hitler, you fucker!"

The man's arm shot forward; his heels clicked like the bolt of a rifle. "*Jawohl! Sieg heil!*"

"Oh, shit!" Sam turned and walked back into the room. In exasperation, he kicked off his shorts. Then he absently studied them as they lay on the floor. Perhaps it was the angle of the fabric, he was not sure. But suddenly they looked strange.

He bent down and picked them up.

211

Christ! *What* games?

The elastic waist had been cut deliberately in three places! The incisions were *incisions*, not tears. There were no loose threads or stretched cloth. Someone had taken a sharp instrument and sliced the goddamn things! On purpose. Immobilizing him by the simplest method possible!

"Lawdy! What's all that shoutin' about?" Regina Greenberg yawned and stretched, modestly pulling the eiderdown quilt over her enormous breasts.

"You bitch," said Devereaux in quiet anger. "You devious bitch!"

"What's the matter, honeychile?"

"Don't 'honeychile' me, you Southern retardant! I can't get *out* of here!"

Ginny blinked and yawned again. She spoke with calm authority. "You know, Mac once said something that's been a comfort to me all through the years. He said, when the mortars are falling all around you and things look terrible—and, believe me, there were times when the world looked pretty terrible to me—he said, think of the good things you've done, the accomplishments, the contributions. Don't ponder your mistakes or your sorrows; that only puts you in a depressed state of mind. And a depressed state of mind is not equipped to take advantage of that one moment that could arise and save your ass. It's all a question of mental attitudes."

"What the hell has that bullshit got to do with the fact that I don't have any clothes?"

"Not an awful lot, I guess. It's just that you sounded so depressed. That's no way to face the Hawk."

Devereaux started to answer blindly, angrily. Then he stopped, looked at the sincerity in Ginny's eyes and began again. "Wait a minute. 'Face the Hawk.' You mean you want me to fight him? *Stop* him?"

"That's your decision, Sam. I only want what's best for everyone."

"Will you help me?"

Ginny was pensive for a moment, then replied firmly. "No, I won't do that. Not in the way you're thinking. I owe MacKenzie too much."

212

"Lady!" burst out Devereaux. "Do you have *any idea* what that lunatic is up to?"

Mrs. Hawkins number one looked at him with an expression of suddenly imposed innocence. "A lieutenant doesn't question a general officer, Major. He can't be expected to understand the intricacies of command——"

"Then what the hell are we talking about?"

"You're a smart fellow. The Hawk wouldn't have promoted you if you weren't. I just want him to have the finest advice he can get. So he can do whatever it is he wants to do the best way possible." Ginny rolled over under the eiderdown quilt. "I'm really very sleepy."

And Devereaux saw them on the bedside table next to her head.

A pair of scissors.

CHAPTER NINETEEN

"Sorry about the clothes," said the Hawk in the huge drawing room. Sam glared and retied the curtain sash he used as a belt around the eiderdown quilt. "You'd think the laundry would have more than one key, wouldn't you? These big fancy places don't trust anyone; shows the kind of house guests they must be used to, I suppose."

"Oh, shut up," mumbled Devereaux, who found it necessary to double-loop the sash because the silk kept slipping. "The laundress *will* be here in the morning, I presume."

"I'm sure of it. She's one of the few who go home at night. To the village. That'll change, of course; there'll be a lot of changes."

"Just tell me there'll be *one* change and I'll go back and have dinner with Azaz-Varak."

"Come on now, Sam, you've got a one-track mind. Let's get on to other things. You sure you don't want a shirt and a pair of trousers? Just take me a minute to go upstairs. . . ." Hawkins made a gesture past a dozen or so overstuffed, antimacassared armchairs toward the great hall.

"No! I don't want anything from you!—I take that back. I *do* want something. I want you to call off this crazy business and let me go home!"

MacKenzie bit off the chewed end of his cigar, spitting it between the feet of a suit of armor. "You *will* go home, I promise you that. The minute you centralize the company finances and make a few deposits that can be tapped under certain conditions, I'll drive you to the airport myself. That's the word of a general officer."

"It's the reasoning of a brain soaked in linseed oil! Do you have any idea what you're asking me to do? That's not chopped liver you're talking about, it's *forty million dollars*. I'm marked for life! They'll have a record sheet on me in every Interpol headquarters and police station in the civilized world! You don't put your name on forty million dollars' worth of bank transfers and expect to go back to a normal law practice. Word gets out."

"That's not so, and you know it. All that Swiss banking stuff is confidential."

Devereaux looked around to make sure no one else was within hearing. "Even if it's supposed to be, it's not *going* to be once a . . . certain attempt is made to snatch a . . . certain person in Rome! And that's *all* it will be! An attempt! You'll have your ass in a net, and every contact you've made since China will be put under a microscope and my name will surface and so will forty fucking million dollars in Zurich and that's the *ballgame!*"

"Now, goddamn, boy, we've been over that! Your job's finished now. Or will be soon's you take care of the money. You don't have to be involved anymore. And you're *clean*, son. You're a hundred percent Clorox!"

"I'm not." Devereaux choked as he whispered and clutched the eiderdown quilt. "I just *told* you: The minute *you're* nailed, *I'm* nailed!"

"For what? Say you happened to be right—which I don't for a second consider remotely possible—what can they nail you for? Banking funds for an old soldier who told you he was raising money to support an organization dedicated to spreading religious brotherhood? Let me ask you a question, Mr. Attorney. Could you, under oath, testify to any wrongdoing?"

"You're *insane!*" broke in Sam, stumbling slightly as he stepped forward. "You *told* me! You're going to kidnap——" Devereaux stopped and made charade-like gestures that included hauling a body over his shoulder and the sign of the cross.

"Well, *hell*, boy, there are *oaths* and there are *oaths*! Be reasonable. Anyway, that's hearsay. Not admissible."

Sam closed his eyes; he began to understand what

215

martyrdom was all about. He continued, his whisper strained but controlled. "I walked out of those archives with that fucking briefcase chained to my wrist!"

"Outside of that," mumbled MacKenzie. "Anyhow, that's army stuff; neither of us has much use for the army. Anything else?"

Devereaux thought. "Circumstantially, it's the mother-loving end. There hasn't been a single aboveboard transaction."

"That's subjective," said Hawkins, shaking his head, confirming his own judgment. "There's been no violence; no one's lied. No theft, no collusion. Everything voluntary. And if the particular methods *seem* unusual, that's the prerogative of every individual investor, as long as he doesn't infringe on the rights of others." Mac paused and held Sam's eyes. "There's something else, too. You said yourself that a lawyer's first responsibility was to his client, not abstract moral dilemmas."

"I said that?"

"You surely did."

"That's not bad——"

"It's goddamned eloquent, that's what it is. You've got a silver tongue in your head, young man."

Sam stared back at the Hawk, trying to see beneath his guile. But it wasn't guile; he meant what he said. And since personal sincerity was the momentary leveler, Devereaux decided to be personally sincere.

"Listen to me," he said quietly. "Say you go through with this—this insanity, because that's what it is, you know. Say you really do it. You actually kidnap the pope and get away with it. Even for a few days. Do you know what might happen? What you could trigger?"

"Surely do. Four hundred million green samolians from four hundred million howling mackerel snappers. No offense intended, just a harmless phrase."

"*No*, you gung-ho son of a bitch! There'd be international *revulsion*! *And recrimination*. And then mainly *accusations*! Governments would point their fingers at other governments! Presidents and chairmen and prime ministers would use blue lines and red lines and then very *hot* lines. And before you know it, some asshole recites a code

216

from a tiny black box in a briefcase because he didn't like what some other asshole said. Jesus, Mac! You could start World War Three!"

"*Goddamn*! Is that what you've been thinking about?"

"It's what I've tried *not* to think about."

Hawkins threw his cigar into the cavern that was the Machenfeld fireplace and stood arms akimbo, a flame dying in his eyes. "Sam, boy, you couldn't be farther from the truth. You know, son, war isn't what it used to be. Hasn't any spirit to it anymore. Bugles and drums, and men caring for men, and hating an enemy because he can hurt the things you love. That's all gone now. Now it's buttons and shifty-eyed politicians who blink a lot and wave their hands without meaning very much. I hate war. I never thought I'd hear myself say it, but I'm saying it and learning it now. I'd never allow a war."

Devereaux bored into the Hawk's eyes; he would not let MacKenzie look away. "Why should I believe that? Everything you've done reeks of con. Immense con. Why should a war stop you?"

"Because, young man," replied Hawkins quietly, returning Sam's stare in full measure, "I just told you the truth."

"All right. Suppose you provoke one without meaning to?

"*Goddamn*! Now you're pushing me too far!" MacKenzie strode from the fireplace to a second suit of armor to the right of the mantel. The face piece was open so he slammed it shut. "I put in damned near forty years and got fucked by the plastic men! *Your* words, boy! Now, I don't feel sorry for myself because I knew what I was doing and was accountable for my actions! But, goddamn, don't ask me to feel sorry for *them* or be accountable for *their* stupidity!"

So much for personal sincerity, thought Devereaux. Like Options One, Two, Three, and Four in the morning, it was shot to hell. This time in a burst of self-righteousness. There was nothing for it but to find another way. One would present itself, Sam was convinced of that. The Hawk had a way to go before the pontiff of the Catholic Church blessed the edelweiss at Machenfeld. Something would turn up; and Option Seven—Options Five and Six happily avoided—was coming into focus. For the moment he had to calm MacKenzie down and under no circumstances lose his confidence. And then Mac did have a point. A legal point.

He, Sam, was clean. Legally clean. In every other way the mud was an inch thick, but in evidentiary considerations, he was not a good case for any prosecutor.

"Okay, Mac, I'm not going to fight you. You were screwed and I did say it, and I believe you. You hate war. Maybe that's good enough. I don't know anymore. Personally, I just want to go back home to Quincy, and if I read about you in the papers, I'll remember the words of a scarred but honest warrior spoken in this room."

"A tongue of silver, boy! I admire that."

"As long as it's not a head of lead, I'll accept that. Do you have the papers for the Zurich bank?"

"Don't you want to hear the amount I've . . . accrued for your participation? How do you like that 'accrued'? I'm a corporate president, you know; we don't fuck around with second-rate vocabularies."

"I'm impressed. What's the entry figure?"

"The what?"

"The accrual; that's the noun root of the verb 'to accrue.'"

"Smartass shavetail. What do you say to a half a million dollars?"

Sam could not say anything. He was numb. He saw his hand move in astonishment, and he watched it with a certain fascination, not sure if the appendage belonged to him. It must have; when he thought about jiggling the fingers, they jiggled.

A half a million dollars.

What was there to think about? It was as insane as everything else. Including the fact that he was not indictable.

It was Monopoly time. Let's buy *Boardwalk* and *Park Place*.

Stop. Go To Jail.

Why worry?

It didn't do any good anyway.

"That's reasonable—severance pay," Sam said.

"That's all you've got to *say*? With what I banked for you in New York, you can hire that Jewish fella and he'll be happy to take the job." MacKenzie was the injured party. He obviously expected Devereaux to practice a little bit of his well-advertised overreaction.

"Let's say I'll erupt with enthusiasm when I'm looking at those figures—in a bank book—in Boston—with my mother sitting across the room complaining about the new management at the Copley Plaza. Okay?"

"Do you know something?" said Hawkins, his eyes squinting. "You're kind of weird."

"*I'm* kind of..." Devereaux did not finish the sentence. There was no point.

There was the abrupt, episodic clicking of high heels. Regina Greenberg walked through the cathedral arch into the drawing room. She was dressed in a beige pants suit, the rather severe jacket buttoned over Titanics. She looked, well, rather efficient, thought Sam. She smiled briefly and addressed Hawkins.

"I've met with the staff. Five will stay. Three couldn't; they'd have to live in the village and I explained that wasn't acceptable."

"I hope they weren't hurt."

Ginny laughed confidently. "Hardly. I spoke to each individually, and gave all three two months' wages."

"The rest understand the conditions?" MacKenzie reached into his pocket for a fresh cigar.

"And their bonuses," said Ginny. "Minimum three months. All with families to explain that they've been hired for resident staff work in France for the duration. No questions are to be asked."

"No different from overseas duty," commented the Hawk, nodding his head. "And the money's a hell of a lot better than combat pay—without a weapon in sight."

"The logistics are in your favor, too," continued Ginny. "Only two of the five are married. Not too happily, I gather. They won't miss, or be missed."

"We'll have to get women, though," countered MacKenzie, "for R and R. I'll scout the grounds later; spec out tent arrangements—far enough away from the maneuvers, of course. And the counselor here is going into Zurich to
219

take care of several financial items for me. What do you think, Sam? How long do you figure it will be before you're finished?"

Devereaux had to force himself to consider the Hawk's question. He was stunned by the obvious control MacKenzie wielded over Ginny. According to the data banks, she had divorced MacKenzie over twenty years ago; yet here she was deferring to him like a schoolgirl with a crush on her teacher.

"What did you say?" Sam knew the question but wanted a few seconds to evaluate.

"How long will Zurich take?"

"A day. Maybe a day and a half, with no hitches. A lot will depend on the account clearances. I think the transfers are coded through Geneva, but I may be wrong about that."

"Can 'hitches' be eliminated with a little honey in the pot?"

"Probably. Relinquishing-of-interest could apply. The time period's minor but the sums aren't. The depositories would pick up several thousand—on paper. That might act as a general incentive."

"Goddamn, son, you hear yourself? You hear how *good* you are?"

"Elementary bookkeeping. A trial lawyer figures litigation with banks is prime meat. They've got more ways to lie to themselves—and everybody else—than anyone since tribes started to barter. A decent attorney simply picks the lies he knows will suit him best."

"You hear that, Ginny? Isn't that boy something?!"

"You're mighty impressive, Sam; I've got to admit it. And, Mac, since the m*ay*jor here's got everything under control, maybe I could go up to Zurich with him and kind of keep him company."

"Why, that's a splendid idea! Don't know why I didn't think of it."

"I can't imagine how it escaped you," said Devereaux quietly. "You're all heart."

From all points of the compass the Hawk's subordinate officers arrived. They were met at the Zermatt railroad station by the bereted, gold-toothed, cat-eyed chauffeur whose name was Rudolph. And Rudolph had a hectic two days.

Crete showed up first, without incident. That is, he managed to cross international boundaries under the scrutiny of very professional authorities without incident (but with a forged passport) and got as far as the Zermatt station, where his troubles erupted. For Rudolph refused to acknowledge Crete to be Crete in spite of the proper identity markings on his clothing, and consequently would not let him into his Italian taxi.

Because, for reasons that escaped Hawkins, none of the G-2 data bank entries on Crete had established the fact that he was Black. Yet there it was. Crete was a brilliant aeronautical engineer, a Soviet sympathizer as long as the Ruskies paid him, a defected espionage agent complete with a doctor's degree and very black skin. Rudolph was totally bewildered, so MacKenzie had to use some very harsh language over the telephone with Rudolph, and finally the bereted maniac let the *schwarzer* in the back seat of his car.

Marseilles and Stockholm were next. They flew in together out of Paris because they met each other on the previous night at Les Calavados on the Boulevard George Cinque and renewed an old acquaintanceship that went back to the days when both were making money from the Allies and the Axis. They were delighted to discover that they were both on a trip to the same yellow mountain in Zermatt. Rudolph had no trouble with Stockholm and Marseilles because they spotted him before he spotted them and they criticized him for his stupidity at being obvious.

Beirut did not take the train from Zurich; he hired an ambulance, instead. He had his reasons; they went back to several contraband run-ins with the Zurich police. So he flew into Geneva, drove a rented car in the name of a socially elite transvestite, dropped it in Lausanne, contacted l'Hôpital des Deux Enfants in Montreux and leased the ambulance, ordering it to transport him as a coronary wishing to spend his last days in Zermatt. He timed everything to the Zurich train however and all would have gone smoothly except for Rudolph. Unfortunately, Rudolph had a flat tire on the back roads of Machenfeld, and in his subsequent haste to reach the Bahnhoff on time he had a minor collision in the railroad station's parking lot. With the ambulance.

Therefore it was difficult for Rudolph to identify the highly agitated coronary patient, who climbed out of the rear door yelling about imbeciles, with the figure whose markings identified him as Beirut.

But Rudolph was beginning to shrug more and more. The master of Machenfeld, he was beginning to suspect, was not all there in the head. And neither were the people he was sent up to Zermatt to meet.

And the lovely lady of his late-night dreams, the beautifully breasted fraulein, had left the château for several days. Things were not the same.

Rome and Rudolph got along splendidly. Rome lost his luggage on the train. The combined chaos of finding his three suitcases and his contact from the château proved a strain nearly too much for Rome. Rudolph sympathized and allowed him to sit in the front seat on the trip to the château.

Biscay was extremely secretive. Once he displayed the coded identification (a pair of white gloves with black roses stitched on the back) Biscay excused himself to go to the men's room and disappeared through a window. After a half hour, Rudolph's impatience turned to curiosity and the curiosity, in turn, became panic when he discovered the men's room empty. He tried to remain inconspicuous as he looked in nooks and crannies and luggage bins. Biscay followed him discreetly. And it was only after Rudolph called Machenfeld in panic that Biscay, listening from an adjacent booth, decided that his contact was authentic.

Biscay sat in the back seat, and Rudolph did not say a single word all the way to Machenfeld.

The last to arrive was Athens. If Biscay was suspicious, Athens was paranoid. To begin with, he pulled the emergency cord on the train, stopping it in the freight yards just outside the station. Conductors and engineers ran through the cars looking for the emergency, while Athens jumped off and raced over the tracks to the platform, where he concealed himself behind a concrete pillar. It was not difficult for Athens to spot Rudolph.

The train finally proceeded into the station. Rudolph examined all the disembarking passengers; Athens could see his anxiety. When there was no one left on the platform but railroad personnel, Athens approached Rudolph from the rear and tapped him on the shoulder. As he did so, he displayed his identification (a red ascot) and gestured for Rudolph to follow him.

At which point, Athens raced back to the end of the platform, jumped down onto the tracks and started running toward the freight yard. He soon outdistanced Rudolph and started a series of *I-See-You's* between the immobile cars.

Five minutes later a distraught Rudolph was being comforted by the energetic Athens as they walked out of the freight yards toward the taxi.

And as MacKenzie Hawkins watched the car approach from the ramparts of Machenfeld, he congratulated himself once more on his professionalism. Seventy-two hours had passed since he had begun making his coded contacts from the D'Accord; and in that seventy-two hours every one of his subordinate officers was physically on the premises.

Goddamn!

Based on the accepted principle that larceny goes a long way in the banking business, Sam's trip to Zurich—more specifically his trip to the Staats Bank to centralize the Shepherd Company's capital—was so successful so rapidly that he would be able to catch the early afternoon train back to Zermatt. And since Regina Greenberg was out shopping, he left a message for her at the Hotel D'Accord: *Have gone bowling. Will be home late.*

He wanted those hours on the train by himself; to think, to refine. For Option Seven was becoming more sharply defined as the hours passed. Due mainly to the papers he carried out of the bank given him by a perspiring trust officer who was considerably richer than he was before he'd met Sam.

Among the fourteen documents, four pertained to the account transfers from Geneva, the Cayman Islands, Berlin, and Algiers—minus accrued interest, of course; one listed the total assets of the Shepherd Company, with its bond of confidentiality, its codes of release and the account number; one was in the name of the family Devereaux (Sam did not explain it and the banker had asked no questions, treating the item as though it did not exist); and eight separate documents defined eight separate trusts.

One of these accounts was larger than the others and within it were four individual sets of figures . . . obviously meant for four individuals. It did not take much reflection on Devereaux's part to identify them: Mrs. Hawkinses one, two, three, and four.

That left seven trusts, each with an identical maximum figure.

Seven.

The Hawk's *support personnel*.

MacKenzie had recruited seven men to kidnap the pope. (Sam couldn't imagine that any were women; the Hawk's four ex-wives were capable of *anything* calling for feminine skills.) These seven were his—what was it?— subordinate officers. MacKenzie had allowed that his subordinate officers would be arriving at Machenfeld shortly.

"What do you mean 'subordinate officers'?" Devereaux had asked.

"The troops, son, the troops!" the Hawk had replied, the flame reignited in his eyes.

"What do you mean 'shortly'?"

"We're on blue alert, boy. That means all posts are manned, contact expected from here on in."

"Like in a few days?"

"Maybe sooner, depending on enemy counterpersonnel blockades. Our troops will have to cross hostile territory on their way to base camp."

"What the fuck are you talking about?"

"Nothing you have to be concerned with. Just bring back that money stuff from Zurich. Before I give my first briefing on the mission, I want my subordinate officers to see for themselves just how thoroughly command center has taken care of their interests. It'll give 'em a real sense of purpose, of comradeship; it emanates from the top, you know. It always has."

That was the other reason why Option Seven was coming into focus. *Bring back that money stuff . . . before I give my first briefing . . . command center has taken care of their interests.*

The Hawk's troops had been recruited without knowing precisely what the war was all about. Militarily speaking there was nothing unusual in that, but considering the enormity of the projected enemy's resources—namely, the whole world—a few well-chosen words like, *"Do you realize what this maniac intends to do? Kidnap the pope!"* and *"You're dealing with a certified mental case!"* and *"Your commander is a fruitcake!"* and *"This lunatic shot the jade balls off a Chinese monument."*—things like that could very well make the support personnel look to other fields of endeavor.

It was a question of timing. And psychology. If Sam read him correctly, Hawkins was going to hit his subordinate officers with a double-barreled salvo: a highly technical, strategically "feasible" description of the abduction, *and* bona fide documents from the Staats Bank du Zurich that guaranteed each man a fortune, *regardless of outcome*! It would be a tough act to cripple, but that's what Option Seven was all about.

Sam would reach the subordinate officers *first*. He would shoot off cannons of doubt regarding the Hawk's fundamental sanity. There was nothing more frightening to criminal underlings than the possibility that their employers were unbalanced. Lack of balance meant lack of judgment, no matter how well disguised. And lack of judgment could spell ten-to-twenty-to-life; in this case, probably a long rope and a blindfold.

Even the criminal element in Europe had to have heard of the paranoid general who was thrown out of China. It wasn't that long ago. And when he had finished this part of his oral summation, Sam would place his high card on the table.

High? There were none higher. It was irresistible.

For on the train to Zermatt he would go through the documents from the Staats Bank du Zurich, specifically

225

the trust accounts, and write out all the numbers and the sequential codes of release, and put them on seven pieces of paper.

He would give each man a card with the information written on it. Each could leave Château Machenfeld without so much as sitting through a meal, head for Zurich— *and claim his money.*

Each subordinate officer would make a fortune! For doing absolutely nothing. Irresistible!

Giovanni Bombalini, Vicar of Christ, walked out into his beloved garden to be alone. He did not wish to see anyone or talk with anyone. He was angry with the world, *his* world, and when one was angry it was always best to meditate.

He sighed. If he was to be truthful with himself, he had to admit he was angry with God. It was so senseless! He raised his eyes to the afternoon sky and a single word emerged plaintively from his lips.

"Why?"

He lowered his head and continued down the path. The sprays of lilies were in spring bloom, greeting life.

As he was about to leave it.

The doctors had just delivered their collective report. His vital signs were diminishing with increased acceleration. He had no more than six or seven weeks.

Death itself was easy. Good heavens, it was a relief! *Life* was the struggle. But struggle or no, he had not consolidated the necessary forces to carry on his and Roncalli's work. He needed more time; he needed the authority of the office to bring divergent factions closer together. Why could not God understand that?

Eh, my beloved Lord? Why? Just a little more time? I promise not to lose my temper. Nor will I insult the nasal-toned—pardon, most Holy Father—the cardinal or his band of antediluvian thieves. Six months would do nicely. Then I shall rest in the arms of Christ with grateful devotion. Five months, perhaps? Much could be accomplished in five months. . . .

Giovanni tried with all his heart to perceive a heavenly

226

response. If there was one, it was too weak to get through his vital signs.

Perhaps, dear Father, if you would speak to the Holy Virgin? She might find more eloquent words to convey my supplication. It is said that women are more persuasive in these matters. . . .

Still nothing. Just a minor pain in his knees which meant the weight was hard on his old bones and he should sit for a while. What was it that lovely *giornalista* had said? There were certain exercises—

Basta! All he needed was to collapse doing push-pulls. Ignatio Quartze would roll his body under the bed and they would not find him for a week. In the meantime, Quartze would pack the Curia.

The pontiff reached his favorite white bench and lowered himself on the cool stone. A breeze came from the garden walls, fluttering the leaves of the tree above him. Was it a sign? It *was* refreshing. Then the breeze stopped; the still air returned and the fluttering of leaves was replaced by footsteps clattering over the path.

It was the new papal aide. A young Black priest from the diocese of New York City, a brilliant student who had done much good work in the Harlem districts. Francesco had sought out just such a deserving young prelate—over considerable opposition. It was a small part of a large design.

"Your Holiness?"

"Yes, my son. You look agitated. What's the matter?"

"I think I did something quite wrong. I was bewildered and you weren't in your rooms and there didn't seem to be anything else to do. I'm very sorry."

"Well, now, we won't know the extent of this calamity until you describe it. You didn't, by any chance, find Cardinal Quartze in my closet and call the guards?"

The Black priest smiled. Ignatio had made clear his disapproval of the aide's appointment. Francesco took every opportunity to lessen the insult.

"No, Your Holiness. I heard your private telephone ringing. The one in the drawer of your bedside table; it just kept ringing."

"It would, my son," interrupted the pontiff. "It is not connected to the Vatican switchboard. A minor indulgence. So you answered it. Who was calling? Only a few old friends and an associate or two of long standing have the number. There is no great harm in what you did. Who was it?"

"A monsignor in Washington, Holy Father. He was very upset——"

"Ahh, Monsignor Patrick Dennis O'Gilligan! Yes, he calls frequently. We play chess together long distance."

"He was very excited—and he thought I was *you*. He didn't give me a chance to speak. He rattled on so fast I couldn't stop him."

"Yes, that sounds like Paddy; he's had his problems. The Berrigans again? Those two keep busy——"

"No, Holy Father. Much worse. The *President* called him. Something about the confidence of the confessional, and whether it was *admissible*. He wants to *convert*, Holy Father!"

"*Che cosa? Madre di Dio!*"

"It gets worse, Your Holiness. Sixteen White House aides want to find Jesus right away. Under certain conditions of Vatican privilege and something called Christian immunity."

Giovanni sighed. There was *so much* to do.

Four months, Oh, Lord?

CHAPTER TWENTY

The unfamiliar faces had one thing in common, thought Sam. Very muscular bodies. As though each enjoyed the outdoors, kept in trim by moving rocks under the eyes of penitentiary guards. And speaking of eyes, that was another thing in common. All their eyes seemed a little sleepy at first, the lids half closed. But it was only appearance. On closer examination the eyes could be seen spinning in their sockets like pinballs caught between magnets; very little went unobserved.

There was a tall, blond man who looked like he jumped out of a television commercial for Scandinavian cigars; a Black who nodded silently a great deal and spoke an English refined in university lecture rooms; another dark-skinned fellow with distinctly sharp, northern features whose accent was like all those people in formal clothes at the Savoy; two Frenchmen who had something to do with boats; a long-haired man in very tight trousers who strutted when he walked like a tango dancer, aware of his ass—unmistakably Italian; and finally, a rather wild-eyed Greek who wore a red kerchief and kept telling jokes no one quite understood.

There was a soft-spoken politeness among them that was positively unctuous, complemented by manners that seemed born of breeding and wealth, were it not for the shifty eyes. They certainly were very much at home in the huge drawing room of Château Machenfeld, where the Hawk had everyone gather before the late dinner.

Gathered, but in the interests of international security, not introduced. No names were used.

Sam had returned to the château at seven. It would have been an hour earlier but he had to walk the last three miles because no taxi out of Zermatt was allowed to travel beyond certain zones and Rudolph was nowhere to be found. When Sam called information for Machenfeld's telephone number, he discovered there was no such place.

It all might have taken the heart out of him, but Option Seven kept him going. He knew when a case was won.

MacKenzie had greeted him with mixed feelings. The Hawk was pleased that he had brought back the financial papers so promptly, but felt that his treatment of Regina was most ungentlemanly. She was a fine girl, and now Sam could not properly say good-bye to her.

Why not?

Because her luggage had been sent to the airport. Ginny was on her way back to California, with a stop in Rome to look at the museums.

So much for Ginny, thought Devereaux. He was a little sad, but there was Option Seven to think about. And he began to think the timing was perfect.

MacKenzie told him that there would be no business discussed the first evening. Just social chitchat and strolls through the gardens and cocktails and dinner and brandy. Why? Because the troops would like a chance, he believed, to size each other up, check their rooms for bugs, oil their weapons, and generally assure themselves that Machenfeld was no Interpol trap. Sam could expect to hear noises during the night; most of the men would carry out their own surveillance, and that was good because they would undoubtedly run into one another and realize further that everything was on the up-and-up.

In the morning, when all were refreshed, the Hawk would hold his first briefing. Before he did that, however, he would certainly take the time to say good-bye to Sam. He was going to miss his young friend, no question about it. But the word of a general officer was his bond; it was the glue that held his battalions together.

Devereaux's work was finished. Rudolph would drive him into Zermatt, where'd he'd take the morning train to Zurich and the late-afternoon flight to New York.

There was one thing Sam should be aware of, however, just in case he became nervous or was afflicted with hypertension. For the next month or so, several associates of the Shepherd Company's first investor, Mr. Dellacroce, would stay in close touch with him. Their names were Fingers and Meat, Hawkins believed; it was just a temporary arrangement, no offense intended.

Yes. Sam understood. There was no point in MacKenzie being redundant.

Devereaux had terminated the conversation, saying he would shave and shower the sweat of three mountain miles off him, and return for cocktails.

In his room, Sam found the scissors Ginny had used on his underwear and cut out seven strips of paper five inches long, one inch wide. He wrote out the identical message on each.

Vitally important you meet with me in my room—third floor, rear of house, last door in the north hallway on the right. 2:00 A.M. sharp. Your life depends on it. I am a friend. Remember two o'clock this morning!

He folded the strips of paper neatly so they fit into the palm of his hand and put them in his jacket pocket. He then removed the seven index cards from his briefcase, the ones with the account numbers and sequential codes-of-release written on them and put them in his trousers pocket. They were his high cards. Irresistible!

He returned to the drawing room downstairs and put to use all the social graces a fine Boston upbringing provided. He shook hands with the men.

And passed each his message.

By one thirty in the morning he was ready. The Italian came first, his hands encased in sheer, skintight black gloves, his feet laced in ballet-like slippers with ridged rubber soles. And then, one by one, the rest showed up in apparel not much different. There was a proliferation of gloves, and soft shoes or sneakers, and black sweaters, and narrow trousers with thick belts holding thicker knives, and small holsters with single straps across small pistols, and in several cases coils of wire.

Altogether a very professional group of psychopaths, thought Sam, as he told them with quiet, not completely heartfelt authority to relax and get comfortable, and smoke if they wished.

Since they all *were* relaxed, and most smoking already, he wasn't sure it was a good opening. But the best summations were those that built from quiet even awkward beginnings.

So he began. Softly, at first. Starting with a man as a tribal being, looking to the heavens for meaning beyond his daily battle for survival, finding solace in that which he could not really comprehend, because there was comfort in primitive faith. There was structure, an organization to natural phenomena, and that meant there had to be a force, a mind, a profound all-knowing intelligence that conceived the whole. Yet could never be truly understood.

There was beauty in that lack of understanding, for men strove beyond themselves for the all-seeing, all-knowing force that created the earth, created *them*, knew *them*— loved *them*.

Without this search, man was an animal. With it he reached out, and compassion became a part of him.

Sam explained that symbols and titles were not important in themselves, for correlations could be drawn between all religions. The essence was the differentiation between good and evil. But symbols and titles held mystical meaning, and profound comfort, for millions everywhere. Faith. The poor and the oppressed prayed to them, held them in reverence and hope. And for millions these symbols were the warm light in their unceasing winters of darkness.

Devereaux paused. It was the moment for a crescendo.

"Gentlemen, facing you is a crime of such monstrous porportions, a crime of such profound evil—a crime which *cannot possibly succeed* and can only lead each of you to your death, or to a life endured, not lived, in a brutal prison cell. For within the walls of this château is a man who would rob you of your most priceless possessions! Your *freedom*! Your *very lives*! For he conceives the *impossible*. In his unbalanced—woefully unbalanced—mind he is convinced he can overcome the swift and terrible reaction, the vengeance, of the entire world! He expects to lead you into the gaping jaws of oblivion. He intends to kidnap the pontiff of the Catholic Church! He is, in a word, *insane*!"

Sam stopped. He bored his eyes into the face of each man. Cigarettes were suspended in midair, mouths were open in disbelief, eyelids were stretched, stares conveying a paralysis born of shock.

He had them! The jury was in the palm of his hand! The phrases had come out like thunder!

It was time for his high cards. Those irresistible figures and sequential code words that would make each man in the room rich. Very, very rich. For doing nothing but avoiding the risk of oblivion.

"Gentlemen, I realize the state of shock you're in and it pains me to see it. It pains me to have caused it. As that great Roman, Marcus Aurelius, observed: We must all do what we have to do, at the moment fate demands that we do it. But as the Indian prophet, Baga Nishyad, also observed: Buckets filled with tears can be spread over grain and the rice will grow like jewels. I do not have jewels, gentlemen, but I do have riches for each of you. Deserved rewards. Sums of money that will lessen your pain, and send you back to the lands of your choice, to live in freedom, freedom from fear, from oblivion. And from want. Here. I pass among you these small index cards. Each is a passport to your personal nirvanas. Let me explain."

And Sam did.

And the seven subordinate officers studied the cards, glancing at one another as they did so.

"Do you speak French?" asked one of the Frenchmen.

Devereaux laughed—a touch too gaily he felt. "Not really."

"Thank you," said the Frenchman, turning to the others. "*Vous parlez tous français?*"

To a man they nodded affirmatively.

So they all began speaking French.

Quietly. Rapidly. Until seven heads nodded once again affirmatively. Sam was touched; he knew they were trying to find a way to thank him.

Which was why he was bewildered when two of the men suddenly approached and grabbed him, spun him around, and began wrapping his wrists in wire.

233

"What the hell are you doing?" he yelled. "What are you doing to my hands? And what the hell is that?"

He gestured his head at the red kerchief the Greek had whipped from his neck and was now twirling.

"And what the hell are they?!"

He referred to a number of metallic cracks that sounded strangely like weapons being inspected.

"We have that compassion you spoke of, monsieur," said the Frenchman. "We offer a man the choice of a blindfold before we execute him."

"*What!?*"

"Be brave, signore," said the Italian. "We all know this business. We accept the odds or we do not play."

"Ya," added the Viking. "It is a game. Some vin. Some lose. You lost."

"*Whaaat?!*"

"Take him down to the patio," said the second Frenchman. "We'll tell the staff it's target practice."

"*Mac! Maac! Maaac!*" He was led down the hallway. Several pairs of hands clapped themselves over his mouth; he bit them. "*For Christ's sake! Hawkins! Where the fuck are you?!*"

Again the hands clamped over his face. The cordon marched with precision down the hallway toward the magnificent winding staircase. Devereaux again forced his mouth open and bit furiously at the flesh around his teeth; hands and arms whipped back momentarily. It was enough for Sam to kick out behind him and for an instant free himself.

He raced and plunged bodily down the curving steps, tumbling over and over as he fell.

"*Hawkins! You son of a bitch, get out here! These maniacs want to shoot me!*"

He bounced over the treads, careened against the wall, and plummeted shoulders over backside down into the last straightaway. His shouts were progressively blurred, but the overall meaning was unmistakable.

"*Shit-kickers! Blindfolds—ouch! Pistols! Goddamn—you—oh—ohh—. Hawkins! Uhu! Jesus—my head!*"

He reached the bottom of the staircase, a disheveled

234

heap. The Hawk strode through the cathedral arch from the drawing room, a cigar clenched between his teeth, several folded maps in his hand. He looked at Sam on the floor and then up at the band of subordinate officers.

"*Goddamn*, boy! This changes *every*thing!"

Once again his clothes were taken. Only now there weren't even any dresses in the closet. His meals were brought up by Rudolph.

The Hawk explained that it had taken a command counterdecision to save his life; and the troops did not like it one bit.

"For a fact, I nearly had a mutiny on my hands before the brigade set its colors," Hawkins had told him the next morning.

"Set its what? Never mind, don't tell me."

"I mean it, son. I had to take stern measures and let them know right off that in matters of extreme prejudice, no authority—regardless of consensus—exceeded that of a field general. It was touch and go for a while, but I've handled the roughest in my day. Those pups, good as they are, weren't any match. It's in the eyes, boy. Always the eyes."

"I don't understand," Devereaux had moaned sincerely. "I spelled everything out beautifully. I unraveled the whole ball of wax. The background, the motive. Jesus! Even the money! I had them!"

"You had nothing," the Hawk replied concisely. "You made two big mistakes. To begin with, you assumed that such a group of men, such a fine contingent of officers, would accept money surreptitiously, without earning it——"

"Get off it!" Devereaux had roared his interruption. "You can't sell that honor-among-thieves bullshit because I won't buy it!"

"I think you're misjudging, boy, but if that's the way you see it, there's your second mistake to consider."

"What mistake?"

"One of the oldest traps in Interpol is to set up a hot bank account and send someone after it. I'm surprised you didn't know that. You set up seven all at once."

Sam had retreated under the eiderdown quilt and pulled it over his head. Unfortunately, he could not block out MacKenzie's words.

"You know, Sam, life is a series of compartments, some related to each other, most separate. But every once in a while these parallel compartments, as I call them, have to acknowledge one another's existence. Now, you saved my life in Peking. You brought to bear your skills and your experience and kept me from that oblivion I hear you talked about. And last night, here in Switzerland, I saved *your* life. Using what skills and experience *I* have. We're even. Our compartments in this area aren't parallel anymore. So don't fuck up, son. I can't be responsible. And that's the word of a general officer."

By the end of two weeks, Sam was sure he'd lose what was left of his sanity. The mere thought of clothes drove him mad. Throughout his life clothes were an accepted part of living—sometimes pleasant, even ego-fulfilling—but they had not been a subject he ever dwelled on for any length of time.

That's a nice jacket; the price is okay. Get it. Shirts? His mother said he should get shirts. What's wrong with Filene's? So I'm a lawyer. Okay, J. Press. Shirts and gray flannels. Socks? His bureau drawer somehow always had socks in it. And shorts and handkerchiefs. A suit was a pretty big occasion, the few times in his adult life when he went out and bought one. Still, he'd never been tempted to have one tailor-made. And in the goddamned army, his civilian jackets and trousers were on hand only because they meant a change from the goddamned uniform. No. Clothes had never been a major factor in his life.

They were now.

But necessity—part of which was not losing one's sanity—was the mother of invention. And truer words were never said. So Sam began to invent, and the thesis of his invention was that he was undergoing a sincere change of position.

It had to be gradual, based on available alternatives. Since he was so completely, intrinsically, *legally* enmeshed in the Shepherd Company's operations and since all avenues of separation had been blocked, what was the point of fighting any longer? Life *was* compartmentalized; and he was locked into a big vault named MacKenzie Hawkins— which also held some forty million dollars, which was a lot of chopped liver.

Maybe, just maybe, his negative approach was self-defeating, all things considered. Perhaps, just perhaps, he should be putting his energies into productive channels; find areas where he could contribute. After all, there was one indelible bottom line. If the Shepherd Company got blown up, a hell of a lot of shrapnel would find its way into the hide of the second and only other corporate officer of record.

These were the conjectures he began to put into words—haltingly, without much conviction at first—during MacKenzie's daily visits at the start of the third week. But he realized that simply saying them was not very persuasive. The Hawk had to see his mind working, observe the transformation.

By Wednesday he had built up to the following:

"Mac, have you considered the legal aspects after—you know, after——"

"Ground Zero's good enough. What legal aspects? Seems to me you've obliged nicely in that department."

"I'm not so sure. I've been involved in a fair amount of plea bargaining. From Boston to Peking."

"What are you talking about?"

"Nothing. I was just—oh, nothing."

By Thursday, this: "There could be consequences after . . . this Ground Zero . . . that you haven't thought out. A cancer could be growing on the presidency of the Shepherd Company that ultimately may cripple the office."

"Spell it out, boy."

"Well. . . . No, never mind. It's just conjecture. What was all that noise this afternoon? It sounded very exciting."

The Hawk squint-eyed him before being pulled into the question. "Goddamn, it was exciting," he answered after several seconds. "Nothing like the evolvement of precision in maneuvers! It fires up a man's heart! What the hell were you talking about? This cancer stuff."

"Oh, forget it. The old legal brain was just wandering. Are the maneuvers really all that . . . top drawer?"

"Yeah . . ." Hawkins rolled the cigar from one side of his mouth to the other. "They're all right, I guess."

On Friday: "How was the practice today? Sounded great."

"Practice? Goddamn, it's not practice, it's maneuvers!"

"Sorry. How were they?"

"A little sloppy; we've got some minor difficulties."

"Sorry, again. But I've got confidence in you. You'll straighten things out."

"Yeah . . ." The Hawk paced at the foot of the bed, his cigar a mashed pulp. "I may have to pick up a few diversion troops. Two or three, that's all. I wasn't concentrating. And, goddamn, Sam, I would have been on-the-barrel-sight except for the trouble you've caused!"

"I told you. I really regret all that. *I* wasn't concentrating———"

MacKenzie stopped and blurted out the words. "Do you mean that?"

"Yes," replied Devereaux slowly, with conviction. "The first thing a lawyer learns is to deal with facts, hard evidence. All of it, not just the bits and pieces. I isolated. I'm truly sorry."

"I won't pretend to understand that bullshit, but if you feel the way I think you're saying, what the hell were you talking about yesterday? And, damn it, the day before. Those 'consequences' after Ground Zero."

Bingo! as they said in Boston, thought Devereaux to himself. But he showed no emotion; he was the calm, probing attorney with his client's best interests at heart. "All right. I'll spell it out. I know those trust accounts, Mac. Excluding the one major trust, which I gather is yours, your seven men can draw (or have their consigners draw) up to three hundred thousand on the basis of the first code releases. The second code releases are on a printout sheet in one of the other documents. The printout requires your countersignature and I assume you'll send it to Zurich just before you leave for Ground Zero. Am I right so far?"

"I really skull-sessioned that trust business. What's wrong?"

"Nothing. Yet. With the second release each man has a

total of five hundred thousand, correct? That's his fee, right? A half a million for Ground Zero. Everybody the same."

"Not bad for six weeks' work."

"There are other things to consider. Plea bargaining on a large scale can include more than immunity. And not just through writing a book, although I understand a lot of cash is funneled through publishers these days."

"What are you talking about?" The Hawk quashed his cigar out on the bedpost.

"What's to prevent any or all of your subordinate officers from going straight to the authorities—through intermediaries, of course—and making separate deals? After the fact. They have your money; they avoid prosecution because they cooperate. Remember, we're talking about one of the biggest scores in history. They would make a few thousand on top of what they've got."

MacKenzie's squinting eyes suddenly widened in relief. And self-satisfaction. There was definitely a sense of triumph in his grin. "Is that what you've troubled yourself over, boy?"

"Don't make light of it——"

"Hell, no, I won't. And I didn't. None of my men would do anything like that. Because they're going to want to disappear like jackrabbits running from a brush fire. They won't surface anywhere for fear of colliding with *each other.*"

"Now *I* don't understand," said Sam dejectedly.

The Hawk sat on the bed. "I've covered all that, son. Sort of in the same way I lashed you to the loaded howitzer. You gave me the idea. I intend to say good-bye to each officer separately. And with each I'm going to hand him an open-faced bearer bond worth an additional half million. And tell him *he's* the *only* one getting it. Because like a good general officer I've kept my combat logs, and in rereading them I realized the mission could not have been successful without *his* particular strategic contributions. They're hung. Both ways. A man won't inform on a crime that couldn't have been committed without *his expertise*—especially when it's worth an additional half million—and he sure as hell doesn't want his fellow conspirators to know he got preferential treatment to the tune of a half million."

"My God!" Sam could not stop the admiration from creeping into his voice.

"Clausewitz makes it clear that you don't engage the Berber in the same way you do battle with the king's dragoons. It's a question of applicable tactics."

Devereaux, once again, was struck by the Hawk's sheer boldness. He spoke softly, barely above a whisper, "You're talking about—Jesus!—three and a half million dollars!"

"That's correct; you add real quick. And a million apiece for the girls, that's four more million. Plus the original compensation for the officers, another three and a half. And for your information, though I should probably reconsider, I've got another bearer bond for you. That's a million on your paysheet."

"What?"

"I kind of suspected you never understood the forty-mill capitalization. I didn't just come up with a figure, you know. That sum was arrived at after very careful deliberation. I got a booklet from the Securities and Exchange Commission which told what to look for in sound corporate financing. You see, before the company even *markets* its services, we have a preoperation salary outlay of close to fifteen million; then there was the capitalization expenses, including travel and front money and finder's fees—I kinda screwed you on that, son, but I knew you had good things coming—and the corporate real estate and the equipment indigenous to the marketing sources. . . ."

Involuntarily, Sam's ears distorted the sound waves. Isolated phrases such as "aircraft purchases estimated at five million," and "shortwave communication relays coming in at a million-two," and "refurbishing, and supplies," and "additional company offices"—all these came through with sufficient clarity to make Sam wonder where he was. Stark naked under an eiderdown quilt somewhere in Switzerland, or fully clothed in a boardroom somewhere in the Chrysler Building. Unfortunately for the state of his stomach, everything came together with the Hawk's brief summation.

"This SEC booklet was very specific about liquid assets available for reserve capital. It recommended a point spread of twenty to thirty percent. Then I checked out the custom-of-the-trade practices with limited partnership agreements and found that the overcalls were generally ten to fifteen percent, which struck me as inadequate. So I skulled a bit and decided on twenty-five percent plus. And that's what we've got. The budget projections prior to marketing come to just about thirty million. Taking that as the base figure, you add twenty-five percent plus, or ten million for contingency. That makes forty million and that's what I raised. Damned sound economics, I'd say."

Devereaux was temporarily speechless. His mind was racing but no words came. MacKenzie the military fruit-cake was suddenly Hawkins the conglomerate financier. And that was more frightening than anything he had previously considered. Military principles (or lack thereof) when combined with industrial principles (of which there was a lack thereof) did a military-industrial complex make. The Hawk was a walking military-industrial complex!

If there was strident urgency in Sam's stopping MacKenzie before, it was tripled now.

"You're invincible," said Sam finally. "I rescind all my previous reservations. Let me join you, really join you. Let me earn my silly million."

CHAPTER TWENTY-ONE

Each officer had been assigned a color in French. Not only was French spoken by everyone, but the sounds of the color words were more distinctive in French than in any other language.

The Ameican Negro from Crete was *Noir,* of course. The Viking from Stockholm, *Gris;* the Frenchman from Biscay was *Bleu,* while his countryman from Marsilles was *Vert;* the dark-skinned non-Black from Beirut was *Brun;* Rome was *Orange;* and finally, Athens was *Rouge,* in honor of his ever present kerchief. To instill a sense of discipline and identity among the men, the Hawk further insisted that the word "Captain" precede each color.

This aspect of authority and identity was desirable because MacKenzie's second command by necessity stripped his men of their specific individualities. For Ground Zero's assault was to be made in stocking masks. Head and face hair were to be at a minimum; skins powdered or bleached to medium Caucasian hues, and all ambulation which, no doubt, had been studiously disguised, drastically changed.

The men accepted the order without question. Razors and scissors and bleaching agents went to work; none had any desire to stand out any more distinctly from his fellow officers than basic nature dictated. There was security in anonymity, and they knew it.

The maneuvers progressed into the fourth week. The forest road bordering the Machenfeld field had been shaped to conform as accurately as possible to the site of Ground Zero; boulders had been moved, trees uprooted, whole areas of bush transplanted. A second location had been selected and cosmeticized: a winding, narrow, back road that descended a relatively steep hill in the woods.

In redesigning both these sites the men worked from enlarged photographs—123 photographs, to be exact—sent by an agreeable tourist in Rome by the name of Lillian von Schnabe. However, Mrs. von Schnabe did not take credit for her films. As a matter of fact, the rolls were sent undeveloped by two relays of couriers unknown to each other and delivered to a bewildered Rudolph in Zermatt. In several cases of tampons. Rudolph put the strange cargo in the trunk of his Italian taxi, underneath the tools. A man had his dignity to consider.

On the third day of the fourth week the Hawk scheduled the first complete run-through of the assault. By necessity it was a start-stop hold-to-position exercise as the men switched around, assuming the pivotal roles of the adversary. Motorcycles raced, limousines sped, figures in stocking masks leaped from their stations to perform the tasks assigned. Using a stopwatch, MacKenzie clocked each phase of the maneuver; he had developed eight basic phases for the entirety, from incursion to escape. And goddamn, his officers were progressing beautifully! They knew that the overall success of Ground Zero depended on the complete success of each individual assignment within each specific phase. The concept of failure was not attractive.

Which was why the captains objected unanimously to the Hawk's prime tactical innovation: total absence of hand weapons. A well-placed knife or a rapidly exercised garrote had served them all in past skirmishes, more often than not being the difference between survival and capture. But MacKenzie was adamant: It would be both guarantee and proof that no harm would come to the pope until the ransom was paid. Therefore, all pistols, knives, coils, foot studs, knee cleats, finger points—even pig-iron knuckles—were eliminated. Forbidden, too, were any forms of hand-to-hand above the level of basic jukato.

Eventually, they accepted the limitations. "In Sweden there is a saying," intoned Captain Gris in his Nordic lilt. "One Volvo in the garage is worth a lifetime of passes on the Scandinavian railroad. I shall accommodate the commander."

"*Oui,*" agreed Captain Bleu, the Frenchman from Biscay.

"For the recompense involved, I shall sing them to sleep with Gascogne lullabies, if it is required."

But lullabies were not required. Instead, sleep was to be induced by half-inch hypodermic needles dispensing solutions of sodium pentothal. Each officer would be outfitted with a thin bandolier across his chest, which carried tiny hypodermic needles in small rubber receptacles—where once had been bullets. They were easy to extract swiftly. If administered properly, within a three-inch diameter on the lower right area of the neck, the anesthetic would take effect in seconds. The problem was merely to immobilize the victim for those brief moments until the drug caused collapse. It was not a difficult problem and since there'd be considerable noise from the vehicles, even a partial scream or two might go unnoticed.

So the officers, heeding the words of wisdom from Gris and Bleu, reevaluated their objections to the Hawk's order. In a way it was a challenge; and none were interested in lifetime passes on the Scandinavian railroad. Not when he could own a fleet of Volvos.

Each captain's expertise was called on. Captain Gris and Bleu were masters of camouflage and escape cartography. Captain Rouge was an expert in demolition; he had personally blown up six piers in the Corinth strait when it was rumored the American fleet was sailing in. Sedative medicines were a specialty of the Englishman, Captain Brun, who had darkened his skin for a life in Beirut; most narcotics held interest for him. Aircraft technology and electronics were covered brilliantly. The first, of course, was the bailiwick of Captain Noir, whose exploits in Houston—and Moscow—were legend. The second was the province of Captain Vert, who found it necessary in Marseilles to devise an extraordinary variety of radio communications. It was such a busy port; and Interpol was always underfoot.

Lastly, native orientation was left to Captain Orange, who knew Rome like the back of his constantly gesturing hand. He would write out full descriptions of eight innocuous-looking sets of clothing that blended into the current dress, and further, he would provide a minimum of four separate methods of transportation, using public conveyances where feasible, to the site of Ground Zero. For during the final days of the fourth week, each captain was to travel to Rome and personally survey the assault area.

The airfield at Zaragolo would be no problem; they agreed to that. And neither would the helicopter at Ground Zero. It would be flown in the night before the assault. Gris and Bleu assured them the camouflage would be undetectable.

Goddamn, thought MacKenzie as he snapped the stopwatch at the end of the maneuver's Phase Eight. Twenty-one minutes! In another day or so it would get to the optimum eighteen. He felt a surge of pride in his once bemedaled chest. His machine was emerging as one of the finest ministrike forces in the military books.

Even the three privates (the diversionary troops) were splendid. They had but two functions: scream and lie still. But as was proper for the lowest enlisted ranks, they knew nothing. They had been recruited by Captain Brun from the poppy fields high in the Turkish hills, to which they would return the instant Ground Zero was terminated. They'd been hired to perform at a fixed price, did not care to know anything and, naturally, were housed by themselves in enlisted quarters and did not eat at the officers' mess.

They were called simply: Privates One, Two, and Three.

The run-through completed, the officers gathered around the Hawk beside the huge blackboard he'd set up on an A-frame in the field. Sweat was pouring through their stocking masks. Those in priestly habits took them off carefully, studying them for repairs that might be needed; and the inevitable cigarettes and matches came out of pockets. No lighters; fingerprints could be lifted from lighters.

The three privates, naturally, went off by themselves. In sight but not within hearing. Enlisted personnel were not privy to tactical analyses; it was not proper.

The analysis began. Although immensely pleased Hawkins did not dwell on the positive; he told them their mistakes, marking up the blackboard with his criticisms with such sharp authority that the officers cowered like rebuked children.

"Precision, gentlemen! Precision is everything! You must never allow your concentration to lapse, even for a second! Captain Noir, you're cutting your time too close between Phase One and your station in Phase Six. Captain Gris, you had trouble with your cassock over the uniform. Practice it, man! Captains Rouge and Brun, your execution of Phase Five was just plain sloppy! Take out that radio equipment! Go over your moves! Captain Orange! Yours was the most serious lapse of all!"

"*Che cosa?* I make *no* mistakes!"

"Phase Seven, Captain! Without the proper execution of Phase Seven, the whole mission goes up in mortar smoke! That's the *exchange*, soldier! You're the one who speaks Italian best. I put this Frescobaldi in the pope's car and take the pope. Where the hell were *you?*"

"In position, *Generale!*"

"You were on the wrong side of the road! And Captain Bleu, for an expert at camouflage, you stuck out like a plucked duck in your Phase Four station! *Cover*, man! Use the foliage for cover!

"Now, as to this latrine rumor that some of you are unhappy over Phase Eight, the escape routes to Zaragolo; that a few of you figure we should have two copters at Ground Zero. Well, let me tell you, there's no contingency for radar, gentlemen. One small bird with Italian air force markings, flying low, can get through. Two choppers would be picked up on a scanner. I don't think any of you cotton to having your asses a thousand feet in the air, surrounded by the whole guinea air force. No offense, Captain Orange."

The captains looked at each other. They'd obviously discussed Phase Eight among themselves, and since the small helicopter at target center was lifting out only the Hawk, the pope, and the two pilots, they had grumbled. But the commander painted a convincing picture. The escape routes on the ground had been exhaustively analyzed by Gris and Bleu, who were not only the best in the business, but who would be using them as well. It was conceivable that the ground was safer.

"We withdraw our objections," said Captain Vert.

"Good," said MacKenzie. "Now let's concentrate on——"

It was as far as he got. For in the distance, across the south field, running through the grass was the figure of Sam Devereaux in sweat pants, shouting at the top of his lungs.

"One, two, three, four! What do we like to *jog* for? *Good* health, *good* health! Five, six, seven, eight! Get the weight! Out of the freight! Four, three, *two*, *one*! Jogging is a lot of *fun*!"

"*Mon Dieu!*" cried Captain Bleu. "The soft-headed one never stops! He has carried on so for five days now!"

"Before we rise in the morning!" added Gris. "During rest periods, whenever there is a peaceful moment he is below the windows, shouting."

The other captains joined in a chorus of agreement. They had accepted the general's decision not to shoot the idiot, even grudgingly allowed that there was no harm in letting the fool out of the room to exercise—as long as two guards from the Machenfeld staff were assigned to him. The jackass wasn't going anywhere; not in sweat pants, with no top, over a high barbed-wire fence that led only to impenetrable Swiss mountain forests. But they had drawn the line regarding the clown's participation in Ground Zero.

So here he was, trying to impress them with his training. A pathetically poor athlete who cannot make the team, but will not stop trying.

"All right. All right," said the Hawk, suppressing a laugh. "I'll talk to him again, make him quiet down. He's just doing it for your benefit, you know. He really wants to join the big fellas."

He was driving them all crazy, and he knew it. Of course there were times when he thought he might collapse from exhaustion, but the knowledge that his grotesqueries were having their desired effect kept him going. Everyone avoided him, some actually ran at the sight of

247

him. His insane behavior had become an irritating, aggravating joke. Already three dogs which had appeared out of nowhere to guard him were taken from the corridor outside his room to the staff quarters below because of their incessant barking. And he made it a point to run by the staff area repeatedly. The hounds, themselves weary of being screamed at for their perfectly natural reactions, now merely raised their heads and stared with hatred at him from behind the gates as he passed by.

As did the staff—and MacKenzie's officers. Sam was a loud nuisance, a joke that had worn thin. What was happening, of course, was that he was being taken for granted. And in a few days he would take advantage of that scorn.

Although he was not allowed to eat with Mac and his band of psychopaths, the Hawk was considerate enough to continue visiting him every day in the late afternoon when Sam was brought back to his room and the sweat pants removed. Devereaux understood. Hawkins needed a sounding board for his enthusiasms. And, bragging, he dropped the information that he and his men would be away for a day or two to execute a surveillance check of Ground Zero. They would then return for any last-minute alterations of strategy.

But Sam shouldn't be concerned. He would not be lonely at Machenfeld. What with the guards, and the dogs, and the staff.

Sam smiled. For when the Hawk and his freaks left the château, it was his own personal Ground Zero. He had begun to prime his guards, the wild-eyed Rudolph and some obvious killer with no name. He had convinced Rudolph and No Name on several occasions to sit in the middle of a field as he ran around it. It was not difficult; they were grateful to be stationary. They simply sat in the grass with two ominous looking pistols trained on him as he jogged and intermittently stopped to perform calisthenics. On each occasion he had gradually widened the distance between him and his guards so that this afternoon he was nearly 250 yards away from them.

The army had taught him *something* about small weapons; he knew that there was no handgun that was any damned good beyond thirty yards. Not in terms of accuracy; scatter shot was something else, but he had to take *some* chances. Stopping the Hawk was the kind of objective that in war made heroes of unheroic soldiers. What had MacKenzie said? "It's commitment. Nothing takes its place. All the ammo in the world can't be a substitute. . . ."

Sam was committed. The prospects of World War III loomed larger every day.

His plan was simple . . . and relatively safe. He had been tempted to give it an option number, but his options had not been noticeably successful so he decided against it. He would jog here in the south field, as he was doing now, where the bordering forest was thickest and the grass higher than in the other pastures. He would widen the distance between himself and the guards as he had done this afternoon and institute intermittent calisthenics. Among them pushups. Which naturally brought him close to the ground, below the level of the grass.

At the proper moment, he would crawl away as fast as he could toward the forest, then race to the fence. However, when he reached the fence, he would *not* climb it. Instead, he would remove the sweat pants—properly torn—and throw them over. And then, if all went as it should, if Rudolph and No Name were racing in several directions at once, he would scream as though severely hurt and get the hell out of the area. Into the thickest woods.

Rudolph and No Name would naturally run to the spot at the fence, see the sweat pants on the other side, and undoubtedly take the appropriate actions: One would go over the fence, while the other raced back to the château for the dogs.

At which point Sam would wait until he heard the barking. Then he would return to Machenfeld, go in through the door, steal clothes and a weapon. From that point to an automobile in the circular drive, and a pistol to threaten the gatekeeper, had to be clear sailing.

It had to be!

What could go wrong?

The Hawk wasn't the only one capable of strategies. He'd learn not to mess with a Boston lawyer who worked for Aaron Pinkus!

The shouts interrupted his thoughts. He was within sight of the maneuver area; he could see the strange looking road signs and the vehicles. Rudolph and No Name were yelling at him to come back. Naturally, he would oblige; he was not permitted to observe maneuvers.

"*Sorry fellas!*" he yelled breathlessly as he reversed direction, his legs pounding the soft earth. "Let's head down to the gate and back and call it a day!"

Rudolph and No Name grimaced and got up from the grass. Rudolph gave him a finger; No Name a thumb to the teeth.

Sam made it a point every afternoon to end his jogging with a run down to the main gate. It was a good idea to study the premises as thoroughly as possible in anticipation of his escape. It was conceivable that he might have to operate the mechanism himself, depending upon the state of panic at the moment. If it was maximum (as MacKenzie would say) the gate might even be left open.

He contemplated this possibility as his feet clattered over the boards on the moat, when suddenly his musings were replaced by a feeling of discomfort. For down at the gate a long, black limousine was being admitted with much bowing and obsequious grinning on the part of the gatekeeper. And when he heard the words shouted from the driver's seat as the automobile was expertly whipped out of the gate area toward him, he froze and instantly considered drowning himself in the Machenfeld moat.

"I don't believe it!" yelled Lillian Hawkins von Schnabe at the wheel. "Sam Devereaux in *sweat pants*! God almighty, you took my advice. You're toning up that wreck of a vessel you live in!"

And if he considered drowning himself at Lillian's words, the next voice he heard drove him to the railing.

"You surely look better than you did in London!" shouted Anne from Santa Monica, Mrs. Hawkins number four— Sloping yet Argumentative. "Your little trip must have done you a world of good!"

CHAPTER TWENTY-TWO

Devereaux's escape plan did not become unglued as had Options One through Four. Neither was it bypassed as Options Five and Six had been. Nor had it exploded in a torrent of abuse as was the fate of Option Seven. It was, however, postponed.

He suddenly had two additional guards to contend with, one of whom was as much a shock to the Hawk as both were to Sam. MacKenzie admitted it. Casually, without letting it upset his schedule; merely using the reality to bolster his overall strength—turning a liability into an asset.

"Annie's got a problem, counselor," the Hawk said back in Devereaux's room. "I think you might give it some legal thought. Do something about it when this is over."

"All problems pale into insignificance——"

"Not hers. You see, Annie's family—the whole goddamn family—spent more time *in* prison than *out* of it. Mother, father, brothers—she was the only girl—they had record sheets that took up most of the precinct files in Detroit."

"I never came across any of that. It's not in the data banks." Devereaux was momentarily sidetracked from his own concerns. MacKenzie wasn't trying to con him now. There was no fire in the eyes, only sadness. Truth. But there *hadn't* been any mention of a criminal record in Anne's dossier. If he remembered correctly, she'd been listed as the only daughter of two obscure Michigan school teachers who wrote poetry in medieval French. Parents deceased.

"Course not," said the Hawk. "I changed all that for the army. And everybody else, mainly her. It was a big hangup for the girl; it was holding her back." MacKenzie lowered his voice, as if the words were painful, but nevertheless a reality that could not be brushed aside. "Annie was a hooker. She fell into poor ways—very artificial ways for her—when she was growing up. She worked the streets. She didn't know any better then. She had no home life, most of the time no home. When she wasn't hooking she'd spend her time in libraries, looking at all the pretty magazines, imagining what it would be like to live decent. She was constantly trying to improve herself, you know. She never stops reading, even now, always after bettering herself. Because underneath there's a very fine person. There always was."

Sam's memory went back to the Savoy. Anne in bed with a huge, glossy paperback of *The Wives of Henry VIII* on her lap. Then later, the words spoken with such conviction in the foyer doorway as she was about to get dressed. Words that meant a great deal to her. Devereaux looked up at the Hawk and repeated them quietly. "'Don't change the outside too much or you'll mess up the inside.' She said you told her that."

MacKenzie seemed embarrassed. It was obvious he had not forgotten. "She had problems. Like I just said, underneath there was a very fine person she didn't recognize. Hell, *I* did. Anybody would."

"What's her legal problem?" Sam asked.

"This goddamned gigolo-waiter husband of hers. She's stuck with that fucker for six years; helped him go from a hot-pants beach boy to owning a couple of restaurants. She *built* those restaurants. She's damned proud of them! And she likes the life. Overlooking the water, all those boats, nice people. She lives descent now, and *she did it*."

"So?"

"He wants her out. He's got himself another woman and he doesn't want any lip from Annie. A quiet divorce and just get the hell out."

"She doesn't want the divorce?"

"That's immaterial. She doesn't want to lose the restaurants! It's principle, Sam. They represent everything she's worked for."

"He can't simply take them. There's the property set-
252

tlement to consider, and California laws are rough as hell."

"So's he. He went back to Detroit and dug up her police record."

Sam paused. "That's a legal problem," he said.

"You'll work on it?"

"There's not much I can do here. It's a confrontation problem, big attack variety. Fire for fire, dig up counteraccusations." Devereaux snapped both his fingers—the legal *wunderkind* making a brilliant decision. "Tell you what. Let me out of here and I'll fly straight to California! I'll hire one of the best LA private detectives—like on television—and really go after this prick!"

"Good thinking, boy," replied the Hawk, clucking his tongue in respect. "I like that aggressive tone; you bear it in mind for later. Say, in a month or two."

"Why not *now*? I could——"

"I'm afraid you can't. That's out of the question. You're here for the duration. Talk with Annie, though. Learn what you can. Maybe Lillian can help; she's a resourceful filly."

With these words MacKenzie dispensed with his liability and gained an asset: Sam now had two additional people to keep an eye on him. He might outwit Rudolph and No Name; the girls were something else again.

Within hours after their arrival, however, it was apparent to Sam that Lillian would have very little time to pay attention to him. In her usual forthright manner she plunged into furious activity, commandeering two of the Machenfeld staff to help her. The work began first thing in the morning when the brigade went out for maneuvers.

Upstairs. In the top floor rooms and on the ramparts of the château.

There was the banging of hammers and the whirring of saws and the cracking of plaster. Furniture was carried up and down the long winding staircase; those pieces too large or too awkward were raised and lowered by pulleys and ropes over the outside walls. Scores of potted plants and bushes and small trees were placed around the battlements—seen from the ground by Sam for he was not permitted above the third floor. Paints and brushes and panels of wood were transported daily by Lillian and her two helpers and when Sam could no longer politely ignore her labors, he asked her what she was doing.

"A little arranging, that's all," she replied.

Finally, crates of crushed stone and washed gravel were hoisted up the walls, accompanied by several concrete benches and (if Sam was not mistaken, and being from Boston he was not) a marble *prayer* stall.

It was suddenly very clear to Devereaux exactly what Lillian was doing. She was turning the top floor and the ramparts of Château Machenfeld into a full-fledged papal residence! Complete with apartments and gardens and prayer stalls!

Oh, my God! A papal residence!

Anne, on the other hand, spent most of her time with Sam. Since MacKenzie had deemed it improper for the girls to eat at the officers' mess—it was diversionary for women to break bread with a strike force prior to combat—Anne and Lillian were assigned their meals in Devereaux's room, Sam under the eiderdown quilt, of course. But Lillian was rarely there; she spent most of her time upstairs—arranging.

So Sam and Anne were thrown together. On a surprisingly platonic basis. True, he made no pass, but she made no offer either. It was as though both understood the insanity whirling around them, neither wanting the other to be involved, each, in a very real sense, protecting the other. And the more they talked together, the more Sam began to understand what MacKenzie meant about Anne. She was the most genuine, guileless person he had ever met in his life. All the girls were devoid of artifice, but there was something different about Annie. Whereas the others had reached certain plateaus, conscious of their worth, Annie was not satisfied. There was about her a delightfully irreverent sense of purpose that proclaimed for all the world to hear that she *could* expand, *could* experience—but *good heavens*! one did not have to be *gloomy* about it.

Devereaux recognized his imminent danger: he could get really sidetracked. He began to think that he had been looking for this girl for about fifteen years.

And he *couldn't* think about that. Another plan had come into focus. One he knew would work.

The very day Hawkins and his brigade of banana captains took off for Ground Zero!

The last sweet and sour strains of the orchestra filled the theater. Guido Frescobaldi took his curtain calls, wiping a tear from his eyes. He had to shed his art and think of things plenipotentiary now. He had to hurry to his dressing room and lock up his makeup box.

The call had come! He was going to Rome! He was going to be embraced by his beloved cousin, the most beloved of all popes, Giovanni Bombalini, Francesco, Vicar of Christ! Ohh! Such blessings had come to him! To be reunited after all these years!

But he could say nothing. Absolutely *nothing*. That was part of the arrangements. It was the way Bombalini— *Madre di Cristo*—Pope Francesco wished it, and one did not question the ways of so munificent a pontiff. But Guido did wonder just a little bit. Why did Giovanni insist that he tell the management that small lie that he was going to visit family in Padua, not Rome? Even his friend, the stage manager, had winked when he told him.

"Perhaps you might ask your *family* to pray to Saint Peter for a little sacred lire, Guido. The box office has not been good this season."

What did the stage manager know? And when did he know it?

It was not like the Giovanni of old to be secretive. And yet who was he, Frescobaldi, to doubt the wisdom of his beloved cousin, the pope.

Guido reached his small dressing room and began to take off his costume. As he did so his eyes fell on his Sunday church suit, pressed and hanging neatly in the center of the wall. He was going to wear it on the train to Rome. And he suddenly felt very ungrateful and ashamed of himself.

Giovanni was being so *good* to him. How could he even *think* a compromising thought?

The lady journalist who was bringing them together had

asked for all his measurements. Every last one. When he asked why, she told him. And he had wept.

Giovanni was buying him a new suit.

The Hawk and his subordinate officers returned from Rome. The final check of Ground Zero had gone off without a hitch; no alterations were required.

Further, all intelligence data had been gathered and processed. Using basic surveillance techniques employed in hostile territories, Hawkins had donned an enemy uniform (in this case a black suit and a clerical collar) and obtained a Vatican pass, and identification that certified him to be a Jesuit doing an efficiency study for the treasury. He had free access to all calendars and personnel schedules. From apartments to barracks.

They all confirmed the Hawk's projections.

The pope would leave for Castel Gandolfo on the same day he had chosen for the past two years. He was an organized man; time was to be allocated properly with regard to needs and functions. Castel Gandolfo expected him, and he would be there.

The pope would use the same modest motorcade he had employed previously. He was not a wasteful or pretentious man. One motorcycle point with two front and rear flanks. Basic. The limousines were restricted to two: his own, in which his most personal aides accompanied him; and a second, for secretaries and lesser prelates, who carried his current working papers.

The route of the motorcade was the scenic road he had spoken of with feeling whenever he mentioned Gandolfo: the beautiful Via Appia Antica, with its rolling hills and remnants of ancient Rome along the way.

Via Appia Antica. Ground Zero.

The two Lear jets had been delivered to Zaragolo. It was an airfield for the rich. The small Fiat sedan, which was the diversion equipment for the Turk privates, had been purchased by Captain Noir, in the name of the Ethiopian embassy. It was parked in an all-night garage next to a police station where the crime rate was at a minimum.

Guido Frescobaldi was on his way to Rome. Regina would handle him. She'd put him up at a *pensione* she rented called The Doge, on the Via Due Macelli, right near the Spanish Steps, and take good care of the old man until the morning of the assault. And first thing that morning she'd load him up with a thiopental solution that would keep him on a harmless high for damn near twelve hours.

The Hawk planned to pick Guido up in the Fiat on his way to Ground Zero. Of course, Regina would have him properly dressed by then, with a very large overcoat that covered his fancy clothes. Skirts, really.

There was only one last item to take care of. The two limousines used in maneuvers had to be driven to a place called Valtournanche, several miles northwest of the Alpine town of Champoluc. To a little-used private airfield frequented by the jetsetters heading for their ski chalets. The limousines were a natural. They were registered to nonexistent Greeks, and the Swiss *never* bothered Greeks who could afford such automobiles.

Lillian could take care of the transfer. Oversee it, actually. She could use the two men who had helped her shape up the pope's BOQ. Once the cars were in position they could vanish along with Lillian. Mac, of course, would give them bonuses.

He'd get rid of Rudolph, too, and that psycho, what's-his-name, the minute they were back from Ground Zero and the pope was safely—secretly—in his quarters. The chef had to stay; what the hell, even if he did find out who he was cooking for, he was a French Huguenot wanted by the police in sixteen countries.

That left Anne. And Sam, of course.

He could handle Sam. Sam was so lashed to that loaded howitzer he was part of the casing. But he couldn't figure out Annie. What was the girl up to? Why wouldn't she leave? Why had she used his own oath against him?

"You gave your solemn word that if ever any of us came to you in need, you'd never abandon us. You'd never allow an injustice to be done if you could prevent it. I'm here. I'm in need, and an injustice has been done. I've nowhere else to go. Please let me stay."

257

Well, of course, he had to. After all, it was the word of a general officer.

But *why*? Could it be Sam?

Goddamn!

So he would die in Gandolfo. It could be worse, thought Giovanni Bombalini, gazing out the windows of his study. A half century ago all he had to look forward to was a gravesite in the Gold Coast, preceded by a long, drawn-out Last Rites ceremony delivered half in Latin, half in Kwa with swarms of flies circling hs head. Gandolfo certainly held advantages over that exit.

He would be able to work better, too, at Gandolfo; use the weeks left to straighten out his own affairs, which were minimal, and do his best to set a course for the immediate future of the Church. He would bring with him several hundred analyses of the most powerful dioceses throughout the world and issue scores of promotions; balancing, but balancing in favor of younger, more vigorous perspectives. Which often had nothing to do with youth.

He had to keep reminding himself that the intractable old guard was not to be scorned, and should not be. The old war-horses had gone through ecclesiastical battles unknown to the vast majority of those who screamed for reform and change. It was not easy to alter the philosophies of a lifetime. But the *fine* old war-horses knew when to step aside and graze in the pastures, ready with an affectionate eye to offer advice when asked, compassion regardless. The others—the Ignatio Quartzes of the world—needed a push.

Pope Francesco decided that among his last acts would be a little pushing. It would take the form of a Last Rites Dissertation to be read to the Curia after his death, and then made public. It was a bit presumptuous, he supposed, but if God did not want him to complete it, He could always summon him at His will.

He had begun the dissertation, dictating to the young Black priest. And he had sent a papal memorandum to every office in the Vatican appointing his young aide as executor of his personal effects in the event he was called to the arms of Christ.

258

Giovanni was told that Ignatio Quartze threw up for nearly an hour after receiving the papal instruction. It must have wrecked havoc with the cardinal's nasal passages.

"Your Holiness?" The young Black aide came through the door of the bedroom carrying a suitcase. "I can't find the miniature chessboard. It's not in the drawer with the telephone."

Giovanni thought for a moment, then coughed an embarrassed laugh. "I'm afraid it's in the bathroom, Father. Since Monsignor O'Gilligan solved his conversion problems by explaining penance, he's been an absolute terror in his moves. Concentration was required."

"Yes, sir." The young priest smiled as he put down the suitcase. "I'll put it in the vestment trunk."

"Are we about packed? I say 'we,' but you've done the work."

"Almost, Holy Father. The pills and the tonics will stay in my briefcase."

"A little fine brandy could do just as well."

"I have that, too, Your Holiness."

"You are truly a man of God, my son."

CHAPTER TWENTY-THREE

RIGIRATI! COSTRUZIONE!

The large metal sign was secured to the center of the wooden barrier which stretched across the width of the back country road.

It looked very official, right down to the last tiny red reflector, and the imposing insignia of Rome's municipal government. It also officially closed off a section of the Via Appia Antica to all approaching vehicles, offering instead a detour cut out of the forest down the Appian hill. And since this particular stretch of the Appian road was the narrowest on the entire route, there was no feasible alternative to the detour if the vehicles in question were larger than the smallest Fiat. Not even the size of the Fiat sedan which the Hawk had driven out of the garage next to the police station and which now lay overturned at the bottom of the hill.

Any larger automobile would not have room to turn around. To reverse direction a driver would have to steer his car backward for the better part of a mile, over countless potholes and around numerous blind curves. Of course the same driver might opt for negotiating the wide expanses of fields that regularly interrupted the Appian forests, but they were filled with rocks and mounds and intermittent stone walls, some built in ancient times. The fields were not only treacherous, but it was against the law to drive on them.

These thoughts went through Captain Noir's head, his black face powdered under the stocking mask, as he lay motionless in the bushes off the side of the road beyond the barrier. He had heard the sounds of the motorcycles in the distance.

All was ready.

Ground Zero had arrived.

The location was perfect. Only trees and fields and hills; the general had planned well. The abduction could probably be carried out on this isolated stretch of road without the detour but in some ways the detour was the most important aspect of Ground Zero. The vehicles *could* turn around by inches—but they wouldn't. They would use the detour.

Still, in case they didn't, Captain Noir held in his hand a piercing, high-frequency whistle. Its use meant that Plan Able, Phase One, Positions One through Three were aborted, instantly implementing Plan Baker, Phase Double Zero, Positions One Hundred One through One Hundred Ten: abduction farther up the Appia.

Down the road beyond the barrier, the blue helmet with the white cross enameled on the steel stood out like an enormous jewel in the Italian sunlight. It was on the head of the motorcycle patrolman in front of the papal column; the Vatican point, as the general termed him. The uniformed officer was traveling at medium speed; any faster on the old road would be uncomfortable for those in the limousines.

The patrolman spotted the barrier with the large official sign and drove up to it. Captain Noir held his breath. The officer jumped off his motorcycle, kicked out the stand, and walked up to the obstruction. He raised his eyebrows in bewilderment, looked beyond the barricade for signs of construction and grumbled unintelligibly.

He turned and held up his hands. The lead automobile had reached a point approximately a hundred feet from the barrier.

The patrolman returned to his idling bike, mounted, swung the bars, drove swiftly to the lead limousine, and spoke excitedly to those inside.

The rear door opened; a priest in a black cassock got out. He and the patrolman walked back toward the barrier, their attention on the sloping road down the Appian hill.

There was rapid, indistinguishable chatter between them; and then a series of gestures that conveyed only indecision. The priest turned, picked up the cloth of his cassock, and trotted back past the lead car to the papal limousine.

Captain Noir could not see too well, but the slight Appian breeze carried the sounds of more excited chatter. Noir swallowed and gripped the high-frequency whistle in his hand.

Then to his great relief he heard laughter. And the priest returned to the lead car, nodded his head, gesturing to the left at the patrolman, and climbed back into the limousine.

An adventurous decision had just been made; the general knew his enemy.

The motorcade turned left down the hill, led by the patrolman. All the vehicles entered cautiously, at very slow speeds, and when the two rear motorcycles reached the first curve on the slope, Noir got out of the grass and raced to the barrier, pulling it across the opening of the detour. He ripped off the top sign revealing the second:

DINAMITE! FERMA! PERICOLO!

He had done it! By God, he'd done it! He had escaped from Machenfeld and was on his way to Rome, and if everything held firm, no one would know he was gone until morning! Then it would be too late! The Hawk would be on his way to Ground Zero!

There was no way they could know he was gone. Unless they broke down the door to his room, which was highly unlikely under the circumstances. Anne wasn't talking to him; she'd stamped off to her room in the south wing. He had provoked an argument that could be heard on the peaks of the Matterhorn, eliciting language from her she must have learned from her felonious family.

Rudolph and No Name wanted absolutely nothing to do with him. Especially proximity. After the battle with Anne he had proceeded to complain to his guards of sudden, agonizing pains in his groin. He had doubled up and screamed.

"Oh, Jesus! It's Kuwaiti encephalitis! I saw it in the Algerian desert five weeks ago! Oh, my God! I caught it! The testicles swell like basketballs, but heavier! I've got to have a doctor! Get me a doctor!"

"No doctor. No outside communications until the master of Machenfeld returns." Rudolph was stern.

"Then you better watch it!" Sam continued. "It's highly contagious!"

Whereupon he had fainted, clutching himself through the sweat pants. Panicked, No Name and Rudolph moved back swiftly against the wall in the drawing room. Revived but in agony, Sam crawled out of the room and up the staircase. To meet his Maker in peace, and with enormous testicles.

Rudolph and No Name stayed well behind until Sam reached his room and closed the door. When he opened the door for one last time—he saw that his guards were far down the hallway with double handkerchiefs tied around their faces, aerosol cans of disinfectant billowing clouds of spray around them.

The coast was clear! For a beautiful, foolproof exit from Machenfeld.

Lillian and two of the staff were driving the limousines to an airfield somewhere south. He'd overheard the Hawk explaining the route to Mrs. Hawkins number three; the trip was four hours long and it was vital that she position the vehicles on a road by the west highway of the airfield.

An airfield!

That meant airplanes! And airplanes flew to Rome! And even if they didn't—or wouldn't—there were telephones! And radios!

His new plan had jelled instantly. He would be inside the trunk of the second limousine, the one being driven by a member of the château staff. It had been a simple matter to jam the lock of the vehicle's trunk while he had been saying good-bye to Lillian, helping her with the suitcases.

As soon as his guards disappeared in the cloud of disinfectant, Sam tied three blankets together, scaled down to the ground from the balcony, raced to the limousine in the drive, and crawled into the trunk.

Once inside, he wrapped the blankets around his upper body, grateful he still had his sweat pants, and waited. He was counting on nature to provide him with a shortcut to his objective and he was not disappointed.

The limousines sped through the gate and the trip had

begun. After three and a half hours of bouncing, plunging, climbing, and racing through the Swiss mountains, Sam heard the rapid blasts of the limousine's horn. Within seconds there'd been a corresponding reply in the distance, from the lead automobile, and the car slowed down and stopped. The driver got out quickly. Devereaux could hear the footsteps outside the trunk. And then he'd heard the unmistakable muted splashing.

He opened the trunk, climbed silently out, and hit the urinating Swiss with a jack handle.

Before a half minute had passed, Devereaux had removed the man's trousers, jacket, shirt, and shoes. Pulling on the trousers and the jacket—enough to obscure him in the night darkness—he had raced around to the door and leaped into the driver's seat, tapping the horn twice as a signal to resume the trip.

Lillian honked back, and started off immediately.

The airfield at Valtournanche (that's what the sign had said) did present a minor problem, but it was more than compensated for by the extraordinary sum of money Sam found in the jacket he had taken from the Swiss. Five thousand dollars, American! The Hawk must have given the staff member a bonus!

It automatically gave birth to another, incredible plan! A magnificent finale!

He could stop the Hawk without the police! Without the authorities! Stop him cold, dismantle Ground Zero and disperse the brigade all at the same time! With no firing squads or hangmen or life imprisonment in the offing! It was perfect. Beyond error.

There was a curve in the road on the west border of the airfield. Sam slowed his limousine, and the instant Lillian's vehicle rounded the turn, he stopped the car, turned off the ignition, grabbed the shirt and the shoes, jumped out, and raced into the woods.

He waited in the darkness for the inevitable. Lillian's automobile could be heard in reverse gear. She and her escort got out and ran back to the abandoned second car.

"Isn't that the limit!" Lillian was angry. "The ungrateful worm chickened out at the last moment! And after Mac gave him all that money. Well, it doesn't surprise me. His neck

muscles had no tone; it's always a sign of weakness. Come on! Get in! We're almost there."

An hour later Devereaux, dressed in a leather jacket and baggy trousers oddly too large for his frame, was counting out $2,500 to a stunned pilot in a Valtournanche hangar, the fee for a rushed, unscheduled flight to Rome. Sam had chosen a man quite a bit smaller than himself, with no apparent muscle tone whatsoever. Pilots who took this kind of employment were not generally considered to be of the highest moral character. He didn't care to be rolled and dropped off into an Alpine mountain pass.

But he had made it! They were airborne! They'd reach Rome well before dawn. And then he, Sam Devereaux, the finest young attorney in Boston, would deliver the best summation of his career.

Captains Gris and Bleu, dressed in tight-fitting police uniforms, stood erect and motionless behind the trunks of two Appian maples on opposite sides of the winding road—motionless except for their right hands, which they flexed at their sides, thumbs caressing the short hollow needles that protruded from the inverted rings.

As the commander had predicted, the two motorcycles at either side of the papal limousine had dropped back and now rode parallel in front of the bikes flanking the rear. And again, as the commander had projected, the noise was deafening.

One by one the vehicles passed. As the final two patrolmen came between the two maple trees, Gris and Bleu leaped out, hammerlocked both men with their left arms, and each plunged a small needle into his man's neck.

Within seconds the patrolmen were limp.

Gris and Bleu lowered the motorcycles between their legs and dragged each body off into the underbrush. Together they entered the woods and raced diagonally downhill through the tangled foliage to position themselves for their next assignment. Secreted in these positions were the cassocks they would slip over their uniforms.

Captains Orange and Vert lay on their stomachs across from one another hidden by the tall weeds. Their posts were at the start of the second curve on the descending side road. Through the dense reeds they saw—and smiled as they did so—that the two final motorcycles failed to appear. The other team of patrolmen struggled to keep their bikes upright, riding behind the second limousine.

Captain Orange crossed himself as the pontiff's vehicle passed.

Captain Vert spat. It was long past time for the Church to install a *French* pope; the Italians were pigs about that.

The papal car turned into the final downhill curve. Orange and Vert sprang up and out and executed the practiced maneuvers with lightning-swift dispatch against the motorcycle escorts.

The patrolmen collapsed; the papal limousine was entering the turn at the base of the Appian hill. There were only seconds remaining before the detonations of Phase Four, the smoke bombs from the overturned Fiat. Orange and Vert ran to their next assignments—the most prestigious of all: Phase Seven. Phases Five and Six, the destruction of the communications equipment and the sedation of the papal entourage, would be occurring any second.

Phase Seven was the zenith of Ground Zero: the exchange of the popes. Guido Frescobaldi for Giovanni Bombalini.

The explosions from the Fiat were positively frightening; the screams of the hysterical Turks terrifying. The Hawk grinned in appreciation. *Goddamn!* What a beautiful sight! All that smoke and noise and—well, the screams were overdone.

The motorcade stopped in shock, agitated voices swelling. One motorcycle and two limousines in an isolated back country road bordered by a steep hill on the south side and a tall, thick forest on the north.

Optimum, observed the Hawk, holding a weaving Guido Frescobaldi in the bushes.

Captain Noir reached his post and signaled Captains Rouge and Brun; they were strung out at ten-yard intervals, prepared for the moment to implement Phase Five: the destruction of all communications equipment.

It came.

The single Vatican policeman jumped off his motorcycle and ran toward the smoking Fiat with the trapped, screaming passengers. Every door of both limousines was swung open. The drivers and the priests screamed and waved their hands and shouted orders at everyone and no one, then ran toward the overturned car.

Now!

Dressed as priests, Noir, Rouge, and Brun dashed from their hidden recesses. Brun and Rouge plunged into the front seat of the first limousine, ripping out every wire in sight. Noir raced to the second automobile, the papal car, and dove through the open door toward the equipment.

Suddenly a hand lashed out over the seat, followed by an arm extending from a white cassock. But the hand and the arm were not white. They were *black*!

And the grip that held Noir's neck—accompanied by the swift, hard rabbit punches that hammered his head—was a street tactic Noir knew well. It was indigenous to a plot of turf called Harlem!

Noir wrenched his aching, pounding head and was suddenly, astoundingly, face to face with a brother!

A *brother* in the honkey white robes of the Church!

It went against Noir's grain to coldcock a brother, but there was nothing for it. The Catholic kid was good, but he hadn't taken advanced training above 138th Street and Amsterdam. Noir twisted his thumb and forefinger into the sensitive flesh; the Black priest screamed and released Noir's head as Noir yanked him halfway over the seat. He sighed as he chopped the Catholic kid at the base of the skull. He immediately went about his business, ripping wires and smashing dials. The fat old honkey in white robes—the *man*, himself, figured Noir—leaned forward and pulled the kid into the back seat, cradling the kid's head as if the kid was really hurt.

"He'll be okay, pops. I don't know how you boys do it. I *swear* I don't! The Baptists got his turf tied up in ribbons. They've got *rhythm*! Course, you've got the cops. . . ."

Son of a bitch! What the hell else could go wrong? What other delays were concealed in the blinding sunlight of Rome's Leonardo da Vinci Airport? It was a nightmare being played out in the bright morning without benefit of sleep!

The goddamned, dwarf son of a bitch of a pilot from Valtournanche insisted that his aircraft be cleared by the narcotic inspectors! Nobody gave a damn if a plane flew in six vaults of stolen gold, or undeclared diamonds, or eyes-only defense plans for all of NATO, as long as there wasn't a joint on board! No amount of protesting on Sam's part made any difference whatsoever—Well, yes it did. It caused him to be stripped and searched.

"Per favore, signore. Where is your underwear? Where did you leave it?—Search the plane again!"

"That's crazy!" screamed Devereaux. "How could a pair of shorts——"

"Che cosa?" inquired the capitano suspiciously.

"Shorts!" Sam outlined a pair of briefs. "Where could I hide . . ."

"Ah haaa," interrupted the capitano. "The mountain Swiss wear long underwear. With pockets. And flaps. And many buttons. Buttons are hollow."

"I'm not Swiss! I'm American!"

The capitano's eyebrows shot up as he lowered his voice. "Ah haaa——Mafia, signore?"

And so it went until Sam had dispensed ten one-hundred-dollar American bills, which happened to coincide with the end of the capitano's shift, whereupon Sam was released.

"Where can I get a taxi?"

"Have your money exchanged first, signore. No taxi has change for American one-hundred-dollar bills."

"I don't have any hundreds left. Only five hundreds."

"Then they will call the police. For certainly such money cannot possibly be authentic. You will need lire."

Oh, my God, the police! thought Sam. *The police and hysterical taxi drivers were the last thing he wanted. They definitely were not part of hs grand finale to thwart the Hawk.*

And so he spent the better part of an hour in the

exchange line only to be told by the lady with a moustache that bills of such denominations had to be examined by spectographs.

"Thank you, signore," said the face of fur finally. "We have processed these under four different machines. They are very nice. Here is your lire. Do you have an empty suitcase?"

It was 9:45. Still time! A taxi into Rome took about an hour when one considered the traffic, and then perhaps a half hour to get to the southern outskirts where he could pick up the Via Appia.

The ride down the Appia couldn't be more than twenty minutes or so. He would recognize the signs he had seen during maneuvers, he was sure of that. He'd reach Ground Zero with at least a half hour to spare!

He'd stop the Hawk, prevent World War III, eliminate the specter of life imprisonment, and go home to Boston with a real Swiss bank account!

Goddamn! If he had two cigars, he'd smoke them both at the same time!

He ran across the terminal to the doors under the signs that read Taxi in three languages. He raced breathlessly onto the concrete.

Up and down the whole area were hundreds of immobile dollies filled with luggage. Groups of men were gathered in the street, close to riot.

Sam approached a tourist. "What's going on?"

"Goldanged guinea bastards called a cab strike!" Sam backed away. He had several million lire stuffed in his pockets like football pads. There had to be somebody in one of the parking lots with an automobile.

He found him. At twenty minutes past eleven. And offered money. The faster he drove the more thousands of lire he would get. The man agreed.

11:32! He would make it!

He had to!

It was the summation of his life!

Why was he kidding himself? It was his life.

Gris and Bleu pulled at the clerical ropes around their cassocks. They were on their knees, concealed by the

269

dense underbrush and cascading branches at the base of the hill by the edge of the old road. Both were prepared to spring through the foliage to execute Phase Six, the immobilization of the motorcade. The overturned Fiat was directly in front of them, the smoke billowing everywhere, the five papal aides, the two chauffeurs and the remaining patrolman all making genuine attempts to reach the screaming Turks.

The numbers presented no problem. Once Gris and Bleu joined the smoke-engulfed melee, they would work swiftly, their church habits adding to the confusion. It would be a simple matter to incapacitate one adversary, then another. Rouge would join them on the west flank, intercepting anyone who might discover the conspiracy prematurely, and make a dash for the limousines.

Now!

Gris and Bleu lunged out of the brush into the confusion of smoke, screams, and flailing arms, their wide cassocks billowing, rings at the ready.

One by one the members of the papal entourage collapsed to the ground, beatific smiles on their peaceful faces.

"Tie them! Give me some cord!" yelled Gris to the Turks as the three "victims" crawled out of the windows and from under the car.

"Not tight, you maniacs!" added Bleu harshly. "Remember what the commander said!"

"Mon Dieu!" roared Bleu suddenly, grabbing Gris's shoulder, pointing to the ground beyond the rising smoke. *"Qu'est-ce que c'est ça?"*

In the middle of the road, halfway to the limousines, lay Rouge flat on his back, one arm raised, the wrist bent, as though frozen in mid-pirouette. The stocking mask could not disguise the expression of Olympian repose underneath. In the confusion, he had tripped over his cassock, plunging his needle into his stomach.

"Quick!" yelled Gris. "The antidote! The general thinks of everything!"

"He has to," said Bleu.

"Now!" ordered the Hark, holding Guido Frescobaldi, who had suddenly raised his voice in song.

Across the dirt road, Mac could see Orange crossing himself as he leaped out of the bushes toward the papal limousine. It was wasted motion, he thought; the pope was not going to attempt any escape. He had helped his aide down on the seat and was getting out of the car, his face wrathful.

The Hawk took Frescobaldi by the hand, and led him toward the limousine.

"I bid you good day, sir," said the Hawk to the pope. It was a proper military salutation for a surrender.

"Animale!" roared the pontiff in a roll of thunder that reverberated throughout the Appian forests and hills. *"Uccisore! Assassino!"*

"What's that?"

"Basta!" The thunder cracked again. And the lightning was in Francesco's eyes; the eyes of a giant in the body of a mortal. "Take my life! You kill my beloved children! The children of God! You slay the *innocenti*! Send me to Jesus! Kill me, too! And may God have mercy on your soul!"

"Oh, for Chri——for heaven's sake, shut up! Nobody's going to kill anybody."

"I see what I see! The children of God are slain!"

"That's plain horseshit! Nobody's hurt, and nobody's going to get hurt."

"They are all *morto*," said Francesco, with less conviction, his eyes darting everywhere in bewilderment.

"No more than you are. We wouldn't be tying them up if they were, would we? Orange! Over here!"

"Sí, Generale." Orange came around the hood of the limousine, crossing himself repeatedly.

"Get that colored boy out of the car. Must be a house guest of the pope here."

"That man is a *priest*. My personal aide!"

"You don't say? Must be a fine lad with the choirs. Easy, Orange," said MacKenzie as the Italian pulled the unconscious Black prelate from the automobile. "Put him in the brush and loosen that big robe. It's too damn hot for ponchos."

"You mean," asked Giovanni incredulously, "they're all alive?"

"Certainly, they're alive," replied MacKenzie, signaling

Vert to prepare Frescobaldi for the exchange; the pope's double sat serene.

"I don't believe you! You've murdered them!" roared the pope suddenly.

"Will you keep quiet!" The Hawk did not ask a question. "Listen to me. I don't know how you handle your command, but I assume you can tell if a soldier's alive or not."

"Che cosa? . . ."

"Captain Gris!" yelled MacKenzie to the masked Scandinavian tying up a priest by the hubcaps of the first limousine. "Lift that man up and bring him here, please."

Gris complied. MacKenzie took the pontiff's right hand.

"Here! Put your fingers on the side of the throat next to the collar bone. Now, see? Do you get pulse?"

The pope's eyes narrowed, his concentration on the touch. "The heart—. Yes. You speak the truth. The others? They are the same? The hearts beat?"

"I gave you my word," said the Hawk sternly. "I must reprimand you, sir. Opposing commands do not lie when capture is secure. We're not animals, sir. But we haven't much time." The Hawk gestured for Vert to bring over the narcotized Frescobaldi. "I'm afraid we'll have to change some of your clothes. I'll have to——"

MacKenzie stopped. Pope Francesco was staring at Frescobaldi. It was the first moment he had taken cognizance of the singer who was clean shaven and now, without his moustache, looked more like Giovanni Bombalini than did Bombalini himself.

"Guido! It is Guido Frescobaldi!" The pontiff's voice could have been heard in the Bay of Naples, so loud was his roar. "Guido, my own flesh! My blood! It is Guido! *Madre di Dio!* You are a part of this—this heresy?!"

Signore Guido Frescobaldi smiled.

"Che gelida . . . manina . . . a rigido esanime . . . ah, la-la . . . la-laaa . . . ."

"It's him, all right, but he's been a little out of things since this morning. And will be for a while longer. Come on, now. We've got to get some of that hardware off you and on him. Captain Orange? Captain Vert? Give Mr. Francesco a hand."

"There!" The Hawk spoke in the tones of a victorious general officer. He held the grinning Guido Frescobaldi by the shoulders, admiring the final result. "He looks real fine, doesn't he?"

Francesco, transfixed, could not help himself. *"Jesus et Spiritus Sanctus.* The ugly Frescobaldi is myself. It is a miracle of God."

"Two like-spits in the gunnery pool, Mr. Pope!"

The pontiff was barely audible. "You put . . . Frescobaldi . . . in the *chair* of St. Peter?"

"For about two hours with luck—by my calculations."

"But *why?*"

"Nothing personal. I understand you're a very nice fellow."

"But why? In the name of God, *why?* That is no answer."

"Didn't expect it to be," replied the Hawk. "I just don't want you screaming your head off. You've got a mighty loud voice."

"Then I shall be—screaming my head out—if you do not tell me. . . . Aiyeeeee! . . ."

"All right! All *right!* We're kidnapping you. Holding you for ransom. You'll be fine; no harm will come to you and that's the word of a general officer."

The conference was interrupted by Captain Gris and Bleu, who raced up and snapped to attention.

"The area is secured, General," barked Gris.

"All sedations are completed," added Bleu. "We are prepared to move."

"Good! Let's move then. *Troops!* Evacuate the area! Prepare to execute escape procedures! By your numbers! *Move!*"

As if on cue, the sounds of the revving helicopter could be heard from the camouflaged area fifty yards away from the center of Ground Zero.

And then there was another sound. From the road at the top of the Appian hill: A car screeching to a halt.

"Stop!" came a plaintive wail from the woods. "For Christ's sake, *stop!*"

"What?"

"Mon Dieu!"

"Che cosa?!"
"I say!"
"Tokig!"
"Bakasi!"
"Shit!"

Sam stumbled down the old dirt road on the hill. He came racing around the last curve and fell to one knee.

Giovanni Bombalini watched in astonishment; automatically he gave the kneeling figure his rather confused benediction, *"Deus et figlio—"*

"Will you shut up!" MacKenzie glared at Francesco. *"Goddamn,* Sam! What the hell are you doing here? You're supposed to be sick as a *dog——"*

"Listen to me, everybody!" broke in Sam. "Everyone gather around!" He struggled to his feet; the captains stood where they were, their faces betraying a certain insensitivity. "Escape! Run for your lives! Leave this man alone! It's a trap! Machenfeld has fallen! It happened last night! Hundreds of Interpol police are swarming..." Sam's jaw was suddenly a gaping orifice as he stared at the Hawk. *"What did you say?"*

"You're a real pistol, son. I respect your moxie, like I said before. But I can't say you have much respect for my know-how." MacKenzie snapped one of the straps that crisscrossed his chest over his field jacket. It was attached to a large leather case that was lashed over his hip. "No assault operation ever stays out of contact with its command center. Not since 1971, anyway. Hell, I used to patch relays from Ly Sol in Cambodia right straght down to the Mekong units."

"What?"

"Tri-arced, high-frequency radio contact, boy. Set a schedule and receive-send simultaneously. You're *dated,* Sam! As of an hour ago the only thing swarming around Machenfeld were butterflies. I don't know how you did it, but you're mighty lucky you got here alone.... Come to think of it, you'd be a damned fool to get here any other way. —All right, men! Resume Phase Eight! —Come on, Sam. You're going for a ride. And I tell you this now, boy. Any more trouble and I'm going to open a door at two thousand feet and you can fly by yourself!"

274

"Mac, you can't! Think of World War *Three!*"

"Think of a nice free-fall—without a parachute—straight into a plate of spaghetti!"

And then there was another sound. A frightening one. From the top of the hill. From the road again.

The captains and the Turks froze.

The Hawk whipped his head around—and up—toward the Via Appia.

The pontiff said one word.

"Carabinieri."

The whining, jarring, two-note scream of the Italian state police sirens could be heard in the distance. Drawing nearer.

"Goddamn! How?! What the hell happened? Sam, you didn't!"

"My God, *no!* I didn't! I *wouldn't!*"

"I think there is a—miscalculation, signore," said Pope Francesco softly.

"What? What mother—what miscalculation?"

"The motorcade was to stop at the small village—well, not so *much* a village—of Tuscabondo. It is a mile or so past the *deviazone*, your detour."

"Jesus!"

"He can be merciful, Signore Generale."

"Those bastards will be swarming the hills, the fields. Goddamn!"

"And the air, Generale," said Captain Orange excitedly, breaking out in a sweat under his mask. "The *carabinieri* have fleets of *elicotteri*. They are the *pazzi* of the sky!"

"Jesus H. Christ!"

*"Figlio di Santa Maria—Figlio di Dio—*He is the way, Generale."

"I told you to shut up. *Men!* Check your maps! Quickly! Gris and Bleu, evaluate escape routes E-Eight and E-Twelve. Our previous routes were faster but more exposed. Deliver your decision in one minute! Orange and Vert. Give me Frescobaldi! Join the others! Sam, you stay here!"

The screams of the sirens were nearer, almost at the intercept point of the Appia. Frescobaldi, weaving in MacKenzie's grip, sang louder.

275

"Signore." Giovanni Bombalini took a step toward Mac-Kenzie. "You speak of the word of a general. You have great sincerity when you say it."

"What? Yes, of course. You're not much different, I suspect. Command's a big responsibility."

"Indeed it is. And truth is responsibility's right arm." The pope looked once more at the unconscious figures of his motorcade, each body comfortably stretched out, none harmed. "And compassion, naturally."

The Hawk was barely listening. He was holding Frescobaldi, keeping an alert eye on a stunned Sam Devereaux, and watching Captains Gris and Bleu make their final evaluations over the maps. "What are you talking about?"

"You say you have no wish to inflict harm on my person."

"Of course not. Wouldn't get much ransom for a corpse. Well, maybe with *your* people———"

"And Frescobaldi is as strong as an ox," said the pope, as much to himself as to MacKenzie, while studying the half-conscious Guido. "He always was. Signore Generale, if I said I would go with you without interference, perhaps even in the spirit of cooperation, would you grant me a small request? As one commander to another?"

The Hawk squinted at the pontiff.

"What is it?"

"A brief note, only several words—in English—to be left with my aide. I would want you to read it, of course."

MacKenzie took out a combat pad from his field jacket, ripped off a page, unclipped the waterproof pencil and handed both to Francesco. "You've got fifteen seconds."

The pope put the paper against the limousine and wrote swiftly. He gave the page back to the Hawk.

I am safe. With God's blessing I shall reach you as the chess-playing O'Gilligan reaches me.

Honkey

"If it's a code, it's pretty piss-poor. Go ahead, put it in the colored fella's pocket. I like that part that says you're safe."

276

Giovanni ran to the figure of his papal aide, stuffed the note under his cassock and returned to the Hawk. "Now, Signore Generale, you waste time."

"What?"

"Put Frescobaldi in the limousine! Hurry! Inside is a briefcase. With my pills. Get it, please."

"*What?*"

"You would last five minutes in the Curia! Where is the *elicottero?*"

"The copter?"

"Yes."

"Over there. In a clearing."

Captain Gris and Bleu had completed their swift conference. Gris called out. "We have briefed the men, General. We go! We meet at Zaragolo!"

"*Zaragolo!*" said the pontiff. "The airport at Monti Prenestini?"

"Yes," answered the Hawk, staring with sudden concentration on Pope Francesco. "What about it?"

"Tell them to stay north of Rocco Priora! There are battalions of police in Rocca Priora."

"That's east of Frascati——"

"Yes!"

"You heard him, Captains! Outflank Rocco Priora! *Now, scramble!*" roared the Hawk.

"*No!*" screamed Sam, backing away on the road, looking up at the hill. "Everybody's crazy! You're out of your minds! I'm going to stop you. All of you!"

"Young man!" Giovanni stood erect and addressed Sam pontifically. "Will you please be quiet and do as the general says?!"

Noir emerged from the clearing. "The bird's ready, General! We've got a clean lift-off area."

"We've also got an extra passenger. Get the counselor, Captain. You might show him a needle, if you can manage it."

"With real pleasure," said Noir.

"One dosage, Captain!"

"Shit!"

And so Giovanni Bombalini, the Holy Father of the Catholic Church, and MacKenzie Hawkins, two-time winner of the Congressional Medal of Honor, put Guido Frescobaldi into the papal limousine and ran like hell through the Appian forest to the helicopter.

It was difficult for Francesco. The pontiff swore mildly at Sebastian, the patron saint of athletes, and finally in desperation pulled up the skirts of his habit, displaying rather thick peasant legs, and damn near beat MacKenzie to the aircraft.

The Lear jet soared above Zaragolo's cloud cover, Captain Noir at the controls, Captain Rouge in the co-pilot's seat. The Hawk and the pope sat in the forward section, across from one another, each by a window.

Bewildered, MacKenzie glanced over at Francesco. He knew from long years of experience that when command was stymied, the best thing to do was to do nothing, unless the combat at hand required immediate counterstrike.

Such was not the case now. The problem was that Francesco did not behave like any enemy the Hawk had ever fought.

Goddamn!

There he sat, his heavy robes unbuttoned down to his undershirt, his shoes off, and his hands folded casually across his wide girth, looking out the Lear's window like some kind of happy delicatessen proprietor on his first airplane ride. It was amazing. And confusing.

Goddamn!

Why?

MacKenzie realized that there was no point in wearing his stocking mask any longer. The others had to, for their own protection, but for him it made no difference.

He removed it with a grateful sigh. Francesco looked over at him, not unpleasantly. The pope nodded his head, as if to say, Nice to meet you face to face.

Goddamn!

MacKenzie reached into his pocket for a cigar. He lifted one out, bit off the end, and pulled out a book of matches.

"*Per favore?*" Francesco was leaning toward him.

"What?"

"A cigar, Signore Generale. For me. Do you mind?"

278

"Oh, no, not at all. Here you are." Hawkins extracted a second cigar from the pack and handed it to the pontiff. And then, as an afterthought, reached into his other pocket for the clipper.

But it was too late.

Francesco had bitten off the end, spat it out—somehow without offense—taken the matches from Mac's hand, and struck one.

Pope Francesco, the Vicar of Christ, lighted up. And as the circles of aromatic smoke rose above his head, the pontiff sat back in the seat, crossed his legs under his habit, and enjoyed the scenery below.

"*Grazie*," Francesco said.

"*Prego*," replied MacKenzie.

PART

IV

The ultimate success of any corporation is dependent upon its major product or service. It is imperative that the projected consumer be convinced through aggressive public relations techniques that the product, or service, is essential—to his very existence, if possible.

Shepherd's Laws of Economics:
Book CCCXXI, Chapter 173

CHAPTER TWENTY-FOUR

Sam sat in the cushioned, wrought iron chair at the northwest corner of the Machenfeld gardens. Anne had picked the spot after careful deliberation; it was the area of the gardens that provided the best view of the Matterhorn whose peak could be seen in the distance.

It had been three weeks now since the awful thing: Ground Zero.

The captains and the Turks had departed—for unknown parts of the world, never to be heard from again. The staff had been reduced to one cook, who helped Anne and Sam with the housecleaning and the gardens. MacKenzie was not very good at either chore, but he did take turns driving into the village for the newspapers. Too, he checked daily with the high-priced doctor he had flown in from New York, just in case. The doctor, a specialist in internal medicine, had no idea why he was being paid such extraordinary sums of money to do absolutely nothing but live lavishly in a lakeside residence, and so in the spirit of the AMA he accepted the unreported cash and did not complain.

Francesco (Sam could not bring himself to say pope) had settled comfortably into the sealed-off top-floor apartments and could be seen daily walking on the ramparts through his rooftop gardens.

MacKenzie had really done it! He had won the biggest military objective of his career.

And he was currently, through a convoluted series of extraordinarily complex, untraceable conduits, making his ransom demands of the Vatican. Ultrahigh-frequency radio codes arcing from the Alps to Beirut to Algiers; relayed by desert and ocean towers from Marseilles, to Paris, to Milan, and on to Rome.

According to the schedules he had imposed, the Vatican reply was to be radioed out of Rome and relayed from Beirut by 5 P.M.

MacKenzie had left Machenfeld to drive to the isolated transmission center—a lone cabin high in the upper Alps, in which was installed the finest, most sophisticated radio equipment obtainable. It had been delivered to Machenfeld by Les Château Suisse but put into operation by the Hawk himself. No one but MacKenzie knew the location of the mountain retreat.

Oh, my God! Five o'clock this afternoon! Sam forced his thoughts away from the awful thing.

There was movement up at the château. Anne had walked out the terrace door carrying the usual large, glossy picture book under her arm and a silver tray with glasses on it in her hands. She started across the lawn to the gardens. Her walk was firm, feminine; a graceful, natural dancer oblivious to the subtle rhythms inherent in her grace. Her light brown hair fell casually, framing the clear pink skin of her lovely face. Her wide, bright blue eyes reflected whatever light they faced.

He had learned something from all the girls, thought Devereaux. Something different and individually their own—gifts to him. And if a normal life was ever to return, he would be grateful for their gifts.

But perhaps he had learned the most important thing from Anne: Try for improvement—but don't deny what's past.

There was laughter on the lawn. Anne was looking up at the ramparts where Francesco, dressed in a colorful ski sweater, was leaning over the parapet.

It had become their private game, Anne's and Francesco's. Whenever the Hawk was out of sight they held conversations. And Sam was sure—because Anne would not deny it—that she had made numerous trips up to his private apartments bringing him glasses of chianti, which was specifically forbidden from his diet. Anne and Francesco had become good friends.

Several minutes later that judgment was confirmed. Anne placed the silver tray with the drinks on the table next to Sam. Her eyes were smiling.

"Did you know, Sam, that Jesus was a very practical, down-to-earth person. When he washed Mary Magdalene's feet, he was letting everybody know she was a human being. Maybe a very fine one, in spite of what she used to do. And that people shouldn't throw rocks at her because maybe their feet weren't so clean, either."

MacKenzie climbed the final precipice by means of an Alpine hook. The last two hundred yards of the spiraling summit road were too deep with mountain snow for the motorcycle, so it was faster to make the final ascent directly. It was eleven minutes to five, Zurich time.

The signals would commence in eleven minutes. From Beirut. They would be repeated after an interval of five minutes, to double-check for decoding errors. At the end of the second series he would confirm reception by transmitting the air-clearance code to the relay in Beirut: four dashes, repeated twice.

Once inside, the Hawk started the generators and watched with satisfaction as the myriad wheels spun with a smooth whirring sound within the casing, and the dials began registering *output*.

When the two green lights went on, signifying maximum performance, he plugged in the single electric heater, feeling the warmth of the glowing coils. He reached over to the powerful shortwave equipment, flipped on the receiving switches and turned the amplifier spools to high volume. Three minutes to go.

He walked to the wall. Slowly he began to turn a handle, hearing the gears mesh. Outside, beyond the iron grillwork of the tiny window, he could see a webbed disc swing out and up on its track.

He returned to the radio receiving panel and revolved the parallel megacycle and tetracycle dials with delicate precision. The voices of a dozen languages emerged from the amplifiers. When the needles were in the exact parallel cycle points there was silence. One minute to go.

MacKenzie took out a cigar from his pocket and lighted up. He inhaled with real contentment and blew out the smoke in ring after ring.

Suddenly the signals were there. Four short, high-pitched dashes; repeated once. The channel was cleared.

He picked up a pencil, his hand poised above a page of notepaper, prepared to write out the code as it was beamed from Beirut.

The message terminated, the Hawk had five minutes to decode. To convert the signals into numbers, then transfer the numbers into letters and the letters into words.

When he had finished, he stared in disbelief at the Vatican reply.

It was impossible!

Obviously, he had made several errors in receiving the Beirut transmission.

The signals began again.

The Hawk started writing on a fresh page of notepaper.

Carefully.

Precisely.

The transmission ended as it began: four dashes, repeated once.

MacKenzie put the decoding schedule in front of him. He believed he had memorized it thoroughly, but this was no time to make a mistake. He cross-checked every dot, every dash.

Every word.

There were no errors.

The unbelievable had happened.

Relative to the insane request regarding the contribution of four hundred million American dollars, by assessing worldwide dioceses on the basis of one dollar per communicant, the treasury of the Holy See is in no position to consider such a request. Or any request at all for this particular charity. The Holy Father is in excellent health and sends his blessings in the name of the Father, the Son, and the Holy Spirit.

> Ignatio Quartze,
> Cardinal Omnipitum,
> Keeper of the Vatican Treasury

The Shepherd Company suspended operations.

MacKenzie Hawkins walked the grounds of Château Machenfeld, smoking his cigars, staring blankly at the infinite beauty of the Alps.

Sam made an accounting of the corporation's monetary assets, exclusive of the properties and equipment. Of the original capitalization of $40,000,000, there remained $12,810,431.02.

Plus a contingency expense fund of $150,000, which had not been touched.

Not bad at all. Especially since the investors, to a panicked vulture, refused reimbursement. They wanted nothing whatsoever to do with the Shepherd Company or any of its management personnel. None would even bother to file for tax losses as long as Shepherd's corporate executives promised—on the Bible, *Burke's Peerage, Mein Kampf,* and the Koran—never to get in touch with him again.

And Francesco, now sporting a Tyrolean hat along with his favorite ski sweater, was allowed out of the top-floor apartments. For the sake of everybody's sanity, it was agreed to refer to him as Zio Francesco, somebody's uncle.

Since he showed no inclination to go anywhere or do anything other than enjoy the company, Zio Francesco roamed freely. There was someone always nearby, but not to prevent escape; for assistance. He was, after all, in his seventies.

The cook was especially taken with him, for he spent long periods in the kitchen, helping with the sauces, and every once in a while asking permission to fix a particular dish.

He made one request of the Hawk. The Hawk refused it.

No! Absolutely no! Zio could not telephone his apartment in the Vatican! It made no difference whatsoever that his telephone was private or unlisted *or* concealed in the drawer of his bedside table! Telephone calls could be traced.

Not if they were radioed, insisted Francesco. The Hawk had impressed them all, frequently, by telling them about his complicated methods of communicating with Rome. Of course, a simple telephone call would not have to be nearly so complex. One little relay, perhaps.

No! All that spaghetti had gone to Zio's head. His brain was soft.

The Hawk's was softer, perhaps, suggested Francesco. What progress was the general making? Were not matters at a stalemate? Had not Cardinal Quartze outflanked him?

How could a telephone call change that?

How could it make things any worse? persisted Francesco. The Hawk could be at the radio, his hand on a switch, prepared to break the connection should Zio say anything improper. Was it not more advantageous to the general for at least two people to know he was alive? That the deception was *truly* a deception? There certainly was nothing to lose, for the Hawk had already lost. And possibly there was something to gain. Perhaps four hundred million American dollars.

Besides, Guido needed help. This was no criticism of his cousin, who was not only strong as a bull but a most gentle and thoughtful person. But he was new at the job and would certainly listen to his cousin Giovanni Bombalini. Helped, of course, by Giovanni's personal aide, the young American priest from Harlem.

The situation might *not* be remedied overnight— for there were matters of health and logistics to be considered. But when all was said and done, what alternative did the Hawk *have*?

He obviously had none. And so MacKenzie came down from the Alpine cabin one afternoon carrying three canvas-wrapped cartons of radio equipment and proceeded to install the instruments in a Machenfeld bedroom.

When all was completed, the Hawk issued an irrevocable command. Only he and Zio Francesco were allowed inside during radio transmissions.

That was fine with Anne and Sam. They had no desire to be there. The cook thought everybody was crazy and went back to the kitchen.

And at least twice a week from then on—very late at night—the huge disk antenna was wheeled out and raised above the battlements. Neither Sam nor Anne knew what was being said or whether anything was being accomplished, but often when they sat in the gardens to talk and look at the glorious Swiss moon, they heard great peals of laughter from the upstairs room. The Hawk and the pope were like small boys thoroughly enjoying a new game.

A secret game, played in their personal clubhouse.

Sam sat in the garden absently looking at his copy of the London *Times*. Life at Château Machenfeld had become routinized. For instance, every morning one of them would drive into the village to pick up the newspapers. Coffee in the gardens with the newspapers was a wonderful way to start the day. The world was such an unholy mess; life was so peaceful at Machenfeld.

The Hawk, having discovered the existence of riding trails on the property, purchased several fine horses and rode frequently, sometimes for hours at a time. He'd found something he'd been looking for, thought Sam.

Francesco discovered oil painting. He would trek over the fields in his Tyrolean hat with Anne or the cook, set up his easel and paints, and render for posterity his impressions of the Alpine splendors. That is, when he wasn't in the kitchen, or teaching Anne to play chess, or debating—always pleasantly—with Sam over points of law.

There was one thing about Francesco that nobody talked about, but all knew had something to do with his attitude. Francesco had not been a well man when he was taken out of the Appian hills. Not well at all. It was the reason Mac had insisted on the availability of the New York specialist.

But as the weeks went by, Francesco seemed to improve in the Alpine air.

Would it have been the same, otherwise?

No one, of course, would speculate, but Francesco had said something at dinner one evening that registered on them all.

"Those doctors. I shall outlive every one of them! They would have had me buried a month ago."

The Hawk responded with a coughing fit.

And Sam? What of him?

Whatever it was, he knew that it included Anne.

He looked at her now in the late morning sun, sitting in

289

the chair reading the newspaper, the ever present book on the table beside her. *A Pictorial History of Switzerland* was the title today.

She was so lovely, so gloriously—herself. She'd help him became a better lawyer, by making the law seem not so important.

Now he began to think about other things.

Like reading quietly. Understanding. Evaluating.

Like—Judge Devereaux.

Oh, Boston was going to like Anne! His mother would like her, too. And Aaron Pinkus. Aaron would approve wholeheartedly.

If Judge Devereaux ever got back to Boston.

He'd think about that—tomorrow.

"Sam?" said Anne, looking over at him.

"What?"

"Did you read this article in the *Tribune*?"

"What article? I haven't seen the *Tribune*."

"Here." She pointed but did not give him the paper. She was engrossed. "It's about the Catholic Church. All kinds of things. The pope has called a Fifth Ecumenical Council. And there's an announcement that a hundred and sixty-three opera companies are being subsidized, to elevate the spirit of creativity. And a famous cardinal—my God, Sam—it's that Ignatio Quartze! The one Mac yells about."

"What about him?"

"It seems he's retiring to some villa called San Vincente. Something to do with papal disputes over Vatican allocations. Isn't that strange?"

Devereaux was silent for several moments before he replied. "I think our friends have been very busy up on the ramparts."

In the distance were the sounds of galloping hooves. Seconds later MacKenzie Hawkins emerged on the dirt road from beyond the trees and the fields where only weeks ago maneuvers were held. He reined in his horse and trotted up to the northwest corner of the gardens.

"Goddamn! Isn't it a glorious day? You can see the peak of the Matterhorn!"

There was the music of a triangle coming from the other direction. MacKenzie waved; Devereaux and Anne turned and saw Francesco on the terrace outside the kitchen door, the triangle and the silver bar in his hands. He was dressed in a large apron, the Tyrolean hat firmly on his head.

Zio Francesco called out.

"Lunch, everybody! The *speciale di giorno* is *fantastico!*"

"I'm hungry as a horse!" roared back the Hawk as he patted his mount. "What've you got, Zio?"

Francesco raised his voice to the Alpine hills. And there was music in his words.

"My dear friends. It's *Linguini Bombalini!*"

EPILOGUE

MacKenzie Hawkins, pleasantly surfeited with Zio's linguini and the splendid *chianti classico* that Francesco had had his cousin, Frescobaldi, ship to the railroad station in Zermatt, wandered across the Alpine pasture to the edge of the field, its glorious view of the majestic mountains as always moving him. It was another ritual that had become part of his day. A few minutes alone, really alone, without even his horse beneath him, or the sound of human voices, only the rustle of the tall grass caressed by the gentle Alpine breezes. He needed these moments, for a man had to face both his accomplishments and his failures by himself, accepting the results without regret as long as he knew he had done his best with what was in him.

Regarding Zio, he had both lost and won. He had hardly reached the four hundred million dollars he envisioned, but what was left of the forty million capitalization wasn't exactly C rations. Yet he had won something else, something far more important, a restored, healthy, *vital* Pope Francesco I, the pontiff who wanted more than anything else to finish the job started by John XXIII. To blow the cobwebs out of the catacombs and bring his church into the twenty-first century, Zio would have to go back—without telling the others, they both had agreed to that—sometime soon, somehow. They could work it out. Somehow.

Well, that was just goddamned *fine* for Uncle Zio, but

what about *him*, what about the Hawk? What the hell was *he* supposed to do? Sit on his ass in edelweiss and let the world pass by while he *vegetated*?

"Find another cause, Mac, perhaps a somewhat more earthly one," Francesco had suggested. "The world abounds with them, and you have extraordinary talents, my son—"

"Cut the 'my son' crap, Zio."

"Sorry, it goes with the office. If I had so many 'sons,' I'd make an extraordinary mockery of celibacy—which I intend to bring up one day. It's really so unnatural, so foolish, and there's nothing explicit in the Scriptures."

"Maybe I should just keep you here so they don't hang you in St. Peter's Square."

"No, no, I must go back . . . But what about you, my friend? What *will* you do?"

The Hawk had not replied, for he had had no answer then. He thought about it now, gazing at the breathtaking skyline of the snow-capped Alps, when suddenly an eagle swooped down from some unseen high-altitude perch, in search of ground-bound prey that would sustain it.

An *eagle*. A lone eagle, soaring in splendor and splendid freedom, the master of the air and the earth, its wingspread incredible and mesmerizing. The magnificent bird circled in the winds, descending lower and lower, then abruptly dove with marvelous speed into a field far below. . . . Something *happened*! The eagle's massive wings were flapping furiously—it was caught, something had snared it, binding it to the ground! Then, after agonizing moments, the bird broke free, its movements frantic until it found the unencumbered air and soared aloft.

MacKenzie stared across at the would-be killing field, wondering what had caused the near tragedy. The answer came in seconds: Two men were racing out of a nearby cluster of brush, obviously angry that their decoyed trap had malfunctioned. They picked up the lethal animal-covered instrument, one man throwing it into the grass in disgust.

The incident brought back memories to the Hawk, images from long ago when he was a young officer posted to a Ranger training base somewhere in the hills of Nebraska or Iowa—or was it Kansas? No, it was Nebraska. The eagle itself was not the sole prodder of these memories, but the great bird was a large part of it, because of what it historically stood for in pictures and symbols, even in name. Full headdresses crowning the heads of once powerful chiefs, the single, double, and triple feathers earned by deeds of bravery performed by the young tribal males.

The American Indian.

There had been an Indian reservation perhaps twenty miles from the secret training base, certainly no secret to the Indians who pathetically came to beg whatever they could from the strapping, well-fed troops. So pathetic were these pilgrimages that many of the young Rangers, the Hawk among them, trekked over to the reservation to get a clearer understanding. It was a *disgrace*! These original inhabitants, the *owners* of the land, lived in abject poverty, scandalously shafted by the white invader! Naturally the Rangers stole the quartermaster bare, and until the soldiers left for scaling cliffs on D day, the Indians lived better than any of them could remember.

The *American Indian*—screwed by the same kind of pricky-shits who threw General MacKenzie Hawkins out of the army! That noble savage would be his *cause*! It might take months, even years, but *goddamn*, it was a quest worth serving.

The Hawk turned and raced back across the field, the tall grass whipped by his gathering speed. He saw Francesco by the vegetable garden, watering his precious herbs. "Zio, Zio, I've *got* it!"

"What have you got, my son—forgive me, I mean Mac?"

"I'm going to free our American Indians, I mean *really* set them *free*!"

"They are in *chains*?" asked the bewildered Francesco, his watering can drenching his lederhosen.

"Worse, they're in economic bondage, shafted by the white pricky-shits!"

"Sometimes you can be obtuse, MacKenzie—"

"Don't you *see*, Zio? It's my grail, my quest, my *cause*! Hell, it may take me a long time, maybe even a few years, but the right *shaftees* are there, I know it, I *feel* it!"

"May this humble country priest bless in advance those you would free from this bondage? . . . In the name of the Father, the Son, and the Holy Ghost, pray to your Maker, my children. The Hawk is on your horizon."

ABOUT THE AUTHOR

ROBERT LUDLUM is the author of seventeen novels published in nineteen languages and twenty-three countries with worldwide sales in excess of one hundred sixty million copies. His works include *The Scarlatti Inheritance*, *The Osterman Weekend*, *The Matlock Paper*, *The Rhinemann Exchange*, *The Gemini Contenders*, *The Chancellor Manuscript*, *The Road to Gandolfo*, *The Holcroft Covenant*, *The Matarese Circle*, *The Bourne Identity*, *The Parsifal Mosaic*, *The Aquitaine Progression*, *The Bourne Supremacy*, *The Icarus Agenda*, *Trevayne*, *The Bourne Ultimatum*, and *The Road to Omaha*. He lives with his wife, Mary, in Florida.

THE ROAD TO OMAHA
by
Robert Ludlum

Sam Devereaux and General MacKenzie Hawkins will cross paths again in Robert Ludlum's
hilarious new novel, *The Road to Omaha*, on
sale in hardcover from Random House in Feb-
ruary 1992. Here is a special preview of the
opening chapters.

The small, decrepit office on the top floor of the government building was from another era, which was to say nobody but the present occupant had used it in sixty-four years and eight months. It was not that there were dark secrets in its walls or malevolent ghosts from the past hovering below the shabby ceiling, quite simply, nobody *wanted* to use it. And another point should be made clear. It was not actually on the top floor, it was *above* the top floor, reached by a narrow wooden staircase, the kind the wives of New Bedford whalers climbed to prowl the balconies, hoping—most of the time—for familiar ships that signaled the return of their own particular Ahabs from the angry ocean.

In summer months the office was suffocating, as there was only one small window. During the winter it was freezing, as its wooden shell had no insulation and the window rattled incessantly, impervious to caulking, permitting the cold winds to whip inside as though invited. In essence, this room, this antiquated upper chamber with its sparse furniture purchased around the turn of the century, was the Siberia of the government agency in which it was housed. The last formal employee who toiled there was a discredited American Indian who had the temerity to learn to read English and suggested to his superiors, who themselves could barely read English, that certain restrictions placed on a reservation of the Navajo nation were too severe. It is said the man died in that upper office in the cold January of 1927 and was not discovered until the following May, when the weather was warm and the air suddenly scented. The government agency was, of course, the United States Bureau of Indian Affairs.

For the current occupant, however, the foregoing was not a deterrent but rather an incentive. The lone figure in the nondescript gray suit huddled over the rolltop desk, which wasn't much of a desk, as all its little drawers had been removed and the rolling top was stuck at half-mast, was General MacKenzie Hawkins, military legend, hero in three wars and twice winner of the Congressional Medal of Honor. This giant of a man, his lean muscular figure belying his elderly years, his steely eyes and tanned leather-lined face perhaps confirming a number of them, had once again gone into combat. However, for the first time in his life, he was not at war with the enemies of his beloved United States of America but with the government of the United States itself. Over something that took place a hundred and twelve years ago.

It didn't much matter when, he thought, as he squeaked around in his ancient swivel chair and propelled himself to an adjacent table piled high with old leather-bound ledgers and maps. They were the *same* pricky-shits who had screwed *him,* stripped him of his uniform, and put him out to military pasture! They were all the goddamned same, whether in their frilly frock coats of a hundred years ago or their piss-elegant, tight-assed pinstripes of today. They were *all* pricky-shits. Time did not matter, nailing them did!

The general pulled down the chain of a green-shaded, goose-necked lamp—circa early twenties—and studied a map, in his right hand a large magnifying glass. He then spun around to his dilapidated desk and reread the paragraph he had underlined in the ledger whose binding had split with age. His perpetually squinting eyes suddenly were wide and bright with excitement. He reached for the only instrument of communication he had at his disposal, since the installation of a telephone might reveal his more than scholarly presence at the Bureau. It was a small cone attached to a tube; he blew into it twice, the signal of emergency. He waited for a reply; it came over the primitive instrument thirty-eight seconds later.

"Mac?" said the rasping voice over the antediluvian connection.

"Heseltine, I've *got* it!"

"For Christ's sake, blow into this thing a little easier, will you? My secretary was here and I think she thought my dentures were whistling."

"She's out?"

"She's out," confirmed Heseltine Brokemichael, director of the Bureau of Indian Affairs. "What is it?"

"I just told you, I've *got* it?"

"Got what?"

"The biggest con job the pricky-shits ever *pulled,* the same pricky-shits who made us wear civvies, old buddy!"

"Oh, I'd love to get those bastards. Where did it happen and when?"

"In Nebraska. A hundred and twelve years ago."

Silence. Then:

"*Mac,* we weren't around then! Not even you!"

"It doesn't matter, Heseltine. It's the same horseshit. The same bastards who did it to *them* did it to you and me a hundred years later."

"Who's 'them'?"

"An offshoot of the Mowhawks called the Wopotami tribe. They migrated to the Nebraska territories in the middle 1800s."

"*So?*"

"It's time for the sealed archives, General Brokemichael."

"Don't *say* that! Nobody can *do* that!"

"You can, General. I need final confirmation, just a few loose ends to clear up."

"For *what*? *Why?*"

"Because the Wopotamis may still legally own all the land and air rights in and around Omaha, Nebraska."

"You're *crazy,* Mac! That's the Strategic Air Command!"

"Only a couple of missing items, buried fragments, and the facts are there. . . . I'll meet you in the cellars, at the vault to the archives, General Brokemichael. . . . Or should I call you co-chairman of the Joint Chiefs of Staff, along with me, Heseltine? If I'm right, and I know damn well I am, we've got the White House–Pentagon axis in such a bind, their collective tails won't be able to evacuate until we tell 'em to."

Silence. Then:

"I'll let you in, Mac, but then I fade until you tell me I've got my uniform back."

"Fair enough. Incidentally, I'm packing everything I've got here and taking it back to my place in Arlington. That poor son of a bitch who died up in this rat's nest and wasn't found until the perfume drifted down didn't die in vain!"

The two generals stalked through the metal shelves of the musty sealed archives, the dull, webbed lights so dim they relied on their flashlights. In the seventh aisle, Mackenzie Hawkins stopped, his beam on an ancient volume whose leather binding was cracked. "I think this is it, Heseltine."

"Good, and you can't take it out of here!"

"I understand that, General, so I'll merely take a few

photographs and return it." Hawkins removed a tiny spy camera with 110 film from his gray suit.

"How many rolls have you got?" asked former General Heseltine Brokemichael as MacKenzie carried the huge book to a steel table at the end of the aisle.

"Eight," replied Hawkins, opening the yellow-paged volume to the pages he needed.

"I have a couple of others, if you need them," said Heseltine. "Not that I'm so all fired-up by what you think you may have found, but if there's any way to get back at Ethelred, I'll *take* it!"

"I thought you two had made up," broke in MacKenzie, while turning pages and snapping pictures.

"*Never!*"

"It wasn't Ethelred's fault, it was that rotten lawyer in the Inspector General's office, a half-assed kid from Harvard named Devereaux, Sam Devereaux. He made the mistake, not Brokey the Deuce. Two Brokemichaels; he got 'em mixed up, that's all."

"Horseshit! Brokey-Two put the finger on *me!*"

"I think you're wrong, but that's not what I'm here for and neither are you. . . . Brokey, I need the volume next to or near this one. It should say CXII on the binding. Get it for me, will you?" As the head of Indian Affairs walked back into the metal stacks, the Hawk took a single-edged razor out of his pocket and sliced out fifteen successive pages of the archival ledger. Without folding the precious papers, he slipped them under his suit coat.

"I can't find it," said Brokemichael.

"Never mind, I've got what I need."

"What now, Mac?"

"A long time, Heseltine, maybe a long, long time, perhaps a year or so, but I've got to make it right—so right there's no holes, no holes at all."

"In what?"

"In a suit I'm going to file against the government of the United States," replied Hawkins, pulling a mutilated cigar out of his pocket and lighting it with a World War II Zippo. "You wait, Brokey-One, and you watch."

"Good *God*, for *what*? . . . Don't smoke! You're not supposed to *smoke* in here!"

"Oh, Brokey, you and your cousin, Ethelred, always went too much by the book, and when the book didn't match the action, you looked for more books. It's not *in* the books, Heseltine, not the ones you can read. It's in your stomach, in your gut. Some things are right and some things are wrong, it's as simple as that. The gut tells you."

"What the *hell* are you talking about?"

"Your gut tells you to look for books you're *not* supposed to read. In places where they keep secrets, like right in here."

"Mac, you're not making sense!"

"Give me a year, maybe two, Brokey, and then you'll understand. I've got to do it right. Real right." General Mackenzie Hawkins strode out between the metal racks of the archives to the exit. "*Goddamn*," he said to himself. "Now I really go to work. Get *ready* for me, you magnificent Wopotamis. I'm *yours!*"

Twenty-one months passed, and nobody *was ready for Thunder Head, chief of the Wopotamis.*

The President of the United States, his jaw firm, his angry eyes steady and penetrating, accelerated his pace along the steel-gray corridor in the underground complex of the White House. In seconds, he had outdistanced his entourage, his tall, lean frame angled forward as if bucking a torrential wind, an impatient figure wanting only to reach the storm-tossed battlements and survey the bloody costs of war so as to devise a strategy and repel the invading hordes assaulting his realm. He was John of Arc, his racing mind building a counterattack at Orleans, a Harry Five who knew the decisive Agincourt was in the immediate picture.

At the moment, however, his immediate objective was the anxiety-prone Situation Room, buried in the lowest levels of the White House. He reached a door, yanked it open, and strode inside as his subordinates, now trotting and breathless, followed in unison.

"All right, fellas!" he roared. "Let's *skull!*"

A brief silence ensued, broken by the tremulous, high-pitched voice of a female aide. "I don't think in here, Mr. President."

"What? *Why?*"

"This is the men's room, sir."

"Oh? . . . What are *you* doing here?"

"Following you, sir."

"Golly gee. Wrong turn. Sorry about that. Let's go! *Out!*"

The large round table in the Situation Room glistened under the wash of the indirect lighting, reflecting the shadows of the bodies seated around it. These blocks of shadow on the polished wood, like the bodies themselves, remained immobile as the stunned faces attached to those bodies stared in astonishment at the gaunt, bespectacled man who stood behind the President in front of a portable blackboard, on which he had drawn numerous diagrams in four different colors of chalk. The visual aids were somewhat less than effective as two of the crisis management team were color-blind. The bewildered expression on the youthful Vice-President's face was nothing new and therefore dismissible, but the growing agitation on the part of the chairman of the Joint Chiefs of Staff was not so easily dismissed.

"*Goddamn* it, Washbum, I don't—"

"That's Washburn, General."

"That's nice. I don't follow the legal line."

"It's the orange one, sir."

"Which one is that?"

"I just explained, the *orange* chalk."

"Point it out."

Heads turned; the President spoke. "Gee whiz, Zack, can't you tell?"

"It's dark in here, Mr. President."

"Not that dark, Zack. *I* can see it clearly."

"Well, I've got a minor visual problem," said the general, abruptly lowering his voice, ". . . distinguishing certain colors."

"What Zack?"

"*I* heard him," exclaimed the towheaded Vice-President, seated next to the J.C. chairman. "He's *color*-blind."

"Golly, Zack, but you're a soldier!"

"Came on late, Mr. President."

"It came on *early* with me," continued the excitable heir to the Oval Office. "Actually, it's what kept me out of the *real* army. I would have given *anything* to correct the problem!"

"Close it up, gumball," said the swarthy-skinned director of the Central Intelligence Agency, his voice low but his half-lidded, dark eyes ominous. "The friggin' campaign's over."

"Now, really, Vincent, there's no cause for that language," intruded the President. "There's a lady present."

"That judgment's up for grabs, Prez. The lady in question is not unfamiliar with the *lingua franca*, as it were." The DCI smiled grimly at the glaring female aide and returned to the man named Washburn at the portable blackboard. "You, our legal expert here, what kind of . . . creek are we up?"

"*That's* better, Vinnie," added the President. "I appreciate it."

"You're welcome . . . Go on, Mr. Lawyer. What kind of deep ca-ca are we really into?"

"Very nice, Vinnie."

"Please, Big Man, we're all a little stressed here." The director leaned forward, his apprehensive eyes on the White House legal aide. "You," he continued, "put away the chalk and let's have the news. And do me a favor, don't spend a week getting there, okay?"

"As you wish, Mr. Mangecavallo," said the White House attorney, placing the colored chalk on the blackboard ledge. "I was merely trying to diagram the historical precedents relative to the altered laws where the Indian nations were concerned."

"What *nations?*" asked the Vice-President, in his voice a trace of arrogance. "They're tribes, not countries."

"Go on," interrupted the director. "He's not here."

"Well, I'm sure you all recall the information our mole at the Supreme Court gave us about an obscure, impoverished Indian *tribe* petitioning the Court over a supposed treaty with the federal government that was allegedly lost or stolen by federal agents. A treaty that if ever found would restore their rights to certain territories currently housing vital military installations."

"Oh, yes," said the President. "We had quite a laugh over that. They even sent an extremely long brief to the Court that nobody wanted to read."

"Some poor people will do anything but get a job!" joined in the Veep. "That *is* a laugh."

"Our lawyer isn't laughing," observed the director.

"No, I'm not, sir. Our mole sends word that there've been some quiet rumors which may mean absolutely nothing, of course, but apparently five or six justices of the Court were so impressed by the brief that they've actually debated its merits in chambers. Several feel that the lost Treaty of 1878, negotiated with the Wopotami tribe and the forty-ninth Congress, may ultimately be legally binding upon the government of the United States."

"You gotta be outta your *lemon* tree!" roared Mangecavallo. "They can't *do* that!"

"Totally unacceptable," snapped the pinstriped, acerbic Secretary of State. "Those judicial fruitcakes will never survive the polls!"

"I don't think they have to, Warren." The President shook his head slowly. "But I see what you mean. As the great communicator frequently told me, 'Those mothers couldn't get parts as extras in *Ben-Hur*, not even in the Colosseum scenes.'"

"Profound," said the Vice-President, nodding his head. "That really says it. Who's Benjamin Hurr?"

"Forget it," replied the balding, portly Attorney General, still breathing heavily from the swift journey through the underground corridors. "The point is they don't need outside employment. They're set for life, and there's nothing we can *do* about it!"

"Unless they're all impeached," offered the nasal-toned Secretary of State, Warren Pease, his thin-lipped smile devoid of bonhomie.

"Forget that, too," rebutted the Attorney General. "They're pristine white and immaculate black, even the skirt. I checked the whole spectrum when those pointy-heads shoved that negative poll tax decision down our throats."

"That was simply *grotesque!*" cried the Vice-President, his wide eyes searching for approval. "What's five hundred dollars for the right to *vote?*"

"Too true," agreed the occupant of the Oval Office. "The good people could have written it off on their capital gains. For instance, there was an article by a fine economist, an alumnus of ours, as a matter of fact, in *The Bank Street Journal*, explaining that by converting one's assets in subsection C to the line item projected losses in—"

"Prez, *please?*" interrupted the director of the Central Intelligence Agency gently. "That bum's doing time, six to ten years for fraud, actually. . . . A lid, please, Big Man, okay?"

"Certainly, Vincent. . . . Is he really?"

"Just remember, none of us remember him," replied the DCI, barely above a whisper. "You forgot his line item procedures when we had him at Treasury? He put half of Defense into Education, but nobody got no schools."

"It was *great* PR—"

"Stow it, gumball—"

"'Stow it,' Vincent? Were you in the navy? 'Stow it' is a navy term."

"Let's say I've been on a lot of small, fast boats, Prez. Caribbean theater of operations, okay?"

"*Ships*, Vincent. They're always 'ships.' Were you by way of Annapolis?"

"There was a Greek runner from the Aegean who could *smell* a patrol boat in pitch dark."

"Ship, Vincent. *Ship*. . . . Or maybe not when applied to patrols—"

"Please, Big Man." Director Mangecavallo stared at the Attorney General. "Maybe you didn't look good enough into that dirtbag character spectrum of yours, huh? On those judicial fruitcakes, as our high-toned Secretary of State called 'em. Maybe there were omissions, right?"

"I used the entire resources of the Federal Bureau," replied the obese Attorney General, adjusting his bulk in the inadequate chair while wiping his forehead with a soiled handkerchief. "We couldn't hang a jaywalking ticket on any of them. They've all been in Sunday school since the day they were born."

"What do those FBI yo-yos know, huh? They cleared *me*, right? I was the holiest saint in town, *right?*"

"And both the House and the Senate confirmed you with rather decent majorities, Vincent. That says something about our constitutional checks and balances, doesn't it?"

"More about checks made out to 'cash' than balances, Prez, but we'll let it slide, okay? . . . Owl Eyes here says that five or six of the big robes may be leaning the wrong way, right?"

"It could simply be minor speculation," added Washburn. "And completely *in camera*."

"So who's takin' pictures?"

"You misunderstand, sir. I mean the debates remain secret, not a word of them leaked to the press or the public. The blackout was actually self-imposed on the grounds of national security, *in extremis*."

"In who?"

"Good heavens!" cried Washburn. "This wonderful country, the nation we love, could be placed in the most vulnerable military position in our history if five of those damn fools vote their consciences. We could be *obliterated!*"

"Okay, okay, cool it," said Mangecavallo, staring at the others around the table, quickly passing by the eyes of the President and his heir apparent. "So we got us some room by this top-secret status. And we also got five or six judicial fruitcakes to work on, right? . . . So, as the intelligence expert at this table, I say we should make sure two or three of those zucchinis stay in the vegetable patch, *right*? And since this sort of thing is in my personal realm of expertise, I'll go to work, *capisce*?"

"You'll have to work quickly, Mr. Director," said the bespectacled Washburn. "Our mole tells us that the Chief Justice himself told him he was going to lift the debate blackout in forty-eight hours. In his own words, Chief Justice Reebock said, 'They're not the only half-assed ball game in town'—that's a direct quote, Mr. President. I personally do not use such language."

"Very commendable, Washbum—"

"That's *Washburn*, sir."

"Him, too. Let's *skull*, men—and you, too, Miss . . . Miss . . ."

"Trueheart, Mr. President. Teresa Trueheart."

"What do you do?"

"I'm your Chief of Staff's personal secretary, sir."

"And then some," mumbled the DCI.

"*Stow* it, Vinnie."

"My Chief of Staff . . . ? Gosh 'n' crackers, where *is* Arnold? I mean this is a *crisis*, a real zing doozer!"

"He has his massage every afternoon at this hour, sir," replied Miss Trueheart brightly.

"Well, I don't mean to criticize, but—"

"You have every *right* to criticize, Mr. President," interrupted the wide-eyed heir apparent.

"On the other hand, Subagaloo's been under a great deal of stress lately. The press corps call him names and he's quite sensitive."

"And there's nothing that relieves stress more than a massage," added the Vice-President. "Believe me, I know!"

"So where do we stand, gentlemen? Let's get a fix on the compass and tighten the halyards."

"Aye, *aye*, sir!"

"Mr. Vice-President, give us a break, huh? . . . The compass we're locked into, Big Man, should better be fixed on a full moon, 'cause that's where we're at—looney-tune time, but nobody's laughin'."

"Speaking as your Secretary of Defense, *Mr. President*," broke in an extremely short man whose pinched face barely projected above the table and whose eyes glared disapprovingly at the CIA director, "the situation's utterly preposterous. Those idiots on the Court can't be allowed to even consider devastating the security of the country over an obscure, long-forgotten, so-called treaty with an Indian tribe nobody's ever *heard* of!"

"Oh, I've heard of the Wopotamis," the Vice-President interrupted again. "Of course, American history wasn't my best subject, but I remember I thought it was a funny name, like the Choppywaws. I thought they were slaughtered or died of starvation or some dumb thing."

The brief silence was ended with Director Vincent Mangecavallo's strained whisper as he stared at the young man who was a heartbeat away from being the nation's Commander in Chief. "You say one more word, butter skull, and you're gonna be in a cement bathrobe at the bottom of the Potomac, do I make myself clear?"

"*Really*, Vincent!"

"Listen, Prez, I'm your head honcho for the whole country's security, right? Well, let me tell you, that kid's got the loosest mouth on the beltway. I could have him terminated with extreme prejudice for saying and doing what he didn't even know he said or did. The hit off the record, naturally."

"That's not fair!"

"It's not a fair world, son," observed the perspiring Attorney General, turning his attention to the White House lawyer at the blackboard. "All right, Blackburn—"

"*Wash*burn—"

"If you say so. . . . Let's zero in on this fiasco, and I mean zero to the max! For starters, just who the hell is the bastard, the *traitor*, who's behind this totally unpatriotic, un-American appeal to the Court?"

"He calls himself Chief Thunder Head, Native American," answered Washburn. "And the brief his attorney submitted is considered one of the most brilliant ever received by the judiciary, our informer tells us. They say—confidentially—that it will go down in the annals of jurisprudence as a model of legal analysis."

"Annals, my ass!" exploded the Attorney General, once more working his soiled handkerchief across his brow. "I'll have that legal banana peeled to his bare bones! He's finished, eliminated. By the time the department's through with him, he won't get a job selling insurance in Beirut, *forget* the law!

No firm'll touch him and he won't find a client in the meat box at Leavenworth. What's the son of a bitch's name?"

"*Well*," began Washburn hesitantly, his voice squeaking briefly into a falsetto, ". . . there we have a temporary glitch, as it were."

"Glitch—*what* glitch?" The nasal-toned Warren Pease, whose left eye had the unfortunate affliction of straying to the side when he was excited, pecked his head forward like a violated chicken. "Just give us the name, you idiot!"

"There isn't any to give," choked Washburn.

"Thank God this moron doesn't work for the Pentagon," snarled the diminutive Secretary of Defense. "We'd never find half our missiles."

"I think they're in Teheran, Oliver," offered the President. "Aren't they?"

"My suggestion was *rhetorical*, sir." The pinch-faced head of the Pentagon, seen barely above the surface of the table, shook back and forth in short lateral jabs. "Besides, that was a long time ago and *you* weren't there and *I* wasn't there. Remember, *sir*?"

"Yes, yes, of course I don't."

"Goddamn it, Blackboard, why *isn't* there a name?"

"Legal precedent, sir, and my name is . . . never mind—"

"What do you mean, 'never mind,' you wart? I want the *name*!"

"That's not what I meant—"

"What the hell *do* you mean?"

"*Non nomen amicus curiae*," mumbled the bespectacled White House attorney barely above a whisper.

"What are you doin', a Hail Mary?" asked the DCI softly, his dark Mediterranean eyes bulging in disbelief.

"It goes back to 1826, when the Court permitted a brief to be filed anonymously by a 'friend of the Court' on behalf of a plaintiff."

"I'll kill him," mumbled the obese Attorney General, an audible flatus emerging from the seat of his chair.

"*Hold* it!" yelled the Secretary of State, his left eye swinging back and forth unchecked. "Are you telling us that this brief for the Wopotami tribe was filed by an *unnamed* attorney or attorneys?"

"Yes, sir. Chief Thunder Head sent his representative, a young brave who recently passed the state's bar, to appear before the Justices *in camera* and act as temporary counsel anticipating the necessity of the original anonymous counsel should the brief be held inadequate. . . . It wasn't. The majority of the Court deemed it sufficient under the guidelines of *non nomen amicus curiae.*"

"So we don't know *who* the *hell* prepared the goddamned thing?" shouted the Attorney General, his attacks of duodenal gas unrelenting.

"My wife and I call those 'bottom burps,'" snickered the Vice-President quietly to his single superior.

"*We* used to call them 'caboose whistles,'" replied the President, grinning conspiratorially.

"For Christ's *sake!*" roared the Attorney General. "No, no, not *you,* sir, or the kid here—I'm referring to Mr. Backwash—"

"That's . . . never mind."

"You mean to tell us we're not allowed to know who *wrote* this garbage, this swill that may convince five airheaded judges on the Court to affirm it as law and, not incidentally, *destroy* the operational core of our national defense!"

"Chief Thunder Head has informed the Court that in due time, after the decision has been rendered and made public and his people set free, he will make known the legal mind behind his tribe's appeal."

"That's nice," said the chairman of the Joint Chiefs. "Then we'll put the son of a bitch on the reservation with his redskin buddies and nuke the whole bunch of them off the goddamned map."

"To do that, General, you'd have to wipe out all of Omaha, Nebraska."

The emergency meeting in the Situation Room was over; only the President and his Secretary of State remained at the table.

"Golly, Warren," said the chief executive. "I wanted you to stay because sometimes I don't understand those people."

"Well, they certainly never went to *our* school, old roomie."

"Gosh, I guess they didn't but that's not what I mean. They all got so excited, shouting and cursing and everything."

"The ill-born are prone to emotional outbursts, we both know that. They have no ingrained restraint. Do you remember when the head-master's wife got drunk and began singing 'One-Ball Reilly' at the back of the chapel? Only the scholarship boys turned around."

"Not exactly," said the President sheepishly. "I did, too."

"*No,* I can't believe it!"

"Well, I sort of peeked. I think I had the hots for her; it started in dancing class—the fox trot, actually."

"She did that to all of us, the bitch. It's how she got her kicks."

"I suppose so, but back to this meeting. You don't think anything could come of that Indian stuff, do you?"

"Of course not! Chief Justice Reebock is just up to his old tricks, trying to get you mad because he thinks you blackballed him for our Honorary Alumni Society."

"Gee, I swear I didn't!"

"I know you didn't, I did. His politics are quite acceptable, but he's a very unattractive man and wears terrible clothes. He looks positively ludicruous in a tuxedo. Also, I think he drools—not for us, old roomie. You heard what that Washboard said . . . he said Reebock told our mole that we 'weren't the only half-assed ball game in town.' What more do you need?"

"Still, everybody got so angry, especially Vincent Manja . . . Manju . . . Mango whatever."

"It's the Italian in him. It goes with the bloodlines."

"Maybe, Warren. Still, he bothers me. I'm sure Vincent was a fine naval officer, but he could also be a loose cannon . . . like you-know-who."

"*Please*, Mr. President, don't give either of us nightmares!"

"I'm just trying to prevent 'em, old roomie. Look, Warren, Vincent doesn't get along too well with our Attorney General or the Joint Chiefs, and definitely not with the whole Defense Department, so I want you to sort of cultivate him, stay in close touch with him on this problem—be his confidential friend."

"With a *Mangecavallo*?"

"Your office calls for it, Warty old boy. State's got to be involved in something like this."

"But *nothing* will *come* of it!"

"I'm sure it won't, but think of the reactions worldwide when the Court's arguments become public. We're a nation of laws, not whims, and the Supreme Court doesn't suffer nuisance suits. You have some international spin-control in front of you, roomie."

"But why *me*?"

"Golly gosh and zing darn, I just *told* you, Warty!"

"Why not the Vice-President? He can relay all the news to me."

"Who?"

"The Vice-President!"

"What *is* his name, anyway?"